EMPIRE FOR LIBERTY

Dangerous Lullaby

I0564073

Previous Legend

HEARTLAND
On the Side of Angels

EMPIRE FOR LIBERTY

Dangerous Lullaby

TERRI SEDMAK

THE
LIBERTY & PROPERTY
LEGENDS

Visit www.terrisedmak.com
Official website of THE LIBERTY & PROPERTY LEGENDS
A Saga of The West & Gilded Age America

As always, heartfelt thanks to Francis, my wonderful and steadfast companion
in all things Tank & Ferry; my gorgeous reader, Anastasia; and Gem, traveler
intrepid. Also to Michael at Blow–Up Design Pty Ltd, who consistently and
cheerfully saves my art; Wyoming State Archives; thanks so much to Jason and
the team at Vivid for the trusty path the Legends now tread and books to be
proud of; and to Jane at Jake PR, for her encouragement, friendship,
enthusiasm and opening many doors; lastly, to all those readers who have
made a place in their hearts for HEARTLAND *On the Side of Angels*.

Credits: *I Ride an Old Paint* and *Git Along Little Dogies*, Cowboy Traditional;
We Will Not Be Slaves, Sons of Liberty Traditional; *The Starlight Night* by
Gerard Manley Hopkins; *Love's Philosophy* by Percy Bysshe Shelley;
My Lost Youth, Keramos, Emma and Eginhard, and *Song: Stay at Home*
by Henry Wadsworth Longfellow.

Published by VIVID Publishing
P.O. Box 948, Fremantle
Western Australia, 6959
www.vividpublishing.com.au

National Library of Australia Cataloguing-in-Publication entry:
Sedmak, Terri
Empire for liberty
ISBN 9781921787638 (pbk.)
Series: The Liberty & Property Legends
A823.4

To Rosario Previtera, my Dad
for watermelon, spaghetti,
stuffed artichokes, and peppers,
for strong arms, sweet peas and
Sunday best.

'The birthright we hold, shall never be sold,
But sacred maintained to our graves,
And before we'll comply, we'll gallantly die,
For we must not, we will not be slaves, brave boys,
For we must not, we will not be slaves.'

The Sons of Liberty

Cliff...

State Penitentiary
Cañon City, Colorado
January, 1885

"The prisoner is always kept in solitary confinement?"

"His sentence stands. Nothing's changed."

"And his health?"

The guard, his face expressionless, turns his key in the lock.

"Prisoner Five One Three ain't in good health, Sheriff. Don't get too close then." He yanks open the door; pulls it wide enough for one man to enter. "I'll be right outside."

Cliff enters the small, dark cell.

The air is rank, and he can hear moisture collecting, dripping and plopping in poignant distortion; from one corner there emanates a paltry glow, and as a result he is able to make out a slumped figure.

"More light, guard," he calls out.

Within moments a lantern is handed to him. He holds it high and the prisoner's dejected personage is wholly revealed in the light, trying to shield his eyes from the brightness.

"Hello, Ed."

Slowly, the hand shield is lowered and Cliff is examined through slotted eyes. "Not you again. Nothing better to do?"

Cliff lowers the lantern to a crude table by the door.

"It's been a while, Ed. Hear you're not feeling too well."

"What's it to you," Parsons replies in a raspy voice, and then coughs.

He has wrapped himself in a couple of thin prison-issue blankets and sits huddled on the cot; even so, it is obvious that the once stocky build of Ed Parsons has wasted considerably in a short time.

"What do you want, Ryan?"

"Information."

Another cough. "I told you before, I don't know who killed the Keaton girl."

"Yes, you do, Ed."

The old man peers up at him. "No, you sonofabitch, I don't, so clear off and leave me in peace." The exertion of this causes a long bout of coughing.

"Guard!" Cliff shouts. The iron door creeps open and the guard appears. "I want this man examined by a doctor at once."

During the half an hour it takes for Ed Parsons to be moved to the hospital wing and be examined by the prison doctor, Cliff reflects on the harsh conditions of Ed's incarceration...

For a start, the temperature inside these dense stone walls turns everyone's breath white; all the guards wear thick woolen coats. Gloominess pervades, and echoes abound: footsteps rapping, iron doors slamming, the prisoners calling out in their cells behind their ice cold doors. Every sound in this huge grim dungeon rebounds off its telltale walls...

Outside, a chill wind swirls and whistles with sleet in its icy tentacles, and the ground is deeply permafrosted and paved with compacted snow. Above the gate of iron bars and icicles, engraved into thick stone, is the number 1875, the year this hard place first opened its doors to welcome guests that civil, law-abiding society could no longer accommodate. Why any man would want to be included in their number defies comprehension, as do their deeds; but he knows outlaws and criminals enough to know they never think the law will catch up to them... The prison doctor emerges from Ed's assigned room in the hospital wing.

"Well?" Cliff asks.

"It's pneumonia. He has a fever and he's weak."

"Will he recover?"

"Hard to say. With the very best of care and in normal circumstances, possibly. In these conditions..." The doctor shrugs. "I will keep him here until there is some definite improvement."

"I need to be getting on with my interrogation."

"I don't suppose there's much point me advising you to go easy on him. He *is* suffering, you know."

"I thought that was the point of him being in this hellhole, Doc," Cliff says and leaves the doctor in the outer room.

Ed Parsons is tucked up in clean white bed linen and plenty of blankets; there's a fire blazing in the corner of the room and a guard who has positioned himself sensibly right next to it, with his eyes fixed on the prisoner.

Cliff stands over the bed. "Well, Ed, you can thank me any time."

Ed's glassy eyes stare up at him. "Am I dying?"

Cliff shrugs. "The doctor can't be sure, but it's likely."

"I feel like I'm dying." Ed's eyes drift away and he stares straight ahead.

Cliff folds his arms. "The promise of death has a way of putting a certain spin on a man's life."

"I don't know who killed the Keaton girl."

"Maybe not the killer exactly..."

Ed's eyes come back to Cliff's face. "What are you getting at?"

"You know who orchestrated the killing."

"It wasn't me."

"I know."

"How do you know?"

"A hunch. Besides I have in my possession a small piece of evidence that someone else is involved. Now before you die I want you to confirm my suspicions."

Ed coughs, laughs, hard to tell which. "You stuck up little piece of shit. You're nothing but a piece of crap, who would give a damn about your small piece of evidence..."

"Strength coming back, is it, Ed? Guard, extinguish that fire."

The guard's eyes fling open wide.

"You heard. The heat in here is unbearable and the prisoner can't concentrate."

"Bastard," Ed mutters.

"And you can wait outside," Cliff adds.

The guard, having smothered the fire, and mumbling under his breath, leaves them alone.

"Now, you listen, Ed, listen hard. The evidence I have…"

"You don't know what you're dealing with, Ryan."

"You didn't let me finish, Ed. The evidence is…"

"You're outa your league. "

"Don't think so. But thanks for caring."

"What do you think you're doing, Ryan?"

"I'm trying to tell you, Ed. Luke Taylor's file has a lot more in it than you can imagine…"

"Taylor!" he rasps and coughs.

"You never got to see Luke's file did you, Ed. Such a pity, too, because then you would have seen not only the things you yourself got up to while you were extorting the Alliance, bribing that pea-brain sheriff, Vincent McCurdy, and conspiring to have Wilson Cutter murder Mart Keaton, but also a very fine sketch of Loren Bodecker." Cliff is not disappointed by Ed's response; the pale old man almost dissolves into his white sheets. "You see, Ed, Luke sketched Loren Bodecker into his file not knowing who he was but most probably considering him part of the problem. At some point he saw Loren Bodecker and you. Curious, wouldn't you say?"

"And where do you think that is likely to get you, Ryan?"

Cliff shrugs. "To the truth."

Ed just stares at him.

"So, Faraday and I are of the opinion, Ed, that Loren Bodecker might know who murdered Miss Keaton."

Ed's mouth tightens. "What do you want from me, Ryan?"

"Will Loren Bodecker know who murdered Miss Keaton?"

"Why don't you ask him and find out?"

The reply is outwardly sarcastic, but it is Cliff's job to probe beyond the sarcasm and force the truth. Parsons knows that Cliff asking Loren Bodecker such a question and acquiring an answer is tantamount to political suicide for a sheriff, but Ed's response can also be interpreted another way.

"I will ask him, Ed, and I'll tell him you suggested it."

Ed's eyes widen instantly.

"No," he gasps, "you don't know what you're doing."

4

"Because Bodecker is one of the most powerful businessmen in Wyoming? Because he happens to be a good friend of the governor, because accusing him of being involved in criminal activity could see the end of my career, and Cam Faraday his, because in asking Bodecker I could be further endangering the lives of the Keatons and the Taylors, because if Loren Bodecker has just a inkling of the source of my confirmation something might happen to you?"

Cliff has worked up a full head of steam and Parsons lies there as though he's being hammered to the bed.

"Something has already happened to you, Ed. You are in prison, for life. Bodecker helped you become a member of his Association, and probably a heap of other stuff, but did he help you at your trial? It would have ruined him, and we couldn't have that. But maybe, knowing what a revengeful bastard you are, he helped with something else, something close to your heart… payback for Luke and Mart putting you behind bars for good."

"Shut your goddamn mouth, Ryan," Parsons grinds out, and he struggles to raise himself onto his elbows. "Leave it alone, for God's sake."

"I can't do that, Ed. So many of us thought it would all be over when the trial finished, when you came here, and Wilson Cutter got what was coming to him, but it's not over, is it?"

"Shut up!"

"You thought that the Alliance would just lay down and die, didn't you? That somehow you had scored a victory because with Miss Keaton assassinated in broad daylight the Alliance would just crumble into the dust. But, at some point in the trial, you gave up caring about whether you got your hands on their ranches and a couple of other things got much more important. Number one, revenge. And number two, making sure someone else was safe. Someone who could help you. That was your buddy, Bodecker, wasn't it, Ed?"

"So you know; bully for you." Ed sinks back into his pillow and bed sheets. "Go to hell."

"I was planning on going home."

"That'll feel like hell soon enough."

Cliff calls for the guard. "So long, Ed. Thanks for the chat."

ONE

There are things of which I may not speak;
there are dreams that cannot die;
there are thoughts that make the strong heart weak,
and bring a pallor into the cheek,
and a mist before the eye.

Henry Wadsworth Longfellow
My Lost Youth

Dermot

Provincetown, Massachusetts,
January 26, 1885

Dermot puts flaming match to trimmed wick.

In the growing darkness of the room the candle-glow drifts up from the mantle and illuminates her portrait, the beauty of her round green eyes and flowing chestnut hair. Her vitality and sweetness are perfectly captured. She was twenty-five when the painting was done. He had it commissioned for her birthday. Three years later she was dead… his Aisling was gone…

Having poured himself a large whiskey, Dermot sinks into his leather wingback, drags his feet onto the footstool and stares up at her. Her eyes glisten as they stare back at him. Her dimpled smile mingles with the whiskey to warm his cold innards. He raises his glass to her.

"Well, my beauty, my Aisling, happy birthday. Yet another year has gone by. And you know what that means. Your daughter is now just two years younger than you were when you left me here… all alone…"

He takes a large swig.

On this anniversary he usually likes to remember Aisling as she was on their wedding day, seventeen years of age and so full of life and beauty. They were wed in July when the weather had finally given Boston a summer. The following year, Joseph was born. Miles, two years after.

Aisling knew how obsessed Dermot was with the sea, that, but

9

for his strict upbringing, he would have preferred a livelihood that consisted of reading the heavens for navigating the sea at night and the formation of clouds on the horizon by day to reading law books; preferred the smell of brine, sight of whale blubber and the bustle of the port to the sights, smells and bustle of the courtroom.

This upbringing and dogged family expectation scored a victory of sorts; he was miserable until Aisling... and she, with her youth and energy, came up with a solution that the rigidity of his trained mind rebuked at first; indeed it took him time to treat her unharshly and fully realize the treasure he had in his possession, not to mention the miracle that he had come by it in the first place. He needed her, he knew that much. When he learned to open his mind in those first months with her, his existence changed...

Her idea was simple. They bought this house in Provincetown on the knuckle of Cape Cod, a holiday home, when Joseph was four and Miles two. Frank came next. Aisling was so proud of her boys. They occupied many glorious days in this charming old sea-captain's house named *Liberty Keep*. When it appeared for sale they snapped it up, much to the bother of the locals who were, at best, ambivalent about outsiders, even Bostonians, treating their busy fishing town as a holiday resort.

The house itself was – is – uncharacteristically made of stone, not wood, white-washed of course, with an eight-window cupola that gave them three hundred and sixty degree views of the ocean, the bay, the town and everything in between. The sea-captain's ship had been the *Liberty*. The house was called *The Keep*, where he held safe his dearest possessions: his wife and his son. But they both died one winter and the distress drove the captain back to the sea; he never returned to Provincetown.

Dermot and Aisling thought *Liberty Keep* a splendid and apt name. Here they were away from Boston for a time and at liberty to pursue what they loved. And so they had the best of both worlds. Occupation that afforded them superior material comforts and a secure future; and recreation that nourished their spirit and made them content. The people of Provincetown became used to them in time, since they were so often in their midst, negotiating narrow, bustling Commercial St, about the wharves or along the seashore.

Liberty Keep was the perfect base for exploring the natural beauty and pilgrim history of the bay, roaming the wild and endless dunes, romping in the sea, wondrous fishing, digging for clams and trapping lobster, and scampering excitedly over the wharves as the fishing fleet either set out from or returned to their beautiful topaz-blue harbor, laden with cod, mackerel, haddock and halibut. The boys were always intrigued by the Portuguese fishermen. And any day they decided on a voyage to the Vineyard or Nantucket to go 'a-whaling' (as Miles called it) was a perfect day. Aisling cared not for whaling, and she kept young Frank at the house with her.

"Francis will not be going a-whaling with you barbarians," she would say. "Whales are grand creatures and we'll have no part in their slaughter." There was no changing her thinking, no matter how hard he tried to explain the commercial importance of whaling to everyday life, including hers. Somehow she managed to turn her mind from Provincetown's impressive and prodigious whaling industry and see beyond it to what was more important to her... what made her family happiest.

No, no... Aisling's favorite was being able to watch the sun rise over the Atlantic at Race Point Beach and the sun set over the Bay at Herring Cove. Like living on an island, she said... "how many people on the East Coast get to see the sun set on water...?"

These are tortuous memories of the days when Dermot was content. In retrospect, Dermot had placed far more importance on his life with Aisling than he ought. He should have been like most other men he knew then, whose wives were little more than the trophy in their cabinet or their assurance of immortality. Aisling was his life, his soul...

Dermot hears the door open and close behind him.

"Well, Joseph?" he asks.

"I sent the telegram as you requested," his eldest son replies.

Dermot gulps another mouthful of whiskey. "Thank you. Is Marianne feeling better this evening?"

"A little, I think."

"You know, you are welcome to stay here for as long as you need to, until Marianne is feeling well again."

He hears Joseph sigh and say, "We are both very grateful."

Joseph moves quietly across the boards and appears at his side. His son is tall, seems even taller, standing there looking up at his mother.

"It's been a long time, Father."

"I know."

"I think it is time you forgave her."

"Your mother for being weak, or your sister for being the instrument of her death?"

Joseph moves about in a restless fashion while Dermot finishes his drink.

"Can't you see it any other way, Father, after all this time?"

"There is no other way."

Joseph throws up one hand. "And this is how you'll greet her, if she in fact agrees to come?"

"She'll come."

"And when you tell her that you... when you tell her, what do you expect her to do, to say?"

"Nothing. She has said nothing to me for eight years, but by God, I'm going to tell her to her face."

"You disinherited her when she was eighteen, why would she come? She feels nothing for you. You saw to that."

Dermot cranes his neck to look at his son. "Is that a reprimand I hear from you, Joseph? When was the last time you were in contact with your sister? When did you ever take an interest in her? You *or* Miles, for that matter. Frank is the only one who cares. Frank is like her..." he raises his empty glass in a toast to Aisling, "...with his good heart and endless patience. God bless Francis Patrick... I need another drink."

"Well, I'll leave you to it then," Joseph says and strides to the door. "I'll let you know when I receive a reply."

"Thank you, Joseph."

The door closes quietly. Dermot pours more whiskey into his glass and gazes up at Aisling.

"She just had to look so much like you. What kind of a torment is that to bequeath a man for the rest of his life?"

He never understood it or accepted it; however, now the sands of time are running low and all his affairs are in order except one.

Jennifer

Boston, Massachusetts, 1867

From the window of my room on the second story of our Boston house I see his carriage round the corner and head for home. The father of my brothers keeps two beautiful horses for his carriage, their chestnut coats slick from the drizzle that has been falling all afternoon. Harold, our coachman and possibly the oldest living American, turns the pair into the drive and the lot disappears down the avenue of red pebbles and full grown cherry trees, whose spring leaves are wet and softly glistening. Now the street is quiet again, misty gray and empty. I turn from the window and sigh. And wait, while the sound of my breathing rivals the beating of my heart in my ears.

Presently, the door of my room bursts open. My heart rears up like a frightened horse and tears into a gallop within my chest.

Clémence, my French nanny, oblivious to anything other than her own feelings, enters in an excited state; she flounces around me, straightening my clothes and smoothing my hair. I push her hands away.

"Leave it, Clémence."

"Your papa, he wants to see you, tout de suite."

"Yes, yes, I figured as much. Library?"

Clémence frowns. "Oui. Oui, ma cheri. La bibliotheque…" Her voice falls away.

That my nanny is afraid of her employer makes me all the more determined not to be afraid of him. Fear could be useful up to a point; however, in dealing with the man who is father to my three brothers, fear puts you on the back foot and he can smell it like a predator. I stare straight into Clémence's eyes; Clémence winces. I flick my hair behind my shoulders. I straighten my dress. As I stride from my room Clémence calls after me, "You know you should not have done it, Genevieve (my name Frenchified), you must be penitent, ma petite. He is your father. He only wants what is best for you."

Frank stands in the hall. His expression is strangely grown up and solemn for a thirteen-year-old boy. And he probably heard Clémence's pleading.

"Does he, Frank – want what's best for me?" I ask him.

Frank shrugs. "I'll come in with you."

Something close to fear flutters in my stomach then. "He'll think I'm afraid."

"Are you? What have you to be afraid of?"

I think about this for a moment. I have been challenged and nothing tramples fear in me faster than that, and Frank well knows it since it has been he who has taught me how to conquer fear with intellect. "We will see who is afraid when I come back out of the library."

Frank's eyes glint. "I guess I'll see you then."

By the time I reach the library door butterflies flutter delicately around in my stomach. I'd floated down the stairs on their wings, I think. Now it is time to steel myself, and I do it.

He is waiting by the hearth, the firelight casting a huge silhouette of his figure against the opposite wall. This room is always dark, even in summer when the sky is brightest blue and the sun intense enough to bring freckles out on my nose. In here it is dark and I always suppose he likes it that way for a reason. Strangely, I don't find it menacing; in fact, the long shadows bent across the floor and shooting up the walls have always intrigued me and while I wait for him to begin I often try to work out the science of light and shadow. He always interrupts before I can make my conclusion.

"Did you complete your piano lesson?" he demands to know.

"I did, sir."

"A small mercy."

Not true. I love my piano lessons. My tutor, Maestro Vieri, is Italian and he considers me exceedingly proficient. Maestro is amusing, even in his strictness, and I obey him without question. I used to dream that it would be so pleasant if the father of my brothers could be more like Maestro; they are of a similar age, but that's the end of it.

"Well, I met with your school teacher. He told me everything." He looks at me for the first time, expecting I know not what. I stare blankly in return at his hard expression. I do not understand how my loving, gentle brother Frank can physically resemble this harsh, cruel man, but he does, and this is why I often stare; I'm curious…

"You have no shame."

Not true. I feel ashamed every day of my life; he sees to that. Constantly. Expectedly.

"I have three sons. You are supposed to be my daughter, but I may as well have four sons for all the use you are as a female in this family."

Not true. My chest begins to hurt. I glare back at him, smarting. Don't think that because I am used to his insults that I am immune. He can think up new things as quickly as I can snap my fingers and this is not something he's ever mentioned before. He is disputing my femininity. Should I be confused? A boy? His son? Better that I was. Then I would not be the mirror image of my deceased mother. Maybe he wouldn't hate me so and accuse me of killing her, maybe I would be treated with respect…

"Stop daydreaming and listen!"

Am listening. I receive a start anyway, which should satisfy him.

"Brawling with a sixth grade girl. You attacked her. She had to defend herself. She had a black eye and a bruised cheek…"

Serves her right. Aren't boys who stand up to bullies considered brave? Not so girls, it seems.

"Her parents are outraged. Your teacher no longer knows what to do with you. The headmaster has suspended you. He says for your pitiful sake he won't expel you, but that I, who have better things to do with my time, must deal with you in an appropriate manner…" He doesn't yell, but his voice has that quality peculiar to attorneys who are well practiced in the art of cross-examination and accusation. I know he is working up to something dreadful and I would prefer he shouted the house down. He hisses, "You could at least have the decency to look sorry for what you have done."

My heart is beating so fast I think it will burst.

"You don't want to hear my side of what happened?" I ask.

He marches towards me then, and because I am only an eight-year-old girl he is big and tall, and my stomach lurches and I start to shake. *Please don't let him see me shaking.* Determinedly, I keep my eyes straight; they eventually fix themselves on the third button of his waistcoat onto which his fob chain is fastened.

"I know what happened," he barks. "There are no sides."

"You are a lawyer and you think that?" I ask breathlessly.

His whole body stiffens and I think my heart will burst right out of my chest. If it did all my guts and blood would cover him and stain him and my blood would be on his hands forever...

"You will not speak to me in that manner," he says. I imagine the words coming through teeth viciously clenched.

Not sorry.

Then it comes. The tirade. And indeed it is very loud. "You are nothing but a supreme disappointment to this family. You are defiant and disobedient in the extreme. You refuse to do anything that is asked of you..."

Not true.

"Why can't you be a normal female child in grade three? Why must you persist with this nonsense? Grade six in mathematics and science. Grade five in spelling, composition and social studies. Reading adult books, unsuitable and forbidden to you. Analyzing everything. Remembering every detail you read... the gall to think you are smarter than your teacher, for God's sake..."

I know better but I interrupt him. I am outraged and my heart beats so fast that I can hardly breathe so that the words come out stilted. "Don't call me a freak, don't say I belong in a circus or a display case in a museum. Don't say my mother and father must be freaks too. Don't say it, don't say it..."

"Silence!"

My eyes prickle. Sting. I whimper as I gasp for air. "That's what she said. Clarice Nolan-Brown. In her nasty stuck up voice. With her gang of bullies standing in a circle around me. I had to protect myself."

"You are changing schools. You will do the level of schoolwork required of a girl your age. You…"

"Don't you understand? I had to protect myself."

His hands come up, in frustration I suppose, but still I flinch and gasp. His hands shake in the air above my head. As hard as I try I can't steady my breathing, so I press on regardless, praying I don't faint.

"If I were one of the boys you would be proud of me for standing up for myself…"

"You are a stupid girl."

No, no, no…

"In the first instance you will not be allowed to have meals or communicate with myself or your brothers for the next two weeks. Now as for your schooling…"

All of a sudden an idea comes to me. "What… what is this new school?"

"A public school," he announces with an oily streak in his voice.

So, the private girls' school is gone for good.

I find myself calming little by little as the outcome of this sinks in. Doesn't he realize this is an answer to prayer? No more Clarice Nolan-Brown and her cronies. His eyes are narrowed on me in suspicion.

"Boys and girls together?" I ask.

"Of course."

I didn't mind boys in the least. The pounding in my ears eases.

"So let us see how well you can stand up for yourself now, Miss Smarty-pants."

I draw myself up to stand as erect as I can and look him in the eyes. Those stony, dark recesses send a shiver up my spine and I feel cold. Isn't it time that I take this fear in hand and do something?

He continues, "You will continue with your music, sewing and drawing lessons."

"And you will also be having a lesson," I tell him. "I am sure we will learn a lot."

"Get out of my sight," he hisses at me.

I bob the required curtsey and leave the library quickly. On the other side of the door again, I stand with my eyes closed for several moments and steady my heart. Public school. This wasn't going to be easy, but I figure people are the same everywhere. If a person wants to be good, they will be good, and if they want to create mischief they will do that too. There are good and bad public people, just as there are good and bad private people. If money makes people respectable in the eyes of society in general, in spite of what good or bad is in their hearts, then people with very little money have nothing to hide behind and might just be more honest. If teachers in public schools don't get paid as much as those in private schools, which I know to be the case, then maybe they teach school because they like to teach and they like children. Maybe they would like me.

The lesson I decide to teach my father is very simple.

I cut my waist-length red-brown hair short like a boy's; I know how to do this because I have seen Frank get his hair cut many times and studied the barber's technique. I rummage through Frank's clothes and find several articles he no longer wears. He reasons with me unsuccessfully not to do what I'm going to do – no inducement he can think of dissuades me. I become a boy for the first day of public school. Clémence refuses to take me to school even though it is her duty. I take myself. In persistent drizzle I walk the thirty minutes to the school. Much to my satisfaction I look similar to the other boys, although I decide I'm too neat and muss my clothes a little. When I eventually locate the grade three classroom, the teacher – a kind-looking young woman who introduces herself as Miss Palmer – asks my name.

"George Sullivan."

She looks confused and says, "I'm sorry, George, but on my class roll here it says my new pupil's name is Jennifer A...Aisling Sullivan... to tell the truth, I'm not sure how that middle name is pronounced..."

I resist telling her that it is Irish and pronounced Ashlin.

"I'm George... er, Ashley Sullivan," I say, deepening my voice some. "It can happen to anyone, a mistake like that. Where do you want me to sit, Miss?"

"Well," says she, bewildered, "you may be seated next to Daisy-Rose Peters. Daisy-Rose, make room for George please."

Daisy-Rose is a pleasantly average looking girl with dark brown hair and eyes, and pleasantly small for her age too. I can only imagine how pleasant it would be to be named for not one flower but two. She doesn't know what to make of me when I sit down, however, so I say pleasantly, "Your name has nice flowers in it."

Her eyes go big and round and she stares at me like a stunned mullet (a vulgar, boyish expression). The rest of the class stares at me also. Well, I do look pretty good as a boy so I don't mind.

The teacher comes towards me with some papers in her hand. "Now, George, you have arrived on a very good day because we are doing some tests to see how much we've learned so far this term. I want you to do the work on these papers. If you can't do something, just leave it and I will try to get you up to date with the others later. Do you have a pencil?"

"Yes, Miss," I say and yank one out of my pocket.

I take the papers. I complete the tests in arithmetic and grammar in five minutes and raise my hand.

"Yes, George?"

"I've finished, Miss Palmer. Is there something else I can be getting on with?"

By the end of the day the public school has me seated in the second row of grade six next to a rather alarming looking boy with red blotchy skin, unkempt hair and a very strange smell emanating from his clothing. I'm honored; I don't think they'd put a girl next to this feller. The headmaster gives me a letter for the man he calls my father before I leave for the day.

I never give the father of my brothers the letter, and when two weeks later I am finally allowed to return to the family table for meals, with Clémence sobbing at my side and trying to explain what I have been up to all this time behind his back and unable to stop me, the father of my brothers has his lesson. His face turns beet red. He cannot talk for a full minute and in his angry eyes I can see him thinking that the whole time he thought he was punishing me I had been humiliating him. And not even the boyish style walloping that I receive can dislodge the satisfaction.

Poor Clémence; the inevitable happens.

My new nanny's name is Frau Schmidt. She is German. She calls me fraulein. But, no matter who speaks to me, I only answer to George.

Boston, 1872

I love summer purely and simply because I can read in my favorite tree. It's a tallish, voluptuous crab apple, lusciously green and thick. The perfect camouflage. I am able to hide here, with provisions, for hours, and no one cares – well, Frank does, but as long as I'm happy he's happy, and that suits me fine. And as the tree is situated beside the back gate of our extensive grounds, I may watch the comings and goings like a regular spy.

The grounds of the house are indeed beautiful, well tended by the oldest living American's brother; he's not as old and he has help. There is something comforting in watching our gardener with his hunched back as he wanders from garden bed to orchard to lawn to rose bush.

Today things have been slow in the espionage department. No matter. I survey the peaceful garden from my hide with relief. If things are slow then I am not in trouble – that is how I see it. Sometime later, however, I am alerted by voices coming my way.

It is Miles; his voice is unmistakable. Urgh!

Then I hear another voice; an unfamiliar voice. What kind of spy would I be if I were not curious? I lean forward carefully as Miles and his male companion stroll through the gate. What is Miles doing bringing visitors through the back gate?

"I'll wait here, shall I?" says the stranger; he's standing directly beneath me.

"Very well, old man. Won't be a tick." Miles does that stylish jog on which he prides himself. Urgh! The stranger, however, is worth my attention. He is tall and broad shouldered, smartly dressed although not ostentatious, and as he has removed his hat I see his dark brown hair.

Unfortunately, unless he moves, I won't make out his face.

Mm.

I snap off a small, insignificant branch within my reach and toss it at his feet. Immediately, he looks up; impatiently I peer through the greenery for a glimpse of his face. What I see makes me smile. Miles' friends usually warrant bombardment by a whole tree of crab apples, but not this face. Even in its suspicion over the branch coming its way that face is kindness itself. And intelligence, and perhaps even sympathy. All right, I may be getting carried away, but Frau Schmidt tells me that's normal for thirteen-year-old girls, even abnormally smart ones.

I close my book, climb a silent descent, and then jump from the tree to land solidly right in front of my stranger. The expression of shock on his otherwise kind face reduces me to giggles.

His hand on his chest, he says, "I'm glad you think it funny..."

"I only do that to people I like the look of," I say jauntily.

"I'm flattered," he says.

A sense of humor – excellent! So what was he doing with Miles?

"What were you doing up there?"

I study his face before I answer. It's rather a handsome face, smooth features and chocolate brown eyes.

"I was reading. Darwin."

"Darwin?"

"You have heard of Darwin."

"Ah, *The Origin of Species* Darwin."

"One and the same."

My handsome stranger is giving me the once over, politely of course. This young man has impeccable manners.

"My uncle gave it to me."

"Why are you reading it in a tree?" he asks, looking up at the leafy branches swaying gently in the breeze, as is their summertime duty.

I shrug. "Why are you here?"

He gives me a dry smile. "My name is Cam Faraday; I'm a friend of Miles from college. We are studying law together. And you are?"

"George Sullivan," I tell him.

The chocolaty eyes widen. "Miles did mention he had sister."

"Did he? Well, I'm her... Please to meet you, Cam Faraday."

I tuck my book under my left arm and hold out my right hand; very gallantly he takes it. His fingers are warm and his eyes are twinkling at me. Yes, this is a very pleasant encounter.

But just then: "Fraulein... Fraulein..."

Frau Schmidt's voice is most distracting and I glance around to see her half running across the lawn towards me. At once my heart jumps into my mouth and any pleasant feelings induced by Cam Faraday's chocolaty eyes and nice manners leech out of me to be replaced by dread.

"What is it, Frau Schmidt?"

"It is your papa. He has found your secret library. Fraulein, I am so sorry, but he has found it."

I can hardly breathe, barely see. "No, no... What... but how?"

"I do not know how, but he destroys it, Fraulein. He has lit a fire in your room and he is tossing your books into it. They are burning as we speak."

"Burning books?" I hear Cam Faraday asking. "What books?"

I am standing there, numb, groaning, picturing my beautiful books aflame, the fire blackening the covers, consuming the pages, reducing the precious words to ashes...

"Miss Sullivan?"

...he despises me and what I love *that* much?

I detect Cam Faraday's hand on my arm. "Miss Sullivan?"

My eyes are burning too as I look up at him. "My Uncle has been giving me books since I was very young, books my father wouldn't let me read, like... like Darwin... they were hidden in a secret place."

"Fraulein, you must come now!" Frau Schmidt is saying in a shrill voice. "You must come now!"

"How can I stop him?" I reply.

Frau Schmidt's cold gray eyes pierce mine. "Any way you can, Fraulein. Together, yes? Let's go."

She takes my hand and encourages me along. I feel something slip from beneath my arm and look around.

Cam Faraday is clutching Darwin in his sure fingers. "Perhaps I should mind this for you." His chocolaty eyes regard me with such kindness that I find myself uplifted.

"Yes," I breathe, "thank you."

"I will keep it safe, I promise," he says. "Thank you, Frau Schmidt. Off you go." This is said with authority and both Frau and I respond at once.

My books are decimated. My hands are singed as I try to retrieve them. My body is bruised from being flung across the room by the father of my brothers as I repeatedly attempt to save them. Frau Schmidt is dismissed.

"We tried, my little fraulein, we tried, and now I must go."

She completes the bandages on my hands with circumspection and typical German efficiency.

"I will miss you," I tell her simply, heartfelt.

"Uh, you will never forget why I go. We try to save your books. We stand up for what we believe, ja?"

I nod miserably. "Ja."

That evening, when all is finally quiet, Frank comes to my room and sits with me. He brings with him a brown paper package that I cannot open for myself. As he removes the paper I catch my breath. *Darwin!*

"Cam Faraday called back with it a little while ago. I am to tell you to look inside the cover."

With clumsy fingers I open the cover; a white card rests inside. On one side of it is printed a name and address, the name being William D. Faraday, and on the other is written:

Dear Miss Sullivan, my father possesses one of the finest libraries in the country. It is at your disposal whenever you wish to use it.
Kind regards, Cam Faraday. P.S. What do you think of Darwin's theories so far?

Darwin offers no explanation as to why some people possess the milk of human kindness and some are completely devoid of it. Perhaps the answer lies with another scientific discipline altogether.

Then, as if he can read my mind, Frank says gently, "You will survive this. I promise you."

I sigh and say, "Survival of the fittest dictates that I must be stronger than him."

"Conventionally, anatomically, yes, but you are in other ways just as effective."

I study him pensively; he takes the book carefully from my sore hands, ensures the card is safely tucked inside and starts looking around the room.

"Where to put this? – no more hiding…"

This rouses me. "What?"

"There's some room on your shelves over there; of course it will look sort of lonely until you can build up your collection again."

"Frank, what are you talking about?"

He strides across the room and starts shifting various objects on my shelves. He finds the book a satisfactory niche. "I spoke with Father earlier, about your books. I told him they were gifts from Uncle and that Uncle will most likely be very upset to find his surrogate library destroyed. Father expressed his disappointment in me for keeping your secret, and declared – somewhat irrationally, as he was still angry – that he found a young girl reading such material as unnecessary, unwholesome and inappropriate. In reply, I pointed out that most of your collection comprised the classics of literature, science and philosophy, read by the most learned people in society…"

"All my Jane Austens," I weep, smudging my bandaged hand across my cheeks.

"I took the opportunity to get him to give his word that he won't touch your books again, and that they can sit openly on your shelves since it makes no difference now. He agreed; I think the thought of facing Uncle weakened his resolve."

I beam at Frank across the room. Maybe I am the fittest. Frank, who is loved by his father as much as I am detested by him, is my ally. This is definitely in my favor. How bizarre is it that one man can love his sons so gently and rationally and yet treat his female offspring like dirt beneath his shoes.

"I don't care for the study and practice of science for its own sake," I say.

"No? Science is as beautiful as art, as literature."

I smile. "I believe you will do something splendidly applicable with your beloved mathematics, or at least end up teaching it to someone who one day will do something splendidly applicable with it."

"That's comforting, George."

I shake my head. "No, I'm going to be a doctor, Frank. I've made up my mind. Your father is a lawyer, Joseph and Miles are lawyers, and they only take on pro bono cases when it promotes their careers or furthers the Law. And you will be a professor of mathematics one day. So what this family needs is someone who uses science to answer human need."

Frank's eyes twinkle in amusement. "Oh?"

"Caring for the health and welfare of all kinds of people."

"Reversing survival of the fittest," he muses.

"Well, I don't know that anyone can reverse it, Frank, but I think scientists can redefine who the fittest are. They are doing it all the time. Each new scientific discovery that benefits human beings, and there are a great many, increases their life expectancy or reduces the risk of disease. Can you imagine being able to do that, Frank?"

"Not really," he says, looking a little overwhelmed. "I wouldn't toss Darwin out the window just yet."

I let out a laugh. "Never going to happen, Frank."

Then I remember Frau Schmidt and sadness comes over me.

"I'm going to miss Frau. She barely tolerated Jane Austen and we had some ever so juicy discussions about her. Frau loathed Fanny Price, but well... I always felt I understood Fanny. Elizabeth Bennett was more to Frau's liking."

The last tear I wipe that day with my Frau-bandaged hands is for her. "I just hope the next governess is fit enough to survive me."

Boston, 1875

Forcibly dragged by my arm into his library, I am immediately thrust into a chair. The darkness of the room with those long foreboding shadows shooting up the walls frightens me not. But his temper does.

And the fact that Uncle, my mother's brother, dogs him as he paces the room causes me further agitation.

"You cannot do this, Dermot," my Uncle shouts.

"She is *my* offspring, Michael, I will do what I like. Besides a sixteen year old girl…"

"Sixteen or twenty-six, it makes no difference, Jennifer must stay in medical school. I will not allow you to remove her…"

"You! Not allow me! How dare you, Michael! You have no rights where she is concerned."

"I beg to differ. I've been paying her piano tuition…"

"You are ridiculous, Michael."

"She is a gifted musician and you know it. She could be great."

"Don't talk to me of such unmitigated nonsense."

"And then there are her university fees…"

"You both tricked me, you lied to me, and she is full of lies and deceit."

"She is my niece and she needed my help. I gave her my help willingly, because you and I both know that Aisling would have wanted her to be the best she can be…"

"How do you know what Aisling would have wanted? The girl is to marry Sheldon Reynolds and that is final. End of discussion."

"Oh no, brother-in-law, she is going to be a doctor. It's what she wants, she is brilliant and the university seems to agree. She is in the top three percent of her class. I will pay every single penny, do you hear me? I will pay."

"Don't be absurd, man! There is nothing in this for you. She'll forget you as soon as the last bill is paid."

"How wrong you are, Dermot."

"She's nothing but a trouble-maker and has been all her life. No, Michael, it is time someone outside this family had the dubious pleasure of taking care of her. Sheldon Reynolds has expressed interest and I believe that once he has subdued her…"

"Subdue her! You speak of your own flesh and blood as if she were an animal."

"Wild as one, you can't deny."

"I can and I do. Most fervently. Reynolds is too old, too mean and not at all suitable. The man is indelicate and we both know what he wants; I can't say it in front of the child. Dermot, he has been a widower for five years and is seen all over town. The condition of his health I cannot imagine. He will make her ill. I will NOT let you do this, Dermot. Give her to me. She can live with me. I will be her guardian. I will see that she finishes her education and begins her internship in a suitable medical institution."

"She's a woman, for God's sake! What medical institution will take a female doctor! She will get married and bear children and keep a decent home for Reynolds..."

"She's a girl who has deceived her way into university by means of her own true brilliance two years before she even had a right to sit for the entrance exams – when are you going to pull your head out of the sand? You have an extraordinary daughter, Dermot, and you cannot treat her the same as every other young woman."

The father of my brothers sucks in his breath and glares at my Uncle. The uncompromising coldness in his expression chills me to the bone and fear like I've never known in my whole life over-whelms me. I rush from the room, and the sound of my Uncle screaming my name is the last thing I hear before I leave the house.

I run to the university, and to Jim McGregor, a fellow student. I have been resisting his overtures for a long time because he thinks I am older than I really am. But suddenly I am very mature and I tell him that if he still wants me I will lay with him this one time, as long as he swears to tell no one. He gives his word, since he also requires his first lesson in these matters.

Mr McGregor's self-gratification is not mutual, but I bear his lustful fascination for my body, the awkwardness, and discomfit, for an extended biological understanding of the male of the species.

And the job is done.

When I return to the library of the father of my brothers that evening I tell him that Sheldon Reynolds will no longer want me. I am no longer 'intact'.

"You're lying!" the father of my brothers screams. My Uncle seizes the hand that bears down on me before it strikes. Both men are shaking as much as I am.

"No. I am not lying," I say. "Have me examined if you wish.

What do I care! I will not have Sheldon Reynolds and he will not have me, and that's all I care about."

Indeed they do stare at me, and in my eyes they see the truth.

"Who did this?" the father of my brothers demands to know.

"The blame is yours, Dermot, and yours alone," my Uncle rasps. "Now give me my niece and let me make a doctor of her."

I leave the house of the father of my brothers that night for good.

I am numb and wild and detached all at the same time. My maidenhood is irretrievable, and my virtue tarnished, a test for those who truly love me. Oddly, and despite everything that has happened, I am relieved that I no longer embody that overprized Boston commodity – a wealthy, eligible young woman – and that this part of being a female is over, and that now I can be a scientist and a single-minded woman with a passion to heal the sick; but, I swear by my mother's blood in my veins that my sanity is very much intact, and my life and my future are no longer in doubt.

My Uncle takes me to his house, which I love, a house full of light and sweet smells, the comfortable ticking of clocks, and his Irish housekeeper – the incomparable, twice-widowed Duffy. She insists on a hot bath; when this is accomplished I find Frank waiting for me in the parlor, where the hearth is ablaze with a roaring fire. Jeanne, his bride of twelve months, is with him. As Duffy potters around the room, pouring tea and pretending to be useful, Frank and I stare at one another; it is now that my eyes flood with tears.

"All will be well, George," he murmurs and folds me in his arms. We stare into the flames and I realize for the first time that Frank will always be the father that Dermot Sullivan should have been.

"There's nothing that time and a little tender loving care can't fix," says Duffy. "You'll see, Miss Jennifer." And she gives my chin a shake. There is a deeply caring smile in those experienced eyes.

"Come and have your tea," suggests Jeanne. She takes me by the hand and leads me to the cozy chair by the fire; she places a cup and saucer into my hands. "Drink."

I do as I am told.

Over the rim of the cup I watch my brother join his bride by the hearth. Because of Frank I know love; because of Frank and Jeanne I know how a man and a woman should love one another. She is sparkling and pretty, blonde hair and bright blue eyes, supremely domesticated, kind, feisty, smart and older than myself by only three years. They are comfortably settled; Frank is no slouch in the genius department either; at nearly twenty-two he is already an associate professor in mathematics at the university and I am extremely proud of him. I consider them thus, as I sip my tea; they anchor me to life while the storms rage all about me.

All *will* be well; the profound goodness of my Uncle and the abiding love of Frank and Jeanne will see it so.

Haven't I just been liberated?

I *am* filled with hope; I must not grieve for all the things I have lost. I am child enough, resilient enough, to endure this. I still believe that I can make a difference to the world using the intellect with which I am gifted.

I may never have what Frank and Jeanne have together, but I will always know it does exist because of them, and that just may be enough, to keep me sane, to keep hope trickling through my blood like a lifeline. They will never know how much I owe them, and yet already this is how I repay them, with a most cynical act.

They regard me solicitously. My brother bends down and kisses my forehead. Dear, dearest Frank. Death would have claimed me long ago if not for this brother, this friend, this teacher, this surrogate father…

I do not deserve him.

Luke

"So now you know everything," she concludes, her voice hoarse, as though her throat is fully grazed from speaking so long and hard.

Luke's eyes have been fixed on her trembling mouth for what seems like a lifetime, and from out of those sweet, soft-red lips has come such a history... such a barbaric, insane story.

He doesn't know whether to weep or rage; he gazes into those gorgeous green eyes with the firelight wriggling in them and realizes that he has already been weeping, the whole time, deep inside him; every place inside of him hurts.

He charges to his feet, the blood pounding in his head.

"I'll kill him."

"Luke..."

"You want me to kill Dermot, I will," he declares, sounding strange even to himself.

"No..." she says and throws herself against him, hugging his neck, pressing her face against his. "Just hold me. Very tight."

That's the easy part; well it would be if he weren't so dang agitated. Still, he does what she asks of him; holds his dearest one, his darling Jennifer, very tight to him.

"How much sweeter it was when you knew nothing about me..." she whispers.

Sweeter? Innocent and naïve – sweeter, no. No... To fall for a woman he knew was brilliant and compassionate and loving while

30

everything else about her had been a mystery, he had thought amazing and commendable – huh! Well, that was the easy part after all. And it was naïve in the extreme. Now their relationship is exposed to reality, like new grass to a late frost, and at the fickle mercy of the truth. He senses it, deep down inside of him: Dermot Sullivan has crushed the last surviving remnant of the innocence he was born with and which Jennifer's love had been protecting; ground it into dust like it was nothing. Only it wasn't nothing; he loved that she could do that; keep his soul safe. But it's crushed, that innocence. It survived the worst of death and heartbreak and guilt all life long, but now the crushing of Jennifer has crushed him.

There is nothing – *nothing* – sweet about the way he feels.

His agitation spills over and he lets her go. He removes her arms from around his neck and avoids looking into her eyes. Maybe he wouldn't be so emotional if he weren't still grieving the loss of Mart and K… who can say. All he knows is that anger and hatred have taken over him, they are unworthy of her and he can't control them.

"I need you to tell me what you're thinking…" she says.

She wants him to *speak*?

He struggles. "I need to be *angry*…"

"We should talk about why you're angry," she mutters quickly, breathlessly.

"Later – when I *can* talk."

"No, you don't understand…" she pleads. "I'm still me; I haven't changed just because you know, do you understand that, Luke…"

"This has *nothing* to do with that, believe me."

Against his better judgment, but desperate to release these vile emotions, he leaves her.

He runs to the harbor and charges onto a pier where a cold, stiff wind off the water pulls him up short. If only it could rip the angry heart out of him. Would even jumping into the icy deeps kill the heat inside of him?

Tears of rage swell in his eyes. His beautiful Jennifer…

Not once in his life has he ever felt unloved and disrespected – despised – by any member of his family. It doesn't make sense: every person who knows Jennifer respects her. And yet her own father… what kind of man would do this?

He thought he was mature enough to cope with whatever she told him.

Maybe he loves her too much.

Or his anger is justified.

Or he wishes she'd never told him at all.

Or maybe he's just come face to face with the real demands of loving her.

Maybe... maybe if he shoots her father, and her two older brothers, it would rid her of them for good. Her father would get what's coming to him...

"Luke..."

At the sound of her voice he turns.

His bright shining angel appears, illuminated by the pier lamp under which she is poised, a little breathless, her chestnut hair rippling in the breeze and her eyes ablaze. He is in awe of her, her courage and resilience.

Memories of their time in Cheyenne spring to life in his mind, of her kindness and her compassion, her understanding and her gentle humor. He's relieved that he cherished her then, but in the end he left her and forced her to cope with yet more heartache. He should fall at her feet and beg her forgiveness, assure her that from now on everything will be all right.

"How did you find me?"

"This is where the *Pacific Treader* was docked." She steps up to him; strokes his hair off his forehead. "Look at you... don't be so angry."

"How can I not be angry?" he grinds out against her softness.

His scolding tears are wiped with her cool, gentle fingers.

"All right, Luke. You can be angry and hurt and shocked."

He locks her inside his arms and buries his face in the chestnut cloud on her shoulder.

"I wanted to spare you this," she says, her voice trembling.

"I know, and I understand."

"The truth hurts, Luke, in remembering, in the retelling..."

He feels her body shaking; she's crying.

"I don't know how to make it better," he mutters.

"Or how to make it go away?"

There is an edge to her voice that scares him, accuses him. He lifts his head and looks straight into her drenched eyes. Defiance alters the line of her chin; tears on her cheeks trap the pier lights and glisten. He starts to panic and knows he can't keep it off his face. He desperately wants to say the right thing, but which is it:

Without her past they wouldn't be together now.

Or her past has made her the extraordinary woman she is.

Or he loves her beyond the heavens and for all time.

Or all three.

But all three seem trite and not how he feels exactly, or what he thinks she would want to hear. He needs time to think. To grieve, to understand, and to rage. And to work out what to do next so that his actions will be true.

Jennifer steps out of his grasp. "You need time to think. And I will give it to you. If anyone deserves time it's you. I never expected this anger from you; in fact I wasn't sure what you would do. True, I feared your pity, but that's not been your first response, who knows, it may come." She backs away from him. "I'm so sorry, Luke."

"You have nothing to be sorry for," he says. But another wave of anguish surges through him and he must fight it in order to declare what is at the heart of his frustration. "I love you, Jennifer, so much that it hurts, and I can't bear to think of you as disrespected and mistreated. For God's sake, you were just a baby... don't you understand... I want to go back in time, to stop him from hurting you, protect you..."

"Luke..."

"Why can't I ever seem to stop bad things happening to the people I love?"

All at once she rushes at him, and kisses him. She lingers close for one heady moment and murmurs, "So that's what you meant by you don't know how to make it better..." Then, as she slowly backs away again, she says, "I suspect that all your life, since what happened to your sister, you've wanted to protect the world against wickedness. And you may think that your gun is your weapon, but in essence it is your honor and gallantry and determination all rolled into one fine character."

"What are you talking about?"

"Such a character is more than I have ever imagined, or wanted, but only you can decide if it is what I deserve."

"Where are you going?" he says, choking on the words.

She doesn't answer; she turns and walks away quickly.

"Jennifer," he murmurs to himself. Sadness washes over him, turning that rage inside him into a lonely shore.

They are not individuals in this, not any more. If anything it has made him realize just how much they belong to each other, and with each other, and when you belong together to live one without the other hurts in the cruelest way, and your insides feel like one enormous empty cavern.

She deserves everything and anything that he can lay at her feet. She deserves to be happy. But his actions must be true. Hollow sounding platitudes are not worthy of either of them.

He watches her disappear into the shadows at the end of the pier. She knows that he loves her, but he's got to do better.

Just let me be angry, Jennifer, just this one time, and then I will be all that I can be, I promise.

Dermot

The following morning Dermot walks to the point and watches the North Atlantic grasping the wintry shore. For a man with a limited time on God's earth he feels remarkably strong. Being here makes him strong. Aisling's spirit is so very close.

Way out to sea he spies the signs of a nor'easter in the blue-gray clouds appearing on the horizon. The wind blusters and he wraps his coat tighter. He'd have to make tracks if he didn't want to get caught in the tail of the storm.

It won't be long, Aisling darlin', then we'll be together again.

We'll be like we use to be. There's something I've got to do first though.

I need to know how she turned out.

If the damn girl ever thinks of keeping the fourth commandment and comes and sees me!

By suppertime that evening, while Dermot is eating his lobster by the window overlooking the bay, Joseph returns with the reply to his telegram.

"Frank has sent the reply. He says that Jennifer has gone to Cheyenne and San Francisco and he doesn't know when she'll be back."

"Where on God's earth is Cheyenne again?"

"Wyoming territory, Father," says Joseph.

Dermot hears the forced patience in his son's voice and feels old.

"Ah, I remember now. That's where the trial was that Miles' old college friend Faraday won for those ranchers. You see, Joseph, I'm not so decrepit."

"I never said you were, Father. Anyway, Frank says he will tell her when she returns."

"Let me see the telegram," Dermot demands. Joseph hands it to him and Dermot holds it into the light of his lamp.

```
FATHER. JENNIFER IN CHEYENNE OR SAN FRANCISCO. DO NOT
KNOW HER RETURN DATE AT THIS STAGE. WILL TELL HER OF
YOUR REQUEST TO SEE HER WHEN SHE RETURNS. REGARDS. FRANK.
```

"Short and to the point." Dermot gives a chuckle. "Still looking out for her, aren't you, big brother Frank?"

"Will that be all, Father?"

"Yes, Joseph." Dermot studies him momentarily. "Why do I get the impression that you are not comfortable with this whole idea?"

Joseph buries his hands in his pockets. "What you do with Jennifer is neither here nor there to me, Father. She loves Frank because Frank is, and always has been, good to her. She hates you and I think you like it that way. It means that you can hate her with a clear conscience. It's a damnable legacy and, personally, I would not care to be lining up at heaven's gate with that as my ticket of entry. Now will that be all, Father?"

Dermot nods his head slowly. Joseph leaves him with his lobster supper. Will she come, the daughter who always called him the father of her brothers? Will she face this last cruelty? It irks him that the bane of his existence holds the key to his eternal life.

The days pass by like the waves on the Atlantic shoreline.
Endless.
Insistent.
Unforgiving.
Winter ravishes Cape Cod; it howls and storms and leaves no grain of sand undefiled.
Dermot waits…

TWO

Westward the star of empire
takes its way.

Ed. Cheyenne Leader
26th October, 1867

Ben

Omaha, Nebraska
January 28, 1885

Ben checks his look in the mirror.

He can't see his whole reflection because he's outgrown the mirror. That tends to happen when a tall man of twenty-six peers into the mirror that long ago suited a boy... and a much smaller house. It's been his mirror since he can remember; and it got packed with all their furniture when they quit Montana twelve years ago and set up here – as a family heirloom it's an oddity; who the heck keeps a mirror as an heirloom?

He recalls the day he asked his mother that question; he was told to have more respect for something of value, that his great uncle greatly prized it. Why, she couldn't seem to tell him.

Once a week she takes if off the wall, dusts and polishes the ornate walnut frame, and cleans the looking-glass, like some ritual that connects her to her past life; so the mirror is as immaculate as the day his great uncle left it. Maybe it holds fond memories for her, he doesn't know.

For him, Montana is always present in his mind when he looks into it. It is a good thing to be a boy raised on a ranch: no matter what his parents might think of that difficult existence now; despite the three lonely years he attended college back East; and regardless of the kind of life he is expected to live as a businessman in Omaha.

Things go to plan, run on schedule, in his family. That's why his father excelled in business where he crashed out in ranching.

The scheduled precision of the day-to-day suits Richard Taylor, who thrives on running a tight outfit. Anything not planned gets pushed out of the way, dealt with, chopped...

He cringes and squeezes his eyes shut. This is his future. A man doesn't question a future in which everything is laid out for him.

He steadies himself and opens his eyes. His image is perfect; there is nothing he needs to adjust.

Shouting in the street below his window draws him across the room, where he parts the curtain and peers out. The sun is shining on a thick cover of snow. And two of their neighbors are airing their grievances on the sidewalk...

This is *her* favorite time of year: *Christmas is over and the New Year stretches ahead with so many bright promises.*

He never really understood what she was on about; she could be a flibbertigibbet at times and yet beneath that veneer there persisted a quiet conviction that he couldn't help but admire...

There's a knock on his door, disturbing his daydream. His father enters, dressed similarly to himself; well-cut three-piece suit and necktie, hair smoothed back and face deadly serious.

"Just checking that everything is on track for the board meeting this morning."

"The figures are exact; the books are up-to-date," Ben tells him.

"Good," his father says and then studies him silently.

"Something the matter, Father?"

"I was going to ask you the same question."

The something-the-matter-with-Ben Richard Taylor's son cannot, under any circumstances, talk about with his father.

"The neighbors are arguing again. Breakfast, then?"

His father frowns thoughtfully and nods his head. "Sure."

Later that morning

When the last board member has left the room, Ben sinks back into his chair, sighs heavily and presses his fingers into his stinging eyes. He hears his father returning, so he straightens up and busily gathers his books and papers.

His father is beaming. "That went well, don't you think?"

"Yes."

"So, what did you think of our new man?"

"Mr Bodecker?"

"Mm. Got a lot to offer, I think."

"Sure, Father."

"Powerful connections."

Too powerful. And arrogant. Smiled too much…

"He was impressed with our set up. Yes, sir, he's going to help us expand this sand, gravel and limestone operation into something big, right into the extensive coal mining operations of Wyoming, Ben. Coal low in sulphur and perfect fuel for this booming nation. It's just the direction we need to go and Loren Bodecker is just the man we need. Everyone is going to sit up and take notice of us, mark my words. Oh, he said you were the best figures man he'd ever come across."

"Very flattering," Ben says and wishes he hadn't. His father's eyes narrow on him.

"Something bothering you, Ben? Because if you don't like a powerful man like Bodecker paying you compliments…"

Ben picks up his pile of books and papers. "Not at all, Father. Good of him to acknowledge the effort it took to get this ready in time. Got work to do… I'll see you at supper."

His father nods and Ben strides out of the room and into his office two doors up. He drops his armful on his desk and heads straight for the pitcher in the corner. He dumps some water in a tumbler and gulps it down. Why does he still feel like he's choking?

Again, he finds himself gazing out the window at the street; it's busy, productive, vibrant… and then her voice intrudes.

"If only you knew your heritage, knew Luke… You have his eyes, you know; we both do. Our great great grandfather Matthew's eyes. I won't give up on you, Ben. No matter how long it takes."

What on earth was she talking about?

Many months have passed since she uttered those words and he still can't get them – or her sad, tear-washed face – out of his head. He didn't care for Luke, his 'cousin', son of a Confederate; but this forebear Matthew – who was he?

She knew, but he didn't. And what was so special about their heritage that it causes a loving, obedient child to rebel against her parents, marry a man they disapproved of, and then expect them to help her when the husband is killed and she and the child she is expecting need a home. And yet as bad as all this sounds, he knew his sister. They were close once, before Mart Keaton, the husband. Once she took up with him there was no getting through to her. And yet, did she change all that much?

And what does she mean by she won't give up on him?

To his very core he wishes she'd never said anything before she left the house that day; it's haunted him day and night to the point that the desire to know about this great great grandfather pushes every other thought out of his mind and causes his hands to shake.

His eyes, his eyes… what does she mean? The color? His own are a dark blue, similar to Tressa's. Their cousin's are the same then? And how does Tressa know what color Matthew's were?

It all goes round and round in his head like it always does, a potter's wheel of unwieldy clay, and he can't stand not knowing what it all means.

Damn you, Tressa.

He rushes out of his office, barely stops to tell the office secretary that he will be gone for the rest of the day, and gets himself outside into the bracing chill. Despite it, he loosens his tie and collar and heads for home.

Since the day Tressa left he has been forbidden to communicate with her, an edict he has only just begun to realize he was observing with puerile compliance. The fact is she has the answers to end this torment and get his life back on track, which is and always will be to follow in his father's footsteps.

So he will mark the beginning. He will fix this once and for all and stop this madness. And the place to begin is a pile of old news-papers and letters tied up with string in a locked drawer in the bedroom that once belonged to his sister.

Emmaline

Cheyenne, Wyoming
January 28, 1885

Emmaline steps down from the train into the icy world that is Cheyenne in the depths of its long winter. Thankfully, she had the sense not only to buy woolen drawers but put them on. It is not long, however, before the cold has seeped into her lungs and her chest stings. She's shivering all over as she pays a porter to deliver her trunk and other luggage to the boarding house in which she has arranged to be accommodated.

Welcome to Cheyenne the sign reads. Mercy. Barely three o'clock and already pre-dusk gloom is creeping across the town. Well, no one forced her to come here; she wanted a frontier job and the Cheyenne Tribune wanted her:

Young, enthusiastic journalist, ambitious to succeed and keen to expand investigative experience. Someone not from around these parts. Far away parts actually. Distant, warmer parts…

She consults her scribbled instructions… she heads out of the passenger depot and looks up and down what is 15th Street; she's supposed to head west but a good long look in that direction has seediness written all over it, and she'd rather that was not her first impression of Cheyenne. So she proceeds directly north up Hill Street, prepared to make a left at 16th Street instead; that done, she eventually arrives at Eddy Street, as required, where she veers right.

She shivers all the way.

This is one busy town… The wide, snowy streets are lively with commerce. There are emporiums and mercantile, grocery stores, hotels, banks, bars and cafes. Distinctive buildings of two and three stories. She wasn't expecting it to be so sophisticated, wealthy-looking, and civilized; after all, it began its life as a 'hell on wheels' town (she had researched all she could), and the frontier, beyond the reach of the railroad, is just over the frozen prairies on the horizon; although she suspects that eighteen years of stupendous growth might not be long enough for this leopard to completely change its spots. At least dodging people, wagons and horses keeps her mind off the extreme chill. She crosses the intersection and in the next block locates the Tribune's front door. She dives inside and pushes the door shut. The climate is still 'hell'...

While she shudders aloud, a too-young-to-be-balding man who happens to be walking by remarks, "Wait till next month."

She tries to speak, or even smile, but her lips are frozen; a little disconcerting.

"Cup your hands around your mouth and blow on them."

She removes her gloves and does as he suggests.

"That's the ticket. Now, what can I do for you?"

There is some improvement and she is able to ask, "Where's the boss?"

"Who wants to know?"

"Emmaline Roberts, new reporter."

"In that case, you go down the hall..." He stops. "Say, what is this? Does the Chief know you're a woman?"

"I believe so," she says and this time manages the grin.

"What's the world coming to," he mutters and walks off.

"Down the hall you say?" she says to his back.

"Last door on the right." Mr Balding-too-young is still shaking his head when he disappears into a room and shuts the door. The door opens again and his head appears. "And don't think for a minute I'm gonna be watching my language."

"As long as that doesn't include swapping recipes, the price of lace and what color works best with green, your language won't bother me in the least. Mr...?"

The door slams shut again. A woman in this game is only as good as her last story and hers happened to win an award. She can tolerate a few slammed doors.

Her boss, Charles E. Quaid, editor-in-chief of the Tribune, and who she immediately decides looks like a 'Chuck', is decidedly more hospitable. For a start, there is a large potbelly stove heating his office and he insists that she sit near it while he puts a mug of hot coffee into her hands.

Chuck is aged about forty, strong features, a good head of hair, which is silvering above his ears, medium height and physique; his three-piece suit hangs on him as though he is required to wear it but would rather not. The coat and waistcoat are unbuttoned and his necktie dangles in uneven strands down his shirtfront.

She sips her coffee.

"Now, Roberts, you are aware that we are not the biggest news-paper in town…"

Her insides begin to thaw. "Cheyenne boasts numerous news-papers and journals, as I understand it, but presently the Bugle has that distinction I believe."

"Mm, but if you can get the story that I hired you to get, I think the Bugle's days of wearing that crown are numbered."

"I relish the prospect. In your letter you said that you believe the Bugle did an uncharacteristically poor job of reporting a sensational story that broke some months ago. What is that story, Mr Quaid, now that I am here?"

"Well, I'll give you a stack of files and such for you to read for yourself, and you can draw your own conclusions, and then we'll talk some more in the morning. The main thing I want you to keep in mind is that I believe there is a cover-up going on in this town and I want you to find out what it is. Have you got that, Roberts?"

"Certainly." She places her cup down. "If you give me the files now, Mr Quaid, I'll get started at once."

Chuck gives her a shrewd look. "You'll have to excuse the anti-female sentiment around here, Roberts. The last female we had on staff went over to the Bugle. She was my secretary, helped out in the office and such. We don't appreciate that kind of disloyalty."

She stands up. "I understand, Mr Quaid. "

"Your sex ain't necessarily disloyal by nature but you do tend to become romantically attached."

She is unsure as whether to hide her surprise or declare it.

"Yes, Cora Daniels decided to fall in love with the Bugle's sub-editor, and I decided not to replace her."

Decided? She thinks she begins to understand him. Poor Cora.

"You won't have any problems with me on that score, Mr Quaid, I assure you."

Chuck gives her an amused look which adopts a more serious quality as his outstretched hand comes toward her.

"Shall we shake on it, Roberts?"

She stares at him and then at his hand.

This was a first. For anywhere.

You want this job more than anything, Roberts; pull yourself together.

Right… She clutches Chuck's hand firmly.

Chuck chuckles. "Excellent. You know, Roberts, you might just win some respect for your gender in this business, if you can hold to that promise and get the story."

She nods brusquely, fiercely holding her tongue since she wants to debate how forming a romantic attachment (of which she has no intention, good grief) could possibly interfere with her doing her job properly and professionally.

"The files, Mr Quaid? I shall get started."

Chuck places a juicy stack of files and back copies of the Tribune, the Bugle and various other publications into her arms. "See you in the morning. I'll get Simons to show you your desk."

Chuck opens his door, hollers for this Simons who appears as though he materialized out of thin air, and barks orders at him like a cavalry sergeant. She decides that calling Mr Quaid 'Chuck' in her mind, where it could at any moment slip out, might not be the best idea. Mr Quaid bids her good day. She also decides not to call Simons 'Mr Balding-too-young'. He could just turn out to be her best friend. Her mother would say, as she often has, *you are not at home now, Emmie, remember that.*

At the far end of a large, darkening room of desks there is a window encrusted on the outside with snow; she dumps her armful on the table Simons had indicated and crosses the room to peer out. Evening is fast approaching; citizens scurry about the street. *Home before dark,* her mother used to say. And the old hymn: *Night may come down.*

Ben

Omaha

In Tressa's lonely and discarded room, Ben succumbs to the chill and lights a fire in the little hearth. The flames burst into life, leaping about, wriggling to release their warmth...

He misses her; he admits it, not something he has ever allowed himself to do. He gazes over his shoulder at the collection of letters from her husband and other papers strewn across her bed behind him. Facts he can deal with, but the emotion... he was not prepared for that.

Like many things his father considered useless, his imagination had been pretty much drummed out of him and replaced by a cold reality, but that doesn't prevent him from picturing what had befallen his sister.

Mart Keaton, a rancher from Bright River, Wyoming, strolls into their mining offices right here in Omaha three years ago and sees Tressa. According to the letters, they fall in love at first sight, not something he would ascribe to himself. Yet, in his mind, the letters of Mart Keaton are definitely those of an honorable, sincere man. The man who loved his sister deeply, and desperately... They are married one week later in Omaha without anyone knowing except for Tressa's friend Layla Wilkes.

A deep, shaky sigh wells up inside of him.

Layla Wilkes.

Resentment towards the woman fidgets in his stomach. He never thought Layla was good for much; perhaps he's right, but she was a true friend to his sister and so could now be quite valuable to him.

For the second time this day, and only one of a few times in his adult life, he acts on impulse. Leaving everything as it is, he rushes from the room; at the bottom of the stairs he grabs his coat and thrusts his arms into the sleeves.

Along the dark and icy streets he marches, to the house of Layla Wilkes. She is married herself now, with a child. He thumps on the door and ignoring the protestations of the housekeeper, pushes his way in; he strides into the living room, demanding to see Layla.

While the housekeeper endeavors to stand her ground, Layla appears.

He glares at her.

The housekeeper is reassured and dismissed.

"Well?" Layla demands of him.

"You knew. You were there," he accuses her.

"It's late, Ben."

"You. Were. *There.*"

Layla's eyes flash. "Of course I was there. I was all she had. Anyway, what's brought this on, how did you find out?"

"I read her letters…"

Layla stares at him. Then, with irritating calmness, she walks to the fireplace. "So, you finally read Mart's letters, the words that meant so much to her, that she cherished – and yet she left them behind, what could she have been thinking?"

"You are insinuating that it wasn't an oversight on her part?" As galling as it is, he secretly agrees with her.

"So Tressa wanted you to know that your father forbade the marriage and threatened to cut her off from her family, that Mart insisted that she never disclose their marriage, never get herself cut off, that she pretended and lied about it because she loved him so much, that eventually she discovered he was hunting down an outlaw to protect his family and your cousin's family and he thought he might be killed and that's why he didn't want her to say anything about their marriage, that they fought about it, that they lived a nightmare instead of happily ever after. And do you know the rest?"

"Oh, you are so clever, why don't you tell me."

"I have received a letter from Tressa every two weeks since she left. I know everything, while you, her own brother, know nothing. Do you even care, Ben, what she has suffered, do you even know that she has a *son*?"

He swallows, feeling pain in his throat. "No."

"What *do* you care about? Your father's company? Inheriting it? Becoming a big man in this town like Richard Taylor... a man who disowns his daughter in her hour of need?"

"Enough, Layla," he mutters.

She lowers herself into a chair by the fireplace.

"What else do you want to know?" she asks quietly.

"I want you to tell me everything."

The suspicious glare she sends him from across the room makes him even more uncomfortable. "Who are you doing this for, Ben? Your folks, Tressa or yourself?"

He deserves this, but he won't give Layla the satisfaction of seeing the blow. "It's none of your business, Layla."

Layla throws back her head and laughs. "None of my business!"

She gets up and crosses to a writing desk by the window. She scoops something up and strides toward him, holding out a folded letter. "Here. Read this. Tressa's most recent letter. I received it two days ago. Read it, Ben, and then tell me if your reasons are none of my business."

He takes the letter; he stares at it for some time, unsure, afraid of what it contains.

"It won't bite you," Layla taunts, "or maybe you're afraid it will condemn you."

No man likes to be accused of cowardice – he unfolds the letter to reveal Tressa's fine, gentle hand.

My dearest Layla,

I hope this letter finds you and your dear little family well and happy. I myself am well, and little Adam, too, which is amazing considering the weather – we are almost snowed in.

Amy and John continue to brighten a little as the

long days trudge on. They grieve so deeply for Kelley, more so than for Mart because Mart died such an honorable death, and Kelley's so futile. I miss her terribly. And I miss my Mart. Adam is so like him and I am glad of that because I feel Mart's presence every day and his love made manifest in our dear little boy.

Motherhood is a joyful occupation and I believe that I am better at it than I thought I would be. Of course I have Amy's excellent help and guidance.

But Layla, here is my very best news. Luke is not leaving America after all. He sent Ethan a telegram and Ethan came over especially to tell us. I am so happy. To have Luke back again is more than I ever dreamed possible after everything that has happened. Why he has decided to stay and when he is to return exactly we do not know, but in these dark days it is something to look forward to. He will lift our spirits, renew our courage.

Of course, when I think about Luke I inevitably think about Ben. I think of Ben every day, praying that he will forgive me for leaving him, hoping that his heart will be softened, and that he will begin to see.

Well, my dearest and most loyal friend, I hear Adam waking for his supper, so I will close for now.

Write soon and tell me all your news.

Affectionately, as always, Tressa.

Tressa… *what has happened to you…* his stomach collapses. Shakily, he refolds the letter and glances at Layla.

Surprisingly, her harsh expression has completely softened.

"So, what will you do?" she asks.

He hands her the letter. "There is so much I need to know."

"You know and I know that there is only one person who can answer all your questions."

He agonizes. "I don't know if I will be welcome."

Layla shakes the letter in his face. "You read this, what do you think?"

"I think she will be happier to see my cousin than me!"

"Jealous of a man you don't even know, or care to know? Ben Taylor, I am ashamed of you. I know a great deal about your cousin, a great deal more than you, from Tressa's letters and newspaper reports of the Ed Parsons trial last year. He is an honorable man, and Tressa loves him because he is her cousin and because his best friend was her husband and they were like brothers. There is a rich vein for you to tap into, waiting for you, but you've got to shake off your prejudices. Do you understand, Ben?"

He has been steeped in extreme prejudice towards his cousin and that side of the family from his earliest memory; his father would denounce his brother Morgan Taylor's family as southern scum...

...we don't want people in this family who would hold back this grand nation by endorsing slavery and dividing our people and prosperity with secession from the union...

Ben's mother would argue that family is different, that blood is thicker than politics, or even principle; but his father would brush her opinion aside.

Something in Richard Taylor will not forgive people's differences – where is the freedom in that?

He looks up at Layla, whose eyes betray her excitement.

If he is ever to know peace of mind again, he must do this.

"How do I find the Keaton ranch in Bright River, Wyoming?"

Faraday

Cheyenne
January 28, 1885

Faraday pours himself a drink and crosses to the hearth.

He gazes into the fire, appreciates the warmth on such a night; he remembers and contemplates and imagines, all done in good faith of course. A man in his position cannot afford to be cynical. It would be so easy to slide into cynicism. Even comfortable. But these times are not simple, and a man's principles tend to complicate matters considerably.

He knew the investigation would be problematic and dangerous, but so far it has proved well nigh impossible. He and Cliff, despite Cliff being the most fastidious sheriff this town would have ever known, have very few leads; an investigation such as this requires the utmost care, so it must proceed cautiously, and this damnable weather slows everything down even further. Even Cliff's planned expedition to interrogate Parsons in the Colorado State Pen had to be postponed while they waited for a string of blizzards to subside; he got through eventually, and now Faraday had to hope he could get back again before something else blew in. Anything Cliff could coax, squeeze or coerce out of that despicable old man should be worth something.

Faraday places his glass on the table and picks up Luke's file that's been sitting there. It's a unique document, without a doubt, as one-of-a-kind as its creator. The skill and the imagination and the daring of that creative mind are the very things he needs right now.

When he set out on this discreet investigation of tycoon Loren

Bodecker, he never imagined that he'd need Luke to do it. Luke's part in all this was surely over. He'd suffered enough, done enough, sacrificed enough. But the truth is that Luke is the heart and soul of the investigation because it all stems from his file. This amazing chronicle, packed with sketches of people and places, and factual accounts signed by various witnesses, and Luke's own conclusions drawn from all he had collected, helped condemn two despicable men to prison and a murdering outlaw to the gallows...

Faraday locates the page – *that* page! Luke's sketch of Bodecker's face floats there before him in the flickering light of the fire. There, inadvertently, is incriminated a man so powerful that one mistake by Faraday now could mean the end of his career.

Cliff also feels the heat in this regard, but they vowed it must be done. Faraday had given his word.

"So! What are you doing there, husband of mine?"

Meg's abrupt and typically vivacious entrance jolts him to the core. The file nearly slips from his grasp. Meg's quick hands dive under it before there is a disaster.

"I'm sorry, Cam," she says, righting the pages. She looks up into his face and he wishes she wouldn't see the concern he can't hide from her. "Luke's file again, I see."

"Mm..." is all he can mutter.

She places the file on the table and rather sweetly puts his drink back in his hand instead. She's altogether sweet, with her dark curls and flashing eyes, and with her round, protruding belly. Gently he places his other hand on it, and imagining the child within, brings himself back to a calmer, safer place.

Meg's warm hands cover his cold one. "What's the matter, Cam? You must tell me. What is it about Luke's file that has you so worried?"

Should he tell her, or protect her? – the ongoing dilemma.

"I wish Luke were here..."

Meg grins softly. "So do I. Then you would stop fretting over that old file, and Jen would be here too."

It's Faraday's turn to smile. "You think so, do you?"

"She won't return without him, be sure of that!"

Faraday laughs at her.

Then, they are serious together.

"It's her birthday," Meg murmurs, and her eyes begin to glisten. "Darling Jen…"

"Mm."

"Do you think she has told him everything?"

Faraday strokes her cheek, so soft beneath his finger. "It was her intention, but I don't know."

"A secret deep and dark," Meg murmurs. "Sometimes I don't feel right about knowing."

"You know, Meg, Dermot Sullivan saw to it that every day of George's young life was punctuated with shame. And that is how she sees it even now. She feels chained to it, like a convict. But she needs her very closest friends to know so that we can be a place of refuge. She loves you… trusts you."

Meg grins engagingly. "She loves and trusts Luke."

"Mm, but I think it is different because…"

"How do you think Luke will react when he knows?"

Faraday leaves his explanation of why the situation is different, and admits he has often asked himself the same question. "Without a doubt he loves her a great deal. Difficult to say… When he left for San Francisco after Wilson Cutter's hanging, with Miss Keaton murdered, he was in no fit state to handle his *own* life, let alone one as complex as Jennifer's."

"I can't imagine him abandoning her though. Her telegram said she had found him, that he wasn't leaving, that they were going to work it all out. That all sounds very promising to me. And you yourself said a number of times that Luke never gives up."

"Well, he has her measure all right, so we can hope for the best."

Meg's eyes blaze approvingly. Then, intriguingly, she quietens, softens… "Cam, there is something else, something I think I should tell you. I… well, I know you don't want me to know what it is about Luke's file that worries you, but I already know."

She has the gall to look contrite, while Faraday experiences an odd mixture of relief and disappointment.

"Everything in Luke's file makes sense in relation to the trial of Ed Parsons and Wilson Cutter's hanging, except for one…"

He covers her mouth with his hand. Her eyes bulge.

"Don't say it," he mutters.

Meg removes his hand impatiently. "Cam, I want you to know that you should do what you feel you must."

"What do you mean?"

"You know what I mean. You worry about it constantly."

"Do you really understand what you are saying, Meg?"

"Of course. It's not over, Cam, the fight. If you want to fight, with everything you've got, whole-heartedly, with all the means at your disposal, if you think it necessary and worth everything, then so do I."

He deposits his glass and puts his arms around his Meg.

"Where would I be without you to say all will be well?"

"I have no idea. I just hope Jen and Luke are doing the same right now and they are on their way back to us."

Strangely, he's not so worried about George.

Luke, on the other hand, is a man who feels things very deeply; sometimes that can be a good thing, and sometimes it can leave a man in a very precarious place.

Emmaline

Cheyenne

Emmaline looks directly into the mirror at her reflection in order to practice what she will be discussing with Mr Quaid in the morning and get it straight in her own mind.

"The facts are these," she says, pinching one cheek pink and then the other. "An evil rancher named Ed Parsons resorted to extortion, bribery and murder in order to acquire the ranch belonging to the Keaton family and the Diamond-T ranch belonging to the Taylor and Benchley families. In the trial, Parsons' defense attorney Walter McKinnon argued that when the Keatons, the Taylors and the Benchleys refused to renew Parsons' contract to water his cattle in their river, the rancher did what he needed to do. But the truth is that Parsons wanted the land, he used an outlaw named Wilson Cutter to harass and intimidate Mart Keaton, and the outlaw eventually murdered him..."

She stops and frowns at the complexities of the case, creating a wrinkle in her forehead. She rubs it smooth.

"So... we know Ed Parsons is the bad guy. Where is that trial transcript?" Leaving the mirror, she digs through all the papers spread out on her bed. "Bad guy, yes, yes... Here we go. What does our prosecuting attorney Mr Faraday say in summing up..."

She thumbs through a copy of the trial transcript until she finds the attorney's summation; while not the best transcript she's ever seen, it's certainly not the worst... she slides her finger down the page, skimming through as she needs to, and reading the bits that are significant to her.

When in the last two years of his life, Mart Keaton chose to write down what was and what did happen to him and his family and the Diamond-T families, he concluded, I swear on the Bible that this account is the truth, and then he quotes John 8:32 – Then you will know the truth and the truth will set you free.

"Mm... Mart Keaton's journal was key evidence, of course. No one knew he was keeping it and he had recorded all of Ed Parsons' crooked dealings and how he used Wilson Cutter. Now..."

In September 1882 ... Parsons ... forced Mart Keaton before him and threatened him and the families with bloodshed if the water contract was not renewed ... Mart Keaton specifically states in his journal that he dared not tell anyone ... because the slightest protest would make it very convenient for Ed Parsons to initiate bloodshed...

"Tricky for poor old Mart."

The instrument of this threat was ... the outlaw Wilson Cutter, whom Ed Parsons paid handsomely to intimidate and threaten not only Mart Keaton, but also members and employees of the families. The fact is that Wilson Cutter under the direct orders of Ed Parsons murdered Mart Keaton.

"And he hanged for his crime."
She pushes her shoulders back and forward hoping to ease the stinging knots that had very happily settled themselves there.

And there was a middleman whom we have heard about, particularly from the file doggedly compiled by Mr Taylor and painstakingly verified by Sheriff Ryan ...

"Oh yes, the file! Which no one has seen since the trial; where did that end up, I wonder? With the Taylors? According to all these back copies it was a work of art, and when Mart Keaton's journal was unearthed late in the trial, the two records went together like a key in a lock..."

This middleman was a sheriff ... Ed Parsons colluded with him ... bribed an officer of the law.

Never a good idea to do that.

She rubs her eyes, her thoughts reverting to the file – the prosecuting attorney, what's his name... Faraday... could still have it... The idea gives her heart a jolt. Interesting if he did, considering it is the property of this hero Luke.

We heard ... that at no time ... Ed Parsons' ranch was in dire need of water. The Alliance families ... dared to defy this pirate ... and have been paying the price ever since ... have a fine and noble heritage on the land that they intend to pass down to future generations ... integrity ...

"Integrity, Mr Faraday. I think you liked these people."

... with its backbone of truth cannot be pushed aside. Mart Keaton proved this with his life and his death – and with the triumph of his journal which he wanted his sister to bring into the light because he saw her as the brightest, most fervent exponent of the truth. We should not treat the honor Mart Keaton bestowed on his sister lightly. In her hands you will remember that Mart Keaton's journal became like a sword to carve up the web of lies camouflaging the crimes of Ed Parsons. From her mouth came his words; from her heart came the strength of those words and from her soul, the spirit of them. The truth...

"Mm, Mart's sister, Kelley. She found Mart's journal and that was basically the end of Parsons, Cutter and the crooked sheriff. A worthy young woman; Mr Faraday seemed to think so, as did her brother. She stood up for him and was determined to see justice done."

She thrusts her hand across the bed for the last article ever written about the Alliance. Leaving the transcript aside for the moment, she rereads the article.

Miss Keaton, described in the Bugle article as 'a jewel in the crown of the Alliance, with her flaxen hair and blue eyes', was shot dead by a single bullet to the head after the trial by an unknown assassin, still unknown presumably. This, she assumes, is where the trail to the ultimate truth went cold.

The investigation is ongoing, the article tells, but unless Mr Quaid has withheld something, she concludes that after almost five months the investigation has gone south.

She reverts to the trial transcript.

Ed Parsons is a land grabber of the worst kind ... quite blatantly prepared to lie, cheat, steal, threaten, bribe, conspire and murder to get what he wants ...

"But did he conspire to kill the sister, Miss Kelley Keaton?"

... it is in your hands to stop him right now. Then our community will be free of Ed Parsons and the danger he presents to us...

"Are you sure about that, Mr Faraday? You couldn't have been so certain after Miss Keaton was killed... Oh, I see, Mr Quaid, what is troubling you..."

... then these families who have had their courageous son, brother, husband, father and friend so brutally taken from them will once again be free to live and work on their land, without the threat of danger that Ed Parsons has inflicted upon them for many years.

"How did you feel, Mr Faraday, when that danger did not stop and Miss Keaton was murdered?"

Outraged, angry, determined to fight on?

If so, why hasn't Miss Keaton's killer been apprehended and brought to justice?

What have you and your sheriff been doing all this time?

She spends another hour before bed reading other parts of the transcript, particularly those relating to Luke Taylor's file.

Comparison of the two men, Taylor and Mart Keaton, seems inevitable; Mart was straightforward and noble, perhaps a little stoical; Taylor, on the other hand, seems complex, intelligent and unafraid to speak his mind.

She makes notes from the back copies and transcripts, and as she does, the pictures form and swim about in her head. If Mr Quaid's hunch is correct and there is a cover-up going on for whatever reason, she firmly believes that it does not come from within the Alliance. The Keaton, Taylor and Benchley clans were good honest folk who had fallen prey to something vile and sinister.

Ben

Ben returns to the house.

He picks up the pace when he remembers that he left Tressa's letters all spread out on top of the bed. If his father should see there would be hell to pay, and the demand for an explanation he is not ready to give, nor talk about; all is emotion, feelings of regret and shame, of loss and the need to retrieve what has been lost, and above all, the desire to understand burning away inside of him.

The house is quiet when he enters.

He bounds the stairs to Tressa's room to find his mother sitting on the bed amid the letters. He receives a jolt at first... then he sees that although his mother is surrounded by Tressa's memorabilia, she stares serenely into the low flames in the hearth.

"Mother..."

Her eyes drift to his face. "I've been hoping that one day you would do this..."

He moves to the hearth, picks up the poker and stabs at the fire. His mother, meanwhile, has lapsed back into silence... Concern for the letters grips him and he goes to the bed and begins collecting them, folding each one with care.

"Why?" he says at last.

Her hand reaches for his forearm. "My duty is to stay with your father. I took that vow twenty-eight years ago this April."

Astounded, he stops what he's doing.

"And while you, my son, are a product of that vow, you took no such vow yourself."

He frowns, disbelieving. "Are you telling me that I should disobey Father?"

"I am telling you that a young man must follow his heart, listen to his instincts... find his own way if he must. Fathers and sons can be alike, Ben, but often that is not known until later when the son looks back and says, I never realized how much I am like my father... and daughters say it too, about their mothers," she adds, her eyes dropping to the letters on the bed. "And what most parents want above all for their children is that they don't make the same mistakes."

"Mother..."

She hushes him gently. "You are a strong, intelligent, capable young man with your whole life ahead of you. I wish I'd said these things to you a long time ago – don't make that mistake with your own children." She smiles warmly, stands up and straightens the coverlet where she's been sitting. "Leave the room exactly as you found it."

Thought-provoked by his mother's sentiments, he barely notices her leave, although he hears the door snapping shut. It brings him to his senses, so he finishes gathering the letters and does exactly as she tells him, leaving the room as he found it. The only remnant of his visit is the lingering warmth from the now extinguished fire.

He writes late into the night... a letter for his father. There is nothing he can say that his father would ever understand, so as he thinks of clear, succinct phrases he jots them down, while he fills one large suitcase and a leather travel bag with his belongings.

He realizes he has nothing for the child until he catches a glimpse of his serious, gray-looking reflection in his boy mirror.

From his suitcase he removes the top layers of clothes, lifts the small mirror from the wall and wraps it in a towel. He packs it in his luggage between his clothes. The idea is impulsive, he admits, and probably one he will have a great deal of trouble trying to explain.

He sleeps restlessly, barely at all, waiting for daybreak, at which time he dresses warmly, checks that he has everything, and places the letter on his pillow.

He leaves his father's house stealthily and heads off into cheerless streets sheathed by a freezing mist moving in off the Missouri.

At Union Station, the UP's early bird is all ready steamed up and keen to be moving. This is the train Layla suggested he take; the railroad will shadow the Platte River across Nebraska until the river splits in two in the vicinity of the town of North Platte; the line heads due west to the Wyoming border and eventually arrives in Cheyenne late in the evening; here it will stop over for a brief period before it pushes on overnight to Laramie and beyond.

However, he has decided not to go directly to Laramie, and plans instead to stop over a night in Cheyenne; something tells him he should take a look at the town where the trial and the tragedy took place before he sees Tressa.

Having instructed the porter regarding the fragile nature of his suitcase, he boards with his leather travel bag in hand. He chooses a seat on the outbound side of the car; the temperature is at or below freezing outside and only marginally better inside. A ruddy-faced conductor shuffles down the aisle, reading his mind:

"Don't worry, folks, it'll warm up a bit once we get going... by the time we pass through Fremont you'll be as warm as you please... stops along the way include Grand Island, North Platte and Sidney... 'course no trip across Nebraskee is complete without a set down at Ogallala, one of the most famous cow towns in the West and destination of more Texas herds than you can imagine ..."

He reminds himself he has no imagination, particularly about things relating to a dim memory he has of his never-spoken about uncle and cousin being ranchers from Texas...

"...be in Cheyenne by midnight... coffee's hot, dining car's warm as toast and we got most of the local and syndicated newspapers right on board... breakfast served from seven o'clock..."

Train travel never did excite him much, but this particular trip has his stomach in such a state that he thinks he'll probably skip breakfast. He directs his eyes around the car; there is a scattering of passengers, obviously some who work in outlying settlements of Omaha's booming economy, and maybe some, who, like him, are taking their first anxious steps into unfamiliar territory.

Emmaline

"So, Roberts, what have you come up with?"

Emmaline did not sleep well and Mr Quaid is noticing.

"Coffee?"

"No. Thank you. I'll just get started."

He sits back in his chair. "Sure."

She digs out her notes from her leather satchel. "I've thought up a list of questions."

"Interesting… Let's hear them, if you wouldn't mind."

She had intended to hand them to him and let him read them to himself, expected him to hand them back and tell her to get on with it. "Oh, yes… certainly…"

Mr Quaid chuckles softly. "You'll get used to me, Roberts."

"Yes, Mr Quaid. Er, the questions. I wrote them down as I was studying Faraday's summation from the trial of Ed Parsons, so if they don't flow…"

"I've studied Faraday's summation myself, Roberts, more times than I care to say, and it's pretty darn good, but you just go ahead."

She concentrates on trying not to feel like she's reading out her homework in class. "Who has Taylor's file? – is it Mr Faraday?"

"Good," booms Mr Quaid and her sheet almost flies out of her hands. "You're onto Faraday, ain't you, Roberts – excellent."

She composes herself; sticks a smile on her face.

"Why is the file so closely guarded?"

"You sensed that?" Mr Quaid interjects, but she is ready for it and nods.

"How personally involved was Faraday with members of the Alliance?"

"Roberts," Mr Quaid declares, smacking his hand down on his desk; then he clenches his fist and gives her a meaty look of approval.

"Did Parsons conspire to murder Kelley Keaton?" She pauses automatically.

Mr Quaid's brow creases and he rubs his chin.

"Something rhetorical, Roberts?"

She allows his question to be rhetorical also and continues, "Why has the investigation into Miss Keaton's death gone south? And what have Faraday and the sheriff been up to all this time?"

"Mm. They told us that no one saw the gunman near the scene or after, and that all their enquiries came up empty. We experienced the same problem. However, our sheriff believes that the assassin fired from the rooftop across the street; it makes sense and most people agree with him."

She considers this momentarily before she continues. "In his summation Faraday exhorts the jury to find Parsons guilty so that the community can be free of Parsons and the danger he presents, but that was before Miss Keaton was shot.

"If we assume that Parsons did conspire to kill Miss Keaton, and all his former conspirators, the known ones, were also incarcerated, then there has to be others who helped him, who knew clearly how and what to do without being caught or be incriminated, or even suspected. So how can the community actually be free of danger?

"Because from what I understand about the political climate in this territory, Mr Quaid, there are the major outfits who want the minor outfits gone, like largemouth bass loose in a tub full of sailfin mollies. The Bright River Alliance, while not major but not so minor, is not gone; they are very much alive and are still bringing hope to others, and if I'm not mistaken, Mr Faraday their champion is also a champion of the Homesteaders Act, which cannot be easy.

"From my research, I understand that much of the land pertaining to the Homesteaders Act has been bought up by the railroad and mining companies and such, but some of it is very much in the hands of the people for whom it is intended."

While she takes a breath she becomes the object of Mr Quaid's shrewd observation. "This territory is certainly a hot bed from time to time. It's about coming here and making good."

"Opportunity, yes, I understand that."

"You have to stand up for yourself."

"I understand that, too."

Mr Quaid lengthens his observation of her. "You think Ed Parsons was conspiring with…"

"Someone big," she finishes, unable to hide her excitement at the prospect.

Mr Quaid presses his lips together, then sighs. "You're not afraid of this, Roberts."

"I believe Mart Keaton himself said it best in his journal, you know where he quotes from the Bible: *Then you will know the truth and the truth will set you free*. What an amazing young man. That kind of heroism and faith, Mr Quaid, defies death and reaches out across time. It is ageless. And it says to me that uncovering the whole truth is our quest. Mr Faraday believes it also; he says the laws of our nation exist to ensure justice and protect the liberty of all its peoples. He infers that this will enable us to answer the question 'what is truth?' So my question, for the present, is: 'What is the truth *now* – the *whole* truth?'"

"Faraday never got to the bottom of it," Mr Quaid says.

"At *that* time, in *that* trial, I believe not. He prosecuted Ed Parsons, the crooked sheriff McCurdy, the outlaw Wilson Cutter and that was all. Probably thought it was enough."

"Mm, it's what I've always suspected but I kept bumping against the question of why if there was more did he stop?"

"And did this in some way contribute to Miss Keaton's death?"

"I can't get any answers from anyone or anywhere."

They stare at each other silently for a moment.

Her mind is buzzing.

"Your plan, Roberts?" Mr Quaid asks, once again sitting back in his chair.

"I want to see what kind of man Mr Faraday is for myself."

Mr Quaid nods. "And then?"

"Find out where Taylor's file is and get my hands on it."

"Good luck on that score."

"Then there's the sheriff, of course…"

"He's out of town at present. My source tells me our Mr Ryan is visiting Ed Parsons in the Colorado State Pen."

At this juicy piece of information her heart jumps.

"So he will be all yours when he returns," Mr Quaid adds with a sardonic smile.

"Will he be a problem?"

"Ryan? Hec, no…" he murmurs with a kind of latent sarcasm. "No problem."

So far she has proved herself willing to share her passion for this investigation; now she must prove she is prepared to go that extra mile, or even two…

"And then, of course, there are the Alliance family members, particularly Luke Taylor… the file must be somewhere… surely he would know the whereabouts of his own…"

"Taylor left Wyoming not long after Miss Keaton was murdered. My source says he's in San Francisco."

She feels put out at once. She was thoroughly looking forward to meeting Taylor; she considered squeezing him dry of information a worthy challenge.

"Just take a little longer then," she murmurs, hoping the Tribune can afford to send her to San Francisco.

Mr Quaid laughs. "You know he hates journalists."

"He reads newspapers, I'm sure," she says.

Mr Quaid laughs louder. "Yes. He always seemed to know what we had printed on any given day during the trial."

"Just as I thought."

"Oh, one other thing, there was a gentle rumor around at the time that he and our female doctor, Jennifer Sullivan, were having an affair."

She almost chokes. "You have a female doctor?"

"Had. She left town about three weeks after Taylor. Some said she was the best doctor in this town, even the governor himself swore by her."

"So do you believe the affair rumor is true?"

"Her timing points to it, but…" Mr Quaid shrugs.

"I mean, if they were close she might be worth an interview. And if she attended the governor who knows what she might have been privy to."

Mr Quaid frowns. "The governor?"

She raises an eyebrow at him. "Someone big, remember? You should know, Mr Quaid, that I have no intention of holding anyone above suspicion."

Mr Quaid exhales a very long breath. "All right, Roberts, but you'll need to consult with me before you launch yourself on the governor, understood?"

"Yes, Mr Quaid."

After a quiet moment, he says, "Did you happen to read that collection of letters to the editor in the Bugle?"

"The discussion between Miss Keaton and Mr Faraday? Yes, I did. Miss Keaton certainly had some very definite opinions, and an interesting turn of phrase. *The acquisition of property has not given us true freedom…* that had to upset a lot of people in this territory who believe owning land is their religion."

"Oh, it did that all right…" Mr Quaid's words float about in the atmosphere until she twigs that he is onto something. Something quite significant. Their eyes meet. "Anyone who can so eloquently question Thomas Jefferson's 'empire for liberty' right in the heart of that empire either has guts or no brains. I think Miss Keaton had guts, too much for some."

"And she paid the price for it."

"A very steep price for having an opinion."

"But it seems to me that in her letters she spoke of *property* in its most literal meaning. From my understanding, the *property* of *liberty and property* includes at its heart one's very own being and potential to work."

"Which explains the actions of Luke Taylor on the day of Wilson Cutter's extradition. How he reasoned with the governor. That is definitely his understanding of it."

"Miss Keaton, however, expressed her belief that America has ditched that pure meaning for imperial land grabbing."

"I can't be sure if she ever really understood the pure meaning or if she was driven to make her point."

"We are taught and expected to believe that this nation is the source and bearer of true liberty for all people and places."

"Mm. I believe it was President John Quincy Adams, Old Man Eloquent, who said that America *is the well-wisher of the freedom and independence of all*. I think Miss Keaton believed the nation had lost its way in that regard. I think she regarded Manifest Destiny as a kind of internal foreign policy."

"*How much blood has been spilled across this continent in the last one hundred years, and now from one ocean to another we say we are free...the acquisition of property has not given us true freedom.* There is something deeply spiritual about it."

"If only we were all that pure of heart."

"Did you have much contact with her, Mr Quaid?"

"Not much. She was Faraday's pet witness and he had her flapping 'no comment' to anyone who even remotely looked like a reporter. But, for all that, I liked her. She was a good kid. Had the jury wrapped around her little finger. A waste, that's what it was."

"Yes, I feel very sorry for her."

Mr Quaid rallies. "Now, don't get ahead of yourself, Roberts. It's a hunch and a place to start, and maybe no one else, including Faraday and Ryan, has even thought of it."

"So: who would want Miss Keaton dead and why?"

Mr Quaid gets to his feet. "*Qui bono?*"

"Precisely. Who benefits from her death?"

"The first question after all, mm?"

"Yes, but I have one more: why was the Bugle, obviously a soap box for the Republican Party and the cattle barons, and ideologically opposed to Miss Keaton's opinions, so happy to print each and every controversial letter?"

"Mm," Mr Quaid murmurs.

"Who owns the Bugle, Mr Quaid?"

Mr Quaid's glance is sharp. "Loren Bodecker."

"Do I need your permission before I launch myself on him too?"

Mr Quaid swallows and his Adam's apple bobs up and down; he has a far away look in his eyes. "Leave Loren Bodecker to me."

Ben

In the dining car, three potbelly stoves are intrepidly giving off warmth; Ben seats himself close by one. A black waiter appears at his table, offers a greeting and asks him what he'd like.

"Just coffee," he tells him.

"Yes sir…" The waiter has a nothing is too much trouble tone in his voice, so Ben makes one further request.

"Do you have a Cheyenne paper?"

"They is yesterday's, but we got the Bugle, and the Tribune."

"Both if I may… thanks."

"Yes sir."

He figures if he has to be on this train for the whole day and half the night he might as well do something useful; he's not above a little investigating, particularly now that his father is not standing over his shoulder questioning his every move: if Loren Bodecker is as mighty as he reckons he is, then the Cheyenne papers must tote something about him. After all, Cheyenne is the man's base of operation.

The coffee and the newspapers arrive smartly.

"Sure there ain't nothing else I can get for you," says his waiter. "Breakfast is a mighty fine meal on this trip, sets a body up nicely for the long haul…"

"No. This is fine. Thank you."

As the waiter sashays away to the rocking rhythm of the train, Ben stirs two spoons of sugar into his black coffee, also to the rocking rhythm of the train. Everything must be done to it.

He straightens one of the newspapers, the Bugle.

It's full of articles and references to Bodecker, with comments and summaries on his business interests, and his numerous difficulties with Populist Party members and their supporters, who are trying to give workers, homesteaders and small time ranchers a voice.

Bodecker is given front page space to express his approval of the success of Mr Elliot Morgan's transition to the office of Acting Governor following the death in office on January 13th of Governor William Hale. Then, in another article, Bodecker expresses the importance of unregulated capitalist enterprise to Wyoming if it is to achieve statehood.

There is even an article in which he condemns the territorial prosecutor, Faraday, for his outspoken defense of homesteaders' rights despite the protests of the cattle barons, who clearly want to see the back of the homesteaders. It seems the cattle barons hold sway in Wyoming, and everyone is doing their damnedest to survive in spite of them.

Apart from all this, according to the Bugle, the cattle industry is booming and there is no limit to its potential.

Now for the Tribune.

The lead article reports on the political vitriol spewed forth by the Populists regarding unfair treatment of the struggling homesteaders. The Populists give their support to Faraday and call for the governor to rein in the 'questionable activities' of the cattle barons and their associations.

The Tribune names Loren Bodecker as one of the cattle barons whose questionable activities are damaging 'to the fabric of economic, social and civil life' in the Territory.

> Can the humble homesteader survive?
> In the five months since prosecutor Cameron P. Faraday won the Keaton-Taylor-Benchley Alliance a victory in court over the imprisoned demi-baron Edward Parsons, pressure has been mounting for the respected attorney to fall into line with the governor and so back the cattle barons.

And something else… something intriguing…

> The distinct reluctance of Mr Faraday
> to do so has raised many eyebrows in
> this town, particularly the big end, and
> so begs the question, is there something
> that Faraday knows that the rest of us
> are not privy to?

Very odd. Anyway, the reference to this Alliance of the Keatons, Taylors and Benchleys really piques his interest these days. Mart Keaton was his sister's husband, the one she sacrificed everything for. This Faraday, who seems to have a mind of his own, might have even known the man.

He peruses the remainder of the paper and it makes interesting reading. Loren Bodecker is no hero in the eyes of the Tribune.

The waiter returns with his coffee pot. "So how things lookin' in Wyomin' sir?" With admirable rhythmic ability, he pours more coffee into Ben's cup.

"Fairly interesting," Ben replies. "Tell me, do you know who the proprietors of these newspapers are?"

"Can't say that I do. All I know is that my friend Charlie Quaid, he's the editor of the Tribune. Fine man Mr Quaid. He helped me get this job. That be all sir?"

"Sure," says Ben and gives him a generous tip.

The waiter thanks him.

After he has left Ben alone again, it is not long before a perfect stranger approaches his table and says, "Mind if I join you. Couldn't help but overhear you're interested in the Bugle."

Ben stares straight up into the face of one of the hardest looking men he's ever seen. His face is all sharp angles, his skin stretched tight over them, with a thin mouth and slate gray eyes.

Ben is well practiced in poker faces and he maintains a good one as he says, "What has my interest in the Bugle and you joining me got to do with each other?"

The stranger sits anyway, as if Ben can be easily pushed aside.

"Kinda interested in territorial affairs I see."

"You didn't answer my question," Ben says.

The stranger narrows his squinty eyes even further.

"I'm a friend of the owner."

Casually, Ben folds the Tribune back into its original shape. "Oh? You can help me then, with my inquiry?"

The stranger takes his time in lighting up a cigarette. "Loren Bodecker owns the Bugle. Got a problem with that?" The latter is said through a plume of fresh tobacco smoke.

"This is a non-smoking table."

"A man who don't smoke ain't a man," is the stranger's reply.

Ben decides to look mildly interested in this philosophy. "Well, Mr Smoking Man..."

"You don't know who you're talking to, sonny."

"No, I don't, and I don't like it much; since you interrupted my reading the least you can do is introduce yourself."

The hard-faced stranger stares straight into his eyes; even if the stranger was a snake charmer and Ben a snake it wouldn't work; he knows hard men and they don't scare him.

"Donnelly," the stranger says.

Ben gives a start that he can't conceal. At yesterday's board meeting Loren Bodecker himself mentioned his Laramie partner Donnelly. Some partner, Ben reflects; he looks more like tarted up muscle, who at present is fiddling with his collar.

"Taylor," Ben replies.

"Thought so. Caught a glimpse of you yesterday while I was waiting for Loren. You're a tough guy, Taylor. I like that. Say, ain't you related to Luke Taylor from Bright River? He won the case against Parsons last year; dang nuisance and a troublemaker."

"Why would I want to admit being related to a troublemaker with you sitting there like it wouldn't be the brightest idea I ever had?"

"Cause I heard you ain't too fond of your cousin, and couldn't care what anyone called him."

"Where'd you hear that?'

Donnelly laughs.

"Is there a point to all this, Donnelly?"

"You're heading to Cheyenne, then pushing on to Bright River, I'm guessing. To visit your cousin."

Ben lets him think it, but needing to probe further says, "I reckon you could even tell me why I'd be paying him a visit."

"Call him out, maybe. Maybe buy him out, since your Pa is so keen on doing some coal digging in Wyoming. Loren sure would look on that kindly, I'm telling you. Your cousin could even be sitting on a gold mine, eh? But now I'm getting carried away... he ain't even there; been in San Francisco the last four months, since his best friend's sister got done in. Hey, you'd know all about that, wouldn't you? Taylor's best friend was married to your sister, wasn't he? Hey, I recall she lives in Bright River as well, with her dead husband's folks. My, my, it's a small world."

Ben feels his annoyance curl in his gut.

Donnelly unleashes an ugly grin and stands up to leave. "Just being friendly. Glad to meet you, Taylor."

Ben refuses to release him from the conversation, however.

"Does Mr Bodecker know as much as you claim to?"

Donnelly chuckles darkly. "Everyone knows about the Taylors and the Keatons in Wyoming. They're famous. Say your name there, Taylor, and folks'll be asking you if you're related."

Whether Ben likes it or not, Donnelly gets up and takes his leave, disappearing through the door of the dining car.

As Ben watches the white Nebraskan countryside rock by, the idea dawns on him that this whole meeting wasn't a coincidence. His father would say it was. And if that's what his father would say, then Ben needs to think the opposite.

Donnelly deliberately followed him onto the train. Probably been following him all along. But why?

Does Bodecker always go to these lengths?

His instincts are rewarded and suspicions confirmed when the train makes an unscheduled stop at the next settlement, in all just an hour out of Omaha. He spots Donnelly strutting along the small wooden platform as the train once again pulls out.

Ben watches the sonofabitch until he disappears. What the hell was that all about?

He catches the eye of his waiter. "Did you happen to notice the gentleman who..." He stops and the waiter raises an eyebrow.

"You asking if I know that gentleman sir?"

"Yes, I guess I am."

"Well I know him," says the waiter. "See him all the time on the Cheyenne to Laramie stretch. Sometimes on this leg."

"His name is Donnelly..."

"Reckon it is."

"How come he can just get off wherever he wants?"

"Some people got power, lotta power, yes sir."

"*Him?*"

"The world is a mighty peculiar place."

"Mm. Looks like there's a lot to learn about Wyoming."

The waiter shows all his teeth in a friendly grin.

"Reckon there is."

"How bad is it?"

"Well now, it's pretty as a picture, for sure, but they fight like cats'n dogs over it. Ain't no friendly family spat neither. What with the homesteaders, the sheepherders and the miners wanting their share, the cattle barons are good'n mad, and the others are just plain fed up with being bullied. 'Course there's the railroaders, they got *long* claws, mm, long *sharp* claws..." He bends lower and the whites of his eyes, so vivid in his dark face, widen to the size of small discs.

"What?" Ben asks.

"Then there's the ontrapenooers..."

"Who? Oh... yes... them."

"*...and* the politicians." He straightens and stands tall once more but with his feet set apart, clearly prepared for whatever causes the train to jerk at that precise moment, and clears his throat.

"That's all sir."

Ben thoughtfully observes the snowy Nebraskan terrain as it moves by him. Some people don't care so much about which way they sit in trains, but he always likes to sit facing the direction of his destination. A few hours ago this journey was about finding Tressa, reuniting with her, and raising questions and getting answers about his ancestor Matthew Taylor. But something happened the moment Donnelly sat down at his table. He feels as though his noble quest just got sullied. He might have run away from his father, but it is uncomfortably obvious that he has not escaped.

Emmaline

Cheyenne Courthouse
Northwest Corner of 19ᵗʰ & Ferguson

Emmaline has no luck with Josh Bridger, the assistant to the territorial prosecutor. His desk is strategically positioned outside Cam Faraday's office, contained in its own corral, swinging gate included. Bridger has informed the closeted Faraday that she has requested an audience, but that was twenty minutes ago and Faraday, who sent Bridger back with the message she would have to wait till he was free, doesn't even look like he is coming out. She stares hard at the solid oak door to Faraday's inner sanctum, almost willing him to appear.

She takes out her watch and gives Faraday five more minutes.

"Mr Faraday is aware I am still here, Mr Bridger?" she asks from her seat adjacent to Bridger's cage. He looks up from his bookwork and opens his mouth to comment, but she grins smugly and says, "Well, of course, he does – you would have told him it was safe to come out if I wasn't."

Bridger's bespectacled, well-bred face feigns a grimace.

"Ooh, that hurt."

"I'm so pleased," she says. "What next?"

"Make an appointment."

"And have him cancel it?"

"Suit yourself."

They resume their previous positions.

Faraday's office is located at the end of a long corridor, so although the courthouse and its offices are vibrant with activity,

75

Faraday's section offers more privacy and less traffic. But, emerging from all the activity into the rarefied atmosphere of Faraday's province, there comes a tall man striding with athletic, long-legged grace. As he walks he unbuttons his navy blue, thigh-length wool coat, revealing a fashionable dark gray suit beneath. He holds his hat in his gloved hands so she can see his very weary eyes set into a refined, handsome face. His black hair is longish yet stylishly cut to just below his collar and sits naturally without the use of hair oil.

Self-assured, aged somewhere around thirty (although obvious weariness is aging him just a little), he is an elegant young man with a sophisticated air, from the cut of his clothes to the way he walks.

He is, as her sister Celina would say, quite a specimen.

Curiosity begins to bite.

No one even remotely this interesting has ventured down this way in all the time she's been waiting here…

Except that she was here first.

Suddenly, Bridger is on his feet, a look of surprise giving that now way-too-familiar and bespectacled face an owlish quality.

"Cliff, you're back!" Bridger exclaims.

"Josh, how are you," the newcomer says and the two men shake hands.

"Fine thanks. When did you get in? How was Colorado?"

"Just now. Denver was a revelation as always. Don't suppose Cam is in there?" And the man called Cliff rubs a spot over his right eye… how fascinating to be named for a geological feature, namely a precipice… would you christen someone Mountain, Canyon or Plateau… or maybe you would where he comes from.

Bridger lets out a laugh. "Cam would ask Judge Callaghan for a recess if he found out you were back. But, yes, he's in there."

She sits up straighter. *I was here before you! Wait your turn…*

"Not surprised he's got his door shut," the man Cliff remarks staring at Faraday's drawbridge.

Bridger is a quick study. "You've been reading the papers."

"What's Charlie Quaid's game anyhow…"

Bridger almost breaks his throat he clears it so loudly; uncanny, because just at that moment Faraday's oak door breaks open like the seal in a bank vault. She freezes in her chair.

Cameron P. Faraday emerges, a tall, lean man, clean-shaven and younger than expected… no more than thirty-five. He wears a dapper three-piece suit and necktie, which appears slightly skew-whiff. His dark-brown hair is neatly combed, although a strand at the temple has broken loose. He is holding a rather rumpled wad of papers in his hand, which is the subject of his attention; he's not even looked up yet, almost as though he don't want to.

She cocks her head to the side in an effort to read his face.

I was here first, before that tall black-haired man from Colorado…

"Josh, would you know where Mavis Quigley's affidavit has got to? It's not in her file. Damn woman will have my head…"

"Working you too hard, are they, Cam?" says the man Cliff, with a grin that seems to have reached his eyes and shaken the weary look right out of them.

Mr Faraday's eyes bolt up. They are brown, but richly hued like chocolate, and full of… what? Relief? A smile breaks out on his distracted face and very soon the two men are shaking hands, the warm regard between them genuine and charismatic.

Emmaline presses her lips together and grips the sides of her chair. *Observe, Roberts… but I was here first!*

Bridger is taking the papers out of Mr Faraday's hands. "I'll find the Quigley affidavit."

"Well," Mr Faraday murmurs, "how did you fare?"

"I believe I fared fair enough," says the man Cliff.

"Excellent. Supper tonight and we will review?"

The man Cliff accepts… *good, because I was here before him.*

"How are things here, Cam?" he asks.

But Bridger, the snarly owl, breaks in before she can score some free information… "Ah, Cam, there is someone waiting to see you, remember?"

Pain in the…

Mr Faraday's brow creases and he looks around. His eyes find her pressed back in her chair; good God, she's nervous – since when? She stands at once – *at last!*

"I'm sorry, miss…"

She steps forward with her hand outstretched.

"Emmaline Roberts."

Mr Faraday takes her hand in a gentlemanly fashion.

"Miss Roberts," he says.

Bridger adds, "From the Tribune."

She notes, with perplexity, the spear-like gaze of the man from Colorado. Soon, all three men are staring.

"Your clerk is correct," she says. "I…"

"Excuse me," says Bridger, "but I am the assistant prosecutor…"

"I *do* beg your pardon. What *was* I thinking?"

"Not much, I'd wager," Bridger retorts.

She feigns amusement, then says, "As I was saying, I am the new investigative reporter for the Tribune, hoping you will give me but a few minutes of your precious time, Mr Faraday."

Mr Faraday actually smiles at her. "I see. And what would we be talking about, Miss Roberts?"

"Miss Roberts is Charlie Quaid's new secret weapon," Bridger submits.

"Oh, are we at war?" she replies in kind.

Bridger rolls his eyes and returns to his work.

She glances warily at the man who took her place in the cue, and wonders if that fierce gaze concentrates his efforts on seeing right inside her brain and sucking out her thoughts.

Mr Faraday, however, decides to introduce them.

"Miss Roberts, this is Sheriff Cliff Ryan."

Sheriff? Makes sense. Back from Colorado. Officious, suspicious manner. The pushing-in… She tries a jaunty *how do you do,* but he doesn't seem too thrilled to meet her.

"Roberts?" he mumbles.

"Last time I checked." She turns away, wondering if he has a problem that no one likes to talk about. "So, Mr Faraday, just a few minutes of your time?"

"You never said what it was about," Mr Faraday points out politely.

She finds herself liking Mr Cam Faraday. He *is* trying to put her off, but in such a nice way; in fact, he appears to be a very nice human, not at all what she expected from what she had read and been told. For a man who is embroiled in controversy he has retained a sense of humor; for a man who appears to be straining on the roaring tide of big business and oligopolistic enterprise in the name of justice, he impresses her as wonderfully normal.

"When did you start at the Tribune, Miss Roberts?" the sheriff asks her unexpectedly.

"I believe it was yesterday."

"So you didn't write the article about Mr Faraday?"

"I haven't had the opportunity or the privilege to write anything as yet."

"No," Mr Faraday confirms. "The article has Charlie Quaid written all over it."

"So Quaid has hired you, Miss Roberts, to start investigating *what* exactly?"

"I declare I am not obliged to answer that question, Mr Ryan."

"You will have to excuse our sheriff, Miss Roberts, he has just returned from a very long trip," Mr Faraday says, smiling.

"A little defensive, don't you think?" she remarks.

"Nothing escapes his attention."

"I have done nothing as yet to warrant interrogation by a law enforcement officer, have I, Mr Faraday?"

"Not that I am aware of, Miss Roberts."

Suddenly, Bridger speaks up. "Do I make an appointment for Miss Roberts to come back when you're not busy, Cam?"

The sheriff says, "Don't change your plans for me, Cam, I have work to do."

"Well, I'll see Miss Roberts now, Josh. Take a seat in my office, Miss Roberts; I'll be with you in a moment."

"Thank you. Good day, Mr Ryan," she offers coolly.

He grunts… actually grunts.

Mr Faraday is chuckling as she ventures into his inner sanctum. She hears him say to Ryan, "So Colorado and the Mile High City didn't agree with you, Cliff…"

I'd say not.

She keeps her head down and smiles into her hand; then is immediately curious as to what transpired between Ryan and Ed Parsons in the Colorado State Penitentiary.

Faraday

Faraday enters his office and immediately notices Miss Roberts with her head down already industriously writing in her notebook. She is clearly a well-bred woman, probably about twenty-two or three, petite in stature with a bright face of refined features, large eyes and fair skin. Well-groomed is a word that does not do her justice; she is impeccable, right down (or up) to the sweep of dark blonde hair. As soon as she registers his presence she very politely places the tools of her trade in her lap.

Faraday sits down in his chair behind his desk and says, "I believe, Miss Roberts, that this conversation is off the record. So, what are you investigating for Charlie Quaid that requires my assistance?" Rule number one: never ask a question to which you don't know the answer. So he waits…

She regards him coolly for a long moment (a useful technique that sometimes works on the unsuspecting, and he is not one).

"You have already made some notes, I see. I hope Josh was polite…" Then he laughs gently. "I know Cliff wasn't. You got him on a bad day."

"Oh?"

"You will probably receive an apology."

"That won't be necessary. If I may refer back to your initial question: I have been assigned to cover the ongoing investigation into the murder of Miss Keaton. I believe that the investigation has gone south, Mr Faraday, is that how you would see it?"

"No," he answers. "I believe it's progressing."

"Very slowly then."

"Your words, Miss Roberts, not mine."

"Of course," she says with a faint smile. "Mr Faraday, have you any idea who would want Miss Keaton dead?"

"Well, if I knew that…"

"And kept it to yourself…"

"That would be against the law…"

"Or not in your best interests."

"And against the law."

"I think I know who might want Miss Keaton out of the way. Someone who didn't like her very definite opinions on liberty and property…"

Faraday leans back in his chair, rests his elbow on the arm of it, raises his forearm, drops his head sideways onto his upturned fist, and watches her… and listens.

"… this territory evidently boasts some exceedingly wealthy men who own or want to own large chunks of it, and some appear to be very disgruntled about the small time operators – the home-steaders, the small ranchers, with little or nothing to contribute… I guess I don't need to tell you any of this…"

"You are new in town, Miss Roberts, and everyone needs to get their bearings."

"What would you say, Mr Faraday, if I was to tell you Miss Keaton's murder was orchestrated by persons both powerful and wealthy?"

"Do you have any proof?"

"You don't seem surprised."

"You yourself just related the current business climate. Miss Roberts, to prosecute such persons I need evidence, not a theory."

"Mr Faraday, you don't seem to understand. I'm not here to offer you a case to prosecute, I am here to suggest that you yourself know who murdered Miss Keaton and you are withholding the evidence for some unscrupulous purpose of your own."

Faraday looks straight into her eyes. "I know, Miss Roberts."

She looks straight back at him; her eyes darken in the process.

"Charlie Quaid has been insinuating a cover up by me for some time now and it is simply not true…"

"Mr Faraday…"

"That would go against everything this office stands for and my own ethics. What we need, Miss Roberts, both of us, is evidence. Cold, hard fact. You cannot print without it and I cannot prosecute. It's that simple."

"Mr Faraday, I am determined to get to the bottom of this, and I am not afraid of where it will lead me."

Faraday feels a shiver travel down his spine; how could she possibly appreciate the danger and how on earth is he supposed to protect her...

"Mr Faraday, why was the Bugle, clearly a political platform and apologist for the cattle barons, and ideologically opposed to Miss Keaton's opinions, so happy to print every one of her controversial letters?"

"You will have to ask the Bugle that question, Miss Roberts."

"And you will be very happy for me to pass on the answer Loren Bodecker gives me, no doubt," she says. "Unless, of course, you have already asked him, and in that case you might like to tell me what he said, because I am just dying of curiosity."

Faraday feels sick; however, he responds nonchalantly, "Loren Bodecker is not the editor of the Bugle. Obadiah Williams is your man. His motivation for publishing Miss Keaton's letters, I believe, was that he rather likes a woman's point of view from time to time."

Miss Roberts smiles brightly. "Well, I think I'll pay Mr Obadiah Williams a visit and offer him *this* woman's point of view." She stands up smartly and Faraday follows her to his feet. "Well, Mr Faraday, thank you for your time."

"You are welcome, Miss Roberts."

She flashes a white smile. "It has been such a pleasure meeting you. Good day, then."

And she breezes out of his office.

Faraday sinks back into his chair.

Josh appears.

"Judge Callaghan wants to see you in his chambers; says it can't wait..."

Faraday nods.

"And McKinnon's client wants to plea bargain. Ten years for manslaughter."

"No," Faraday instructs.

"And Brown's client is changing his plea. Not guilty by reason of insanity."

"The whole territory's gone insane…"

"Mavis Quigley's affidavit is now in the file. And Mavis Quigley is outside. She says she just remembered something important."

"Anything else?"

"Obadiah Williams sent a junior reporter over to say ditto to the Tribune's question: is there something that you know that the rest of us are not privy to, et cetera, et cetera."

"A *junior* reporter? Williams is a weasel."

"Precisely the answer I gave him on your behalf."

"At least Charlie Quaid sent his brand new investigative reporter to get an answer to his own question. The man has got more moves than a Swiss pocket watch. When you have a moment, Josh, do some digging on Miss Roberts, make up a profile. Might as well know what we're dealing with."

"If you think it will help," Josh says and leaves.

Faraday saunters over to his window. He doesn't see the view.

He recalls the day when Miss Keaton sat in this very room, searching Luke's file, determined to flush out anything that would help them find Parsons guilty of conspiring to murder her brother.

And he remembers another day, not long after, when she came bursting in to tell him that she had run into someone in court that day whose face she believed she had seen in Luke's file…

It was Loren Bodecker she had run into and Loren Bodecker's face in the file. Not long after that, Miss Keaton was dead. That day had been a defining one in Faraday's life; and now the time had come to fix this thing once and for all, and fix it fast. The vultures are beginning to circle – around the wrong camp.

Caroline

Omaha

Caroline, her head aching, decides to make tea.

Richard's explosions have subsided, or more accurately, he has left the house and taken his temper tantrum elsewhere. Still, she can't help but feel sorry for him. His only son, on whom all his hopes and dreams rest, gone. As sorry as she feels for Richard, she is not sorry that she gave Ben her blessing to leave. Nothing was ever the same since Tressa left. No one felt it more keenly than Ben.

"After all, Richard, the day had to come when he would want to know, deep down you must know that..."

"Your foolish daughter filled his head with nonsense!"

"Our daughter did no such thing; her actions, Richard, said far more than the few words she spoke."

"You side with him!"

"A young man needs to find his own way. Just as you did."

"His place is here! We have just taken on a new venture."

"He knows that, but would you have ever let him go? Would any time have been the right one?"

"My own wife! I can't abide disloyalty, Caroline."

"That's why I am here, Richard. My place is with you."

It was all too much and he stormed out of the house and her head started throbbing. The only course is to ride out his anger and disappointment; it won't be pleasant because he is convinced she is partly to blame; after all she didn't talk Ben out of going and she freely admits it. Richard will not easily forgive her for that.

A cold draught sweeps through the kitchen; the back door is open. Well, that's odd. Richard left by the front... and there is no one else in the house. She locks out the icy blast, and turns to set about making her tea.

Standing there is a man. She gasps and clutches her breast.

"No cause for alarm, M'am."

Her thumping heart doesn't think so.

"Sorry for scaring you, M'am."

He's frightful. Hard-looking. Large.

She wants to know what he is doing in her house, but she can't speak. She stares at him, shaking.

"M'am..."

She starts to back away, straight into the locked door. The bump rouses her, and she says, as she thinks about grabbing a kitchen implement, "What are you doing in my house?"

"Listen up. I understand your boy took the Cheyenne express this morning. Why would he be doing that, mother?"

"What...what are you talking about?"

"Your boy. He took off for Cheyenne."

"For... for business."

The man grits his teeth. "That's a *lie*, M'am. Know for a fact he's gone to see his cousin."

She holds her tongue; she has no intention of putting Tressa in harm's way by telling this strange, dreadful man Ben's true reasons for leaving Omaha.

"Know for a fact his cousin is that troublemaker Luke Taylor. It don't please me that your boy's decided to make contact with his no-good cousin."

"What has any of this to do with you?" she asks.

The stranger makes his eyes into slits. Frightful.

"It ain't a good move. Not if he wants his papa's business to succeed. Now if I was you, mother, I would get him back, pronto!"

"Who are you?"

"You don't need to know. You only need to do as I say. Get your boy back."

"W...what if I can't do as you say? I m...mean, it's impossible; he's his father's son – I can't change his mind..."

"Aw, you're making me sad," he mocks her. "You know you better do as I say. There's a lot at stake here – your husband's business, your children's lives."

"My children's... oh... I don't understand why you are doing this..."

The stranger starts pulling and tugging at his collar, ripples of ugliness contorting his face, scaring her into speechlessness once more.

"Once your boy set foot on that train, there ain't nothing no one can do; you can only do as you're told, understand? Your husband is now an Association member and it's all a question of loyalty, see. Taylor is an enemy of the Association and we wouldn't want any divided loyalties, would we? Seems to me I just heard your husband tell you how he can't abide disloyalty. That kind of attitude goes down well with the Association, but we wouldn't want young Ben to let the side down, now would we? So get your boy back. Clear?"

She nods, or tries to. It seems to satisfy him because he moves to leave. With bruising strength she is pushed away from the back door; she cries out and just manages to keep her balance.

He unlocks the door and wrenches it open. "You wouldn't be stupid enough to tell anyone about this, would you, mother?"

He doesn't wait for her answer; why need he bother?

She clings to the back of a chair as the door hangs open.

Bitter cold once again surges through the kitchen.

Quaking, she launches herself at the door and locks it, even though she is all too aware that the horse has already bolted.

Cliff

Cliff lets go of a sigh now that he's put his office in order and his chair is visible at last; seems like they used it for lost and found while he was gone. With all unclaimed articles now in their rightful place in the locked cupboard out back, he can turn his attention to the next matter; in his absence things have been piling up and he frowns at the stack of files on his desk. His numerous deputies all seem to have acquired an aversion to paperwork.

"Holiday's over, fellers," he says as he grabs half the pile; he saunters out of his office into the general office out front, where sit the deserted workstations of his deputies. "Where is everyone?"

On cue, someone opens the door and enters.

He looks up; their eyes meet across the expanse.

"Miss Roberts," he grunts.

"Sheriff Ryan. You remembered my name."

"You remembered mine."

She looks like she thinks the better of what she was about to say next and instead closes the door behind her.

Interesting…

Coolly, he unloads several files onto the nearest desk.

She's clad in a plain gray travel cloak over a dress made of blue checked material, and steps forward, graceful and purposeful.

"I hope you can spare me a minute of your time."

He dumps the remainder of the files on the adjacent desk.

Flicking back his coat, he sticks his hands on his hips.

"My turn now?"

"I believe we got off on the wrong foot."

"Did we?"

Undaunted, she thrusts out her hand. "Emmaline Roberts. New investigative reporter for The Tribune."

Warily – for it is wise to be cautious of a newspaper reporter disguised as a good-looking woman – he takes the small hand, which feels cold despite being gloved in soft tanned leather, and after a firm shake, he sticks his own hand back on his hip.

"Well, Miss Roberts, what's on your mind, since there'll be no changing it?"

"No *off the record* declaration, Sheriff?"

"My life is an open book."

"I see. How refreshing. Well, I know that you have just returned from the Colorado State Pen. What was the purpose of your visit?"

"Nothing you need to be concerned about."

And he does what he always does with reporters when he's tired and wants to be left alone; he turns his back and walks away. They usually follow anyhow.

"Was it not the purpose of your visit to interrogate Ed Parsons regarding the murder of Miss Kelley Keaton?" she asks, running true to form.

"Maybe it was," he says and returns to his office. "And maybe it wasn't."

"It is a well known fact, Sheriff, that the investigations into Miss Keaton's murder have not been going at all well, so did Ed Parsons have any information that could be deemed helpful?"

He sits in his old chair, wishing it were leather and padded like Cam's. He really should get around to buying a better one. As it creaks under his weight, he tries to recall where he last saw the requisitions book. Meanwhile, he indicates the chair on the other side of his desk where Miss Roberts may be seated also. She declines his offer, so he sits back and while he keeps one ear on her nosy questions, he examines her.

"You didn't answer my question," she reminds him.

"Didn't I?"

"No, you didn't."

"Well, the answer's no," he says. In some very small way she reminds him of Miss Keaton, which is ironic considering.

"Are you saying your visit with Ed Parsons in prison was an act of compassion?"

"Lord knows he could use some."

"Very commendable, I'm sure, but Cañon City is a long way for a busy man like yourself to travel for nothing more than compassion," she ventures. "Are you pulling some re-election stunt perhaps?"

He leans forward and looks straight up into her bright bronze colored eyes. He has never seen eyes this color before – not aged copper-bronze, but golden-brown bronze; and that's just the color; they convey the texture of velvet, amazing and very lovely.

She holds on fearlessly but he senses her dismay.

"The investigation into Miss Keaton's death is progressing as well as can be expected. And that's all I have to say. When I have something to report, you'll be the first to know. Good day, Miss Roberts."

Satisfied, he sits back and ignores her, pulling down a file from the recently shortened pile.

Shame he's got to send her packing; she's the best thing to walk into his office since Jennifer stormed in one day demanding he ban guns from the town because she was tired of fishing bullets out of drunk and disorderly cowboys. (She even charged into Freund's Armory and advised Frank, for reasons of health and safety, to cease selling guns like candy.) Jennifer stood her ground that day, as a respected doctor and citizen, until he promised he'd do something to relieve the situation; he wonders whether Miss Roberts is made of the same stuff.

"Drowning in paperwork, sheriff?"

He looks up. Miss Roberts is planted firmly with her arms folded, glaring at him. He feels strangely pleased with her.

"How do you spell interfering – one *r* or two?" he asks.

"One."

"Thanks," he says and scribbles *interfering* on the top sheet inside the file. He glances upwards while he scribbles. "Still here?"

"Nothing wrong with your eyesight."

He wants to laugh but clears his throat instead.

"Question" she says. "Who would want Miss Keaton dead and why?"

He attends to the file; *drunk and disorderly...*

"Ed Parsons might," she continues, "but surely his business with the Keatons and the Taylors was over by then, unless of course with his vicious nature he decided on one final blow."

...carrying an illegal weapon...

"But who did the deed on his behalf? – all his accomplices were imprisoned. And what would be the point of it when there was no chance of him ever getting his hands on the Alliance's prime grazing pastures."

...resisting arrest...

"I mean, who would stand to benefit from Miss Keaton's death?"

...assaulting a deputy... "That is a pertinent question, but does anyone have to benefit from her death?"

"You or I may not see revenge as a benefit," she remarks.

The file reveals several prior offences, all the same as the last... this feller needs some prison time.

"Did you ask a question, Miss Roberts?"

"No, I did not."

He flicks a glance at her.

"You are not listening to me, Mr Ryan."

Since a glance doesn't do her justice anyway, he gives her his attention.

"*Now* I have a question," she says. "Why was the Bugle, which is obviously a political platform and apologist for the cattle barons, and ideologically opposed to Miss Keaton's opinions, so happy to print her controversial letters?"

He recalls Miss Keaton's letters while he stares into Miss Roberts' lively golden eyes. The question sounded practiced, too much so, but he cuts her some slack. "Ask Obadiah Williams."

A knowing smile sweetens her lips. "You don't think the Bugle had anything to gain by Miss Keaton's death?"

"Now you're not making sense," he says, ignoring her lips and returning to his file.

"I read in the Parsons' trial transcripts that Mr Faraday had you verify the entire contents of Luke Taylor's file before Taylor's file could be deemed admissible…"

"How do you spell disappear, as in 'why are you still here'…"

"That must have kept you pretty busy, Mr Ryan."

Reluctantly, he raises his eyes once more. "Your point?"

"How can we, the public, be sure that everything in Taylor's file saw the light of day? Was there anything you didn't feel the need to investigate and verify?"

He narrows his gaze on her. And those golden-bronze eyes stare right on back at him.

"Just what are you accusing me of, Miss Roberts?"

"Nothing – yet. But we shall see."

He flashes his most charming smile. "You know, Miss Roberts, this has been such a delightful visit, wouldn't have missed it, but don't feel obliged to return. Goodbye – two o's, one word."

"Well, I have *two* words – Loren Bodecker. He owns the Bugle. I have done some digging of my own, Sheriff, and I have discovered that Loren Bodecker helped Ed Parsons buy out the Bright River district newspaper. Ed Parsons was also a member of Bodecker's Association. He is some kind of tycoon, is Mr Bodecker. He despises all the small ranchers and the homesteaders, and his Association works actively to make life hard for them. Parsons made life very hard for the Keatons, the Taylors and the Benchleys, did he not?"

"Miss Roberts…" he begins, dumping the charm.

"Well, Mr Ryan?"

"I believe I said goodbye."

"I'm not very good with goodbyes."

"Snappy," he retorts. "Listen, when you decide that you are not seeking to slather me with indelible mud and that you are genuinely interested in solving the crime of Miss Keaton's murder, then we might have something to say to each other, but up until that point in time, I suggest you go away and stay there."

"I am trying to do my job."

"Your questions are misplaced, so you would do a much better job if you took them some place else."

"I should think you'd appreciate all the help you can get."

She thinks he needs her help? Now he's pissed.

Shame to have to do it, but...

He brings the charm once more. She looks confused.

"Like I said, when you decide which is more important to you, making false accusations or getting to the truth, let me know."

She blinks. "You're serious. I thought you were..."

"Do I look like I'm..."

"Seriously, you would exchange information with me?"

There's one born every minute. He lets her have it...

"What could you possibly have that I would want?"

She catches her breath.

He frowns, irritated.

Those golden eyes blaze with indignation. Her small hands are balled into fists and a deep shade of pink creeps steadily into her cheeks.

"You, sir, are no gentleman," she declares.

"I hear it's a dying art," he retorts.

"I thought so from the first, and now..." Her eyes flash in anger. "Now you have just confirmed it."

She turns on her heel and marches out.

"I think I'll cope," he murmurs to the rush of warm air where she once stood and a soft fragrance reminiscent of orange blossom now lingers.

He gives her a ten second head start.

She takes Ferguson at a fair clip, walking straight through a group of ladies who have congregated outside the Baptist Church.

As he approaches Church Corner himself, he is not so fortunate and the women all bid him good day and expect him to stop.

He must keep one eye on Miss Roberts.

The women all talk at once.

"Sheriff Ryan, you will attend, won't you?"

"We're counting on you."

"It wouldn't be the same."

He has no idea what they are talking about.

"Of course, ladies, I wouldn't miss it. Send me a reminder. Good day."

He makes up ground and spots Miss Roberts veering right at 17th; she's heading for the Tribune.

She has no idea what she's gotten herself into, snooping around Loren Bodecker. He has been scrutinizing Bodecker's operations very closely himself over the last few months and become uneasy by what he's seen. The man does not take kindly to snooping, or negative publicity. Bodecker has spies, and spies that spy on his spies. Up to this point, Cliff has undertaken all his investigations relating to Miss Keaton's murder with the utmost care; he couldn't risk the investigation being shut down, and so, in many ways, it looks like the investigation has lost its way. Nothing could be further from the truth. Now Miss Roberts has come blundering in; well, blundering is not accurate – a woman like her doesn't blunder; there's not one clumsy bone in her body from what he could tell.

She arrives at the Tribune safely and he stops a few doors down, near McDaniel's theater, to think.

Dilemma. If he marches in and tells Quaid to get Miss Roberts to back off the investigation, Quaid is sure to get suspicious, adding more fuel to the fire the editor's nicely stoking. But if he leaves the Tribune to its own devices, the investigation might be jeopardized. And another thing – Miss Roberts could well find herself in danger.

Hell, this could take some explaining…

His best deputy suddenly appears from nowhere.

"Cliff."

"Mac. I left some work on your desk."

"Bad mornin'?"

Cliff shrugs, his eyes on the Tribune's front door.

Mac, he notices, follows his line of vision.

"Somethin' the matter?"

"Got a job for you."

"Well, you know how I never got enough to do…"

"Tribune's got a new reporter. Miss Emmaline Roberts… small, honey-blonde hair…."

"*Honey?*"

"…well dressed. Want you to keep an eye on her."

"A woman?" Mac looks hesitant. "How long for? It's cold to be standing around. Snow piling up everywhere…"

"You won't be standing around much, believe me. Come tell me when she gets home."

"What are you gonna do?"

"Have a chat with Charlie Quaid."

"Okay, boss."

Mac leaves him and sets off for vantage points unknown.

Cliff covers the icy sidewalk to the door of the Tribune and enters. Simons is standing in the hall talking to Miss Roberts.

Her eyes flicker with hostility when she sees him.

"Are you following me?"

"No," he lies.

Simons says stiffly, "Sheriff. Something I can help you with?"

"Charlie in?"

"You're outa luck, Sheriff. Gone to lunch."

"Well, I think I'll join him," Cliff says pleasantly and continues on down the hall.

"Hey!" Simons calls out.

He raps on Quaid's door; Quaid's voice bids him enter. The look on his face says he wished he hadn't.

"Sheriff Ryan, what can I do for you today?"

Cliff saunters around the untidy office for a bit and then stands opposite the editor who is seated behind his desk.

Quaid sighs. "What do you want, Ryan?"

"Off the record."

"What do you want?" Quaid grinds out once more.

Cliff sticks his hands on his hips. "I've had an interesting little chat with your new reporter – she's a peach, by the way – and I told her that not until the Tribune dumps the accusations of a cover-up in the investigation into Miss Keaton's murder will she find herself taken seriously. I'm putting you on notice, Quaid, if this cover-up crap persists..." He stops, painfully aware of what he's doing, but determined to nip Quaid's crusade in the bud before it causes irreparable harm.

Quaid frowns heavily. "This can't be a threat, Ryan, you can't mean it..."

"You can still do whatever you like, Charlie. It's called freedom of the press. If you want to lower yourself to the likes of the Bugle, then that's your look-out, but when can I expect honest and sincere reporting of the Keaton investigation?"

"If you got a conflict of interest, Ryan, then that's *your* look-out."

"Answer my question."

Charlie Quaid's scrutiny could wilt flowers. "You're taking a mighty big risk coming in here telling me how to run the paper. You own an immaculate reputation in this town, Ryan. Could be you don't want anyone spoiling it?"

Cliff stares directly into his eyes. "Listen, Quaid, and listen hard, some things are bigger than a person's reputation, didn't you know that? If you stick with the cover-up accusations, which are untrue, you will unnecessarily damage the very people who are needed to *un*cover the truth. You *are* interested in the truth, ain't you, Charlie? That *is* what the Tribune's about?"

Quaid looks like he'd prefer not to answer; a series of agonizing expressions parade across his face; why do newspapermen have to be so bloody-minded? Eventually, he manages a nod.

"Glad to hear it. Because someone in town needs to have the guts to print it. It's needs to be you, Charlie."

Quaid nods again, sharply this time.

Cliff breathes a sigh. "Now, you've got this Roberts. She's not like anyone you've hired before."

Quaid slowly gets to his feet, slides his hands into his pockets. "What are you getting at, Ryan?"

"I should have thought it was obvious. What the devil possessed you to hire a young woman to investigate the murder of another young woman? Miss Keaton was picked off from the roof without the slightest warning."

"Good God, you are on the level," Quaid exclaims.

"You should send her home."

"I'm not doing that; she just got here and she's smart, just the person I need."

"This was a serious crime, Quaid, and it requires serious people to investigate it. Roberts is a young woman clearly not from around here."

"I need someone with fresh eyes."

"I get that, I could use a fresh pair myself, but with everything else I've got to do, now I've got to keep my eye on her!"

"Aw, shit, Ryan…"

"You'd do well to do the same because if anything happens to her in the course of this serious investigation you just might find yourself responsible."

"That's ridiculous."

"Then send her home."

Quaid sighs, scratches the back of his head.

"All right," Quaid says at last. "I'll watch out for her, but I'm a busy man."

Cliff grunts at him. "You just got busier."

"I won't tell Roberts… you know… got an eye on her."

"Hell, no. Wouldn't want to stifle her creativity."

Quaid shakes his head. "Get out of here."

Cliff runs into Miss Roberts in the hall, literally; they don't see one another; she has her head in some papers as he rounds a bend in the hall apace. He knocks the papers out of her hands and she lets out a gasp.

"I'm so sorry," he says, retrieving her papers from the floor and handing them over. "I didn't see you. Are you all right?" He can't help himself; he looks into her golden eyes. They are shiny with confusion and move rapidly over his face.

Abruptly, she lowers them, shuffling her papers into neatness.

"Yes… I… I wasn't watching where I was going," she says.

"No, it was my fault. Well, if you're back in one piece, I'll be going then."

"Of course," she replies. "Good day, Mr Ryan."

"Good day, Miss Roberts."

Was that gentlemanly enough for her?

Faraday

The mood is a little tense. The Judge has *that* copy of the Tribune in his hand and he's smacked it against his palm more than once.

"Quaid's upped the ante," he declares.

"I know," Faraday replies. "And what's more, he has employed a serious investigative journalist from out of town. And it would be unwise to ignore or underestimate her."

"Her?"

"Yes, Judge. The journalist is a young woman. Miss Roberts."

"That's concerning, in the circumstances."

"Mm."

"What are you intending to do, Mr Faraday?"

"I intend to show a hand that Quaid, or anyone else in this town, is unlikely to forget."

The Judge whacks the Tribune against his thigh for a change.

"So it's time?"

Faraday nods. "Cliff Ryan has returned from Denver; we will be meeting this evening, and intend to proceed at once."

"Cliff Ryan is without reservations in the matter?"

"Totally."

"And yourself?"

Faraday recalls his conversation with Meg last evening. If there had been anything holding him back, that was gone.

"As I said, I believe the timing is right. We need to act."

The Judge tosses the Tribune on his desk. "I don't know what to tell you, Mr Faraday. For all that we try to do here, the desire for people to take matters into their own hands goes on. The political landscape is treacherous for men like you." Judge Callaghan sinks into his leather chair and removes his spectacles.

"I appreciate what you're saying, Judge, but I made a vow to Meg when I married her that my personal ambitions would never take precedence over my duty to the law."

The Judge raises a smile. "Good woman, young Mrs Faraday. All right then, Mr Faraday, begin! Bring this town to its knees, and God help us."

Luke

Cheyenne
January 29, 1885

Luke sits forward against the window of the train. The town is several miles off in the distance domed in a raw white frostiness. To the north, Fort DA Russell and Camp Carlin supply depot have disappeared into the mist entirely.

As the train moves with decreasing speed through the outskirts of town, his stomach begins to churn. Surely he wouldn't be human if it didn't.

He steps down onto the platform and takes his first breath of Cheyenne air in almost five months. The stinging cold immediately stabs at his throat. In that first breath, at the first touch upon Wyoming ground, at the sight of the familiar *Welcome to Cheyenne* at the end of the platform, the memories begin their assault. He pushes through them with a sense that they want to tear him to shreds. He makes his way through the depot crowd, his saddle bags over one shoulder, his hands deep in his pockets, the brim of his hat low against the onslaught of anything real or imagined.

Out of the station, onto 15th... he is determined. No sense in putting it off. Has to be done now.

He takes Hill Street, passing the Phoenix Block on 16th and the Inter Ocean on the opposite corner; he comes to the corner of 17th, where the Opera House endeavors to make a grand statement, turns left soon to pass the Cheyenne Hotel, and arrives finally in the part of town where he almost can't bear to tread. He reaches Eddy Street, crosses over it... retracing her steps... half the block. He stops on the sidewalk in the exact spot where she fell on 17th... he knew he would relive the moment, and he does. His head feels like it will burst with the horror of that memory, but he endures it, as he knows he must, and then swallows it, while people give him strange looks.

The citizens of Cheyenne trample this spot all day, every day, without a thought to what happened here.

The evil that orchestrated it seems to hover in the air, gloating over its wicked deed. He can't have that; it's not right... seems like complicit evil to do nothing...

His skin prickles... tightens, from his forehead to his neck.

Then a voice in his head, clear and distinct, like she's standing beside him... K... uttering those last words she ever said to him... the very ones that tormented him for months in San Francisco... *We did it, Taylor, just as Mart wanted. I could dance for joy about it. Couldn't you...*

A burly middle-aged businessman brushes his shoulder. "Watch it, pal."

K's memory scatters. She won't go far; memories of her are always close. If only... no, he promised himself no more *if only*... it is what it is. Life without her, life without Mart.

He raises his eyes to Jennifer's building, really only a dozen or so strides away, and makes the distance. Gone is the shingle with her name in gold letters. The doors are locked and firmly secured; the windows darkened by those shades...

"Jennifer," he whispers. At once her love jumps to life inside him. A fire. A light. A lodestar. But all too soon there is regret. And confusion... and questions... and exasperation...

"Doc Sullivan ain't there no more, young feller, but I guess you already know that," says a voice from behind him.

He turns right around and comes face to face with a wrinkled old woman whose has wrapped herself up in shabby old pieces of clothing to keep warm.

"Left town, oh, four months ago. Such a pity. Best doc we ever had in this here town. And the best lookin'." She stops and chuckles and adds curiously, "But I guess you know all 'bout that as well. Hope you won't take no offence, but I bin watchin' you. You was stopped on the sidewalk back there, everyone ajostlin' you, and I was thinkin' why don't he git out the way. Then I recalled who you was. You're Luke Taylor, ain't that right? You was famous in this town all last summer. You and Mr Faraday and Sheriff Ryan was some team gettin' that Parsons character put away and gettin' that murderer hanged. Why, you're still famous. They still talk of it."

He stares at her, bewildered. She looks poor and lowly and his conscience receives a hearty jolt.

"Well, I reckon y'are him. An' I reckon that back there you was remembering that golden haired Miss Keaton. Sad business. She was some young woman, that Miss Keaton. I was sorry for yer loss, young feller. But, apart from Doc Sullivan leavin', most everythin' else ain't changed that much since you bin gone.

"Cattle barons still at the throats of us poor homesteaders. You remember how it was an' all? There's a rally comin' up soon; we're gonna make ourselves heard, yes we are. We could use the likes of you. You went to Frisco is what I heard."

"Yes M'am. I'll think about the rally, if I'm still in town that is," he says. He removes the woolen scarf from around his neck and loops it around hers instead. "Stay warm, M'am."

Emotion wells in those age-old eyes. "My eternal thanks, young feller."

"You're welcome."

"That's somethin' she woulda done," she mumbles as her worn hands clutch at the scarf. "Special, the doc was."

"Yes, M'am, she was."

"Stay on yer toes, Luke," the woman delays him. "That young sheriff's got more'n he needs to do and only twenty-four hours in the day to do it."

"Thank you, M'am." He's never seen her before, not once in all the time he'd spent in Cheyenne last year. He gives her a farewell smile and tips the brim of his hat as he moves on. When he glances over his shoulder a moment later the old woman is gone; he stops mid-stride and scans the scene; she is nowhere.

He gives his head a shake. Cheyenne was getting more peculiar by the minute. Well, he can't think about that right now. There is only one thing he needs to do now, only one place he needs to go.

Mac

Nan Morris' Boarding House
Corner of 19th & Warren

Mac observes Miss Roberts disappear through the door of Nan Morris' boarding house; for a moment a warm glow intrudes on the cold dusk, and then she shuts the door and he is left to contemplate an evening of freezing his butt off. He'd made mental notes of all the places she'd been and was ready to report back to Cliff.

Nan Morris draws the drapes across the windows of her dining room. Mac is satisfied that Miss Roberts will soon be sitting down to supper.

Luke

Luke stands on the sidewalk by the Faradays' gate, looking up at the comfortable respectability of the house, surveying Meg's garden of frost and snow. He'd always been welcome here. More than welcome. Expected... like family. With or without Jennifer... now without...

He only has to look at the house to know that Jennifer ain't inside it. The lost and lonely feeling inside of him tells him as much. He takes a deep breath and forces himself to open the gate and walk the path.

Would Cam and Meg resent him for going to San Francisco after K's death, for leaving Jennifer and making her unhappy?

Blame him for her decision to quit Cheyenne after everything she achieved here?

He gets to the front door, is about to rap and then stops himself.

Hate him for her coming to San Francisco to bring him back and then for him to react the way he did and cause her more distress?

He can just hear K... *suck it up, Taylor, and take your medicine...* while she pointed out that his *over-inflated sense of self-importance is showing as usual...*

Jennifer may not be upset with him; she might not care less. She might be handling the whole fiasco as calmly as she handles a medical emergency, and be over the shock he gave her by offering to kill her father. He raises his knuckles again... and again falters. He groans inwardly and flops down on the porch seat. Why can't life ever be simple?

Cheyenne's stealthy chill seeps into his bones.

With the dark purple of evening now settling in around him, that peculiar feeling returns... memories, ghosts... him chasing them to put things right... a missing angel, *his* angel... anyone'd think he didn't have a handle on what's real and what ain't... couldn't blame them... he thinks too much...

A mighty busy imagination, that's what you got.

I can't help it, Ethan...

No one knew him as well as Ethan.

Except maybe now Jennifer does.

He looks up and espies a familiar figure strolling down the sidewalk towards the house, head down, negotiating the ice.

After getting his innards all tied up in knots, this moment was not to be decided by him. He oughta know by now that the moment never is.

Nothing left to do but swallow his self-doubt, recall with a smile that Jennifer would probably be taunting *shy boy* right about now, and prepare to meet a friend.

He steps forward.

Cam looks up from unlatching his front gate.

"Luke..." And grins like he was expecting him.

Luke returns it, relaxing some.

Cam quickly meets him on the porch, and they shake hands.

"Lost something, my friend?"

"Something like that. I'm hoping I've come to the right place."

Cam walks him to the door. "For you, always. You know that."

"Well, I..."

"And I'm glad you never left San Francisco."

"Yeah, well..."

"I'm proud of you. That took courage."

"Thanks. How's Meg?"

Cam gives a chuckle, warm and deep. "Why don't you come in and find out?"

Mac

Mac finds Cliff reading by lamplight, his eyes half hanging out of his head. Their small down-town branch sure could use some handy electric lights.

"So, Mac…"

"Gotta get onto that electric light company."

"So…"

"Last thing you need is a pair of specs attached to that famous mug of yours."

"Mac…"

"This town never had a sheriff who reads as much as you."

No comment.

"Ain't that head of yours full up by now?"

"It could explode at any moment."

Mac chuckles and lifts his Winchester from the rack.

"So…"

"She's eating supper right about now."

"Mm." The boss sits right back in his chair and stretches some; rubs that spot over his right eye. He's beat, anyone can see that. "So, what's she been up to?"

"The Bugle."

"Who did she speak to?"

"Obadiah Williams."

"Damn."

"Yep. She stepped out with Simons for a while. They took a turn around the town; she's new so I guess that's reasonable. Then they

105

went back to the Tribune and stayed there 'til dusk. She seemed okay. Seems kinda nice."

"Well, don't forget she's a reporter."

"I ain't forgetting she's a reporter."

"Anything else?" Cliff asks, impatient all of a sudden.

Mac shakes his head. "Heading off yourself now, boss? Who's on night duty?"

"Clary."

"Well, I guess I'll clean my rifle and keep him company for a bit, then head off myself."

"If anyone's looking for me," Cliff says, reaching for his hat and coat, "I'll be at the Faraday's."

"Okay." Mac, scratching the back of his neck, watches him go. What's eating *him*?

Luke

Luke appreciates his comfy chair by the flaming hearth; but he examines the brandy in his glass, though, to avoid the firelight flickering speculatively in Cam and Meg's wide, interested eyes.

"So," Cam begins, from his armchair, stretching out his legs.

"So," Luke says and swirls his brandy. "Did I mention you both look in good health?"

"Mm, you did," Meg says, perched on the arm of Cam's chair. "In fact, you congratulated us on being in the family way and remarked how well it suited us."

"Ah, so I did."

"So…" Cam begins again.

"So… I did a lot of soul searching in San Francisco."

"Oh, really?" says Meg. "And?"

"Well, I decided that I should find out who murdered K. I did that much for Mart, it would be wrong not to do the same for K."

More swirling.

"Oh," Meg murmurs.

Luke looks up.

Cam's dark eyes are trained on his face.

"Well, that's good, ain't it?" Luke checks.

Cam draws back his legs and straightens up. "It is the very best news you could have brought!"

Luke frowns at his intensity. "Something wrong, Cam?"

"I need you here."

"Regarding the investigation into K's murder?"

"You could say that. It won't be easy for you, Luke, to accept what you will soon find out. But I hope and trust that you can."

Luke hasn't got a clue what he's talking about. "Well, finding who murdered K ain't the only thing… it ain't even the first thing… maybe you think it should be… there's something you need to understand first." He is powerless to stop the pain and regret and desperate longing from flooding his body. In no time at all his eyes are stinging.

"Oh, Luke," Meg murmurs.

The silence is awkward as they both stare at him.

"She's in St Louis," Meg sighs. "She came through here the day before yesterday; she stayed overnight and then went home. When I asked her what happened she refused to go into details, and would only say that she had told you and that I wasn't to interfere."

He swallows hard. "Then I need to go to St Louis first, before anything else."

Cam sits forward in his chair. "I'm beginning to see that. But I wish you wouldn't."

Meg punches his arm. "Oh, Cam, how can you say that?"

"Jennifer will keep while there's important work to do."

"Jennifer will keep!?" Meg stands up and tosses her head, her dark curls bouncing about. "She's *been* keeping, Cam Faraday, *long* enough."

"Luke, just hear me out tonight, and Cliff. He has returned from Colorado."

"What's he…? Parsons?"

Cam gives a sharp nod.

Luke sighs.

"I'm going to be blunt," Meg announces.

"Meg," Cam murmurs.

"No, I think it needs to be said, and if I don't say it I will feel disloyal to Jennifer."

Luke grimaces. "Just say it, Meg."

"Well, it's just this. Miss Keaton, as much as I admired her, and we all did, and as worthy of your time and effort as finding her assassin is, *she* is gone. Jennifer, on the other hand, is alive and needs you, Luke. I honestly believe you are the only one who can make her happy. There I said it."

"Yes, you did," Cam says. He gets to his feet and slides his hands in his pockets. "Drink your brandy, Luke, then, if you want to tell us what happened…"

"Of course, he wants to…"

"I reacted," he blurts out.

Cam and Meg are suddenly very quiet and still. Then:

"How?" Cam asks.

"I…" Luke tables his brandy. "I got angry."

"With Jennifer?"

"No," he says firmly. "I could never be angry with her about anything. I was just angry."

"Oh, you are going to have to do much better than that," Meg reproaches him.

"Look, you two, haven't you ever felt helpless; so useless and… and desperate that the only thing left is anger?"

Cam is studying him mercilessly. "Not really, but you have a tendency to, I've noticed. You want justice and you want it yesterday. It's an innate passion, unmeasured and unapologetic, and we all admire it. And Jennifer's young life is the very personification of injustice and unfairness, so I guess we shouldn't be surprised at your reaction."

"I couldn't control it," he presses on. "This overwhelming sense of outrage. I wanted to kill him…"

"Dermot?"

"Sonofabitch…"

"Luke!"

"You go right ahead, Luke," says Meg.

"Meg!"

"That's no fit state to be in when everything's at stake. No matter what I wanted to say to her it sounded so weak and… and so pathetic, so hollow… If he walked in here right this minute I'd shoot him…"

Cam clears his throat. "The prosecutor in me wishes I hadn't heard that since I know you mean it. So, how did it end?"

"She understood that I needed some time to… My anger scared

her. I didn't expect her to take off like she did. Look, I needed the time to get on top of things, think about what to do next, how I could show her – not just tell her – that I truly believe she deserves to be happy. "

Meg comes across and places her hands on his shoulder. He looks up into that bright perky face with the soft dark curls; she's smiling. "I knew you wouldn't let her down."

"Just promise me," Cam says, "no matter what happens, don't shoot Dermot."

"*Don't* speak that name to me. No, I mean it..."

"Luke."

"Take deep breaths," Meg says. "In... and out..."

"I can't..."

"In... keep trying... and out... better..."

"This is crazy..."

"In... no, it works... and let it out... slowly... good..."

"Luke... promise me. I realize those are powerful feelings you have there, but acting on them won't help Jennifer and it certainly won't do you any favors."

Powerful and scary... he'll never get her back.

He sighs... breathe out... "All right. I swear."

In a way, it's a relief to warehouse his violent anger towards Dermot in this promise to Cam. As for the deep breathing, he'll have to think about it.

"Good man. Now, let's think about something else, shall we?"

"Excellent idea. Supper will be ready soon," says Meg. "And doesn't it smell good? And Cliff will be here."

"Sure." He takes a mouthful of brandy. Lets it settle.

They give him some time to calm himself.

He says, "There is something else I can't seem to get my head around."

"We will do our best," Meg says. "Fire away."

"How in God's name do I live up to Frank?"

Cam pushes his hand through his hair. "Next question."

"Meg?"

"No," she says.

"Maybe Duffy knows."

"No."

"Anyone?"

"No."

"There must be someone…"

Just then, rising on the warm air of Meg's parlor, comes a voice singing like no voice Luke has ever heard before. He thinks it's a woman's, but it's scratchy and croaky and he strains to recognize the tune.

"Oh when I die, take my saddle from the wall, put it on my pony and lead him from his stall, tie my bones to his back, turn our faces to the west and we'll ride the prairie that we love the best…"

"That's just Constance," Meg tells him.

"…ride around little dogies, ride around them slow, for the Fiery and Snuffy are raring to go."

"And who is Constance?"

"Constance McConnell is our cook," Cam announces proudly, "and keeper of Meg."

"Yes, well… she knows lots of cowboy songs," Meg says. "She says cowboys sing to the cattle to keep them calm."

"Well, they do, Meg," Luke grins.

"Oh." She looks confused. Fair enough; a girl from Louisburg Square, Boston, don't need to know cattle. "Why?"

"They're jittery. Tend to stampede. So we sing to them."

"And do *you*?"

"I've been known to warble a tune or two."

"Well, if *that* voice doesn't make a herd of cows stampede I don't know what would," she declares, tossing her curls.

Luke, in spite of his anxiety, laughs. "I gotta meet this Constance. Is she from Texas?"

Meg sweeps her hand in the direction of the kitchen. "Why don't you go ask her? Oh no, not that one, it's her worst…"

"As I was a-walking one morning for pleasure, I spied a young cow-puncher a-riding along. His hat was throwed back and his spurs was a-jingling, as he approached me a-singing this song.

"Whoopee ti yi yo, git along, little dogies, it's your misfortune and none of my own, whoopee ti yi yo, git along, little dogies, for you know Wyoming will be your new home."

"It's a classic, is what it is," Luke laughs some more. "Sung it more than a few times myself. Kinda appropriate, too."

"She's an excellent cook," Cam offers. "And she takes wonderful care of Meg."

"She made the dog across the street howl for half an hour today."

Even Cam starts laughing.

"She'll probably sing this baby into tone deafness. And *what* is a buckaroo? Constance is constantly referring to this child as her little buckaroo."

Luke laughs harder. "Buckaroo? Texan for cowboy."

"Look at the pair of you, laughing your heads off while I have to put up with it morning, noon and night. Is it any wonder I had to learn deep breathing from Mr Wang!"

Cam's laughter wanes to a smug and satisfied grin. He folds his arms and says, "Did I mention Constance is an excellent cook and takes wonderful care of Meg?"

"Why, Cam, I believe you did," says Meg, through gritted teeth, "but I would like to know how Constance amusing *you* is taking care of *me*! And after all I do for you!"

She tosses her head and walks out.

Their grins hover for a spell and then slide off their faces.

"You know, Cam, Ethan says women in Meg's condition have a short fuse and a long memory."

"How long?"

"Ethan never said exactly, but you might find out when the baby's born and it's crying all night long."

Emmaline

Evening

Emmaline moves stealthily down what she thinks is 17th Street heading east, ducking into shop fronts as necessary, all the time her heart pounding. Cliff Ryan is long striding and fast, and very soon her throat is raw and stinging. She imagines that the sidewalk is a fishing line, that Ryan is hooked on the end of it and she's very cunningly reeling him in…

The Opera House comes and goes; then the Cheyenne Club which Simons had indicated earlier. Soon the street becomes more residential. Simons pointed down this way and mentioned something about this part of town becoming 'fashionable'. And she begins to see why. Many of the houses are big and clearly cost a great deal of money to build. Well, society was good at nothing if not impressing upon itself that you can't be fashionable without wealth. This city appeared to have what most other cities have; the transcontinental railroad had seen to that. Except that it sat on a high, ice-cold prairie; which makes stalking its sheriff at night most precarious, for as the noise and lights of the town diminish, any crunching footfall or stumbling on her part could easily give her away. And the cold just seems to grow more intense.

Eventually, Cliff Ryan turns down the front path of a beautiful two-story house. Lights from a number of windows flicker in the darkness. Excellent – whoever lives here has not yet bothered to draw their curtains.

Cliff Ryan knocks on the front door; she ducks out of sight as he executes a cursory sweep of the street behind him. She catches her breath as Cam Faraday opens the door and greets his visitor; but before the door is closed, she glimpses yet another tall young man shaking hands with Ryan. Her heart is pounding in her freezing cold ears. Who is this? Well, whatever is going on, her mission tonight is clear; to gain any leads as to what has happened to the celebrated file of the mysterious Luke Taylor, and… well, keep an eye on these men who Mr Quaid believes have covered up evidence in some kind of conspiracy of their own.

She steals her way across the yard to the front window.

Carefully, she raises herself until she is just able to see over the windowsill. She is peering into the sitting room of an exceptionally charming home. They are all gathered there, including a young, dark-haired woman around whom Mr Faraday has his arm. They are smiling and laughing. Mr Ryan included.

Disagreeable man. He couldn't be more different to what she'd expected. So is Mr Faraday for that matter – shouldn't the pair of them be making her uneasy about this alleged subterfuge, shouldn't their guilt be obvious in their demeanor? Despite being given the brush-off by both (and yes, they are hiding something, from her at least), her proven powers of perception have failed to detect corruption in either of them.

The happy group passes around drinks, except for the young woman, who is quite clearly expecting a child. Mrs Faraday? The lady of the house. The Faradays' home.

The men talk for some time after Mrs Faraday leaves the room. The intriguing sound of their conversation is audible but not the words. It is extremely frustrating.

On top of this, the temperature seems to plummet even further and Emmaline, dressed as plainly and warmly as possible while still able to move, believes her whole body could easily be mistaken for a block of ice.

However, persistence is usually rewarded she reminds herself, and when Mr Faraday goes to a desk drawer and retrieves a leather satchel from it, all her senses are heightened at once.

What's this then?

Mr Faraday discards the satchel. Soon all three men are huddled together in the center of the room looking at something Mr Faraday is holding. She strains to see the object of their attention, but the arrangement of the huddle blocks her view. And then, all at once, the *new young man* breaks the constraints of the huddle.

She cranes her neck.

In Mr Faraday's hand is a thick corrugated wad of rumpled, dog-eared pages...

Could it *be*?

It must be.

Surely.

If only she could get a better look...

Luke

"My file, Cam?"

"There is no easy way to do this, so I need you to keep an open mind."

"About what?"

"For some time now, we have been investigating Loren Bodecker in relation to Kelley's murder. Cliff has just returned from Cañon City where he interrogated Parsons."

"Parsons as good as implicated Bodecker," Cliff says.

"As good as? Well, that's something at least."

Luke watched the words come out of Cam's mouth and then Cliff's; he heard them plain as day... but something blocks the understanding in his brain.

"You want to run that by me again, Cam. Loren Bodecker, the tycoon?"

"You know him, know of him, I mean."

"Of course. Everyone knows who he is."

"But you have never laid eyes on him."

"Can't say that I ever have."

"Well, you have, in a way."

"What are you talking about?"

"It will become clear," Cam says, and locates a particular page in Luke's file. He holds it out.

Luke takes the page. He'd rather not look back at these days... rather keep his sights on the way ahead.

"That face with the words *who is this man* beside it, that is Loren Bodecker. You saw him, with Ed Parsons."

Luke studies the face. "No, that was Ethan. I drew this from Ethan's description."

"Amazing..." Cam murmurs.

Luke clears his throat, clears his head. "What are you telling me, Cam?"

"You would remember the day McCurdy gave his testimony at Parsons' trial, when he pointed to Parsons as the man who hired Wilson Cutter to kill Mart."

"I remember."

"And you recall me asking you and Kelley to study your file?"

"Of course. K did; I didn't."

"I know. That day, after McMurdy's testimony, she ran into Bodecker who had been in court. She, too, had never seen him in the flesh before, but she had a strange encounter with him, in which he seemed to make a point of bumping into her. She was suspicious; his face jogged her memory. She thought it was someone from your file, so she sought out your file and showed this sketch to me."

"What did she say to you, Cam?"

"She said, *Here, Mr Faraday, I think I may have found something. This man was in court today and I didn't like the way he looked at me. I felt very uneasy. Did Sheriff Ryan investigate him?*"

"You remember her exact words?"

"Yes. I can't forget them."

What's that telling him then?

Something stirs inside him. Something very disturbing.

K... he misses her, sorely, and wishes with all his being that he could see her again. His experience on the sidewalk earlier is still so raw. He swallows into a very dry throat... starts to tremble. "You knew for a long time, Cam, that Bodecker's face was in my file..."

"I knew the first time I looked through your file, when you first brought it to me..."

"...knew and did nothing."

"I cannot prosecute a businessman for being seen with another businessman..."

"Being seen with a man you were prosecuting for conspiracy to murder."

"Luke..."

"Even K suspected him, brought him to your attention! After you asked for her help. You knew how smart she was. You ignored her."

"Luke..."

"You *asked* her, Cam, and you ignored her. What was the point of it? She *trusted* you."

"I know..."

"Do you? For God's sake, Cam, Bodecker made her uneasy. Did that mean nothing to you?"

Cliff takes a step towards him. "Luke..."

"Don't speak one word to me, Cliff; you had your part in this. At what point does trust mean something to you two?"

"Bodecker makes a lot of women uneasy."

"And do you ignore their anxiety too?"

"Luke, this is hindsight..."

"I don't give a fuck about hindsight, d'you hear me! K voiced her concerns, after Cam specifically asked for her help, and the pair of you deliberately ignored her."

"Bodecker is not the same as Ed Parsons..."

"He's a man, ain't he? You were just trying to protect your jobs."

"That is not fair."

"*Fair*? If you had questioned Bodecker at the time about his connection with Parsons, and warned him that everyone in the file was under suspicion of colluding with Parsons and were being investigated, don't you think he might have thought twice about having her shot dead? That's what you should have done, Cliff. He had her in his sights. It was the only chance she ever got to save her own life."

"Initially, I did pursue an inquiry with Bodecker's secretary about an association between Bodecker and Parsons. I was told that Bodecker was considering Parsons as a cattle supplier."

"And did either of you bother to tell *me* that she had identified Bodecker and about what happened after court? No, you were scared to, I bet, because you knew I would have gone after him. I *could* have gone after him. I could have done what I promised K that I would always do... protect her."

With his life. If only she had come to him...

Emmaline

It all seems very riveting, but she needs to get closer...

Before she has time to make a move, *new young man* strides out of the room; Ryan takes the file from the hands of Mr Faraday who is looking distressed. Ryan places the pages into its tanned leather satchel and ties the leather strings. When Mrs Faraday comes into the room with her hands in the air in a gesture of confusion, Emmaline begins to suspect who *new young man* might be...

...which strengthens her suspicions regarding the pile of shaggy-eared papers. At that moment she feels so uncomfortably stiff with cold that she must shift her position by the window. But just as she's shifting, a loud blast shatters the silence of her secretive world. She screams... some kind of force streaks by her, stinging her cheek, causing her to lose her balance, and she falls into a mound of snow below the window. She spends several moments gasping for breath, then thinks she ought to make good her escape; but the shock drilling through her is too powerful for her overcome, and try as she might she cannot move. A myriad of sounds erupt... people calling out in shrill voices, and rushed footfall on snow and ice...

"Are you hurt?"

She knows that voice.

"I said, are you hurt..."

Strong arms carefully sit her up in the snow, holding her there.

"Miss Roberts..."

Her head swims in a daze. But it's Ryan, unequivocally.

"It's okay, boss, I got him," some other man calls out. "He and his six-shooter won't be doing no more damage tonight."

"Who is it?"

"Never seen this character before."

"Miss Roberts, are you hurt?" she hears Ryan asking.

"I...I don't think so."

"Can you stand?"

She tries to get to her feet only to fail.

Ryan gets her upright instead, his hands holding her steady.

"Good God, woman, you're half frozen."

The other man chuckles. "She's flinty, that one."

"Why didn't you come in and tell me she was out here, Mac?"

"Well, I was going to, boss, but then I saw this feller; had to keep my eye on him. Just as well."

"I want a sweep at first light for the bullet."

She wants to flee, and she would if Ryan's substantial hand wasn't doing a good imitation of a vice on her arm.

"Throw him in the lockup, Mac, and I'll be there as soon as I can," Ryan says.

"Sure thing, boss," says the other man who finally has a name... Mac.

Ryan soothes the perturbed residents, reassures them it is safe to return to their homes. Emmaline, pushing through the daze, can just see them wandering away, still muttering.

"You want to tell me what you're doing out here?"

"Let me g...go home. I'm c...cold."

"You were trespassing."

"Let me go h...home."

"You're half-frozen." He marches her across the snow.

And seems to have forgotten she is the victim.

Humiliation sets in now. She is taken into the house, passing curious Mrs Faraday, contemplative Mr Faraday, a very pale and shaken-looking *new young man*, and a tall, wide-eyed woman who declares in a very scratchy voice,

"Great God almighty, what's gonna happen next!"

Indeed.

She is deposited in front of the hearth in the sitting room where a delicious fire is blazing. It is heavenly.

"Stay there and don't move," Ryan orders her.

When he removes his hand from her arm, the spot begins to throb. Her legs tremble. Is there not a chair somewhere? The lamps in the room have been extinguished and only the fireplace generates light. Ryan draws the drapes across the windows.

"You have a little blood on your cheek, miss," says Mrs Faraday. "Constance, we must see to it."

"I'm on it, Mrs Faraday."

Meanwhile, Ryan helps himself to Mr Faraday's liquor; he then puts a glass of something amber-colored into her hands and a whiff of fragrant brandy follows.

"Drink, Miss Roberts. You'll need it by the time I'm through with you."

If all this isn't terrifying enough, *new young man* starts to pace up and down in front of her.

She attempts to raise the glass to her lips; it's a tricky business because she's shivering with extreme cold. Then Ryan's hand, encompassing both of her frozen ones, guides the glass to her mouth; she is afraid to look at him, but as she sips her eyes meet his; the concern she sees there causes her to splutter the brandy.

"Just take it easy," he murmurs. "You need more."

She takes more. And then her knees finally give way.

Ryan catches her. "A chair please, Constance."

"Miss Roberts, we need to know what you've been up to," says Mr Faraday at last. "This is a serious situation."

"Cam, leave her be; she's cold and hurt," says Mrs Faraday.

The chair arrives and Ryan has the woman Constance place it close to the fire. Ryan assists her down onto the seat and she suffers the humiliation because it is so relieving to have something beneath her at last...

"Well, Miss Roberts?" says Ryan firmly. "What were you doing? You might as well tell us because your cover is well and truly blown."

Ryan takes the brandy out of her hands and looks down at her with one raised eyebrow. She attempts to make herself more comfortable but he holds her steady by the fire.

"Stay there," he says.

She didn't intend to go anywhere – yet.

"W...why was someone sh...shooting at me?" she asks.

"Welcome to Cheyenne," quips *new young man* as he continues to pace the floor. She believes she knows who he is.

"Your Ch...Cheyenne," she says.

He stops pacing. "Yes, my Cheyenne, and now yours."

"Y...you're Luke Taylor, aren't you?"

He doesn't admit or deny it, but she's right. This is the young man who fought tooth and nail to get justice for his friend, and protect the Alliance from the evil intentions of Ed Parsons; who boldly defied a US marshal at the point of many guns and out-rightly challenged the governor's authority, who risked his life and a serious charge of perverting justice in order to keep the murderer Wilson Cutter in Cheyenne; who flatly refused to give up.

Ryan cuts across them. "You've been asking questions all over town, Miss Roberts, and now you see the result."

"I...I needed to know w...where Mr Taylor's file w...was and I believed that y...you or Mr Faraday w...would know, so I f...followed you hoping for a l...lead."

Ryan's eyes, gutted by firelight, bore into hers.

"I saw you all r...reading it. So I know it's h...here."

"And what do you think the file contains, Miss Roberts?" Mr Faraday asks her in his mild-mannered way.

"Evidence regarding Miss Keaton's murder. Something you withheld from Parsons' trial, something big or you wouldn't have k...kept it secret. Something *very* big, or you wouldn't have kept it from Mr Taylor."

Taylor's face is a picture of mental agony. It's hurting him badly, this discovery. And she feels sorry for him.

"Right," says Ryan sharply. "I'm taking Miss Roberts downtown and detaining her overnight in the lockup."

She glares at him in disbelief. "I didn't do anything. You are the ones who are conspiring..."

Ryan gives her a look of fierce disapproval. "No, we are *not*."

"No?"

"No."

"Are you sure?"

"Yes... no... look..."

"May I quote you?"

"No. Cam?"

"Cam, you absolutely cannot let her stay in the lockup all night," Mrs Faraday protests. "It's inhuman, and... unseemly."

"I ain't attended to her wounds yet," says Constance.

"Cliff, she didn't do any harm," Mrs Faraday continues.

"No, I certainly did not," she says. "Mr Faraday, I apologize for trespassing..."

"Don't forget sticking your nose in where it doesn't belong," Ryan interjects.

"You keep out of this."

"I'm sorry, I'm just the sheriff," he says.

"Mr Faraday, I am only doing my job. I'm supposed to..."

"Snoop," Ryan supplies.

She presses her lips together; counts to three, "...investigate any possible lead; this was one of those. You can't deny it."

Mr Faraday studies her calmly. "I understand the requirements of your job, Miss Roberts, only too well. But you must understand that invasion of privacy and trespassing are matters taken very seriously by our sheriff, particularly considering the danger you brought with you..."

"You are assuming that...that shooter came with me. He could have come with him," she says, tossing her head in Ryan's direction.

"She has a point," says Constance, and Mrs Faraday murmurs and nods her head in agreement.

"Ladies, please stay out of it," Ryan says. "Cam?"

"... considering the danger you brought with you, how can I just over look the whole episode. You picked the wrong house tonight, I'm afraid."

"No, Mr Faraday, I picked the right house and yes, you and Mr Ryan and Mr Taylor are indeed afraid of something."

Ryan lets out a disparaging sigh. He produces a set of manacles from inside his coat. "Come on, Miss Roberts... this is what we do with troublemakers in Cheyenne. Hold out your hands."

Taylor, however, approaches her, with his agony eyes. "You remind me of someone I used to know. She fought like you fight and she pretty much got herself into the worst scraps a female can get herself into; but everyone respected her for her courage. She was murdered, by one bullet."

"Miss Keaton," she murmurs.

Taylor nods sadly. It occurs to her that Miss Keaton meant more to Taylor than anyone has been letting on; after all, Mr Quaid told her of the rumor regarding Taylor and the female doctor.

But Ryan interrupts. "Don't waste your breath, Luke."

Her patience with the man finally gives out. She holds out her wrists. "Fine. I certainly have enough for my first story."

Ryan steps up and fastens them securely, saying, "You certainly have, haven't you. Got what you came here for, very clever. But you'll find, Miss Roberts, that you are about to get more than you bargained for."

Mrs Faraday gasps. "Cliff, you can't..."

Emmaline is forgotten for a moment, however.

Ryan turns towards Luke Taylor and says, "I'm sorry, Luke. Will you try and understand?"

Luke Taylor's woebegone gaze holds the plaintive expression in Ryan's eyes. Undeniably, it's a terrible moment for them both. But Emmaline has a deeper sense of something slipping, perhaps even tearing...

"Please?" Ryan adds, but Taylor turns away, his composure disintegrating, leaving Ryan somewhat downcast.

"Come on, Miss Roberts..." Ryan leads her away.

Taylor's miserable profile is the last thing she sees. Ryan grabs his coat and hat. The door is closed firmly behind them; now all the drapes are drawn and the street is dark, icy cold and still.

On the Faraday's porch the bitter cold hits her hard again. She is shuddering as Ryan arranges his heavy coat around her shoulders.

"What are you doing?"

He gives a soft grunt. "I'm not having all my hard work thawing you out in there undone again."

The coat is terribly warm and smells wonderfully masculine.

"Thank you," she says stiffly.

Another grunt.

Which she assumes is Ryan-speak for *you're welcome*.

Luke

Luke stares across the room at the man he assumed was his friend. His confidence in Cam was one of the strongest emotions he'd ever felt in his life; he had trusted Cam with everything most important to him. And their affinity, which considering the huge gap in their upbringing and credentials should have been unlikely at the very least, had gone some way to easing the pain of losing Mart. Now it is all shot to pieces. He can't believe it.

"Say what you are thinking," Cam insists.

"Do you really want to know, Cam? Really? Because from where I stand, John and Amy lost someone important because you didn't do your job. I lost someone important…"

"I know you lost someone important. No one knows that more than I. And I am sorry for your loss. But I cannot have you thinking that I wasn't doing my job."

"Spare me," he mutters and takes the vacant chair by the fire. Staring into it calls to mind memories of happier days. Days that will never come again…

He made a mistake. Made the mistake of thinking Cam was a friend. Again with the naivety.

"I'm leaving town, Cam. Tomorrow."

"I need you here, Luke. You told me you returned to win justice for Kelley…"

"I can't work with someone I don't trust."

"So that's what it's come to."

"I made a mistake that cost K her life. I trusted you. But then, she trusted you too. She thought she was safe."

"Are you suggesting for one minute that I knew the danger still existed? I thought you and I had stopped it. I'm human, Luke, and I am not a soothsayer."

"You backed away from doing then what you are about to do now, only if you had done it six months ago, there is a chance that K would still be alive."

"I most certainly did not back away. I had a whole territory and its laws to consider! You had your friends and your family."

"Oh, thanks for pointing that out to me. I get it now. Didn't back then."

"I shouldn't have said that."

"No, you are the prosecuting attorney. You have every right to say it. For sure this territory is your overriding concern. All right, Cam, K died because I didn't do *my* job properly, I didn't protect her. It just might have been easier if I had all the facts. But then, I overshot my station, didn't I?"

Cam's expression is bleak. And he offers no argument.

"That's what I figured. K always said I had a nasty habit of thinking too much of myself and one day I would live to regret it."

"It's not true."

"I read you all wrong."

"No, you didn't… you haven't."

"Keep the file, Cam, if it's any use to you. I don't need it or want it." He gets to his feet.

"I don't want you leaving this way…"

"You know, Cam, where I come from, friendships forged in battle go deep. But that's just where I come from… you can't expect folks to be the same everywhere you go. So I think you're gonna do just fine without me."

"If you stay we can work this out…"

"I'll collect my gear and say my goodbyes to Meg. So long, Cam."

Emmaline

Emmaline's thoughts fixate on what deeply bothers her...

A stranger took aim and fired a gun at her head.

In spite of Cliff Ryan's infuriating personality, she is left in no doubt that he can protect her, so she walks close to his side and stays alert.

"Why did someone shoot at me?"

"I thought I already explained that."

"Because I asked a few questions around town?"

"So you were listening after all."

They fall silent; and they walk.

Now what have you got yourself into, Emmie?

Go away, Celina. I got troubles.

You're telling me. He's tall, don't you think?

Celie! I nearly got killed ...

She pulls up smartly.

Feelings... dismay, confusion... crashing over and over her.

"What is it?" Ryan asks. He steps even closer to her and darts his head around like a critter on the lookout. "You're scared..."

She uses his closeness to fortify herself while she deals with her dismay. She raises her hands to her face and covers her eyes; the restraints are heavy, their well-worn metal acerbic to her nose, the kind of smell that makes its way onto your tongue and leaves a bitter taste there. Never has she been in such a situation, but she must have something inside her to draw on.

Papa used to say, "You are one tough china plate, Emmaline Roberts."

Yes, he did. But I'd rather not...

Just use it, Emmie. I won't tell anyone. Besides, it's true.

She'd been in enough scrapes. They come and they go.

Yes, she's afraid, but she's safe now. And she's tough.

She rationalizes her fears away.

All the while Ryan is quiet and close.

Her equilibrium returns. She straightens herself.

By the suffuse light radiating from a street lamp several yards away, Ryan takes a key from his pocket. "Hold out your hands."

"How do you know I won't run off?"

"You won't get far."

While he fiddles with the lock, she attempts redirection of her thoughts. "I felt sorry for Mr Taylor. Whatever you and Mr Faraday did to him, it really hurt him."

He removes the restraints, with care and without saying a word; she risks a glance at his face. Those well-proportioned features are inscrutable.

"What are you going to do with me?" she asks.

"Where do you live, Miss Roberts?" he asks in return.

"Nan Morris' guest house, on Warren Avenue."

"Good," he says firmly. Why it's good she has no idea, and considering the trouble she's in, she decides not to bother him further.

They start walking again. She adjusts her scarf, aware that his stride matches hers and growing more irritated by it every minute.

At last they reach downtown; he keeps them moving along the darker side of the street. By the time he guides her into a small sheriff's office with a corner lockup, a gun rack, a potbelly stove, a coat stand, and a desk and two chairs, she is exhausted. He removes his coat from her shoulders and seats her on one of the chairs. She looks around; it seems this place is a log building with a framed false front, probably from those 'hell on wheels' days; indeed the place to be the quintessential frontier lawman.

The man who apprehended the shooter appears.

"Fetch Doc Prewitt, Mac, pronto," Ryan tells him.

This *Mac* leaves.

"Who is he?"

"Deputy."

"He apprehended the man who shot at me." An idea occurs to her. "Was he following me the whole time? He was, wasn't he?"

"Yes, on my instructions."

She would love to tell him that he is infuriating but even she wouldn't tell that to a sheriff who has her at his mercy. Well, perhaps she would, but she is too exhausted. Instead, she defers to his authority and appeals to his kindness.

"If I may once again have the temporary loan of your coat? It seems the cold is not done with me yet."

The coat is once again arranged around her. She is beginning to like the attention, albeit reluctantly. A moment later he is pouring hot coffee into a tin cup and securing it in her hands. The warmth from the cup penetrates her gloves and begins to thaw the chill from her palms and fingers.

"Where are you from, Miss Roberts?" he asks.

"A town called Orlando in Florida."

"That explains it," he remarks with a smile.

"Explains what exactly?"

His smile broadens. "The southern accent and a lack of know-ledge of northern winters in a mountainous climate."

"Oh," she says, "yes, I can see now why you... that it... Well, it is a great deal colder here than I had anticipated."

His laughter is mellow, almost tender, an unexpected ephemeral delight in which she wonders if she has uncovered the real Mr Ryan...

"You'll get use to it, if you stay around that is."

At least that's what she thinks he said. "I suppose."

"Perhaps it is just a little too cold for someone from Orlando, Florida."

God forbid, she is smiling back at him. "Perhaps."

They sit in silence for some moments sizing one another up; she already did that earlier outside Mr Faraday's office and then again when she interviewed him... perplexed, she resumes her sipping, while he shuffles some papers on his desk.

"I... I'm not a troublemaker," she tells him.

"Not a criminal one, no..."

"Not any kind of a one."

He looks like he doesn't think he should believe her.

On impulse she holds out her coffee to him. "Will you have the rest? Don't you feel the cold?"

Surprise springs into his eyes… followed by a look that suggests he thinks he knows she's up to something. What *is* she doing? She feels warmth in her cheeks.

Emmie, what are you doing?

Not sure.

He is about to say something when an old man, drowning in a thick woolen coat, with half moon spectacles, wiry white hair and rosy cheeks, arrives with the deputy, Mac.

"Sheriff Ryan, what can I do you for?"

"Dr Prewitt, this is Miss Roberts."

"How do, Miss Roberts." The doctor peers at her, takes her coffee cup and hands it to Ryan. She is well aware that doctors who have been around as long as this one know a great deal more than they let on, so he probably knows exactly how she does. Cold and exhausted.

Ryan answers for her. "Miss Roberts has a bullet graze on her cheek."

She'd almost forgotten about that.

Dr Prewitt murmurs disapprovingly as he strips off his gloves and moves her cheek left, then right. "More light please."

"Is it bad?" Ryan asks.

"Hold your horses, sonny. The impatience of youth…"

Dr Prewitt asks Mac to hold the lamp close to her cheek, so close she feels the heat it generates.

"Mm. It's just a scratch, young lady, you'll be pleased to know. How did you manage to avoid the thing?"

"I think I moved just as it happened."

She gulps, and glances at Ryan, who catches her eye.

"There will be a mild graze for a while but it won't scar if you take good care of it; yes, a pity it would have been with such a pretty face."

The doctor dabs her wound with a cotton swab and something out of a brown bottle; it's pungent like alcohol and stings; she gasps and recoils.

"Keep still, Miss Roberts, there's a good girl. Lucky you don't need stitching up; don't think you'd like that very much, eh?"

She opens her mouth to argue that she is quite capable of coping with physical discomfort, but the doctor beats her to it.

"Mouth closed, Miss Roberts."

Ryan's laughter joins the chuckles of the deputy Mac.

The doctor stands back and surveys her cheek. "Good. Now, Mr Ryan, this woman is blue with cold and a little clammy. Tsk, I shouldn't wonder... So, I recommend the three *b*'s, particularly at this time of year."

"What are those?" she asks.

"Hot *b*ath, chicken *b*roth, warm *b*ed, and no arguments from you, missy. Got it?" He peers at her again over his half moons.

"Yes," she says. "Thank you."

The doctor grins and gives a raspy chuckle. "Good girl." He pats her shoulder. "Stay away from bullets. You'll live longer. Ain't that so, Mr Ryan?"

"Sure, doc."

"Good night then."

The deputy Mac tables the lamp and shows Dr Prewitt out.

Meanwhile, Ryan unpegs an oilskin coat from the coat stand, shakes it out and puts it on. "Let's go, Miss Roberts. And hope Nan Morris hasn't retired for the evening."

She feels her spirits lift. "You are taking me home?"

"There is no hot bath, chicken broth or warm bed here."

"But I..." She clamps her mouth shut.

He laughs at her. "Good idea."

Nan Morris is awake, but in nightgown and robe with her hair rolled neatly in rags. Ryan delivers Dr Prewitt's instructions.

"At once, Sheriff," she says. "I'll draw your bath right away, Miss Roberts, and soup will be warming on the stove, when you are ready."

"That is very kind of you, Mrs Morris, but I can..."

"Now don't you worry. Not a bit. You stay right there." She gives Ryan a nod as she leaves.

Emmaline feels Ryan's firm hand on her arm once more.

He takes her aside, and looking her straight into her eyes, he says in a hushed tone, "I live in the next block from here, corner of 19th and Ransom. If you have any trouble, come get me or send for me."

A lump congeals in her throat; she can only nod.

"Lock your doors. And don't stand next to windows. I'll check your room before I go, if that's all right with you."

Again she nods dumbly; she watches him suppress a smile of amusement and doesn't even care. The bottom step seems like a secure place to sit while she waits for him to check her room, or the bath to fill, whichever comes first.

Ryan reappears a few minutes later.

"All clear. Tomorrow will probably be a difficult day, so try and get some sleep. Good night, Miss Roberts."

"What… what will happen; what are you and Mr Faraday going to do?" She can hear the weary, wobbly edge to her voice and it scares her.

He clasps her arms and draws her to her feet. "You're not to worry about that – just do as I say."

"But…" The words disintegrate before they leave her mouth.

Her ephemeral Ryan returns, drawing his coat around her, and gripping her tightly inside it; the physical contact is immensely comforting. "I'm sorry you got hurt and things got a little rough. You've probably gathered you were an unexpected problem at a very awkward moment."

"Mr Taylor," she mutters.

"Luke, yes," he murmurs, with a brief look of anguish. "But never mind that now. Someone will keep an eye on you, I promise. You're exhausted, Emma. Get some sleep."

Did he just call her Emma?

"It's Emmaline," she murmurs.

"I know," he replies, easing his grip.

As he releases her, she feels confused.

"Your woolen coat…" she says.

"I have another."

With a final reassuring smile he is gone, and she is alone and staring at the back of Nan Morris' front door.

Faraday

As Faraday paces up and down in front of the dying embers in the hearth, Cliff makes a subdued entrance draped in his oilskin.

"You should keep that back door locked, Cam," he says, his voice hoarse from the cold.

Faraday grunts his willingness to remember in future. "What about Miss Roberts?"

"Safe and under control for the moment. Luke?"

"Wish I could say the same."

Cliff takes up the poker and prods the fire to life.

"Who then is the assailant?" Faraday asks.

"Says his name is Gordy Jacobs. Decided I'm going to take a sticky beak outside… get that bullet before someone else does."

Faraday watches as Cliff takes the lamp from his desk. The room is left to the waxing and waning light of the embers and Cliff is gone for some time. In the meantime, Meg, sad and distracted, kisses him goodnight; Constance also retires. Then Cliff returns.

"Got it," he murmurs, holding up the bullet for Faraday to inspect. "SAA .44-40 caliber. Stuck fast in your window frame."

Cliff pockets it then, grim-faced.

"And the weapon?"

"Still had it on him. I'll head back down and verify a match with the frontier six-shooter Mac said he used. God, it's damn cold." Cliff helps himself to brandy; it disappears down his throat in one gulp.

Their eyes meet over the lamp.

"Cam, I've known Luke a long time; he'll come round."

"I don't believe he will."

"So…" Cliff sighs. "We are charging Gordy Jacobs with the attempted murder of Miss Roberts."

Faraday gives a sharp nod. "What is this Jacobs like?"

"Young, kind of crazy, refuses to speak. I'm assuming he's from out of town. A resident of Cheyenne would know better than to shoot someone outside the home of the territorial prosecutor. Mac is checking if his name is on the wanted lists."

"And Colorado? Parsons is sick, you said."

"Mm. We already know that Parsons is part of Bodecker's Association and that Bodecker helped him buy out the local newspaper. And when I put it to Parsons he wanted revenge on the Alliance for his conviction, Miss Keaton's murder, and that he needed someone to help him carry this out and that person was Loren Bodecker he said, *so you know, bully for you.* In my book that's an admission of Bodecker's guilt."

"It could be interpreted as trying to be rid of you; he *is* ill…"

"But it's all we need to fire up this investigation; he inferred that the action would heat up once we pursued…"

"Guilt by any association will not do. As the Judge so eloquently phrased it last year: *it is not a crime to be seen with a man.* Even a criminal. We are seen with them every day. You, in particular. The Association has connections all over this territory, even outside of it, but freedom of association is a constitutional right. So Bodecker can visit his Association members wherever and whenever he chooses. An element of suspicion is created by Bodecker's face in Luke's file, but the sketch will never hold up as evidence."

"I still think Parsons' remark is an admission; he was shocked by everything I had to say; surprised that I knew as much as I did. That list of Bodecker's Association members I collated last year, Parsons' name wasn't on it. And I checked every member. All fifteen. They are large landholders, have solid connections, and are fiercely loyal to Bodecker."

Faraday thinks for a moment. "What is the net effect of the Association's activities in recent times?"

"Main activity is acquiring land. I just finished a report that amounts to twenty-two homesteaders in three counties in the last six months that were given an offer they couldn't refuse."

"What are Association members doing with it?"

"You can't guess?"

"Of course... Mining prospects."

"Bodecker has always been interested in what comes out of the ground."

"Something's been going on under our very noses."

"I was hoping you would see it that way."

"It would seem he has his sights set on controlling large tracts of this territory and he wants to do this in such a way that it has happened before anyone notices. Well, okay then – if the citizens of this territory are too dupable to know it's happening, too stupid to allow it to happen. But I'll be damned if I let him get away with shooting innocent women."

"I agree. So we turn a blind eye, so to speak, when it comes to his Association activities and concentrate on conspiracy to murder?"

"His Association activities could have us tied up in knots for years and come to nothing, but the thing is, Cliff, if we get him on a murder charge, he'll be finished and everything else will come tumbling down. It's what we want and I believe it's the quickest way to achieve it."

"So, we keep Luke's file under wraps for the time being."

"Mm, Luke's sketch of Bodecker has been a catalyst for us, and if and when we get that far, likely have its day in court. But until we have something that would make the villainous connection between the two men utterly conclusive..."

Cliff gives him a sympathetic smile. "Luke will come around eventually, Cam."

"I hope so. We're going to miss his help."

Faraday throws Cliff a sideways glance.

Cliff tosses a philosophical smile back.

"The Keatons are like family to him and I've never known him to back away from a fight."

"That's what worries me. What if he tries to do this on his own?"

"He was doing a lot on his own before you or I got involved and he did it pretty well."

"I only hope he doesn't shoot someone."

"He won't. I better get back and start on Gordy Jacobs."

Emmaline

At last she crawls into bed, all the b's completed. The broth was chicken, Nan Morris sprinkled restorative salts in the bath, and the bed is comfy and warm.

And yet, despite her exhaustion, the events of the evening replay themselves in her mind. And the questions... all the questions, but mainly who and why... And when she dwells on the answers...

Fear, unlike anything she has previously known, strikes at the heart of her.

She sits up in bed, shivering.

Emmie... Emmie...What's wrong?

Celie! I'm so alone...

When death slips by, leaving its mark on your cheek like a calling card, what can ever be the same again? She reaches down to the end of her bed and pushes her arms into Ryan's big woolen coat. She inhales the scent, wraps herself tightly inside it and pulls over the quilt.

Em, don't forget. You are never alone.

Cliff

Finally, in the late hours, Gordy Jacobs cracks. He complains of thirst, hunger and lack of sleep; thin and pale, with stringy hair and the patchy beginnings of facial hair, he is a whining, somewhat articulate, highly strung eccentric who's just barely clinging to the margins of society, for whom murder is a job that puts food in his belly and gets him a woman whenever he feels the urge.

The final statement is the result of hours of painstaking work:

What is your name?
Accused: Gordy Jacobs

How old are you?
Accused: Nineteen.

Where do you come from?
Accused: Laramie.

Did you fire a gun at Miss Roberts tonight outside the home of Cam Faraday?
Accused: Yes.

Why?
Accused: It's my job. I wasn't supposed to miss my target, never missed one before. And I didn't know whose house it was.

Which one haven't you missed?
Accused: Don't know their names.

Where did they happen?
Accused: I can't remember everything. Around.

What kind of people?
Accused: Sheepherders and people like that. Don't always shoot
to kill.

Do you shoot to intimidate?
Accused: You mean scare? Sure, I do that.

Why did you miss tonight?
Accused: The girl moved just as I pulled the trigger, and
the deputy jumped me before I could get off another shot.
Didn't see him, didn't know he was there.

Who is your boss?
Accused: Don't know who he is; I get the order from someone
down the line and carry it out.

Where does the order come from?
Accused: Laramie.

Who sends it?
Accused: He calls himself Maverick.

Did you shoot Miss Keaton?
Accused: No.

Do you know who did?
Accused: None of them know the jobs of the others.

What do you mean 'them'?
Accused: Maverick's team.

Team of what?
Accused: Sharpshooters.

What else do you know about Maverick?
Accused: Nothing.

Have you ever seen him?
Accused: No.

Who approached you about working for Maverick in the first
place?
Accused: There was an advertisement in the paper with an
address to reply to.

What was the address?
Accused: I lost it and can't remember it.

Was it in Laramie?
Accused: Don't remember.

Did anyone make contact with you after you replied to the
advertisement?
Accused: I had to try out, you know, show this dude I could
shoot real good. I got the job and he gave me a piece of
paper with job instructions. I don't remember the dude, he
wore a mask, and I lost the instructions.

Was it specified which type of weapon was to be used?
Accused: Colt Frontier Six-shooter and 73 Winchester. Same
ammunition for both, see. Everybody's got them; hard to
trace, if you get my drift. .44-40 caliber. I guess you know
that, you being a lawman.

Are you certain that every shooter uses a Colt Frontier Six-
shooter and a Winchester '73?
Accused: No one can be certain, I guess, but that's what the
job requires. You'd be crazy not to do what you're told.
Feller with the mask insisted.

What happens to the members of the team if they don't' get
the job done?
Accused: We don't get paid.

What if you get caught?
Accused: Don't know. Never heard of anyone getting caught.
Members don't know each other. Maverick will want to know if
the job's done. If I don't contact him and I say I did the
girl he'll send someone else.

How do you make contact with him?
Accused: I send a wire to Maverick at the Western Union in
Laramie. He'll get it.

Write the telegram now.
Accused: I'll just tell it. It's Maverick, Laramie Telegraph.
Nighthawk lullaby.

Nighthawk Lullaby means what?
Accused: I did the job.

Is there likely to be someone here in Cheyenne watching to see if the job is done?
Accused: There might be, I don't know.

You are being charged with attempted murder, Jacobs, do you have an attorney?
Accused: You caught me in the act and I admit doing it, what's to defend?

As I said before, you are entitled to representation.
(Accused shrugs)
Accused: I'd rather be in prison.

What do you mean by that?
Accused: Maverick will pick me off outside. You'll be doing me a favor by locking me up.

How will Maverick 'pick you off'?
Accused: Send someone, probably the same feller who'll come to clean up my mistake with the girl.

How do you know Maverick will send someone to clean up?
Accused: The advertisement said "the applicant must be prepared to take full responsibility for the undertaking of the job". That's code, see. And I remember that part 'cause I like the idea of it. You know, you gotta take pride in your work. Anyway, Maverick pays well for the job or make you pay if the job ain't done. Simple business.

Sign here : *Gordy Jacobs*

For Cliff, exhaustion abides in the pores of his skin and every hair on his head. He locks Gordy Jacobs' statement in his bottom drawer, instructs Clary not to take his eyes off their prisoner, pulls on his oilskin coat and heads down to Nan Morris' boarding house.

He picks up Mac's soft hoot owl in the icy darkness across the street from the guesthouse and joins him.

"All quiet here, boss," Mac says. "Nothing stirring. Guess that little wildcat's just plumb tuckered out."

An amusing thought.

"What about Jacobs?"

"He's been very helpful. Any sheepherders been killed or shot that you can call to mind, Mac?"

White clouds stream from their mouths.

"Yeah, a feller was shot and killed not so long ago; name was Adams, from Dickson."

"Dickson's out Bright River way."

"Sure is."

"Who took over Adams's property?"

"That I can't tell you."

"Find out. And later on I want you to get me the names of all the sheepherders in Laramie and Albany counties."

"What *all* of them?"

Cliff lets go of a weary chuckle. "How many could there be?"

"For a couple of counties that got more cattle than you can poke with a stick, you might poke a few sheep while you're at it…"

"Just the sheepherders, Mac, not the sheep themselves."

"That's good, Cliff, cause we got over a hundred thousand sheep right in this here county alone."

Mac needed hot buttered rum and a spell by the fire.

"There's more, but not before we've had some shut eye."

Mac gives a frosty sigh. "Well, I guess I'd better go get some." He is silent for a moment. Then he asks, "Who are we after, boss?"

"Someone who calls himself Maverick."

"Maverick…" Mac echoes.

"We're going to have to look out for Miss Roberts, Mac. Jacobs reckons this Maverick will send someone to clean up."

Mac gives a soft whistle. "How do you think she'll take to that? She's the kinda gal who needs a full-time body guard."

"We don't have a full-time body guard for Miss Roberts."

"We could get one in, or deputize someone."

"It's a thought. Let's sleep on it."

"Sure, Cliff. Well, 'night."

"Goodnight, Mac."

Mac saunters off down the street; Cliff sticks his hands on hips and runs his eye over the boarding house.

No use pretending; he's worried about her.

And he hasn't worried about a woman in a long time.

Ben

It's after midnight when Ben, feeling stiff and bleary-eyed, finally alights from the train. (The delay had come in Ogallala. There he observed only a few people get on and off, but it seemed to take forever for the train to get going again. And no explanation was offered by UP staff.) As he collects his luggage from the dimly lit platform with the other passengers, a depot attendant is walking towards them.

"Telegram for Ben Taylor…"

"I am Ben Taylor," he says, and the young attendant holds out the telegram.

"It's marked urgent, sir. From Omaha."

He offers a dime in exchange for the telegram, all the while piqued by what is sure to his father's interference.

"The best hotel in town at this time of night?"

"The Inter Ocean. One block north on 16th Street. They'll look after you."

He heads out; two streets lamps illuminate a large sign:

WELCOME TO CHEYENNE

A young woman, who he recalls got on at Ogallala, overtakes him at this point. She strides briskly with her head down and two leather travel bags in her hands.

He sees her again outside the depot; she is looking up and down the cold, deserted street, first one way, then the other, to get her bearings, same as him. She makes a choice and pursues another direction from the one he needs to take. He starts walking, his boots squeaking on the ice and snow. Within moments he can see the lights of the hotel one block straight ahead.

The hotel is a first-class establishment, so accommodation is comfortable and well-appointed. Pleasingly, his room overlooks the street. He unpacks those things he needs for the night, all the while contemplating on what the urgent telegram might contain.

Eventually, he makes himself comfortable by the fireplace and opens it.

DEAREST SON, THINGS GO BADLY HERE, RETURN HOME AT ONCE, I LOVE YOU, MOTHER,

Blood rushes to his head and then drains away like a wave on the shore. This is not what he expected. Again and again he reads the telegram. He can't remember the last time his mother told him she loved him; it probably happened when he callously demonstrated that her love no longer mattered to him. He wrestles this shameful admission aside and concentrates on the rest. His mother knew things would go badly from the moment she gave him her blessing to leave. If anyone knows how to handle his father she does, so she wouldn't be afraid of him. Distressed, fed up, worried – poor Mother. Again he feels deep remorse because she is willing to suffer these things for him. Guilt causes him to think of returning just as the telegram asks, but the desire burning inside of him won't let him be distracted. And Mother was so sure...

He sits at the writing desk by the window. In a drawer he finds an assortment of writing implements, along with several sheets of white notepaper. He pencils a reply to send in the morning:

Dear Mother. Appreciate your help. Tell father not to panic. All will be well. Be strong. Your son Ben.

The night is sure to pass slowly now that he desperately wants it to be morning... To send his telegram... To move on to Bright River...

Cliff

Private residence
Corner of 19th & Ransom
The following morning, January 30

He jerks awake, disorientated.

"Take it easy."

"Mac," he breathes.

"Taken to sleeping on the couch?"

"The couch?"

"Yep."

He sits up. His bedroom is doing a good imitation of his parlor… or the other way round… "What time is it?"

"Time you found yourself a wife to get you out of bed in the mornings."

He gives a muffled laugh. "I don't want a wife like that."

"No man does. But you'll settle like the rest of us. 'Til then, it's nine thirty."

"What's going on?"

"Plenty."

He presses the heels of his hands into his eyes. "I'm listening." He looks up expectantly.

Mac shakes his head. "Folks are supposed to start the day with breakfast. Get some. Then you can listen."

He opens his mouth to protest.

"I don't aim to be nobody's wife," Mac adds; he turns his back to leave. "Just two things maybe. First up," he says as he's walking away, "there's a bunch of reporters outside your office wanting the lowdown on last night *and* what you were doing in Colorado. And second, about that sheepherder Adams, before he went off duty Clary said he remembers that Adams was picked off by a single bullet to the head. And there was no trace of the assassin. It's a mystery, is what they reckon up in Dickson."

"A mystery by the name of Maverick... And Miss Roberts?"

"Nan Morris said she ain't even up yet."

"If she's not at the courthouse by the time I get there, we'd better check on her."

"And you can think of what you're gonna say to those reporters while you shave," Mac calls from the hall.

"Mac, you'll make someone a fine wife some day."

"Oh, one other announcement. Luke Taylor left town early this morning. Got on a UP bound for Omaha. Thought you might like to know."

The door slams shut, leaving him alone again with a heavy heart and wondering why Luke was Omaha-bound.

He washes, shaves and dresses in his charcoal suit, needing the time all that grooming requires for his head to clear and the deep regret at Luke's departure to settle.

As he leaves the house he threads his arms into his other woolen coat. A glance up the street towards Nan Morris' place reveals all is quiet there except for a handful of small boys scooping ice off the sidewalk and tossing it at one another. He adjusts his hat at an acute angle to foil the wind and sets off at a brisk pace along 19th Street towards the courthouse.

Outside his office reporters are mingling patiently. They part like the Red Sea when he approaches; they usually do when he wears his long black coat; for some reason it intimidates them. Once he's told them he won't be long, he heads straight for the coffee.

Mac appears.

"You eat yet?"

"No. Been busy."

"No woman's ever gonna want you if you let yourself get thin'n scrawny. At least you're clean."

"At least," Cliff smiles. "Okay, fill me in."

"Well, you saw our pals from the press."

"Miss Roberts is not among them. Simons is out there for the Tribune. See if you can get Doc Prewitt to make a house call, Mac. What else?"

"Clary gave me the lowdown on MAVERICK, LARAMIE TELEGRAPH, NIGHTHAWK LULLABY. I sent that before I woke you up. According to Clary, Gordy Jacobs slept like a baby."

"Mm, reckons he's safe from Maverick in our lockup."

"Cam wants Jacobs in front of Judge Callaghan before the end of the day."

"How was Cam, Mac?"

"He looked real tired and miserable. Didn't scrub up near as well as you. Scary black coat an' all... Maybe Mr Faraday should get one."

Cliff just rolls his eyes. "Next."

"Charlie Quaid asked if you could spare a moment, go up to the Tribune and see him, you know, about last night."

"That will be my great pleasure. What else?"

"The usual. Tommy Collins swears that Arabelle Watkins threw a dead animal over their back fence during the night. He's made a formal complaint. Last straw he reckons. Wrote Arahell on the form. And... well, it goes on and it can wait till later. No one's wringing anyone's neck just yet. So, d'you want the usual? – Jim said the flapjacks were particularly fluffy this mornin'."

"No flapjacks. Martha's flapjacks are never fluffy. Jim's just sweet on Martha. Just eggs, toast and thin steak."

"You have that every day, ain't you sick of it yet?"

"No."

"You know how Martha's tends to be full of adoring patrons at this time of the morning; you might have to wait a while."

He chuckles. "You're just jealous because you know Martha will drop whatever she's doing to fix my steak."

Mac shakes his head and walks away. "Ain't no accountin' for taste in this world."

Emmaline

Emmaline jerks awake and upright; she can't remember where she is for several moments, and her head feels like there is a little hammer on the inside pounding on her forehead.

Rap, rap, rap…

"Miss Roberts…" *Rap, rap, rap…* "Oh, Miss Roberts, Nan Morris here, are you awake?"

Nan Morris? Nan Morris…

She touches her face where it hurts; all her memories of the previous night join up with the little hammer. Her body aches all over and she is wearing a massive blue woolen coat.

"Oh dear Lord…"

"Are you all right, my dear?" asks Nan Morris kindly, on the other side of her door. "Doc Prewitt is here to see you."

"One moment and I'll unlock the door," she says, but her voice is croaky and hoarse. Surely that can't be good.

"Take your time, my dear. Best not to rush about after your episode."

Episode… She groans and pushes back the quilt. She gets her legs over the side of the bed… her skull is a vast sea in which her brain is drowning. Upon standing, her vision dissolves into bright lights and her stomach rolls. She steadies herself; she must remove Ryan's coat and replace it with her robe. The scent lingering in the wool about the collar penetrates her senses and goes a long way to reviving her.

"Sheriff Ruthless, you smell good," she murmurs as she slides out of his coat and lets it drop to the floor.

Shivering, she reaches for her satin velvet robe and puts it on, fastening it as she wobbles to the door.

"Ah, there you are," croons Nan Morris. "Here is the doctor."

"Good morning, young lady," says Dr Prewitt. "Go and sit on the bed, there's a good girl, I need to look at you."

She obeys and sits on the bed.

Nan Morris, meanwhile, has spotted Ryan's coat. From the corner of her eye, Emmaline watches the woman's reaction: *what's that doing here*? Nan Morris picks it up off the floor and places it over the back of the chintz armchair.

Dr Prewitt, meanwhile, is peering at her. "Mm. Some slight bruising, of course. And the graze, remarkably, is dry; no pus."

"Pus?"

"No, I said no pus, missy. Which is a good thing. You might have skinned your knee as a child and you might remember that they can get rather pustular. But some, you might recall, some just scab over nicely and heal quickly. Of course, the scab gets itchy and you must not scratch or rub. This is one of those."

She blinks. "I wasn't permitted to get grazed or pustular."

Dr Prewitt chuckles. "Now do you hurt anywhere else?"

"Just a headache, a few aches and pains, stiff, you know…"

"Mm, I do know. Get them all the time at my age. Yours are probably due to falling and walking and whatnot. Didn't hit your head at all, did you?"

"I don't think so."

"Sleep all right, did you?"

"Well, as you can imagine, it took a while to fall asleep."

"Mm, I *can* imagine. You had a nasty shock, missy. Someone tried to put a bullet in you. You are going to have to be more careful. Well, the main thing is that you managed to sleep. It is the body's natural healing state after all."

"I don't have to stay in bed or anything, do I?"

"Well, a day in bed won't hurt, you know."

"But I have things to do, and I get *so* bored sitting around."

Dr Prewitt peers at her relentlessly. "After breakfast and a nap, you may get up."

She grins her approval. And he simply looks amused.

"And lock the door, otherwise there will be hell to pay with that pernickety sheriff."

"Good word."

"Mm. I thought so. Now you must keep that graze dry. Clean, but no face creams and all that female palaver, got it?"

"Dry, no palaver. Thank you, Doctor."

"Oh, yes. Almost forgot…" He rummages in his doctor's bag and extracts a small, amber-colored pill bottle. He peers at the label, gives a grunt of satisfaction and then puts the bottle in her hand. "For that headache. Take two of these now and then two every four hours. You'll feel better in no time. Good day then, Miss Roberts."

Dr Prewitt follows Nan Morris out of the room. The wizened old man is wearing a grin from ear to ear. Nan Morris tells her she will bring a breakfast tray shortly.

Emmaline nods, closes the door and goes back to bed.

Barely ten minutes later, Nan Morris brings her fresh squeezed juice, crisp toast and homemade strawberry jam, eggs over easy and coffee. And a glass of water.

"Bless my soul, Mrs Morris, this is a heavenly breakfast."

"Breakfasts are my specialty, Miss Roberts. Important to start the day right. I'll fetch the tray later on when you've had your rest. Don't fuss about those sorts of things like some do. Remember to take your headache pills."

"Mrs Morris, I want to express my gratitude for taking care of me last night. I am ever so grateful for your kindness."

Nan Morris wears a satisfied smile as she leaves Emmaline in peace. Emmaline turns the key. *Lock your doors. And don't stand next to windows…*

She drinks the juice, savors the toast and jam, dabs at the eggs, and sips the coffee. It's all delicious and makes her feel better, just as Nan Morris anticipated. She also takes her medicine.

Breakfast over, she removes her satin velvet robe and slides her arms into Ryan's coat. Nothing can touch her now in her unique armor, her peculiar breastplate…

She sleeps only an hour.

The late morning sun is streaming into her room, creating much needed cheeriness and encouragement, for the time has come to look into a mirror. She imagines that half her face is black and blue, with an unsightly red mark across her cheek. She braces herself and then thrusts her face in front of the mirror at her dressing table.

It is somewhat disappointing.

She moves in, so to examine the graze at close range.

"A bullet did that? What are the chances of a lethal weapon firing a projectile with intent to kill and leaving a trifling scratch that has no pus?"

She turns her face this way and that.

A magnifying glass would be handy.

Still, it is a visible reminder that someone intended to kill her. And it is with this thought that she bursts into tears, which make her pathetic wound sting a little. She wipes the tears and orders her emotions into line. She's a reporter, not a crybaby. She needs to get dressed; she has work to do.

As she loops her second earring into place, someone knocks on her door.

A familiar voice follows. "Miss Roberts, this is Mac."

Mac! The man who saved her life.

She opens her door.

"Afternoon, M'am."

He's shorter than Ryan, and stockier. About thirty-five, with blue eyes, a round face full of excellent character lines and a thick thatch of light brown hair that seems to have a life of its own.

"Good afternoon, Mr…"

"McNamara," he says with a grin.

"Mr McNamara, before we go any further I want to thank you for what you did last night."

"Just doing my job, M'am."

She gives him her most grateful smile. "You do a fine job, Mr McNamara."

"Mighty kind of you to say so. Now, Miss Roberts, the boss sent me over…"

"Your boss or my boss, because I was just about to go to work and speak with my boss…"

"Well, my boss has already seen your boss."

"Oh," says she. "What about?"

"What happened last night. Well, you see, you are required to appear in court this afternoon and give evidence about the shooting. The perpetrator, Gordy Jacobs, is facing a charge of attempted murder. Judge Callaghan will want to hear what you have to say, M'am."

She gingerly threads her arms into her coat, shoulders her hooded cloak and eases her hands into her gloves. "Very well, Mr McNamara. I will come to court. At what time?"

"You are to stay at the Tribune 'til I come for you. Boss's orders. *My* boss."

She reaches for her satchel. Every muscle in her body aches and pretending they don't only makes it worse.

"Is there a Mrs McNamara?"

Mr McNamara frowns. "Yes, M'am. Patricia."

"And are there small McNamara's?"

"Yes, M'am. Two. Lucy and Lola. They're twins, five years old."

"That's very special, Mr McNamara. I myself am a twin. My sister, Celina, lives in Jacksonville. She's married to a banker."

"Identical?" he asks. "Lucy and Lola are. It's mayhem for me and Pat."

"No, we're not. Celina is statuesque and a brunette. And I am, as you can see, the runt of the litter. Shall we go?"

She locks the room; Mr McNamara nods his approval.

They proceed up the hall and down the stairs. Nan Morris takes leave of them at the door and they step out into a cold, bright day that feels as full of danger as it does potential.

Mr McNamara, she notices, slows his stride to keep pace with her; walking quickly produces discomfort, and they need to pick their way through the ice and snow.

"I like walking, usually; excellent physical fitness."

"Good to walk out those aches and pains, M'am."

"Yes, as much as it pains me to agree. Mr McNamara?"

"Ask away."

"I hope you won't take offence at what I'm about to say, and I would urge you not to, but I really must insist that you no longer follow me about the way you've been doing. You have a family and it's not right. I couldn't live with myself if you were killed in the line of duty and left Patricia a widow and Lucy and Lola orphans."

Mr McNamara stops walking. As does she.

"Well, of all the... It's my job, Miss Roberts. Pat knows that. Besides, I'm good at my job."

"I know, Mr McNamara. The fact that I am here right now attests to..." She stops and swallows a huge lump.

"Now, Miss Roberts, you're gone and upset yourself. You're not to worry about me and my family."

She shakes her head. Somehow she manages to say, "No, I don't want you on my case. I'll speak to Mr Ryan about it."

She starts walking again, leaving him behind. He catches up presently, but he doesn't speak to her for the rest of their trek.

At the doors of the Tribune, which he opens for her, she notices he still looks hurt. She can't be worried about that; she must focus on keeping him safe for Pat and Lucy and Lola.

"My thanks again, Mr McNamara. Good day."

She doesn't entertain any emotion, although she'd like to; she wants to plead with him to change his profession.

"Miss Roberts," he says coolly and closes the door behind her.

Ben

It is almost noon when he wakes. He has overslept; missed the morning train to Laramie and the stagecoach; dashed his plan to take a walk around town before he was suppose to leave…

A perfectly rational explanation (although not one his father would accept)… the long trip, the late night, his anxiety about his mother and about facing Tressa… wasn't until the early hours that any decent sleep came. Frustrating. And only one of a handful of times he can ever recall it happening. Everything ran on schedule in Richard Taylor's world.

He consults the hotel clerk. The next train leaves this afternoon and arrives in Laramie in the early evening, but there is no connecting stage to Bright River at that time of the day; he would have to stay in Laramie and wait there all next morning for the stagecoach to Bright River. Laramie doesn't interest him at this point in time, so he decides to stay in Cheyenne for one more day and night, and then take tomorrow's morning train to Laramie. The stage to Bright River would be ready and waiting when he arrived.

With his travel arrangements finally sorted, he locates Western Union. He's made some alterations to his telegram…

Dear Mother. Greatly appreciate your help. Tell Father all will be well and to look into Donnelly. Be strong.

Your son Ben.

Time now to take a good long look at the town where it seems his cousin is famous.

Cliff

Cliff allocates to a very disgruntled Mac the job of escorting Gordy Jacobs to the dock. Not often does Mac get out of sorts; took a woman with a pretty face, a tough hide, startling ethics and a genial backhander to do it.

"Southern women... ain't come across one in a while... dang it, I'm gonna be ready for the next... *I don't want you on my case. I'll speak to Mr Ryan about it*... never in all my born days..."

Probably not, which is why he never saw it coming.

Meanwhile, Jim patrols the perimeter of the courthouse.

And Cliff sees to Miss Roberts.

The Tribune is almost deserted. He puts his head around the doorway of the newsroom. Quaid is with her, resting his behind on the corner of her desk.

"Ryan," he says, getting to his feet.

"Quaid."

"Here she is, all safe and sound."

"I can see that."

"Good luck, Roberts."

"Thank you, Mr Quaid."

Quaid comes towards him, mumbling, "Don't say it..."

"I told you so."

"Ryan, you're a..."

"Uh-uh... there's a lady present."

He grunts and heads off to his office.

"You two don't like each other much, do you?"

154

He swings his attention back to Miss Roberts.

She's on her feet and wrestling with her coat. Her movements are unusually awkward for her and she's grimacing, only managing to put on half her coat and leaving the other half dangling.

He wants to laugh – unwise – so he tells her instead, "He's just peeved because he knows I blame him for getting you into this mess."

"I see," she says, pulling on her gloves. "Never mind my free will."

"Free will? How so, when you didn't have all the information you needed to make a sound decision?"

"That in itself is not a correct assessment."

"It's not?"

"No. And Mr Quaid did not order me to follow you about last evening."

"I think you're splitting hairs."

"Think what you like, Mr Ryan, it's a free country."

"Last I heard," he mumbles.

With a wool cloak over one arm, she walks towards him, saying, "I hope that Mr McNamara is no longer upset with me."

She draws level with him and he replies, "No, not at all, Mr McNamara gets to escort Gordy Jacobs who is much prettier than you."

Her eyes flash at him.

"So, how are you?" he inquires.

He takes up the wayward half of her coat and carefully holds it for her. Obviously, it hurts to thread her arm into the sleeve.

"As well as can be expected. Thank you."

As he finds himself once again adjusting a coat on her, he can't miss the red mark on her fair cheek. And the sight of it, the violence it represents, upon something so delicate and innocent incites a moment of outrage that is quashed with a well-practiced restraint. He swallows hard. Her bronze eyes watch him as he inspects her cheek, takes note of the red glass earbobs quivering from her lobes, the dark red of her dress with the red glass beads at its collar. It seems she has decided to reduce the visual impact of the wound by dressing in red. Intriguing.

Gently, he releases his grip on her coat.

"I just realized I left your blue coat in my room. But you seem to have another. It's rather alarming, you know."

"I know," he says. "It keeps pesky reporters away."

"I myself am not alarmed," she says and their eyes meet.

"And you the peskiest of them all," he jokes very gently.

"Even though my arm is bruised where you grabbed me."

"I'm very sorry," he murmurs. "I promise I won't do that again."

"I should think not."

"You could take Mac back, in case you think I can't be trusted."

"No, I cannot take Mr McNamara back. He has a family. I cannot be the cause of those risks you might make him undertake, but I can certainly have some say…"

"You?"

"Well, how is it that *you* are here, not Mr McNamara?"

Dangerous, stubborn woman. "Are you that determined to ruin a good man's confidence."

"What do you mean?"

"Mac is my best deputy, the best anywhere for that matter. When you sacked him today his confidence took a blow. You want to be responsible for that?"

"Better his lack of confidence, which I'm sure will pass, than his life and the happiness and security of his family. Evidently, I am the only person who has Mr McNamara and his family's long term interests at heart." Her glance sweeps over him sharply. "You are not married, you haven't any children."

"It took you long enough to ask."

"I wasn't asking."

"Meaning?"

"No slight."

"Really?"

"I made the correct assumption."

"Based on?"

"You are too shrewd and ambitious to be married."

"Assuming no one could want a shrewd, ambitious sheriff for a husband…"

"Or a father."

There is something about her tone that begs to be let ring.

And it does for a bit.

Then she attempts to don her cloak, and as he helps her with that as well, she says, "You should know, Mr Ryan, that I can argue a point for a very long time."

"Well, there you have me at a disadvantage," he says.

"I doubt it. I think you would probably go to your grave before anyone got the better of you, Mr Ryan."

While she keeps her poker face, he chuckles, and says, "You think you know me so well already."

"I believe you will run true to form."

"Perhaps I will surprise you."

"You won't."

She's right about one thing; this conversation could go on for hours.

"Come, then, Miss Roberts, we should take our arguing prowess to court."

As he escorts her from the Tribune onto Eddy Street and then 17th, she shivers in the cold. He conducts an assiduous observation of their surroundings, including rooftops. He keeps her close to the storefronts and walks on the outside. As they mingle with the rest of Cheyenne, he feels her press a little closer to his side.

"Don't worry, Emma, I promise I will protect you."

"I don't believe I gave you permission to address me in that familiar manner."

"Then, may I have permission to address you in that familiar manner?"

"I will have to think about it."

"That sounds like a long and drawn out process."

"More importantly, how long will it be until we are free of this terror?"

"Terror… an interesting choice of word."

He considers her predicament and what he now knows of the activities of this Maverick… to live in fear of not knowing when and where the next strike will come and that your death could be the incomprehensible purpose of an unseen evil… terror is accurate.

He is perplexed by her outward show of calm.

"You didn't answer my question," she says.

He revises his estimation; it is only outward; that sounded nervous to his ears.

"Well, once you have given evidence at the hearing in a few minutes, you'll be leaving town and going home to Orlando, Florida. That will be the end of it for you."

A couple of silent moments pass when he realizes she is no longer beside him. He looks around frantically to find her small feisty figure standing like a statue; she is glaring at him.

"What are you doing?" he rasps, striding back to her.

"I will not be told to leave town like... like I'm some sort of unsavory character you can't wait to be rid of..."

"I never said that!"

"I beg your pardon, Mr Ryan, but you certainly did intimate that I am no longer welcome here."

"Emma, we can't stand here and debate this now." Everything in the street seems normal, but how can anyone be sure when there's someone named Maverick with a team of sharpshooters...

"We certainly will. I will not take another step..."

Cliff grabs her hand and pulls her into the nearest store, Mae Jewell's millinery. He pushes the door shut behind them and peers out into the street through the windowpane. Cheyenne parades by as normal...

"Well, Sheriff Ryan, we don't see you in here very often."

He glances across the store to see Mae Jewell beaming at him; with her silvery hair and delicately lined face, she reminds him of his late grandmother.

"Afternoon, Mae."

"You seem agitated, Sheriff, is something the matter?"

"No, not at all," he lies. "Miss Roberts is new in town and she wanted to know who is the best milliner and your name came to mind."

Mae transfers her beam to Emma. "That was kind. Lot of folk would have said the James sisters on Ferguson. They may have a bigger store, but my stitchery and attention to detail are far more desirable than Anna's. And I have the latest fashions."

Emma, wide-eyed and breathless, glances from Mae to him and back again. She sticks a polite smile on her face.

"So. I got some lovely furs, Miss Roberts. Make you a fine hat. The samples are out back. If you care to wait one second I'll fetch them."

"Er... thank you," says Emma.

And Mae disappears through a beaded curtain, which clatters pleasantly behind her.

Emma's stubborn face glares up at him. "You can't make me leave."

"I'm sheriff. I can and I will make you leave. I will put you on the train myself."

"We agreed this is a free country, you can't force me."

"And I will even stay on the train until you are out of the territory, or half way across the country, whatever, but I have a job to do. I'm a sheriff, not a babysitter."

"Well, don't you just blow hot and cold! One minute you swear to protect me and the next you want to send me packing."

The beaded curtain clatters.

"Here we are... lovely aren't they... and this one here, this exquisite black mink would suit your coloring perfectly, my dear."

Cliff swallows hard beneath Emma's irate glare. For someone who only comes up to his shoulders she is scaring the hell out of him.

"Now, for the design... let me see. Of course!" she says, "the new ones from Paris. They don't suit every woman in these parts, but you definitely. And I left those out back too. Landsakes, where is my memory today..." Again the beads whoosh and clatter.

"May we *please* just get into court before Judge Callaghan," he demands.

Her eyes explode. "Everything, and I mean *every*thing, in this town seems to be in your time, on your say so, and done your way. You are infuriating, didn't anyone ever tell you that?"

"Save the whining for your boss, he's the one who brought you here. Not me. I'm just trying to do my job."

She lets out an explosive grunt, followed by, "Hang your job!"

"Charming," he fires back, "just charming..."

"Something you'll never be…"

"This is not personal…"

"No? You disliked me on sight…"

"That's not true…"

"I hardly think you are one to judge what is true or not…"

"What are you inferring?"

Clatter, whoosh… Mae appears. "Sorry for the delay. I declare the Paris design book just got up and walked off somewhere and I couldn't think where it had got to. I think we're all set now."

"I'm sorry, Mae, but Miss Roberts has remembered she has another appointment."

Mae's excited face falls at once.

Emma quickly says, "But I will be back. Ah, soon. Those James sisters sound stuck up, so you're not to worry on that account. And I promise I will think about the mink."

Mae picks up a bit. Emma wrenches open the door.

"Afternoon, Mae."

"Good afternoon, Sheriff. Miss Roberts."

Back in the street, Cliff shadows Emma's feisty pace. Cranky and disgruntled with one another, at least they're moving along now.

They make a left at Ferguson.

Only two more blocks 'til the courthouse.

They arrive without another word spoken between them.

Faraday

The only onlookers interested in Gordy Jacobs' hearing are reporters. The events involving Miss Roberts last evening spread like wildfire through their fraternity and as a result even the smallest publication is represented. They whirr like flies around a carcass before Judge Callaghan brings them to order.

Gordy Jacobs is everything that Cliff described.

He makes an impact nonetheless: his guilty plea and the joyful abandon with which he declares it makes them all uncomfortable, particularly when Judge Callaghan questions his understanding and Jacobs gleefully tells the Judge that he did the crime and he under-stands perfectly. The Judge informs him that he wants to hear the testimony of witnesses, and Jacobs, grinning, giving a wink, says to bring them in.

Mac's testimony is most enlightening:

"I followed Miss Roberts from town as instructed by the boss. She starts looking in Mr Faraday's parlor windows. Just as I make a move to accost her, Jacobs appears. He is standing about fifteen feet away from her in some bushes, and he has a Colt Frontier Six-shooter which he's got trained on her. He fires. Miss Roberts falls in the snow. But he don't get it right. He takes a few steps forward and takes aim again. But I jumped him and wrestled the Colt off him. Marched him down to the lockup."

Miss Roberts has the Judge bewildered:

"Why did you follow Sheriff Ryan to the Faraday's home, Miss Roberts?"

"I was after a lead in my investigations. Mr Quaid hired me to find out why the investigation into Miss Keaton's murder wasn't progressing at a satisfactory pace."

"A pace satisfactory to Mr Quaid, no doubt."

"Well, you know how editors are."

"I believe I do, Miss Roberts. Continue, if you don't mind," says the Judge after clearing his throat.

"I was looking in the window of the Faraday's sitting room, I felt cold and cramped, so I shifted my position. The very next moment I felt some kind of force strike me and I fell. I heard the gunfire. The next thing I remember Mr Ryan is yanking me out of the snow like I was the criminal."

Then there is Cliff's testimony, and uncharacteristically, he is terse and greatly out of sorts:

"The bullet in the architrave definitely came from Jacobs' gun. After several hours of interrogation, Jacobs decided to cooperate. You have his confession, Your Honor."

Finally, Jacobs takes the stand and Faraday questions him closely on the statement he gave Cliff. His answers are consistent with his confession.

"Did you kill a sheepherder named Adams up in Dickson, Mr Jacobs?"

"No, that weren't me. I don't operate in that area."

"What is your area, Mr Jacobs?"

"Cheyenne and Laramie mostly."

"Did you kill Miss Keaton?"

"I already told the sheriff no. I didn't shoot her. Maverick must have more than one man working this area because it weren't me that shot Miss Keaton."

The Judge has one final question, "For someone who was so reluctant to give a statement, you seem mighty happy now about confessing. Why is that, Mr Jacobs?"

Jacobs grins. "Well, you know how it is, Judge, a man's first instincts are to try and get away, you know, protect yourself. The sheriff just wouldn't let up, Judge, and I knew he wasn't gonna be happy 'til I told him everything. He warned me I was facing a long spell in the big house. He said I should have an attorney, but I thought about it some, confessing that is. I'm glad I did it 'cause now I got protection from Maverick, being in the lockup an' all."

"I see. Very well then. I am satisfied, Mr Jacobs, that you are guilty of the attempted murder upon Miss Emmaline Roberts. You are to return to court in two days time for sentencing." Judge Callaghan taps his gavel. "Mr Faraday and Mr Ryan, I will see both of you in my chambers. And, Miss Roberts, if you wouldn't mind joining us please."

Judge Callaghan's chambers

"Gentlemen, this situation is intolerable!"

"Be assured that we are all in agreement, Judge," Faraday says, "including Mayor Warren and Governor Morgan who have been informed of the situation."

The Judge nods. "And their response, Mr Faraday?"

"The governor has contacted the authorities in Laramie and they are to drop everything and find Maverick."

"Mr Ryan, have you any leads so far?"

"The murdered sheepherder Adams, his property was bought by a man named Donnelly from Adams' widow for half its value."

"Donnelly? Who is he? Anyone heard of him before?"

"No. But it turns out he is a Laramie businessman, Judge," Cliff says. "We'll know more in the next few days. The boys in Laramie are cooperating."

"And what about Miss Roberts, Mr Ryan? Is the threat to her life over?"

Cliff eyes Miss Roberts silently for several moments, no doubt considering what is in her best interests.

"Judge, may I speak?" Miss Roberts says.

"In a minute, Miss Roberts, I would like to hear from Mr Ryan regarding this matter."

"It's only that I think it odd that..."

"Let the good sheriff speak, Miss Roberts."

"Are you certain you don't want to hear what I have to say, Judge?"

"This is Wyoming territory, Miss Roberts. Whatever you think is odd, very likely *is* compared to the rest of the nation. Seventeen years ago this town was an assortment of tents and log huts. There were Cheyenne Indians out on the plains behind you and a bunch of people you'd rather not know making a fast buck waiting for the railroad to push through. It was hell all right. And look at us now. Sprouting like a twelve year old boy on summer vacation. We try not to make it up as we go along, but sometimes we have to. Let's just move on, shall we?"

Miss Roberts stares at him, her eyes as large as plates; she swallows and looks straight ahead. "I beg pardon, Judge. Go ahead, Mr Ryan."

"Why, thank you, Miss Roberts," Cliff says.

Miss Roberts looks annoyed.

"Carry on, Mr Ryan," the Judge urges.

"Yes, Judge. Gordy Jacobs is of the opinion that Maverick will send someone to clean up his mistake. It could very well be the same someone who shot Miss Keaton, if what Jacobs says is correct that Maverick has more than one man operating in this district."

Judge Callaghan throws down his spectacles on his desk.

Miss Roberts catches her breath, trying hard not to show her dismay.

"I am appalled on a great many levels," says the Judge.

Faraday exchange glances with Cliff and indicates that he should continue.

"This kind of activity, Judge, has several purposes; at least one of them is intimidation. In the case of the sheepherder Adams, he wouldn't get out of cattle country, refused to be intimidated, so he was shot. And according to Jacobs this Maverick has set himself up as 'the one' to keep the ranchers happy. He fires warnings, then, when they go unheeded, the final shot is lethal."

"I want this Maverick brought to justice *yesterday*, Mr Ryan."

"Whatever it takes, Judge."

"Now I would like to know: what is the connection to Miss Keaton and Miss Roberts?"

"Judge, I..."

"Not yet, Miss Roberts."

"We have a theory. Miss Keaton, if I remember correctly, never took a backward step in making her opinions about certain things known. She even took it upon herself to question our moral right to be here. You may remember, Judge, the reaction of people here in Cheyenne..."

"I remember," murmurs the Judge.

"We believe Obadiah Williams published her letters knowing that they would cause outrage in the cattle community. I have examined records of that time. They show that the number of harassments on homesteaders across Laramie, Albany and Carbon counties increased, and that many of these acts of harassment were instigated by Loren Bodecker's Association members."

"I see."

"Now, Charlie Quaid admitted to me earlier today that he informed Obadiah Williams last week that he had hired a new reporter to hurry along Miss Keaton's murder investigation. Miss Roberts. Miss Roberts' interviewed Williams yesterday, and I have a feeling it wasn't to compare the price of printer's ink. Quaid and Miss Roberts allege, as will we, that the Bugle published Miss Keaton's letters with criminal intent. If she were to challenge Williams on that point..."

"Miss Roberts?" barks the Judge.

The young woman flinches. "Yes, Judge, I did challenge him on that point. That was the reason I went there. Although I did not use the words *criminal intent*..."

Faraday, Cliff and the Judge stiffen in unison, a reaction to her chilling admission on one hand, and on the other for what will surely come out of her mouth...

"The Bugle is Loren Bodecker's newspaper. And we know for a fact that Ed Parsons was an associate of Loren Bodecker."

And there it is.

Cliff jumps in. "Miss Keaton challenges Bodecker and gets shot and killed; Miss Roberts challenges Bodecker and the same style execution is narrowly averted."

"Mr Ryan, you are saying that this Maverick and Bodecker are in cahoots!"

"There is no *other* connection between Miss Keaton and Miss

Roberts than their challenges on Bodecker through the Bugle. Of course Miss Roberts has gone a step further by making the connection between Ed Parsons and Loren Bodecker. The Alliance, Judge, never knew of it. Well, that's not entirely accurate; Ethan Benchley had seen Loren Bodecker with Ed Parsons on at least one occasion, Luke sketched Bodecker from Ethan's description, but in our defense there were more than a few faces and places in Luke's file that meant little or nothing since he kept a record of everything."

Faraday grimaces; he is not happy to discuss the business of the file in Miss Roberts' presence. And he wonders if Cliff coming clean is for Miss Roberts' benefit, since the Judge already knows.

Cliff appears to notice his discomfit and frowns.

"What is it, gentlemen?" the Judge queries.

"Miss Roberts is a reporter, Judge," says Cliff, "and they usually can't be trusted with delicate information. But I think Miss Roberts can be trusted."

The Judge's bristled moustache quivers. "Oh you do, do you?"

"Yes, Judge."

"And what about you, Miss Roberts? Can you be trusted with delicate information? It seems to me that Mr Ryan here appreciates your handle on the situation."

Faraday is fascinated. He regards Miss Roberts with anticipation.

"Of course I can be trusted, Judge. It was only a matter of time before I found this out. As evidence goes, it wouldn't incriminate anyone, except that Miss Keaton was murdered and Mr Faraday and Mr Ryan needed a place to start their investigation. I believe they hoped it would start with Loren Bodecker. I also understand now the reason for the cautious pace of the investigation."

"Good for you. So what will you do, Miss Roberts, now that you have found yourself in an extremely dangerous situation… it would be wise to extricate yourself as soon as possible since these shooters have you in their sights."

"Well, Judge, I have been told to leave town by Mr Ryan for my own safety, and that is what I'll be doing. I don't plan to die here in Cheyenne for asking a few questions, and I am certain that this story will break without my help. It is clear to me now that I should let these bad men, whoever they may be, terrorize me out of my job and run me out of town. I can put their joy and glee at my hasty departure out of my mind because I know I'll be safe. Why I should give my right to free speech and to come and go as I please a second thought? Oh yes, these terrorizers have won this round, Judge. I'm a-leaving town!"

Faraday and the Judge stare at her, dumbstruck.

But Cliff is grinning.

"And you would be smiling, Mr Ryan, because...?" asks the Judge.

"Miss Roberts shows a lot of spirit," he says.

"Mm... A little too much. You have someone assigned to protect Miss Roberts while she is in town, Mr Ryan?"

"Yes, Judge. Subsequently, Miss Roberts will be escorted out of Wyoming to ensure her safety."

"Well, Miss Roberts, it's been a pleasure to have met you. I hope you will cooperate with Mr Ryan in every way possible. He has a difficult job in difficult times. Go safely then. Gentlemen, that is all. Good day."

Emmaline

As Ryan escorts her from the courthouse she is still too annoyed with him to speak. Ruthless, infuriating man… all the pieces of this puzzle are beginning to circle for position on the board and he has to speak of his belief and trust in her to the highest court in the territory; now she must honor it or very likely be charged with contempt! That Judge is one to be reckoned with.

"Escort me back to Mae Jewell's store, if you please," she asks stiffly. They are striding quickly back the way they came – the quicker the better and up until now in silence.

"You don't have to buy a hat."

"Of course I do. I told her I'd be back. You lied to her and I feel bad. In fact, you tell a lot of lies for a law enforcement officer."

"If that's what you care to think, although it probably didn't escape your notice back there that I just told you the truth about Luke's file. I thought you'd be happy… gloating, in fact."

"Largesse on a grand scale, I'm sure – the Judge was still wearing his robes!"

"Sarcasm is unbecoming."

"As is ruthlessness."

"That's a little harsh."

"I'm sure it's nothing that you haven't heard before. And I don't gloat."

"Anyway, why should *you* feel bad because of my lies?"

"Personally, I don't wear fur. I don't think we should be slaying cute furry animals for fashion…"

"You're dodging the question…"

"I understand when native peoples do it to clothe themselves warmly or because it's a part of their culture, but when I see women parading around in the fur of poor dead critters it makes me mad."

"You must be incensed with half the women in town. Aren't we all just trying to keep warm?"

"I've said all I'm ever going to say to you, so I'd take it kindly if you..."

"You still didn't answer my question; why should you feel bad because of my lies?"

"Oh, you have no conscience!" she exclaims impulsively.

"So you want to be my conscience for me, is that it?"

"You are ruthless to the core and I will certainly be glad to see the back of you."

As soon as it is out of her mouth she regrets it. She stops on the sidewalk and feels sick. Now who is telling lies? She sees the black swirl of his coat as he turns and stops also. She looks up into his face; unexpectedly, ephemeral-delight Ryan looks back. And she wonders: could that transient insight into a man she could quite probably like ever be made permanent... He takes two of the three strides needed to be at her side. Before the third is completed a familiar sound shatters her confusion. A gunshot blasts into their tiny little world. The black coat swirls again; Ryan's arms around her force her to the ground. She lays there beneath him for just a heartbeat before he is up and sliding a pistol from his belt. He fires it and the explosion deafens her. Then there is chaos; people are screaming and running; Ryan shouts something and leaves her; some other man helps her to her feet and bundles her inside a store. She sits on the floor just inside the door hugging her knees, shaking. A woman comes to her and puts her arm around her.

Then she hears Ryan's voice, "Emma..."

The woman beside her calls out, "In here, Sheriff."

The black coat swirls in front of her eyes.

"Emma," he says in a breathless voice.

"She's not harmed," says the woman. "Can you stand, my dear?"

She nods, but her body refuses to do what she tells it. Instead, she puts her head in her hands and cries. She is not supposed to get her graze wet...

Gently, she is drawn to her feet by a very strong hand. "Come on, Emma. It's over now. Come on..."

Trembling, she presses herself against the black coat and the strong body beneath it. She feels one arm hold her comfortingly for a while before she is walked back outside. But she hesitates...

"I shot him, Emma," Ryan tells her. "Don't be afraid."

"You... Where was he?" Gingerly, she lifts her eyes to survey the street, wiping moisture from her cheeks with her fingers.

"On a rooftop across the street. I'm pretty sure that's how Miss Keaton was shot. A single bullet from the rooftop on the opposite side of the street. I think we might have Miss Keaton's killer."

She can't believe it. "You didn't kill him?"

"No," he grins at her. "Didn't aim to kill." There is a look of pride and satisfaction in his eyes that goes a long way to ridding her of her fear.

Suddenly, Mr McNamara appears before them.

"The mongrel's squared away, boss. So, how bad is it?"

She has no idea as to what this last question refers, and looks at Ryan in bewilderment. He is inspecting his upper left arm, a hole in the finely woven sleeve of his coat. She catches her breath. A handkerchief is extracted from his pocket and Mr McNamara takes it and binds it around Ryan's arm, with Ryan trying not to grimace. Soon the handkerchief is strained red with his blood.

"Doc Prewitt's gonna be busy," Ryan says, gritting his teeth. "Tighter... yep... Wouldn't hurt to have Miss Roberts checked over either. She hit the ground hard – again."

"Right, boss. Miss Roberts, if you don't mind coming back with us, you can sit a spell 'til the old doc gets to you, give me your statement... unless if you think you should go home, and I'll take you."

She gives her head a shake. "I...I need to get back to work."

"Soon," Ryan murmurs.

She looks at his arm where blood is soaking freely into the handkerchief. It was her fault. She shouldn't have stopped.

"No, I should get back..."

"This changes things, Emma."

"I... I see that... I... I'm sorry."

"Not your fault."

"All in a day's work," Mr McNamara says. "Maybe for you too."

It was becoming that way.

"We can take Miss Roberts' statement at 16th Street, Mac."

"Sure thing."

Ryan guides her forward.

He and Mr McNamara begin planning, leaving her to her own thoughts, although she is very aware of Ryan close by her side, walking to her stride.

Cheyenne citizens part before that black coat. An old woman, however, in shabby clothes and a surprisingly smart woolen scarf, stops him and expresses her concern.

"Mrs Landers, you're not to worry," he reassures her. "The afternoon's growing cold, you had better get on home. Do you have enough firewood?"

Mrs Landers gives him a wide, rather toothless grin. "Still got a heap from what you chopped fer me two days ago. Y' know, Sheriff, that young Taylor gives me this here scarf. Straight off his neck. Ain't it a dandy?"

"Luke?" he murmurs. "Sure, Mrs Landers... very nice."

"Well, so long, Sheriff. Mac. Miss."

Mrs Landers steps aside. Ryan rubs the spot above his eye with his good arm. "What's she doing down this end of town?"

"Beats me," Mr McNamara says as they watch her cross the street. "Jim and Pete see her in the darnedest places. She always tells them she goes where she's needed."

"Strange old woman," Emmaline murmurs.

Ryan takes a shaky breath. "Where were we?"

And they set off again.

"What's the name of this feller, Mac?"

"Swinton Carter."

"Are you sure? Where on God's green earth do they come up with these names?"

"Maybe God didn't want nothing to do with this one..."

"Where'd I hit him? – right shoulder?"

"Yep; he's conscious and making one helluva racket. Doc Prewitt should be there now. Jim and Pete got him covered."

"I don't suppose we could get hold of Luke."

"Long gone I reckon."

"Does anyone know where Dan Hummer is these days?"

"What d'you want him for?"

"He's as mad as a cut snake. When we find out who Maverick is, I want him to be the one to fetch him."

Mr McNamara chortles. "Like he fetched old Ed."

"And find out where Loren Bodecker got to. He hasn't been in town for days. It's time to ask him a few questions."

Mr McNamara, she notices, is almost flushed with excitement. "I got plenty in mind."

"And that Association list, Mac, I want everyone on it brought in for questioning. I want to know who knows Maverick."

"Hey, boss, I like the sound of this."

"Has Carter asked for a lawyer?"

"Matter o'fact, he did mention he wanted one," Mr McNamara takes great delight in announcing. "Part of the racket he's been making. And to think Gordy Jacobs lay down like a dog wantin' his belly rubbed…"

"Who is it?"

"The lawyer? Never heard of him. Name's Marvin Tucker. He's local though."

"Good. When the old doc's finished with Carter, ask Jim and Pete to get around town – I want to know everything there is to know about this Tucker. How is it we don't know about him already?"

"Can't say. But we'll find out."

"I wish Jennifer were here. She has a way with bullets."

"Doc Sullivan's got a way with most things wayward. She's in St Louis, ain't she?"

Ryan sighs. "Last I heard."

They arrive at Ryan's office on 16th Street. Emmaline is out of breath and her throat is stinging. Better than Ryan, however; his face is almost white.

"Take Miss Roberts' statement, Mac."

"Sure, boss. Don't worry, I'll take good care of Miss Roberts."

"Got work to do, Emma. I'll see you later."

He will? How can he possibly still want her around after he was almost killed keeping her alive?

"I'll be with Doc Prewitt in the lockup, Mac. And Mac, send MAVERICK, LARAMIE TELEGRAPH, NIGHTHAWK LULLABY," he says and departs.

As he swings away, she glimpses the Silver Star on his chest beneath the lapel of his black coat.

Mr McNamara gives a great sigh. "Well, Miss Roberts, lets get this statement done. He's kinda finicky about getting the 'i's dotted and the 't's crossed."

She gives Mr McNamara a simple account of what happened, he writes it down, and while he fetches her a glass of water, he gets her to read it. She confirms it with her signature.

"Are you gonna be all right, Miss Roberts?"

She tells him she intends to go to work for the rest of the afternoon and he frowns.

"You know, M'am, I'd be real happy if you would come over for supper tonight. You could meet Pat and the twins. They'd like you for sure and you shouldn't be by yourself after today, and yesterday for that matter."

"You actually get to eat supper at home, Mr McNamara."

Mr McNamara rolls his eyes. "After you finish up at the Tribune just come straight over."

"You are very kind, Mr McNamara. I'd be delighted. Where do you live?"

"Easy to find. You happen to see Mae Jewell's millinery today?"

She bits her bottom lip. "Yes, I believe I did."

"Two doors up from Mae's is a dressmakers. That's Pat. She's the dressmaker. Just come in and the bell over the door will let Pat know you're there. Well, this statement is all done... One more thing. Anyone who eats supper at my house calls me Mac."

She spends the rest of the afternoon at her desk writing, trying to ignore the ache in her head and a slight tremor in her hands.

Eventually, she takes two of the pills Doc Prewitt prescribed and her headache begins to wane.

Mr Quaid wants to know what she's working on.

"It's difficult, Mr Quaid, but I am trying to piece the last two days into some semblance of order."

"Give yourself a little more time," he says benevolently. And he too is concerned about how she is to spend her evening.

"That's very thoughtful of you, Mr Quaid, but I believe I am well-taken care of," she tells him.

He seems relieved.

She feels like she's consorting with the opposition having supper with Mr McNamara... Mac.

As she reads through her rough notes, it becomes glaringly obvious that this story was never going to turn out the way she and Mr Quaid had planned.

Ben

A great many people (and Ben is one of them, for a while at least) congregate outside the various newspaper buildings in the business quarter of town hoping for information about the shooting, the second, apparently, in two days. He wanders around until he comes to the sheriff's office on 16th Street. People of all kinds are milling about here as well.

Speculation abounds; but it is not until he hears someone mention 'Miss Keaton's killer' that he actually takes any notice.

"Who is Miss Keaton's killer?" he asks someone.

The excited man exclaims, "The man in Mr Ryan's lockup, that's who."

"Ryan?"

"The Sheriff, son. He shot and caught the killer today. About time too. The Keatons and the Taylors are gonna be celebrating by tonight, I'll wager." The man moves on.

This is something that Tressa would want to know: the man who killed the sister of her husband has been shot and caught.

No doubt about it, this 'magic city of the plains', as he was told it was called by the clerk in the hotel, as determined as it seems to show maturity, is still very young.

There is every kind of people and every kind of occupation to be seen. Businessmen, bankers and speculators; merchants and shop-keepers; soldiers from the fort north of town; city officials and planners, firemen, factory workers and stagecoach drivers; saloon girls; cowboys; miners; clerks; county hospital employees and those from the public utilities, telephone and electric lighting; scores of railroad employees; construction workers from all the building that was going on in town; the wealthy women and the working class women and the children of both; and the hard-faced men who look like they've never known a day's rest from their labors.

Someone even pointed out the governor deep in conversation with the mayor on the corner of 16th and Hill.

But something bad had happened in this magic city.

Either it still had some growing up to do. Or someone was playing a sophisticated game of hell-on-wheels.

As he heads back to his hotel and contemplates supper, he also thinks about his mother in Omaha, battling his bad-tempered father.

And sure enough, a telegram is waiting for him at the hotel desk.

SON, IF YOU COME HOME NOW ALL WILL BE FORGIVEN, FATHER,

He is not interested in his father's forgiveness.

There is no turning back. Returning to Omaha now would make him feel like a total failure. There is a great thirst inside of him, not just to find Tressa and get the answers to his questions, but also to prove himself, and he will do it or never return to Omaha again.

Father. Not coming home yet. Forgiveness not required. What about Donnelly? Ben.

Quaid

The Tribune, Eddy Street

"She's gone for the day, Chief. Didn't look so good. Told her I'd get tomorrow's copy to you myself… here it is."

Quaid takes from Simons' outstretched hand several pages of Roberts' neat-as-a-pin handwriting… barely a smudge…

Will Dobson, their sub-editor and chief setter, is gonna love her…

The attempt on the life of this reporter came to a head yesterday afternoon when yet another sharpshooter from Maverick's stable of assassins discharged a .44-40 caliber weapon with intent to kill from a 17th Street rooftop.

The attempt was carried out as this reporter was returning from giving evidence at the hearing of Gordy Jacobs, and was thwarted by the quick and heroic actions of Sheriff Cliff Ryan, who not only collected the bullet in his left arm, but seconds later turned, spotted the gunman, and fired a single shot.

The result was the wounding and capture of a valuable piece in the Maverick puzzle, whose name is Swinton Carter, and, significantly, what appears to be a missing chunk in the mystery of who killed Miss Keaton in September last year.

This ongoing investigation had been stalled by lack of evidence. Remarkably, in the last two days, the investigators have broken through the wall of silence and frustration to find themselves with more pieces to puzzle together than they know what to do with.

The attempts on this reporter's life follow said reporter asking the editor of the Bugle, Obadiah Williams, the following question: Why was the Bugle, which is obviously the political platform and apologist for the cattle barons, and ideologically opposed to Miss Keaton's opinions, so happy to print all of her controversial letters?

Mr Williams' response to this question was to say how greatly the Bugle appreciates the opinions of women. However, the events that followed speak rather more eloquently. Perhaps Mr Williams might care to explain why women, whose opinions he values so highly, are in danger of being permanently silenced when what he hears is not to his liking.

But then Mr Williams is only the Bugle's editor. Editorial policy of the Bugle is dictated from the top. Perhaps it is Mr Loren Bodecker, owner of the Bugle, who is keen to do the silencing.

What raw nerve, exposed and throbbing, is Mr Bodecker seeking to numb?

Citizens of Cheyenne could be forgiven for being incredulous of the connection between so-called Maverick and one of their favorite tycoons.

Evidence, however disquieting, is emerging.

Miss Keaton's execution and the attempts made on the life of this reporter bear the same Maverick hallmarks.

Miss Keaton and this reporter vexed the Bugle.

In fact, Miss Keaton's letters provoked a wave of harassment upon homesteaders, some of these by Mr Bodecker's Association members, whose involvement may be widely known but, and this is significant, was never publicly reported. It is easy to see the convenience in publishing Miss Keaton's letters.

One of Mr Bodecker's unlisted Association members is the presently incarcerated Ed Parsons. This fact is little known; however, Mr Parsons' record for harassing small time operators, namely the Alliance families of Bright River, is well documented. Of course, harassment of these families began well before Miss Keaton wrote her letters.

What is not clear is why Maverick waited until Ed Parsons was convicted and sentenced before murdering Miss Keaton. Revenge seems likely, but was it something more?

The next step into these muddy waters is quite possibly a connection between Parsons, Bodecker, Maverick and Miss Keaton's murder. With two of his sharpshooters in custody, it may well be too late for Maverick to cover his tracks.

Swinton Carter's lawyer, Marvin Tucker, one of Loren Bodecker's own lawyers in town, will be doing well to dodge the mud flying in Sheriff Ryan's lock up today.

Mr Bodecker himself would do well to return to Cheyenne and fend off some of the mud flying his way. After all, his lawyer was requested by Maverick's pawn, Swinton Carter.

A great deal of fighting goes on in Wyoming, and every drop of blood spilled in the process must be accounted for.

Indeed, a great deal of fighting for every scrap of dirt, every blade of grass and every drop of water.

And yet there is room for all, cried Miss Keaton.

Not so, decries the cattlemen's associations.

Maverick, meanwhile, has drawn the line in the sand.

Has the time finally come for each citizen to consider and decide what he or she truly believes in?

Our unalienable rights? Or cold, hard ideology?

Whose side are you on?

Emmaline Roberts

"You want Roberts's by-line on this, Chief?"

"Ryan is going to shoot *me* next."

"We could change a word here and there and no one would have to know she wrote it."

Quaid sighs and rubs his eyes. "I need her to write this stuff. We all do. Get it to Dobson. Tell him we want it next to your piece on Maverick."

"Headline?"

"Let's start with: Missing piece in investigation puzzle."

Simons, whose piece on Maverick is purely a regurgitation of Ryan's statement to the press, jots down the headline on top of Roberts' copy and then strides off. It's all they got for now, and it's not enough. Someone has to go to Laramie and do some digging, keep their eyes and ears open. Quaid must stay in Cheyenne; the only person who can do this is Roberts. Even if Ryan declares him morally decrepit; accuses him of taking advantage of a woman wanting to prove herself in a man's job. Fact remains, Roberts came here to do a job and to her credit and in spite of everything she still wants to do it.

Cliff

Not for the first time that day does Mac wake him. Only now it is dark out and instead of shaking him, Mac is lighting a fire.

"Mac," he says groggily.

"It's me all right. So, sleeping beauty, when's the last time you got any decent sleep?"

"Same as you." He makes a doomed attempt at sitting up.

"I got twin girls and still get more shuteye. Least you're in your bed. How's the arm?" Mac finishes up at the hearth and comes across to Cliff's bedside.

"Sore," he replies, grimacing. "I think Prewitt gave me twice the required amount of morphine."

Mac laughs. "Put you out for sure. Well, you needed it."

"What time is it?'

"Nine-ish."

"Developments?"

"Supper first. Your kitchen's got 'bout a week's worth of food lined up. Since when did you get popular?"

"Cut it out, Mac. Developments?"

Mac has a think. "Guess the food can wait a few more minutes. Swinton Carter is resting comfortable; in fact, he looks better than you."

"Mac…"

"I sent those telegrams you wrote out for John Keaton and Ethan. Hard to say where Luke is. As for Dan Hummer, the US marshals' office is gonna try and track him down. Reckon he could be in Utah or maybe Colorado. Handy if he was. And then I gave Mrs Landers a quarter if she'd go into Loren Bodecker's building and say she's got business with him and where is he?"

"You did what? Oh, go on."

"*He he he...*" Mac laughs. "That snooty secretary, Wallace, couldn't get rid of her fast enough. But she did it, Mrs Landers. Bodecker's been in Omaha all week on business."

"What business?"

"Mrs Landers, God bless her, asked that. She's all right, Mrs Landers, she looks loony but she..."

"Mac! We all love Mrs Landers. Will you just get on with it?"

"Setting up a new deal!" Mac announces. "Don't ask what new deal 'cause even Mrs Landers ain't that good." And Mac hitches up his trousers.

"Okay, tomorrow morning get in touch with the chamber of commerce in Omaha and find out what's going on in the business sector."

Mac's look of pride disappears. "Don't ask that like it's the same as asking for a beer at the Eagle. That's complicated that is."

Cliff chuckles. "Only because you had a run-in with them six months ago during that Brisley case. The place is booming, Mac, and all will be forgotten."

"So sure, are you?"

"Don't tell them the city's sewer is crap like you did last time and everything should be fine. Anything else?"

Mac looks amused; jams his hands into his pockets.

"Pete's been working on Bodecker's Association members and reckons they'll all have a 'front up or else' letter by the end of the week. And as for Marvin Tucker, he's one of Bodecker's lawyers. Been in town about ten months."

"Can't believe that one slipped my attention."

"Well, I wouldn't take Tucker's low profile as an oversight on your part, boss, cause it's likely to be strategy of Bodecker's."

"Maybe," he concedes. "Anything on this Donnelly?"

"Too soon for any partic'lars, we'll get more tomorrow. The boys in Laramie wired they're sending a messenger with some stuff for us and the governor; but get this, boss, the wire did mention that this Donnelly has been out of town all week."

He notes the meaningful glint in Mac's eye.

"Coincidence?"

Mac shrugs. "I'd rather have a hunch crawling with coincidences than no hunch at all."

He grins lopsidedly under a wave of weariness.

Mac sees its.

"You should get some more rest, boss. Doc Prewitt didn't dope you up for nothin'."

"Sure, Mac. How is Miss Roberts?"

Mac *he he he*'s again; hitches up his pants again. "She's been at my place all evening. Had supper with us. She and Pat and the twins took a shine to each other. Thought they would. You know, she's all right is Emmaline. She was real interested in Pat's dress-making, and that she had her own business. After supper she told me and Pat to leave the twins with her and she'd bath them and put them to bed. Me and Pat haven't had a whole lotta time together recently. I think she really understands what it's like for Pat."

"Yeah, well, people surprise you with what they…"

"Pat asked her about her family at supper; soon as Pat asked her what her father does for a living, I swear that ornery girl changed the subject, polite of course; let the twins distract her. The twins were as good as gold, sleeping like angels when me and Pat got back. Anyhow, I walked her home to Nan's and then I called in here. Guess I'd better get some of that food into you before I get going."

Eyes heavy after the bedtime story, Cliff tells him not to bother and get on home. He succumbs and sinks into sleep; he doesn't even hear Mac leave the house.

❖

Come morning…

…he feels like a new man.

Amazing what a lot of deep, uninterrupted sleep can do. And although his arm hurts, his appetite has returned.

The sight of assorted dishes and pans full of food sitting on his kitchen table overwhelms him, a reminder of the kindness of his neighbors. He works hard for them and they appreciate it. Being *ruthless to the core* and lacking a conscience obviously doesn't offend everyone. He grins at the pot of rich venison stew he's inspecting, recalling the sight of Emma's small feisty figure on the sidewalk.

A decision between the stew, the bread pudding and the Osgood pie is delayed by the polite knocking on his front door. It won't be Mac again because Mac usually barges right in, so he needs to get a shirt on. In the hall he calls out that he's on his way.

"Just give me a minute…"

In his bedroom he pulls a clean shirt out of his bureau, but to get it on he must remove his sling. The doc strung it up so tight he can't do this without smarting discomfort.

Irritated by his curious lack of coordination, he picks one handed at the sling's knot on the way to the door. The knot finally gives and falls away. Grimacing, he slides his tender arm into the shirtsleeve, and while it stings and brings tears to his eyes, he hastily fastens some buttons. Fumbling with the sling, at last he opens the door onto a dull morning, a draught of freezing air on his lightly clad chest, and the fairest vision ever to grace his doorstep.

Ben

Ben waits until the very last minute to board his train, hoping for a reply to his telegram. Twice he has asked his parents about Donnelly and still there has been no reply. Their forgiveness or even their understanding are not nearly as important as the safety of their business, and if a man like Donnelly is involved with their newest board member, Bodecker, then his parents should know.

Why they are so desperate to have Ben return – when his sin is so grievous and unforgivable – has him intrigued. This is highly unusual behavior for his father. The telegram from Father should have read: you are no longer a son of mine; or, do what you damn well please but don't come back here.

For Richard Taylor to act like the forgiving father in the story of the prodigal son is strange to say the least. Even a small display of independence if not handled right can be construed as an act of betrayal. And Ben's has been monumental. As time is about to run out, Ben quickly scribbles yet another telegram.

Father. En route to Bright River. You must pay attention. Have concerns about Bodecker's partner Donnelly. You must investigate. Ben.

It's all he can do for now; he must not be distracted from his own business. Life can pull a man in too many directions at once and it's up to the man to decide which direction needs his attention, for his own sake and those who are important to him. The train chuffs out of Cheyenne. They are finally on their way. *He* is finally on his way.

185

Cliff

"Emma…"

…perhaps the day looks so dull because she is so lovely…

The idea floats wondrously through his head.

"Good morning," she says, seriously.

A light-blue velvet cloak and hood protect her from the cold, but he notices on closer examination that her complexion is pale. How did Mac describe her… flinty? Not today, not really.

"I hope I am not disturbing you. Well, I can see that I… I am, but I wanted to return this because I felt sure you would be needing it."

His blue coat. He stands back, pulling the door wide.

"Come on in, it's cold," he says.

She'll have to come in because he hasn't taken the coat from her.

"Well, I would be intruding," she says.

"Since when has that stopped you," he says, returning to re-knotting his sling. "Stupid thing… Would you mind hanging my coat on the hallstand… thanks… I just need to get this…"

Her solemn figure crosses the threshold and he quickly closes the door behind her, while she pegs his coat.

"Coffee? Just put some on."

"No, I…"

"And I have doughnuts and prune cake…" He holds up his sling only to find it limp and misshapen; meanwhile his arm is really beginning to ache. "And something labeled… what the…"

"For someone so adept one-handed with a gun," he hears her murmur. She steps up to him and says, "May I?"

"Er… thanks."

He hands over the sling, and while he holds her gloves for her, she shakes it out and then makes it afresh.

"Bend your elbow to where it's most comfortable," she says.

She folds the material around his arm and he holds it in place against his forearm. His main thought is that he's glad he's got on a fresh shirt, until she takes the tips and reaches up around his neck and begins to tie a knot. Something inside him buckles; he puts his free hand on her waist to steady himself.

Her eyelids flicker, but her only comment is: "I'll make it a flat knot; it will be more comfortable."

While she avoids looking at him at all costs, his eyes cling to her serious face; he notices all manner of fascinating details, and while her deft and steady fingers play at the back of his neck, her closeness is fast undoing him. "Emma?"

"Mm?"

"Perhaps if I sit down…"

"No, I'm done."

"Thank you," he says with relief, as she tucks the pointy corners neatly into place.

"The very least I can do, since it is my fault that you are in this predicament."

"It was not your fault," he points out, gently.

She steps back again and puts a respectable distance between them. "You may need to reassess your dressing arrangements."

He returns her gloves. "The doc had me trussed up tight before. That's why I undid the knot in the first place. This is better though."

"I'm glad. Well, I need to be going. I just wanted to say thank you for lending me your coat, and…and most of all, thank you for saving my life."

"I appreciate that, Emma, but I was just doing my job."

"I understand that, Mr Ryan, but taking a bullet for a stranger at risk to your own life is not to be underrated. Certainly I don't, especially since if I had kept walking the whole business may have been preven…"

"You're not a stranger."

"I'm not?"

"No. Anyway, I thought you'd be gloating, since you were right about putting Mac in danger; think how much worse you'd feel if it had been him and not unmarried childless me."

He watches the color rise in her cheeks.

"I told you before, I don't gloat."

He suppresses a smile and leaves her for the kitchen. "So you did." On his way through the parlor he calls out, "Coffee?"

Several moments later she appears at the kitchen door; she has removed her hood to reveal her honey-blonde hair. Her eyes catch the sunlight pouring in through the kitchen window. Their color intensifies and there is moisture brimming along the bottom lids.

"That remark, Mr Ryan, was unkind," she says. "I think of all the things you have said to me over the past two days that was the one thing I wish you had not said."

He thought *what could you possibly have that I would want* from their first encounter would have taken that prize.

Curiosity bites. "Why?"

"Because it disappoints me. I know you are not unkind because I saw myself the way you treated Mrs Landers yesterday. She knew she could come to you for reassurance and kindness and that's what she got, so whatever the reason for saying to me what you did just then, I think you should apologize. If you think for one moment that I would rather see you shot than Mac, anyone shot for that matter, then we have had the last conversation we shall ever have."

One of the things he particularly likes about Emma is her ability to totally overlook his position as Sheriff and tell him what she thinks of him. And he wants to keep it that way.

"Then I apologize," he says firmly, sincerely. "I'm sorry, Emma. You were so serious and I only meant to stir you. I managed to get a whole night's sleep and I'm..."

Her eyes flash suddenly. "I am not meant to take this whole thing seriously? It may be everyday stuff to you..."

"It's not everyday stuff, it's..."

"This is pointless. I will be late for work."

He watches her take off; her blue velvet cloak gives a whoosh. He musters every ounce of restraint and lets her go. "Don't write what a ruthless, lying, unkind bastard I am, will you, Emma..." he murmurs to the place where she stood.

Emmaline

At the Tribune, Emmaline rummages amongst the piles of stuff on her desk for a copy of this morning's paper.

"Looking for this?"

She looks up.

Simons is holding out a copy of the Tribune.

"Yes. Thank you," she says and takes it.

"Any time. So, how does it look?"

MISSING PIECE IN INVESTIGATION PUZZLE UNCOVERED AT LAST – MAVERICK CONNECTION

CHEYENNE, January 31 - The attempt on the life of this reporter came to a head yesterday afternoon when yet another sharp shooter from Maverick's stable of assassins discharged a .44-40 caliber weapon with intent to kill from a 17th Street rooftop.

This second attempt was carried out as this reporter was returning from giving evidence at the hearing of Gordy Jacobs, and was thwarted by the quick and heroic actions of Sheriff Cliff Ryan, who not only collected the bullet in his left arm but seconds later turned, then spotted the gunman, and fired a single shot.

The rest blurs behind a wall of excitement. But it's all there…

Her first published story here in Cheyenne!

In the West! Anywhere that wasn't the South!

"Fine indeed," she says.

Simons chuckles. "Yeah, the Chief and I thought so too."

"What, no gender-related sarcasm, Simons?"

"Can be supplied if desired."

"Think I'll pass."

Another chuckle.

She gathers up her things.

"Now where are you going?" he asks.

"Out," she tells him.

His eyes narrow on her, concerned, cautioning.

"I'll be fine," she says.

Emmaline combs the icy streets for the enigmatic Mrs Landers.

Instead, she discovers the place where Miss Keaton was gunned down, and the building of Jennifer Sullivan, which apparently she still owns. It is empty and locked up.

The chill wind whistles across the street, rippling the hem of her dress, pushing on her cloak. This stretch of sidewalk feels a little eerie. A deserted building; a sidewalk of death …

"I remember you."

Emmaline jumps and swings around.

"You're the girl reporter our sheriff saved yesterday."

"Good morning, Mrs Landers."

"You remember me too. What would you be doin' here?"

She smiles. "Just looking about. Do you live around here, Mrs Landers?"

Mrs Lander's eyes slide from side to side. "Here about. Why d'you want to know?"

"Well, if you did, you would see a great deal that goes on."

"I see what I need to see."

She studies that unfathomably old face. "May I buy you some coffee, Mrs Landers? I would like to know what it is that you need to see."

Mrs Landers grins. Toothlessly. "Hot chocolate?"

"Of course. If you prefer."

Mrs Landers, in ragged clothes and smart woolen scarf, shuffles along by her side towards a cozy-looking restaurant further along the street. A chalkboard sign with fancy lettering stands on the sidewalk:

HOT MEALS

BEST IN TOWN!

"They got mighty fine hot chocolate in this here place. That sign don't lie. You're gonna like it, Miss."

"Emmaline."

"Miss Emmaline."

"Just Emmaline."

Again, the tooth-starved grin.

While awaiting their hot chocolate, Mrs Landers offers bits and pieces of harmless and interesting trivia about the town.

When the hot chocolate arrives, chocolaty fragrant and delicious, Emmaline asks: "So, Mrs Landers, what is it that you see?"

Mrs Landers takes a cautious sip. "When they say hot they mean it."

"There's no rush. Take your time."

Mrs Landers sits back a bit. "I saw young Taylor a lot. He loved that young woman so…" She shakes her head and looks down. "Came back a-lookin' for her."

"Which young woman?"

"Jennifer," she says serenely.

"The doctor?"

Mrs Landers nods sadly. "But he felt so bad about Miss Keaton and after all that happened I don't think he could take being here no more. Guilt can be a powerful emotion. Not always useful neither."

"Why did he feel guilty? Because he loved Jennifer?"

"Loved Jennifer, kinda promised to Miss Keaton. I heard that Miss Keaton didn't want nothin' to do with him but. She broke it off before young Taylor and Jennifer fell for each other, or maybe it was before young Taylor would let himself fall for her."

"That's quite a situation. So when Miss Keaton was murdered, Mr Taylor felt guilty, as though it was his fault."

"So would you when you sweared to protect someone you love and you can't keep 'em from death. Loved two women, did young Taylor."

Emmaline sips her drink while she considers the predicament of the young man she had met briefly at Mr Faraday's two nights ago. Well, he cut a romantic figure then, no reason to suppose it was all in her head.

"Then, a few weeks after young Taylor left town, Jennifer, God love her, left too. She couldn't stand to be here without him, I reckon. She was sad all the time. I think she tried but it weren't no use. She was the fairest girl I ever saw, ain't no wonder he loved her. She had her choice of men anywhere in this whole country and none even turned her head until he came into town. Strangest thing… they never saw each other 'til that day, a sad day 'cause of young Marty Keaton, but she made it better, she did… He called her his angel. Destined to be together."

"That's quite a love story, Mrs Landers. Does it have a happy ending?"

Mrs Landers gives a chuckle. "I wonder…"

"So what else do you see?"

Mrs Landers lifts her cup and takes a more satisfying mouthful. "That's not bad, that." She wipes her mouth on her sleeve. "Let's see. You'd probably be interested in less romantic things…"

Emmaline tries not to take that the way it sounds.

"During the summer when Mr Faraday and young Taylor and our relentless sheriff were puttin' up the trial of Ed Parsons, Loren Bodecker left town. I heard he went to Laramie and stayed there with a friend."

"Which friend?"

"Now that I couldn't say. Didn't see that. Not my place to see that…"

"Then just tell me what you can. When did Mr Bodecker return to Cheyenne?"

"Can tell you that all right. 'Bout the time Ed Parsons was found guilty of conspirin' to murder young Marty Keaton. Why he came back then, can't say, but he did know Ed Parsons personal, so mebbe that had somethin' to do with it."

"Mrs Landers, did you see who shot Miss Keaton?"

Mrs Landers looks extremely uncomfortable and fiddles with the handle of her cup. "I was supposed to. Supposed to be there. But I went for hot chocolate and I didn't see…"

Emmaline examines the downcast face.

"This one here is m'only hot chocolate since that day," the old woman says, looking up… "I didn't see who it was, Miss Emmaline, but I reckon Mr Ryan's got him in his lockup, I see that all right. And you should too. Mr Ryan sees it's him."

"Mrs Landers, did you ever see who sent the man in Mr Ryan's lockup to Cheyenne to kill Miss Keaton?"

Mrs Landers frowns, and stills, like a figure in a painting. Then, a moment later, she pushes her hot chocolate back a little. "I'm sorry, Miss Emmaline, but I gotta go now. Things to do and things to see. But we can talk again soon. And I will answer all your questions, I promise. Glad you're come at last. Mr Ryan's a-needin' you. Without you he'd *never* be a-gettin' rid of that black coat."

The old woman shuffles quickly between tables and leaves the restaurant. Emmaline cranes her neck to see where she's heading but her sight is blocked. She rushes to the door and looks both up and down the sidewalk as well as across the street; Mrs Landers is nowhere to be seen.

Quaid

Quaid realizes it's been a while since he checked on Roberts and finds her at her desk scribbling furiously.

"Roberts…"

"Mr Quaid, you don't suppose there's some connection between this Donnelly from Laramie and Loren Bodecker do you? I have a source who says that Bodecker stayed with a friend in Laramie last summer up until the day Ed Parsons was found guilty."

He feels his jaw drop.

"And what about a possible connection between Donnelly and Maverick? If Donnelly bought out the widow Adams up in Dickson, after Maverick killed her husband, for half the land value or whatever it was, then maybe Donnelly knows who Maverick is?"

Her light brown eyes are alight and shimmering.

"Mac said that the sheriff in Laramie will be sending a dossier on Donnelly today. I'm thinking that if Donnelly is a businessman and Bodecker is a businessman then it stands to reason that they would know each other if they share common interests. Donnelly sounds like he's interested in acquiring land, and we know that Bodecker can't get enough of it."

He nods thoughtfully. Who is her new source? "Well, I think you should…"

"Get down to the courthouse and see what's come in, precisely. If we're not happy with it, Mr Quaid, you will have to send me to Laramie."

He slides his hands into his pockets… studies her from beneath his eyebrows. Meanwhile, she's gathering her cloak and gloves and her notebook and pencils.

"That's a dangerous assignment, Roberts," he says.

"I realize that it could be dangerous, but no more than being here in Cheyenne."

"There are a lot of people looking out for your best interests here in town, that can't be guaranteed in Laramie…"

"Do you think the Alliance families know who is in the lockup?"

He nods. "Ryan would have told them by now."

"Do you think they'll send someone?"

"Hard to say. They may wait until Faraday has Swinton Carter indicted."

"I want to pay them a call, Mr Quaid; while I'm in Laramie I may as well go the extra miles. I think an interview with the Alliance will interest our readers."

He loosens his tie since any minute now he's going to break into a sweat…

"Mr Quaid, you look a little wan," she remarks. "Ryan's got to you, hasn't he?"

"I'd be lying if I said he hasn't," he admits.

"You worry about the Tribune, Mr Quaid; I'll worry about our story; and Mr Ryan can worry about whatever he chooses."

Quaid wishes he'd said that.

Simons sticks his head in the room. "Hey, Chief, thought you might like to know. This morning's edition has sold out right across town. Roberts' story has everyone out in the streets."

The three of them grin at each other.

"And the Bugle?" Quaid asks.

Simons smirks, "What Bugle?"

Faraday

Office of Sheriff, Courthouse
Northwest corner of 19th & Ferguson

Faraday reaches the door and is about to breathe a sigh of relief when Miss Roberts appears at his side.

"Good Morning, Mr Faraday."

"I thought I'd shaken off every reporter in town. In fact, I'm sure someone from the Tribune..."

"Just a quick question," she says. Her eyes are sharp and bright, and there is an undeniable air about her.

"Let's step inside, Miss Roberts. The morning is exceptionally cold."

He directs her inside to the waiting chairs which are unoccupied.

In the background the voices of Cliff's men going about their business are audible, as well as some of the resounding metallic echoes from the jail.

"Fire away, Miss Roberts," he says.

"I've been wondering, Mr Faraday, why you responded to Miss Keaton's letters to the Bugle when it became apparent Bodecker was conveniently using them to incite violence against homesteaders?"

Faraday sighs. "Not that again, Miss Roberts."

"No, please don't mistake my meaning, Mr Faraday. Your correspondence with Miss Keaton I find fascinating, but I have never understood why you would encourage her and foment violence."

"Encourage her, yes. Her first letter expressed a passion for a significant and worthwhile opinion, and a subject that people should be discussing. I encouraged her because it had the effect of encouraging the people of this town to talk about it. And I believed that she had a raw talent that needed a nudge.

"As for the violence, I can only regret it. As you yourself wrote this morning, the harassment was never publicly reported and was not known by me for some time. And why would you think I would want to be a part of that?

"I have been trying to encourage homesteaders to bring their grievances to court, Miss Roberts, to convince them that the law will protect them, and not to take the law into their own hands. The issues raised by Miss Keaton and replied to by myself in those letters are extremely significant to this territory and probably to the whole nation. We need people like Miss Keaton. Your story in this morning's Tribune rekindles the flame, Miss Roberts, and perhaps Miss Keaton would be standing and cheering at this very moment if she was alive, and, going by the town reaction to your article, Miss Roberts, I don't see how Loren Bodecker can avoid the issue."

Miss Roberts, deep in concentration, stares, her light brown eyes fixed on his.

"You are convinced he is guilty of conspiring to murder Miss Keaton," she murmurs.

"I believe that things are going to get a great deal worse before they get better, and considering the two attempts on your life, that is saying something." He smiles at her youthful seriousness. "Do you believe there is room for all, Miss Roberts?"

"I believe that liberty for Americans seems destined to be linked to material property, no matter what Miss Keaton hoped for. I believe freedom is a desire of the human spirit and for most of us it is manifested in a physical way. I think as human beings this is our biggest flaw, because some people just can't be free without hurting others. *Room for all* implies no greed, no viciousness, but kindness and generosity…"

She suddenly looks embarrassed, as if she has said too much, and she lowers her eyes.

He smiles to himself. "Thank you, Miss Roberts, for your article this morning…"

Those bright eyes come back to his.

"The people will debate it, be sure of that." He sighs and folds his arms. "Yes, democracy is not the easy road…"

Loud voices disturb their peaceful exchange. In strides Cliff, agitated from head to boot, with Dillon Kerr on his coat tails. Cliff doesn't see them until Faraday stops both men in their tracks by saying: "Good morning, Dillon."

Dillon Kerr's lanky figure halts in mid-stride.

"Well, well," he murmurs in a voice as oiled as his hair.

He dresses completely and consistently in black; black hat, black suit, long black coat, black shirt, black tie, black leather boots, black belt (pure silver buckle); his hair is jet black and oiled; he sports a waxed pencil-thin black moustache. He carries a black walking cane with an ornate silver handle and is Loren Bodecker's man to the core of his being.

"Looks like I walked into the right place," he says. "Now I can tell both of you."

"And that would be?" Faraday prompts.

"Ryan refuses to warn Quaid regarding that scurrilous story in the Tribune. Linking Mr Bodecker's name with the likes of this Maverick character and those two assassins in your lockup, Ryan, is libelous in the extreme. This Roberts character better think again. If this outrageous vilification of Mr Bodecker continues, Faraday, I will be demanding prosecution…"

"Ah, so it begins," says Miss Roberts. "Fending off the mud…"

Dillon Kerr turns his dark eyes on Miss Roberts, who it seems knows no fear.

"And who are you?" Dillon peers down his nose at her, which is rich considering Miss Roberts is immaculately groomed as always.

"Allow me to introduce you," Faraday says. "Dillon, this is Miss Emmaline Roberts, Miss Roberts, may I present Mr Dillon Kerr, Loren Bodecker's attorney."

If Faraday is not mistaken, the menacing Kerr and the principled Miss Roberts are sizing one another up like opponents in a boxing ring. Kerr's black eyes bulge as recognition dawns.

"You! You wrote that drivel…"

"I beg your pardon, sir, but every word was clear and concise. I do not write drivel. I am incapable of it."

Kerr stiffens. His eyes narrow. "Concise enough to see you in court, Miss Roberts."

"Oh, I don't think when we see each other in court it will be on libel charges, Mr Kerr," she says.

Her nuance is not lost upon Kerr, nor indeed upon any of them.

Kerr's glare would wither a seasoned journalist. "I don't think you understand to whom you are speaking, Miss Roberts. My client is one of the most powerful men in this territory and as such I am a powerful man. We turn the wheels of industry and drive the fortunes of many. We control the lives of more people than you can imagine, even yours. If you persist you will probably rue the day you ever set foot in Cheyenne..."

Cliff sees red. "You're threatening her? In front of us? You..."

Arrogant bastard.

"Always the hero, Sheriff," Kerr says. "What would the damsels in town do without you? Their distress would know no bounds..."

Speaking of damsels, Miss Roberts actually takes a step towards the man; the defiant tilt of her chin should be enough to warn Kerr but the pompous man stands there...

"So you're a lawyer. So what! I've been around lawyers all my life. Two of my three brothers are lawyers, they set up their own law firm, of which my cousin is a partner; his father – my uncle – is a state supreme court judge; my grandfather sat on the Federal bench; and my second uncle on my mother's side is a county defense lawyer in the state of Alabama, he defends Negroes, commonly on spurious charges; and his son my grandfather is putting through Harvard law school as we speak."

"Defending Negroes? Madam, if I'm not mistaken, you are a southerner. We do things differently here."

"You think so? I know how your type likes to play, Mr Kerr. You tie up the courts and people's time and money with a bunch of trumped up charges that take them away from doing what they really need to be doing. But I'm telling you here and now that it won't work. Wearing black clothes and standing six foot two and staring down your nose at folks and blustering about power and influence only fools the weak-minded. There are two men in Mr Ryan's lockup, both of whom tried to kill me; I don't know how far you can intimidate Mr Quaid, but it will be a cold day in hell before you stop me from discovering who sent them and why, you pompous, contemptible... vanilla bean!"

And she storms out.

Dillon Kerr's pencil moustache looks a little droopy. And why wouldn't it? It's just had the wax blasted off it.

It'd warm the cockles of one's heart. Yes, it would.

Emmaline

To her great relief, there is a long bench resting against the wall of the building some little distance from the door and, trembling, she sinks onto it. She receives a jolt when Kerr appears on the sidewalk, and braces herself. Fortunately, he doesn't even glance her way; he crosses the street and heads in the opposite direction. She closes her eyes, her words ringing in her ears. What possessed her? Two attempts on her life perhaps? Burying herself in work and pretending she can ignore them might not be efficacious if her outburst is anything to go by. She feels someone sit down beside her and opens her eyes. Ryan. In his blue coat. And without his sling. Leaning forward, casually resting his elbows on his knees, looking out into the street. Kerr was right about one thing; Ryan *is* her hero.

"You all right?" he murmurs.

"That objectionable man looked at me as though I personally refused to ratify the Fifteenth Amendment."

"Be mightily surprised if Dillon Kerr knows what the Fifteenth Amendment is. He doesn't know what a vanilla bean is either."

"Oh?"

"After you left he asked Cam if being a vanilla bean was bad."

"What did Mr Faraday tell him?"

"That it's a long black bean that gets its middle slashed open and the seeds removed with a sharp knife. Kerr turned a whiter shade of pale and walked out. Highlight of my day, the whole thing…"

"Where is Mr Faraday? I must thank him."

Ryan chuckles. "Having a quiet word with Marvin Tucker about Swinton Carter. That's some pedigree you have there."

"I do not wish to discuss it."

"Two out of three brothers, two uncles and two cousins, and a grandfather... anyone in your family not a lawyer, your father maybe?"

"My fa... Mr Ryan!" she exclaims.

"Miss Roberts!" he mimics.

"You are prying."

"Mm."

Even in profile she catches the teasing twinkle of blue-green eyes.

"Very well. Brother number three is still in school."

"And does he have the same ambitions as his brothers, cousins and uncles?"

"No, he is too much like... Never mind."

"It might surprise you to know that I myself am a lawyer."

"And you ended up a sheriff? What *were* you thinking?"

"That I would like law enforcement better."

She feels the tension in her jaw and her muscles and her hands. "So you can get shot up by criminals? That's ridiculous."

His sigh pours out like soft mist. "Martha's place is a block and a half that way..."

She looks in the direction he indicates.

"Martha makes great coffee. I think you and I should get some."

She shakes her head...

"Why not?"

...and hastily thinks of an excuse. "Because I've already had hot chocolate."

He laughs as he stands up. "So, you've been speaking with Mrs Landers."

"How do you...? Oh. You have..."

"Yep," he says lightly, but then he bends over and reaches for her hand. "Sharp as ever."

Her eyes are almost level with his, and she can't avoid them like she did earlier that morning as she tied up his sling; such a beautiful blue-green, with black lashes. Oh dear. She must stop noticing.

"Mrs Landers told me she hadn't had any hot chocolate since the day..."

Ryan is gently pulling her to her feet. "What day?"

They are at a height disadvantage now; she must look up and he must look down but they seem to be managing it very comfortably, just as they did earlier this morning.

"Don't you have work to do?" she asks.

"I need to take it easy for a day. The old doc's orders."

"What happened to your sling?"

"I reassessed my dressing arrangements."

"I think you don't want people to think your human; I think you want people to think nothing will stand in your way. I think..."

"You're right," he says simply. "Now let's get some coffee before we freeze."

He tosses his handsome head in the direction of Martha's.

"You admit it?" she asks, walking with him – again.

"Off the record, of course."

"Of course," she says, and then decides not to pursue the subject further; walking beside him concentrating on how she'd rather *not* feel is enough until they arrive at Martha's and he holds the door for her. She heads for a table along the back wall and he follows. An excuse is what she needs, but it's very difficult to imagine one into being when the greater part of you won't cooperate.

"You're Emmaline Roberts."

She turns towards the voice.

A middle-aged man of average height... "I can tell 'cause the sheriff here has his eye on you, no surprises there."

"Oh. Yes, well..."

"That's some story you got in this morning's Tribune. Every-one's talking about it. Morning, Sheriff."

"Morning, Chris. Miss Roberts, this is Chris Wiggins."

"A pleasure to meet you, Mr Wiggins."

"And you, Miss Roberts."

"Chris and his family farm one hundred and sixty acres up on Lodgepole Creek."

This is the face of the homesteader; deeply bronzed face, eyes that reveal the weight of the world is upon his shoulders, a world that is one day struggle and the next day contentment, a life etched in hope...

"What do you farm, Mr Wiggins?"

"Some livestock, seasonal crops. You look like a city gal, Miss Roberts."

"Small town mostly. We have a small orchard – oranges."

"You need good warm sunshine for oranges, a lot more than we got here in Wyoming."

"Well, I wouldn't dispute that for an instant."

They share a genial laugh.

"Lotta folks are doing it tough," Chris Wiggins says, "so I sure hope you write some more of that fine prose. Well... good day."

After she bids him goodbye, she observes his ever so slightly hunched figure leave Martha's and head off into the street, coat thrown over one shoulder. She takes her seat and looks up to find other faces are now trained on her; Martha's is full of men just like Wiggins and their female counterparts.

It seems as though Ryan has been watching her, for when she meets his eyes he smiles. "Thought you might like to see the faces of the people who will take you as their champion."

"You read my piece."

"I was curious."

"And?"

"You don't need my opinion."

"I don't... need it... Well, anyway, I thought *you* were their champion."

"Maybe," he says, modestly. "But you speak for them, Emma, and people who feel like they are constantly being pushed around need a voice."

They are still staring at each other when a rotund middle-aged woman says in an extremely resounding voice, "Well, my handsome hero, what will you have this fine morning? And you, young lady? It's on the house for you. Coffee and some of my warm peach preserve pie goes down a treat on a day like today. Everyone in here swears by it."

Emmaline grins as a stream of gladness bubbles to the surface, not something she's felt since she arrived. "Sounds delicious. You're Martha."

"Sure am. Come here on the Overland Route when I was just a

gal like yerself. Set up this place. That's why Cheyenne's here, cause of the overland railroad. I been here ever since the early days…"

Martha barks their order into the air, supposedly someone hears it, and then continues with her history. By the time she leaves to fetch the coffee and pie, Emmaline is left in no doubt that she is about to acquire more friends than she could possibly need.

Ryan says, "Now when you're called to put your life on the line for them it's their faces you see. Ideologies are fine, but they need a human face."

Her breath catches. "You sound like my…."

"Your what?"

Quickly, she dismisses his question with a shake of her head. "Never mind."

"You say that a lot."

"It's of no consequence."

What follows is a remote, almost hard scrutiny under which she prevails commendably. Besides, she wants to enjoy this as a nice moment, not tough it out like the bulk of her Cheyenne experience thus far. Thankfully, the pie arrives. He doesn't seem to eat much of it. She devours hers.

"I wonder what Martha preserves these peaches in," she says, rolling her tongue around her mouth. "I'd say a peach brandy…"

She looks up from her pie to see Ryan's broody expression; he's prodding a piece of fruit with his fork.

"Not hungry then?" she asks lightly.

He rallies himself, almost as if he has finally come to a decision or accepted something and it was hard work and now it's done.

Profoundly curious, she chooses a topic for conversation. "You know, Mrs Landers told me the story of Luke and Jennifer. You know about them?"

"They are good friends of mine. I only had to be in the same room as them to know."

"Mrs Landers said he was supposed to marry Miss Keaton."

"Is there a point to this?"

"I think Luke has gone after his Jennifer. St Louis, Mac said."

"He probably has and good luck to him; he'd be doing the right thing."

"I've never met a lady doctor; rare as hen's teeth, I should think. And people think journalism is a male domain. Imagine…"

"I think you do enough of that for both of us."

She twirls her cup around on its saucer. "Well, I'm thinking that their story is probably one of the great romances in this town's history, if you consider the circumstances and the complications."

"Mm, and it's a *secret* great romance, Miss Words."

"I know, I know; I'm not about to tell anyone. Maybe one day, though, it could be told."

"Write romances do you?"

"No," she retorts. "Just what are you insinuating?"

"Don't get your pencils in a pickle; I know you're a serious journalist."

"Now you are insinuating I'm not romantic."

"Which is it then?"

"Surely it is possible to be both."

"Are you?"

"It's not definite, but I would like to think so."

"I'm glad. It's important to be emotionally balanced. Now would you care for anything else?" He reaches into his pocket for some coins… Emotionally balanced? He should talk. Does he possess a romantic bone in that ruthless body?

"No, thank you." She sips the last of her coffee. "I've been wondering… what happened to your black coat?"

He looks slightly amused. "I'll either have to have the sleeve replaced or throw the coat away."

"A shame to throw it away," she says, mentally comparing the coat in question to the one she'd just seen on Dillon Kerr, "it being so impressive an' all."

Ryan rubs that spot over his eye. "It looks too much like Dillon Kerr's coat anyhow. Don't want to go confusing the townsfolk."

She grins, ear-to-ear.

He lets out a laugh. "Okay, what are you grinning about?"

"Guess," she says.

"You were thinking the same thing, I don't know…"

"I doubt very much that Kerr's would ever suffer the same fate as yours."

"A compliment, Miss Roberts? I think we should leave before it all goes to my head."

"You saved my life; I think you deserve one, at least."

"Oh?"

"You have courage."

He looks down at his hands. "And you have courage," he says, and then directs his blue-green gaze upon her again.

She tells herself to breathe. "I have to go."

Out on the sidewalk, he says, "I take it you have accepted my apology from this morning."

She neatens the fingers of her gloves. "I have."

"Thank you," he says with gentlemanly politeness.

"Considering what happened, what you went through, your injury, I think an aberration is understandable."

"And thank you again," he smiles. "You went through it your-self. We were both edgy."

Overwhelmed, she wants to tell him, by what he did for her.

"I should not have taken you to task – you saved my life. I should have let it go."

"And I should have been more sensitive to your feelings."

"It's no longer of any consequence."

"And we are finally friends, you and I."

She looks this way and that. Why was this happening? It's not as if they haven't been *trying* to despise one another. They haven't stopped niggling and fighting since they met. Besides, she'd shaken on it with Mr Quaid. Given her word.

"I have one question…" she says. "The reason I dropped by in the first place."

"And that would be…?"

"About Donnelly?"

"The information hasn't come down from Laramie yet."

"I see. Well, then, thank you for the coffee and pie, and the human face of ideology."

"You're welcome. Goodbye, Emma. Take care of yourself."

She watches him stride away. In his blue coat, supporting his injured arm in his good hand. Sheriff Ruthless.

An inner voice says, *you are going to have to try harder…*

Faraday

Faraday glances up as Cliff enters and does a double take. As he draws up a chair, their ruthless sheriff seems altered; heaven forbid, mellow. Faraday shifts in his chair to peer at the open door Cliff just came through. Should they expect someone else...? Faraday gets up and closes it. He turns to find Cliff considering Swinton Carter thoughtfully; Faraday clears his throat. Loudly.

Cliff blinks and says, "Well, Tucker?"

Faraday answers instead. "Mr Tucker says his client maintains he is innocent of attempting to murder Miss Roberts."

"That true, Tucker?"

Marvin Tucker nods brusquely. The man is not well known in town; he keeps to himself. He's not older than Faraday himself; and he presents well, is articulate and knows the law.

Their attention switches to the culprit Swinton Carter. He is small, pale and thin, similar age to Gordy Jacobs, with brown eyes and long brown hair secured in a ponytail. His arm is in a sling and he nurses it with his good hand.

Cliff continues, "Your client shot a law enforcement officer, Tucker. The bullet extracted from my arm matched your client's six-shooter. And that six-shooter was recently discharged."

Marvin Tucker shakes his head. "You have no proof that my client fired the gun. But you shot my client, Sheriff."

Cliff leans forward in his seat. "I saw him on the roof holding the damn pistol, Tucker, that's why I shot him. The way it's done, if you didn't already know, Maverick's boys shoot to kill, and if they miss the first time, they try again – without any delay. Bang, bang. Only my bullet stopped your client's second attempt. Of course, my arm stopped the first."

Mellow is gone.

For the first time since Faraday walked in, Swinton Carter begins to look worried. He wasn't exactly cocky before, but it was obvious he had confidence in Tucker.

Cliff eases back in his chair again, holding Carter's eye. "I sent MAVERICK, LARAMIE TELEGRAPH, NIGHTHAWK LULLABY."

Silence. Sweat beads across Carter's forehead.

"What are you trying to do, Ryan?" Tucker mutters. "I told Faraday that my client is innocent of the charge and that's what we'll be telling the Judge."

"I'm just a tiny bit worried about that, Tucker," says Cliff while he looks straight at Carter.

"What are you playing at, Ryan?"

"Well, the Judge might believe your client, Tucker, might take one look at Mr Carter here and think: yes, I believe that boy is innocent of attempting to murder Miss Emmaline Roberts of the Tribune. And he might set Mr Carter free; he might say: I find that Mr Carter has no case to answer in this matter. He might say: Mr Faraday, Mr Ryan, the accused is free to go. I'm telling you, stranger things have happened in Judge Callaghan's courtroom. And then Mr Carter here is *free*."

Faraday watches, marvels, as Swinton Carter's face, shiny with sweat, screws itself up as if he's preparing for a blow.

"You think your client might like freedom, Tucker?"

"Listen, Sheriff…"

"Does your client know what happened to Gordy Jacobs?"

"What are you talking about, Ryan?"

Swinton Carter's eyes, meanwhile, bulge.

"Well, Gordy decided it was safer to confess and take advantage of the safety and security generously offered by Laramie County than face the reprisals of Maverick. In Gordy's words, and I quote, *Maverick will pick me off outside. You'll be doing me a favor by locking me up.* So you see, gentlemen, going free for Gordy was not an option. Why, he feels freer inside than out."

Swinton Carter is swallowing hard and often now.

"But I assume Mr Faraday told you all this before, Tucker, and I wouldn't even be mentioning it, but I figured you would want your client to be fully aware of the ramifications of his decision."

Marvin Tucker starts writing in his notebook. "In case you're wondering, Ryan, I'm noting that in this interview my client was subject to verbal harassment by you. Mr Faraday won't be too happy when my client is exonerated because of this."

Faraday is not perturbed in any way, nor is Cliff by the look of him.

"The law is the law, Mr Tucker," Faraday says. "My job is to prosecute wrongdoers and Mr Ryan keenly feels his duty to keep the town safe from harm. He was shot in the process of doing that, and surely you can understand that he is a little put out."

"He doesn't look shot," Tucker muses, with a disparaging eye on Cliff.

Cliff laughs. "I only hope that your client is *prepared to take full responsibility for the undertaking of the job.*"

Swinton Carter emits a muffled cry and drags his sleeve across his sweaty face. He turns to Tucker and mumbles, "Why's he sayin' *that*, Mr Tucker?"

"Hold your tongue."

Carter's glazed stare inevitably reverts to Cliff's face.

"Well, I think this meeting is concluded," Faraday says. "This being Saturday, Mr Carter's arraignment will be at ten o'clock on Monday morning. He can tell his story to the Judge. Good day, Mr Tucker."

Faraday pushes back his chair, picks up his satchel and leaves the room. Cliff calls for Mac to fetch Carter and return him to his cell. Cliff's long stride is not far behind Faraday's and they step into his office, which is adjacent to the interview room. The room has a door into Cliff's office and another door that leads into the outer office. Dividing the sheriff's office in two and creating a separate interrogation space was a device employed by Cliff when he became sheriff of Laramie County three years ago. The bleak, constrictive environment is effective for interrogation.

Through Cliff's office doorway, they see Marvin Tucker leaving; he's mopping his brow with his handkerchief.

"Give it time," Cliff mutters as he eyes Tucker's back.

"I don't think Tucker realizes the position he's in when Carter goes to trial."

"Obviously hasn't bumped into Dillon Kerr yet."

"Well, that can't be far off."

"Yeah, when Kerr gets his nose out of his backside he might actually smell trouble."

Mac appears before their eyes.

"Hey, boss, thought you might like to know; Swinton Carter just told me…"

"What?"

"You ain't gonna like it…"

"He's a lying murderer, of course I'm not going to like it – unless it's a confession."

Faraday bites back a smile; these two, even in serious matters, are frankly comical.

"I'm lockin' him in his cell and he says Miss Roberts ain't even safe in church. When I said he shouldn't joke about stuff like that, he said: do I look like I'm joking."

Faraday receives an angry blue-green flash from his outraged sheriff. "Admission of guilt?"

Faraday shakes his head. "Anyone could remark that Miss Roberts wasn't safe anywhere since she has been following trouble around from the moment she arrived."

"Yes, but Carter doesn't know what she's like. He knows she's not safe because Maverick is making it *un*safe. If not an admission of guilt, then a threat."

Faraday considers this. "A warning, since *he* no longer poses a threat. You sent the coded telegram. All we can do where Miss Roberts is concerned is watch and wait."

A collective sigh follows.

Faraday says, "I'll be going, Cliff."

"Sure, Cam," Cliff murmurs distractedly.

As Faraday looks back from the door, Cliff and Mac are deep in conference. Cliff is holding his wounded arm to his side. He should be home resting, instead he's plotting to find Maverick, and when that happens, Faraday wouldn't be Maverick for all the tea in China.

Emmaline

The Tribune shuts her doors at midday on Saturdays.

Emmaline gazes out into the street from the window of the news-room considering how to spend her afternoon when she remembers she's not supposed to stand near windows.

She gathers her things from her desk, hollers goodbye to Simons in the front office and hugging her cloak around her, heads off down the street in the direction of Mae Jewell's millinery.

The streets are a mess with slush and mud-stained snow. The sidewalks are marginally better and care must be exercised at all times. Well, for her anyway. Florida is never like this. The problem of how many layers of clothing a person needs to wear never arises. Perhaps that's one reason why she can't abide fur on women's clothing, because in most of Florida it just don't make sense.

But here! A warm, soft, fur-lined hood and muff would be heavenly…

She enters Mae Jewell's store, tempted, but still resolved – no fur! The bell sounds a delicate warning overhead. As she closes the door behind her, a fur muff on display in a glass case catches her eye. She lowers her velvet hood onto her shoulders. The dark beauty of the fur seems fathomless…

"It's a black mink muff, very soft, very warm."

Temptation can be a terrible thing; she is already fighting one very large one, how much more is expected of her?

She smiles weakly at Mae Jewell's enthusiastic face. "It's very lovely."

"Would you like to try it?" Mae Jewell beams.

She fights hard. "Oh… no, Mrs Jewell, I came about a hat, but I'm afraid I can't afford black mink."

Mae Jewell's expectant smile turns to one of sympathy. "I understand, my dear."

Not likely. She *can* afford it, and she'd love it, but she won't give in; and yet she simply must negate Ryan's lie, only now she's told one of her own.

"But I do take lay-away," Mae Jewell says. "You could pay for it in installments. It will be in your hands before you know it."

She capitulates. "Well, since you seem so sure…"

"Oh, absolutely, my dear. In this clime you can't go wrong with fur. And that muff you got your eye on would be a perfect match. Now what style for the hat… the French ones, I think we said. Here's the design book. What takes your fancy?"

What she will do with a mink hat and matching muff when she returns to Florida she has no idea. Particularly when all her friends and her whole family know her views on the fate of unsuspecting critters that happen to be born with fur. She arranges with Mae Jewell to pay for the hat and the muff when the hat is made and ready to be picked up next week. She may as well have them as soon as possible; Ryan is the only person in Cheyenne who knows her views on the matter and she can bear his mockery because she can remind him that it was his lie that got her into this predicament.

She eats lunch in the restaurant where she and Mrs Landers drank hot chocolate before she proceeds to her next stop.

The Faradays'.

The tall, lanky woman with the scratchy voice and a lopsided smile opens the door. "Well, howdy, miss."

"Good afternoon. I was hoping I might see Mrs Faraday."

"I guess it's safe to have you come in."

She steps inside. "Thank you. I must say I much prefer this way of entering this lovely home than being railroaded inside by your sheriff."

"Oh, I dunno. I kinda like the look of Mr Ryan. He's nothing like a Texan but The Rangers sure could use a man like that. So could all the single Texas women. Hah! Anyways, I'll tell Mrs Faraday you're here."

"I'm here, Constance..." Mrs Faraday appears in the hallway. "Oh, hello, it's you. I'm glad you came back. Constance and I have been concerned about you and my husband merely says you are fine and I am not to worry, but that's a man talking. You are fine, aren't you, Miss Roberts? Your cheek does look a little sore, and no wonder. Of course you must be sore and bruised from all that falling about."

"You are very kind, Mrs Faraday, to be so concerned."

Meg Faraday is sweet, with her bright eyes, dark bouncing curls and pert manner. Meanwhile, Constance returns from a foray around the front porch.

"Well, I can't see nothin' or no one, so I guess we're safe. I'll be in the kitchen fixing some tea for you ladies. Make yourself at home, Miss Roberts, and take a seat in the parlor. Mrs Faraday will jabber in the hall all day..." Constance disappears through a door at the end of the hall.

Mrs Faraday looks annoyed.

"I can't stay long, so please don't go to any trouble..."

"Ignore Constance. I do – every chance I get. So come in, Miss Roberts, and sit down."

"Thank you. Please call me Emmaline."

"I'm Meg. Well, it's Margaret actually, but no one calls me that except my mother, and if you ever met her you'd know why."

"A force to be reckoned with?"

"Cam says my mother can organize Boston on her own. I still haven't told her that Jeanne Sullivan taught me to cook."

"Jeanne Sullivan?"

"Oh. A close friend... who really could teach some chefs a thing or two."

They sit and Emmaline looks around at the charming room that up until now has been all shadows and firelight in her mind.

"How long have you been married, Meg?"

"Nearly three years. We are expecting our first child in April."

"Congratulations. Do you like living in Cheyenne?"

"I'm not being interviewed, am I, Emmaline?" Meg asks with a nervous laugh. "What is it I'm supposed to say... off the record?"

"Yes, that's what you say, but I'm not interviewing you... I am naturally nosey, and forgive me if I gave you the wrong impression. I didn't come to ask questions."

"I suppose polite conversation can be tricky when you ask questions for a living. I mean, when you think about it, that which makes the difference between a question being social interaction or a form of interrogation could merely be the tone of your voice. And of course some people love the idea of speaking with a journalist, hoping that they will see they names or their fascinating business in print for the world to read about. I myself wouldn't care, but it wouldn't please Cam."

"He holds a public office, very understandable. But actually, I came to say how sorry I am for what happened here in your home the other night. I placed you in a terrible position and if I may, offer to make it up to you in any way. And, considering the situation, it is probably unwise to stay for tea."

Meg smiles, which is somewhat unexpected. "Don't beat yourself up about it, Emmaline. Apology accepted. You never asked for any of this, so how can you be responsible? And you are definitely staying for tea. And cake... I hope. I am very fond of cake. You know, you remind me of someone... Luke thought it was Miss Keaton, but I don't think so... Oh well, no matter. Besides, who ever feels comfortable being told they are like someone else? We are individuals after all. Oh, here comes Constance. Will you have honey with your tea, or lemon? We have both... I hope. Constance, you remembered the cake?

THREE

Ever been in Omaha
where rolls the dark Missouri down...

Harpers Magazine, 1869

Luke

Luke read an old poem about Omaha once in a magazine from some years back. The first line stuck in his memory... *ever been in Omaha where rolls the dark Missouri down...* he can't remember much of the rest, except that it pictured a town that was dusty, wild, sozzled and loose. And warned people to avoid it. From the train window he could see that it had obviously grown up. No wild dogs to be seen... The streets are mostly paved; the many buildings are large and impressive; electricity and telephone wires crisscross the spaces and everywhere is activity and industry. This is a big, modern and industrious town. Self-aware. Self-important. But he ain't about to ignore that old warning just yet. He reserved the right to make his own judgment. One thing is for sure. The railroad is king. Here is located the headquarters of UP, the Union Pacific Railroad, and of this he is well informed because as he's walking out of the station a proud sign tells him. Such achievements don't go unrecognized, particularly when it's obvious how significant the Union Pacific has been in the organization of Nebraska (they won't let anyone forget it), and posters around the station advertise cheap railway owned land for sale. Well, where would any of them be without the railroad? That roar sounding across the plains is no longer the running of the great bison herds; it's Union Pacific.

First, before anything, he rides a cable car to a riverside park. The famous Missouri...

219

A river so wide and deep, passing by him with sea-like grandeur; famous for her steamboats, the paddlewheels churning, passengers enjoying a more leisurely way of traveling.

Today the surface is encrusted with ice.

No boats, no paddlewheels, no people.

Ethan would say he shouldn't be sightseeing, but he has an excuse. He is, after all, a river man.

Jennifer said so.

He stands on a section of riverbank and thinks about her… out of the depths of his heart into his imagination, to picture her by *her* river in St Louis – the Mississippi – with the wind in her hair and her green eyes smiling, holding her hands out to him, grabbing him tight and never letting go.

He can pine for her all he wants, it don't change the facts: this is Omaha, it's a gateway, not even *nearly* his destination.

From here a traveler can head east to Chicago or south to City of Kansas and onto St Louis, but it is also a gateway for those heading west, so in that sense he is like a fish swimming up stream. That old poem made mention of people back in the day coming and going; looks like a lotta people stayed to call Omaha home…

He's a long way from home, and getting longer by the minute, but he's decided to stop here long enough to do something he should have done before…

He checks in at the Millard Hotel, a first-rate establishment at Thirteenth and Douglas Streets. He ain't exactly dressed the part, but his money is as good as any other well-heeled rancher. And a little charm goes a long way, particularly when you reach into your pocket and pony up before the clerk can open his trap.

After he's dumped his gear and freshened up, he asks the hotel clerk for directions to Taylor Mining Company.

"I seem to recall it's on Farnum. Your cab driver will know."

As the afternoon chill comes down hard, he begins to think that Omaha is actually colder than Cheyenne. He hails a cab and before long it is growing dark. It doesn't seem to be dusk, just dull, and a light snow is falling. The citizens huddle in their coats.

The cab driver stops and announces his requested destination. He asks the driver to wait.

He steps out and fronts a fine, three-story building of smooth gray stone. Affixed to the wall beside the wooden doors is an engraved brass plate:

TAYLOR MINING COMPANY
Trading as "AURORA"

So this is what the brother of his father has been doing all these years.

Despite the steady snowfall, he stands and takes it in…

Two years ago Mart came to this very same spot; he stood here and thought what a sad joke it would be if *this* Taylor were Luke's long-lost and despised relation! He walked in with the intention of finding out, and not only did he discover it to be true, but he found Tressa as well. She was in the office that day, desperately wanting to work but her father forbidding her. Tressa did something that her brother, his other cousin, could not – strike a blow for freedom and leave.

He steps up to the door and tries the handle; the door is locked. He knocks but no one comes. He tries peering in at the window but can't see through the drapes; it is then that he notices a small sign…

Closed
Please call again

He sighs and all that precious heat from inside his body turns to white frost in front of him. Time to move.

"Where to now?" his driver asks.

"City Hall."

Which is not far.

A grand, ornate stone building with a very tall clock tower.

In the lobby, Luke joins several people standing at a high counter headed up 'enquiries'.

A man about his own age, wearing spectacles, a starched white collar and a fancy-patterned necktie, is standing idly behind the counter. The only thing he seems interested in is his thumbnail.

Luke ain't got time for this and he puts himself forward.

"I'm hoping you can help me."

The blue eyes behind the spectacles blink. "I don't believe you were next. Besides, it is Saturday; we are about to close."

"But you ain't closed yet?"

"No, sir, we are not."

"Good. I'm having trouble locating someone…"

"Police Department is in the next block, someone there can help with missing persons… next!"

"No, you don't understand. I'm trying to locate a relative. His business is closed for the day and I need to know where he lives."

The blue eyes stare disinterestedly.

"My name is Luke Taylor, I'm from Bright River, Wyoming, and the father of my cousin, Tressa Taylor, owns Taylor Mining here on Farnum. I'm only here for one night and I need to see him before I leave town."

His eyes narrow. "That would make this man your uncle."

"If you say so."

"Mm. Name?"

"Richard Taylor, and his wife is Caroline."

Suddenly, the eyes fly open wide. "Oh yes. The Taylors. Your uncle is a prominent businessman here in town. I know his son, I knew his daughter a little. She moved to…"

"Wyoming. I know," Luke says, staring him straight in the eye. "The address?"

"You will require a cab."

"I have one."

"Let me write it down for you." He starts writing.

"Is it far?"

"A fine residential neighborhood west of here."

"And west is which way?"

A finger appears and points in the appropriate direction.

Outside the street lamps are lit and the temperature has dropped considerably. Snow flurries whip against his face as he dives back into his cab. This deep and bitter cold calls to mind the months he and John spent searching for Mart only to find him dying in the snow in that forest near Sedalia….

They leave downtown behind and head into the residential neighborhood written down on his piece of paper. Mansion after mansion looms up in the glow of street lamps. House lights are starting to come on as well. And very illuminating they are too; not your average Joe lives on these streets.

"This is it," his driver announces.

Once again Luke asks him to wait.

"It ain't exactly springtime, pal."

"I'll pay you double if you return in half an hour."

"Don't look to me like there's soul at home."

"That's my look-out."

The driver tips his hat. "Half an hour it is."

Standing at the bottom of the porch steps, staring up at the house, he tries to gather his thoughts. But it's too cold to think, and in the end it is the prospect of warmth that impels him to give the great door a good thumping. He waits. Nothing.

He thumps. And waits.

From the other side comes a woman's voice… "Who is it?"

Thin, quivery.

He doesn't intend announcing to the whole neighborhood who he is; truth be told, he doesn't want the world to know he's related to these people.

"I said, who is it?" the thin voice persists.

"My name's Luke Taylor. I'm Tressa's cousin, from Wyoming."

A long pause… "How do I know you are who you say you are?"

He sighs. Raises his voice again; it's beginning to crack with the cold: "I can explain why I've come, but it's kinda cold out here, M'am. If I could just come in…"

"I'm sorry, but I can't admit strangers."

"I went to Richard Taylor's office earlier and it was closed. Coming here was the only thing left to do, hope you can see that, M'am. I don't know why you're so suspicious, this town looks peaceable enough, but I assure you I don't mean you harm. M'am, my father was Morgan Taylor and my mother is Sara. I'm from Bright River, Wyoming. Your daughter Tressa lives with my good friends, the Keatons…"

Suddenly, the door opens and a slither of light cuts the dark. He squints against it, attempting but unable to see.

"You're Morgan's son?" the thin voice asks.

"Yes, M'am. I am."

The crack in the door widens until a small thin woman can be seen. "I am Caroline Taylor. Tressa is my daughter. Is there something wrong with her?"

"Not that I've heard, M'am. May I come in?"

Caroline Taylor peels back the door and admits him at last. He acknowledges the courage this took because she's clearly nervous.

Inside the house is warm, but so dimly lit he can't make out much until Caroline Taylor closes the door and holds up the lamp she's been carrying. He's puzzled because every house in the street is lit up with electric lights.

He removes his hat and snow tumbles off it.

"Is your husband at home?" he asks.

She shakes her head. He can make out some resemblance to Tressa, but the more he looks at this woman the more he realizes Tressa takes after the Taylors. Even so, it's obvious that Caroline Taylor was once a fine-looking woman and Tressa has inherited her refinement.

"I can't believe it," she whispers.

"Is something troubling you, M'am?"

"I've been sitting and... and I've been praying... praying for a miracle... Are you my miracle?"

He's worried she's maybe lost her mind. "I don't think so. I came here to defend Tressa's honor on behalf of her late husband. Now that might sound a little crazy to you but that's why I'm here, so if you could tell me where her father is, I'll be getting out of your hair."

Caroline Taylor lowers her lamp. "That doesn't sound in the least little bit crazy. Her brother has gone to Bright River to reconcile with her."

He is stunned. "What are you saying?"

"Only that Ben has gone to be with his sister, to reunite with her, to see her child, and to find out who he is – at last..." Caroline Taylor lets out a quivering sigh. "I... I can't believe that you of all people should show up here at this time. Look at you, a Taylor through and through. There is a resemblance between you and Ben, and Tressa too, but you would know that…"

Suddenly, she is walking away with the light and Luke, numb with cold and shock, is left standing in the dark.

"Follow me, young man. May I call you Luke? I knew your father once, a very long time ago…"

He obeys and follows the disappearing light. He finds himself in a spacious living room warmed by a huge fire.

"Warm yourself," Caroline Taylor says. "Please, Luke. Warm yourself; you look half frozen."

He does what she tells him and the flames gradually restore him.

"Where is your husband?" he asks.

"I wish I knew. Came to tell him what you think of him, didn't you? Tressa's honor," she laughs weakly. "You do this on behalf of Mart, your friend… There is nothing you can say that will make any difference to Richard. He is implacable. His mind can't be changed. Not ever. His own son betrayed him and he will not forgive him, well, that's how Richard sees it. But Ben is only doing what he should be doing. A shame you are here and not there where he can meet you. It would help him to understand. You are something of a hero in Tressa's eyes and Ben resents it completely, but that would have changed, if he had met you. I can tell by looking at you what kind of man you are. Morgan's son. And Ethan's, too."

"You knew Ethan?"

Caroline Taylor nods. She sits herself in a chair near the hearth. "I suppose Ethan helped Sara raise you."

He feels himself bristling. "I don't want to discuss this with you; this conversation is to be had with Tressa's father."

"You can't even bring yourself to call him your uncle." Then she looks away into the flames; her thin pale features disturb him. She is unwell, he can see that now and his anger subsides. "No matter. At present I don't even particularly want to call him my husband. He refuses to come home. It started when Ben left. But…"

"But?" he prompts gently.

"Ben must come back, only I can't get him to…"

He frowns. "You're not making sense, M'am."

"I tried and I tried. I even offered Richard's forgiveness, something Richard would never do himself, as a bribe, anything to make Ben think of coming back. But every reply he says the same thing; he can't come home, and investigate Donnelly... oh!"

"M'am, what is it?"

Tears fall out of her eyes and she shakes. "I can't do that, he doesn't understand. I can't tell his father, at least I think I can't and... and I'm not sure that the stranger was this Donnelly but in my heart my instincts are telling me he was and I'm not supposed to tell anyone... oh!"

"Again, M'am, you are not making any sense."

"I'm sorry, I've been this way for days, and I don't know what to do. Richard won't come home, I have no one to talk to, and no one I can trust. What am I to do?"

He sits in the chair opposite her. He can't believe he's going to do this, but she is Tressa's mother and it's clear that whatever his no-good uncle is, this woman is as much a victim of it as everyone else in the family. "Start at the beginning."

"No, no, I can't tell anyone, he made that perfectly clear..."

"Who?"

"The stranger."

"Apart from this stranger, M'am, have you noticed anything else peculiar, are you being watched by anyone, or followed, received unusual mail...?"

She shakes her head and then lets out a soft cry. "I'm terrified. I don't leave the house. And I don't know what to do. I told Richard I wouldn't leave him, but I should go to Ben..."

"M'am, you gotta start at the beginning; the very beginning and don't leave anything out."

Her gaunt eyes stare at him. "You will help me?"

"I'll listen to you," he says.

With a frail smile she murmurs, "Tressa was right about you, Luke. And I think you are my miracle."

Caroline

She is bamboozled by the speed with which this young man Luke works.

Once she has told her story, beginning with Loren Bodecker's admittance to the board of Aurora, Luke's interest and understanding are acute, even to the point of being off-putting, but he encourages her every step of the way, frequently asks questions and is not satisfied until she is almost hoarse and utterly fatigued.

Then he announces that they are leaving Omaha for Cheyenne on the early train tomorrow morning in order to tell the sheriff there the whole story – again.

She wilts.

"No time for that, M'am," he says in his charming drawl, with a twinkle in his mischievous blue eyes. "No can't or maybe about it, and you're packing right now and coming with me to my hotel. You ain't staying another night alone in this house... you need a good night's sleep."

"But what about Richard? I can't leave him..."

"You can and you're going to. Once you tell Cliff everything..."

"Cliff?"

"Cliff Ryan. The sheriff in Cheyenne. Once you tell him everything, I'm taking you to Bright River and Tressa and that son of yours."

"He is your cousin, young man, same as Tressa," she tells him, trying to still her quivering bottom lip.

"Yes, M'am," he says obligingly.

They consider one another. She is unsure how she presents to

227

him, probably like a timid mouse, but she likes him, for in spite of his high-handed tactics, he is not a bully, nor is he unkind, just utterly determined. And in these circumstances is that such a bad thing?

"You have to understand, M'am, that what is going on here is very serious. It's dangerous and deadly. Look, I just came from Cheyenne; I was on my way to St Louis on a very important errand. But I can't turn my back on what's going on here. My family and yours and the Keatons are more than likely headed for trouble. Now I don't know who this feller is who terrorized you, but I do know from good friends in Cheyenne that Loren Bodecker spells trouble. So if this Donnelly character is a partner of Loren Bodecker and your son keeps on begging you to investigate him, then we got a whole lot of pieces to a puzzle that need putting together and we need to get back to Cheyenne. And I'm figuring you'd rather be with your children and your grandson than here alone waiting for your husband to get over his disappointment."

Grandson… her heart quickens. Every beat of her heart since the little boy's birth has equated to a powerful longing to see him and hold him, so powerful that…

Luke is quiet, half-smiling at her.

"You know exactly what to say, don't you?" she says.

His smile broadens. "Yes, M'am. Not too much luggage."

Once she concedes, he moves quickly, going about the house, dousing the fire, securing every lock while she packs her bags. He even brings them down for her.

"Does your husband keep any papers relating to the company in the house?" he asks as he places her luggage by the front door.

"Yes, some, in his study, but anything to do with Mr Bodecker is probably all at the office," she tells him. "Besides, I couldn't let you take anything like that with us, Luke, I just couldn't. Think of the position it would place Richard in."

Luke sighs but defers to her wishes; perhaps he thinks she has done all that can be expected of her, and he'd be right; leaving Richard after she swore she wouldn't is pain enough.

After she writes a note of explanation for Richard, placing it on the hall table, they leave the house in darkness.

She doesn't look back.

"Everything will be all right, M'am," Luke says gently as they step out on to the sidewalk.

There is a cab waiting. The evening air is freezing and she tightens her fur stole around her throat.

Once they are seated in the cab, he instructs the driver to proceed to his hotel, and then apologizes for bringing her out in the cold.

"I don't mind the cold, but I am taking a risk trusting you."

"I know. And I ain't doing nearly what I thought I came to do." The young man gives her a sideways glance. "Don't suppose you know where your husband is?"

"Is he in danger, do you think?"

Luke shrugs. "Is Loren Bodecker still here in town?"

"Well, he was a couple of days ago; I haven't seen Richard in all that time so I don't know."

"This is a big town and it's mighty cold to go looking for people who don't want to be found, but once I got you settled in at the hotel, M'am, I'll be looking for your husband or Loren Bodecker or this Donnelly."

She turns to him. "No. The stranger said…"

"I know he scared you, and it's hard. But I'm hoping you have some idea of where your husband might be, or Bodecker."

She feels the cold and fatigue beginning to rob her of her ability to think clearly. She knows where Richard would be, but she wants more time to think before revealing it. "I'll think about it when we reach this hotel of yours. And if I am able to give you some idea of their whereabouts, do you think it wise to confront Bodecker by yourself?"

"I know that's logical, but experience has taught me that there are other ways of flushing out the snakes from the woodpile."

"My husband is not a snake, young man," she protests.

"I've waited a lot of years to tell your husband what I think of him, I can wait a little longer. It's Bodecker I want, M'am. Your husband is just the means to find him."

She stares hard at him. Men, even young ones, can be so ruthless at times. At least he's honest. "What if he hurts Richard, or that stranger does?"

"That's a thought we have to consider when we get to the hotel, but I reckon if your husband is as smart as he thinks he is, he'll protect himself."

"But not me, you're inferring."

"I never said that."

She suspects it is hard for anyone to deny him what he really wants.

"Luke?"

"Yes, M'am?"

"I think you should call me Caroline."

A pause; she glimpses a wry grin. "Yes, M'am."

Luke

After Caroline has three strong cups of tea and some supper she remembers where her husband might be staying – in a businessmen's club not far from their hotel. As for Bodecker's accommodation, she remembers her husband mentioning the Paxton Hotel – he might be there. Luke visits the club first. Oak paneling, leather upholstery and the wafting aroma of aged and fresh cigar smoke. He inquires after Richard Taylor at the reception desk.

"Mr Taylor cannot be disturbed, sir, but if you care to leave a message, I will see that he receives it."

"When will Mr Taylor be available?"

"Hard to say, sir."

Luke leaves, hoping the fool hasn't drunk himself into oblivion because his son did the manly thing.

If Richard Taylor's club is the rich businessman's retreat, then the Paxton is the rich businessman's hotel. In fact, anyone rich. Anyone elite. Anyone who's anyone. The Inter Ocean in Cheyenne couldn't quite match it; Jennifer's hotel in San Francisco could.

He ain't dressed to impress anyone in this establishment, and when he walks in every head turns and with sour expressions confirm it. If he asks for Loren Bodecker now he's likely to get thrown out. Not that he couldn't pass for a rich businessman if he were following the correct dress code… he's just running out of time to get a shave and a hair cut and find some fancy clothes.

There is only one clerk at the reception desk. From his hiding place behind a pair of wide, fancy marble columns, he spies the hotel register perched high on the counter.

Now, to get a look…

He observes the lobby for several minutes for ideas. Most guests are men with their wives, but one larger group contains a very bored looking boy of about eight or nine standing on the glittering train of his mother's dress. He's all dressed up and fancy, and not liking it. She pushes him off with a stern word and returns to her grown up conversation; the kid rolls his eyes and wanders away. Luke stalks him between more columns until he's close enough to get his attention.

"Psst!"

The kid looks around and frowns suspiciously. Luke nods at him and then holds up a quarter. The kid shakes his blond head. Luke digs out another quarter. The kid looks mildly interested. Luke hooks his finger and beckons him over. The kid shrugs and wanders across.

"Got a job for you," Luke whispers.

"Don't do jobs for strangers for less than a dollar."

"That the going rate where you come from?" Luke digs into his pocket for two more quarters he knows are there.

"Sure it is," says the kid and then his eyes light up when Luke puts four quarters into the palm of his sweaty little hand. "What do you want me to do?"

"See that huge book over there on the counter, I need to take a good look at it without the clerk seeing me."

"Oh, I get it. A diversion. Why didn't you say? They're my specialty. Leave it to me, mister."

"How old are you?"

"Ten."

Before Luke can give any further instructions, the kid takes off. He rushes up to his mother and starts pulling on her dress.

"I'm hungry, I'm thirsty, I'm hungry, I'm thirsty…"

As his mother attempts to deal with the situation, the kid races off again running around the lobby, causing more fuss than a wounded bear, and accidentally on purpose upturning a huge arrangement of flowers. The fancy vase is smashed, water streams everywhere and the blooms founder in a tragic mess.

"Oh, Roger, how could you… after I got special permission for you to come..." The kid's mother is distraught; Luke almost feels sorry for her. Roger's far too good at this.

While Roger gets his comeuppance, the register clerk swings into action and leaves his post. Luke springs across the lobby, ducks behind the counter, reaches up for the register and pulls it down on the floor with him, after which he takes a moment to catch his breath. Then he slides his finger down the page until the name Loren Bodecker appears. Room 204. Donnelly's name appears one line below. Room 205. He reaches up and slides the book back into place on top of the counter.

A voice says, "Oh, you there, we have a reservation..."

Luke bobs up. A handsome, well-dressed couple stare at him wide-eyed. "Er, sorry, I'm kitchen staff... Someone will be with you soon." He ducks through the door behind the counter and heads for the staff area. Sure enough, he soon locates the service halls for the hotel. Over one of these is a sign, Guest Rooms. After a short distance it opens into a stairwell. He takes it two at a time until he's on the second floor. Through another door and he's in the hall outside room 201. As he creeps towards room 204, he hears the whir and clunk of the nearby elevator. As the doors are pulled back by the elevator attendant, two men dressed in evening clothes step out. He presses himself back and as far out of sight as possible. Not so far, however, that he risks losing the opportunity to identify them. He realizes he only knows Loren Bodecker by the sketch he drew from Ethan's description in his file; he has never seen the man in person. However, of the two heading for rooms further up the hall, one does look vaguely familiar.

"What news of Cheyenne?" says the familiar of the two.

"You ain't gonna like it," says the other. Then they move out of hearing range.

He watches; they stop at room 204. The familiar man unlocks his door and they disappear inside the room. He creeps up further, past the elevator, towards room 204. He presses himself against the wall and takes a peak at the door beside him. His suspicion is confirmed; the arrogant bastards haven't closed it; it sits ajar with a useful crack big enough for his ear. Already he can hear muffled voices but if he wants to hear properly, he's gonna have to take a bigger risk.

Cadie McClements

Cadie stands close to Burt in the elevator, knowing he don't like it, that she bothers him, but finding that's the reason why it's so much fun. He keeps his eyes front; she bats her lashes. Burt squares his brocaded and lapelled shoulders dutifully; she twists the fringed braid around her finger. He swats her like a bug.

"Aw, Burt, you ain't being nice."

"Ain't my job to be nice to the likes of you. You got yourself plenty of nice in room 204."

She removes her finger from his braid and smoothes her dress over her curves. "Do you like my new dress?"

"Real nice," he says through his teeth.

"I gotta look the part," she says and primps her hair. Bodecker is the kind who decides in a glance if he likes the look of a girl. He sent her away once before and told her to take a bath. She had her bath tonight.

"You shouldn't be using the elevator," Burt complains.

"Aw, don't get your gold brocades in a knot… there was some kinda commotion in the lobby, you must've seen it… no one noticed me. Thought I'd give myself a treat and use the elevator; the stairs make me outa breath."

Burt lets her out on the second floor; she pouts him a farewell, which he ignores and closes the doors almost before she steps out.

She saunters up the hall to room 204. The door is ajar. She hesitates and stands with her ear at the crack, listening to the voices coming from inside. She gives her dress a final smooth, takes a deep breath, and eases the door open; a room of palace-like proportions fills her eyes. Dazzles her. Intoxicates her senses. Two men are standing far across the room by the window and they don't even see her. Instead some small movement on her left catches her eye; she does a double-take. Another man is hiding behind a large armchair not far from the door. He's young, with the loveliest bluest eyes she ever saw. His legs are drawn up to his chest, so he fits behind the chair. He puts a finger to his lips to keep her silent. She sends him a look of reproach. He grins and winks. She raises one eyebrow at him. He taps his finger against his lips to remind her to be quiet. She would much rather be bedding him than the fat old galoot by the window.

"You're late," a voice booms.

She looks up to see her rich client glaring at her from across the huge room. "Sorry."

"What are you doing there?" he demands and moves into the center of the room.

"The door was open so I just walked in..."

"Sit down in that chair until my business is concluded."

Big Bully. Bet Mr Blue Eyes wouldn't treat her like this.

"Sure, honey," she grins, "just pretend I ain't even here."

The other man, who has a hard-looking face, joins him in the middle of the room. They pour brandy, smoke cigars and talk until she is stifling yawns. All the time Mr Blue Eyes with a Wink is crouched behind her chair, like a mouse. The hard-faced one talks about a woman who's 'holed up in her house and too scared leave', about her son 'who don't seem to be taking any notice of her pleas to come home' and someone called Maverick 'who can't get the job done' and whose 'boys are in the lockup'.

Her client blows his lid. "Are they talking, Donnelly? They better not be talking..."

"Relax," says the man Donnelly. When someone says 'relax' like that, they really mean 'I'm lying and it's time to panic'.

She begins to take notice.

Donnelly digs himself deeper, saying, "I got someone to clean up the mess."

"A mess you made," Bodecker says through clenched teeth. "Get Tucker off the case. He'll never handle it. What's Dillon doing?"

Donnelly shrugs. "How should I know, he's your man."

"I want Maverick to stay out of Cheyenne from now on, do you understand? Ryan probably knows more about the whole operation than you do by now." Bodecker steps real close to Donnelly and stares him in the eyes. "You're making mistakes, Donnelly, bad ones. I don't want any more, do you hear me? You are to do *nothing* unless it's what I tell you, you got that?"

Donnelly glares back through a cloud of cigar smoke. "I don't appreciate being spoken to like that, Loren. It ain't productive. Now, what do we do about Taylor?"

Bodecker grunts. "Which one? Father or son?"

"I think papa's got enough on his plate thinking his kid's run out on him. Ain't he happy with the way things are progressing with the board?"

"Yeah, he's happy about that part, so I'm not expecting any problems with him."

"His kid's probably in Bright River by now."

She wonders where Bright River is; it sounds nice, a nice river, or even maybe a town. A town called Bright River would have to be a good place…

"Where's his cousin?"

"Still in San Francisco. Haven't seen hide or hair of him."

"So that at least is going to plan."

Donnelly shrugs again; he starts pulling at his collar and tie.

"Still think we should've made our move sooner."

Bodecker puffs his cigar and shakes his head. "No. I wanted the Alliance to feel comfortable again. Besides, I had other projects to attend to. Keaton and Benchley should be ripe for the picking any day now. When young Ben comes a-calling, should take their minds right off the job that Luke Taylor left them to do all on their own. Is Maverick set to follow Ben to Bright River?"

"There's a Maverick set aside just for him," Donnelly says.

"No one can say he wasn't warned. His own mother warned him." Both men laugh. "You know, Taylor and Keaton should have got hired guns last year when they had the chance."

"What about Faraday and Ryan?" Donnelly asks.

"As long as they don't know who Maverick is, there won't be a problem. And that's your look-out, Donnelly; see it's taken care of. Get back to Cheyenne and tell Dillon I said he's to take care of this Swinton Carter, but no Maverick."

"We should have used Maverick against the Alliance two years ago; it'd be all over by now. Parsons was an expensive waste of time, and you thinking that him knowing the Keatons and Taylors so well would be a good strategic move was a mistake." Donnelly, jigging his collar, sounds miserable; but Bodecker sounds mean...

"Parsons is dying of pneumonia; he won't last long."

"Don't change anything," Donnelly points out.

"Quit grumbling and get to work. And no matter what any of those freakin' papers print about me, I won't be setting foot in Cheyenne. Like I said, Dillon can fix it."

The two men part and Donnelly leaves, slamming the door behind him; she jumps and then her heart skips a beat as Bodecker comes towards her. "Okay, you, in there..." He indicates the bedroom off to the right. She gets up, fearful of the look of power in the man's eyes, wondering about the mouse behind the chair. "Move," he barks. And she must worry about herself now. He undresses her himself with his fat fingers; in bed he's rough, his large body swamping hers. He jabs himself inside her so hard she lets out a scream; he laughs, grabs her hair and pulls back her head. He sticks his cigar soaked tongue into her mouth and grinds her lips. He thrusts with a stabbing motion, accompanied by thudding grunts, his hand around her neck, her body pinned. When he's done he rolls off her, and she lies there breathing hard, dazed, uncertain and sore, her mouth filled with the taste of blood.

"You'll do," he says with a cruel laugh. Then he lights a cigar. A short time later he falls asleep; she removes the smoking cigar from his fat fingers and butts it in the glass dish on the nightstand. Still shaking, she goes to the bathroom and takes care of herself; he's made her bleed. Her stomach churns and turns sicklish. And she bathed for this... She dresses as fast as her trembling hands will allow, takes the money he owes her from his money clip, plus a generous bonus for the rough handling, and tiptoes away.

A glimpse behind the chair. The mouse is gone.

Caroline

Aboard the UP out of Omaha

For Caroline the pre-dawn departure on a Sunday is bad enough, but when the young man makes them travel in the emigrant car when there is sure to be room in the first-class car, she must complain. He smiles, and corrects her... *this is second-class, Caroline,* and says he understands, but this is how it must be... their accommodations seem like emigrant car to her: the seats are wooden and uncomfortable, crowded with passengers and their belongings, cloying with odors, men smoking, and all of them suffocating because the windows are shut tight against the cold, all compounded by noise... before long her head is aching. And Luke made her dress down: no furs, no finery, no jewelry. She feels crude and plain, just like the car she's traveling in. Even after some time spent imagining her precious grandson and how divine it will feel to hold him in her arms, and dwelling upon how good it will be to be with her beautiful Tressa again, the discomfort of their traveling arrangements must be repined. Quietly, she declares her boredom.

He produces a newspaper and hands it to her.

Meanwhile, he reads another, avidly.

She would give anything for a cup of tea; he reaches into his leather saddlebags and produces a flask of water. How is she to survive this long trek across Nebraska on a flask of water? *All these people will be*, he tells her with another of those winning smiles. And food? His saddlebags contain apples, nuts, dried fruit and two small loaves of bread. And is the bread fresh? *Picked up last night,* he winks. She has seen street urchins who wink and grin like that.

238

"I thought you lived on a ranch once," he remarks.

"Don't be cheeky... and that was a very long time ago."

He chuckles and returns to his newspaper.

Several hours out of Omaha, a young blonde girl, small, thin and almost pretty, trying to look older than she really is, defies the incessant rocking of the train and comes up to them.

"I just realized it's you," she says to Luke.

He looks up from his newspaper. "What are you doing here?"

"I came into some money and I'm gonna find a place called Bright River. Ain't that a pretty name? Bright River..."

"So you did all right then, last night," he murmurs with a strained expression on his face.

The girl's eyes sparkle and she simpers a little. "Sure."

"I'm happy for you. Now get lost and don't talk to me again."

"You know, you were much nicer when you were hunched up like a mouse and winking at me from behind that old chair."

Caroline can't believe her ears.

"You heard," he says harshly. "I don't want to see you again."

The girl clicks her tongue defiantly. "I got enough to eat in that fancy dining car." And with her chin in the air she wanders off, her hips rocking with the train.

He watches her momentarily and then disappears behind his newspaper.

"I don't suppose, young man, there is any point in asking who that girl is," Caroline murmurs.

"Whatever your mind is thinking, M'am," says the newspaper beside her, "she's that, but not mine."

"Well, I'm glad. Will they even let her into the dining car?

"I don't know, and I don't care..."

Then, suddenly, Luke crushes the newspaper to his knees and she is staring straight into his dark blue eyes.

"What is it?" she breathes.

"This girl being on this train, it could be trouble, Caroline. Just the kind of bad luck I feared might find us and was trying to avoid."

"Bad luck? Well, if you wanted to avoid bad luck we should

have travelled first-class, worn proper clothes and eaten proper food..."

"She's Bodecker's whore and if she's run away he might come looking for her. She overheard them talking."

"Oh, dear. And how does she know you?"

"We kinda ran into each other while I was investigating last night."

"Oh," she says, lowering her eyes, "I see."

"No, you don't," he says. "I told you, she's not mine. We got to agree now that getting to Cheyenne is more important than any-thing else."

She raises her eyes again. His blue ones are so earnest and so desperate she finds herself nodding. "If anything happens to you, I'm to go directly to your sheriff."

Luke nods. "Cliff Ryan."

"Yes, I remember."

"These men we're dealing with are powerful and dangerous. We don't know who we can trust. What connections they might have. This is important. If anything happens, Caroline, I don't mind if you disown me, lie about me, betray me. Just get to Cheyenne. And," he says and swallows, "I might have to do the same about you. Are you prepared for that?"

No one has ever asked her to exercise heroism before... at least not for a very long time.

"I understand what's at stake. But I'm afraid you have had more practice than I."

A smile from him is truly heartening, she decides as she soaks one up. As tense as he is, that smile says he has faith in her, and that is worth a thousand words.

Cliff

Cliff could probably count on the fingers of one hand the number of times he's spent Sunday morning in Church – any church – since he'd come to Cheyenne.

Maybe it's not something a prominent citizen should be proud of; it's just the way things are. Mac was always saying he didn't know how Cliff got away with it...

He casts his eye around St John the Baptist Catholic Church. From the outside it cuts a fairly modest architectural figure, large brick rectangle and steeply pitched roof with a cross and spire like most Catholic churches. Internally, it seats around three hundred people. The interior arrangements are candy for the eyes, with stained-glass windows scattering rainbows of color across the altar, which is dressed with flowers, a starched white cloth trimmed with lace, tall ornate candle sticks with lit candles and statues of angels on each end. In the middle of the altar is the tabernacle, covered with green satin cloth embroidered with gold thread.

A huge crucifix is affixed on the wall above the altar. Colorfully painted statues of various saints on small stone plinths line the walls. A small organ, aloft, pumps out tunes to accompany the choir who sings in Latin. Father Francis Nugent, attired in a green tunic to match the tabernacle, spends a good deal of time at the altar, his back to his congregation.

Cliff has been inside a number of times, but never for Mass (he's a Methodist after all). His Latin is rusty, but he doesn't mind having his recall of it stretched. Nugent's sermon is an eye opener; *that* is delivered in plain old English in a busy style for which the man is renowned. He acquired land, built a parochial school and manned it with the Sisters of the Holy Child Jesus before anyone knew what was happening. And his congregation was growing. Around one hundred and thirty pupils attended the school, and Nugent was in the mood for additions. Not only did the man have vision, he got things done. And Cliff wouldn't bet on the shrewd man not noticing him sitting on the churchwarden's pew near the holy water in the shadow of a statue of St John just inside the church doors.

Much goes on that he does not understand. Mysterious things.

Things that the Methodists and the Congregationalists and the Episcopalians in general warn their children about. Things that happen when bells ring, things that the congregation can't actually see but perceive. It is beautiful yet frustrating, intimate yet distant, prayerful yet enigmatic, both intriguing and off-putting for someone whose parents thought he was a child who could do with some spiritual guidance and a Methodist church happened to be around the corner so he could walk himself to Sunday School.

For a sheriff, however, the parish notices are informative. Some parishioners are ill, some need help in various ways and two have died. Some families will hold fund raising activities and men are needed to make repairs on the church building.

And despite everything, there is only one reason he's there, a pathetic one-time Methodist attending Sunday Mass. At the vision before him of her attending to her prayer book, with tenderness about her face, the gloved hands held in prayerfulness, the rise of her shoulders as she takes a breath to pray to St Michael the Archangel, the frame of honey-colored hair around her face enclosed in her velvet hood, he momentarily forgets he is the sheriff. The organist applies her feet to the pedals, and plays a resounding melody by which to exit. The congregation stirs; at this point he wishes he *wasn't* the sheriff.

Parishioners start to leave, dipping their fingertips into the holy water by the door and making the Sign of the Cross. Cliff knows or is familiar with a great many of these folk; they are the people he's sworn to serve and protect. However, there are a few that are not familiar and he scrutinizes them from the shadows.

Emma kneels for several moments more and is one of the last to leave (other people near the back were among the first); when she finally rises from the pew and joins the line, he has given all those unfamiliar types a tick of approval. He moves casually out of shadow and towards the door; the last of the parishioners see him and nod politely. Emma comes his way, her face peaceful, her eyes prayerful, and all that exuberance, that competitive spirit at rest. For someone like Emma this House would be one of tranquility and no wonder she stays as long as possible. When she finally sees him, some of that peace falls on him, and although her eyes widen with surprise, there is a smile in their golden light.

"I never picked you for a Catholic," she whispers.

"Because I'm ruthless and tell lies?" he whispers back.

"No," she says. "Because you don't feel guilty about it."

"I'm going to hell, aren't I?"

"While there's life there's hope."

When they step outside into the pale sunshine, the parishioners have broken into clusters around which children of various ages are chasing one another. Mae Jewell, looking very smart in her Sunday hat, appears at Emma's side.

"Miss Roberts, I just had to come and tell you, I've started on your hat. I'm just so excited about it. It will be one of my best. And ready on Wednesday."

"Thank you, Mrs Jewell. That's sounds perfect. Good day."

"Good day." Mae gives him a bewildered glance. "Sheriff…"

"Mae." As they watch her join one of the clusters, he says, "If that hat is mink I'll pay half."

"That seems fair. And the muff?"

"What muff?"

"The black mink muff that matches the black mink hat."

"*Black* mink. Expensive taste…" He fleetingly catches her eye. "You can't look at me, can you?"

"I have no need to look at you."

A stream of children circle them Indian style for a few moments until the one being chased breaks away and the rest follow.

Grinning, on the inside at least, he says, "How much?"

"May we change the subject?"

"Well..."

At that moment, Father Nugent, now in black cassock, comes flying around his church, his purposeful strides crunching over pebbles and slush. He heads straight for them.

"Sheriff Cliff Ryan, this is indeed a pleasure, but you'll pardon me for wondering if something's the matter."

Nugent offers his hand and Cliff grabs it. They shake, the joke hovering on the frosty air.

"Catholic humor, Father?"

"You're a good lad, then, no offence taken."

"Of course not, Father. Have you met Miss Roberts?"

"I don't believe I've had the pleasure. Father Francis Nugent at your service," he says. "New in town?"

Emma replies, "Yes, Father. I am a reporter here on assignment with the Tribune."

"Ah, the Tribune... Fine. Well, you're very welcome. Anything you need, you just have to ask. Now, Sheriff, is there not something the matter? Perhaps you might like to come into the house."

"That won't be necessary, Father. I'm doing my job while we speak, there's no need for anything else."

Nugent's glance slips to Emma. "Ah, you're the young woman. I had heard, you know. But I hadn't got the details. A dreadful lot of people go to God in this weather and a priest can find himself busier than he'd like. Well, if there's anything I can do, Sheriff..."

"I'll let you know, Father."

Nugent places his hands on the small of his back in a gesture of relief. "Fine, then. Well, I'd better see to the others. Good day to you, both. Nice to have met you, Miss Roberts. What did you say is your Christian name?"

"Emmaline," she says softly.

Nugent thinks, then shakes his head. "No, I can't recall that being the name of a saint."

"Oh, that's because my..." She stops abruptly. "Well, it's a long story, Father. My second name is Elizabeth."

"Ah, a fine name that."

"After my mother."

"Just as it should be. And I'm hoping your confirmation name, Emmaline Elizabeth, would be Mary."

"Close," she says. "Eppy."

"Eppy?" Nugent has a merry chuckle to himself. "Neither can I seem to recall a St Eppy. You know, young lady, I'm supposing that you come from a very interesting family. We must have a chat soon. Well, goodbye it is for now though. Take care, children."

When he's some distance away, in the midst of a cluster of women, Cliff exchanges glances with Emma. "Eppy... seriously?"

"Short for Euphemia, fourth century martyr."

"A dare?"

"Your point?"

"Only that I admire your derring-do. Well, Emmaline Elizabeth Eppy Roberts, I'd better escort you to wherever you're going next."

"What's happened?" she asks rather dramatically. "And don't think you have to spare me."

"I saw the way you looked in church. No one should be allowed to take that away from you."

"You were watching me... guarding me in *church*?"

He answers her with silence, his gaze steady.

Eventually, her indignation is resigned with a graceful sigh, and she murmurs, "It's getting cold and I'm hungry."

"So am I. Let's eat something."

"Well, Nan Morris has kept breakfast for me."

"You haven't eaten at all?"

She shakes her head, shrugs lightly. "I was planning just to sit in her lovely kitchen and eat a huge bowl of oatmeal."

"And coffee?" he asks.

"Yes. There's always plenty of coffee. Let's go, before I starting gnawing on my arm."

And they set off.

"Not sure you should be doing all this walking on an empty stomach in this cold weather," he says.

"It's hardly any distance. Anyway, you walked here."

"Walking keeps me fit. Besides I've eaten."

They walk in silence for a bit, while he keeps his eyes peeled, until she says, "Being sheriff is a very physical occupation for you, isn't it, Mr Ryan?"

"Are you implying that I can't keep still?"

"I'm merely trying to understand you."

"If I was doing Cam's job I wouldn't get to guard a fascinating female reporter and keep her from harm. I'd be stuck at home, with my law books."

He feels her eyes on him; he keeps his own on the street.

Other men must have told her she is fascinating... all right, he's flirting with her, or at least he wants to; and it's not professional, but it's Sunday.

"Look, you can't spend your precious time guarding me, it's not right," she declares.

Fascinating, and intense. Well, she hasn't eaten...

"Besides, I need to do things and be places. And so do you."

"Be places?" he queries. Now what's she up to...

"The requirements of our jobs," she explains. "I think it's time you just let go and let God... you don't believe that do you?"

"Believe? Believe what?"

"That God would protect me."

"Emma..."

"Protect you. And the town."

"Emma, you're too hard on me."

She gives him a look of remorse. "I'm sorry. I didn't mean to be."

They walk on in strained silence. She is absolutely right about one thing. He has to give this caper away because he has a complex and dangerous job to do and she has hers.

"My house," he murmurs as they reach it.

"I know," she says, "I pass it every day."

"If anything happens to you..." he says as they walk on towards Nan Morris' house.

"You can keep the black mink hat and muff," she says quickly. "They're half yours anyway."

They don't speak again until they are strolling up Nan Morris' front path. Nan Morris' cat jumps out, meows, and winds itself in a friendly manner around his leg. Emma starts laughing.

"I won't tell anyone that Cheyenne's big tough sheriff is loved by animals." She bends down and picks up the cat; she strokes it and pets it and makes it look like the most natural thing in the world. "I like cats… not quite as much as dogs."

Despite what she thinks about fur, it suits her.

"Go inside, Emma," he says, trying to be a big tough sheriff.

She seems surprised and says, "You have to have coffee."

"I thought you were wanting to be rid of me."

Her golden eyes intriguingly resemble those of the cat in her arms. The animal blinks lazily in his direction.

"I thought I was showing you some hospitality. What I said before, I…"

"Then it would be rude of me not to accept."

She frowns and says, "Then, you will have coffee…"

"Lead on," he smiles.

After a moment her frown dissolves, her eyes sparkle and she informs him, "You are the bossiest person I have ever met."

Hardly true, but he figures not many people ever get the better of her; he just happens to be one.

Nan Morris' kitchen is deserted, although the large work table in the center of the room is partially covered with a cornucopia of unprepared vegetables and a joint of meat waiting for the oven.

"Sunday dinner," Emma murmurs.

They hang their things on a rack by the back door; he notices Emma giving his silver star a second look as she invites him to sit at the other end of the table.

She checks the coffee pot on the stove. "Mm. Fresh coffee…"

Before long he has a steaming cup of it in front of him; he takes his eyes off her for a few moments to sugar it. She is busy now with the oatmeal Nan Morris left to keep warm on the stove.

"I never understand why people don't incorporate more cream into their oatmeal," she says, pouring a river of it into the pot and stirring with smooth strokes. "Would you like some?"

"No, I…"

"Come and taste it, it's good and creamy. I know you'll want some, and I couldn't possibly eat all of this."

She seems oblivious to how lovely she is; everything about the way she looks would give a person the impression she cares about her appearance a great deal. But he watches her work, and there is not one affected, self-conscious bone in her body.

"Are you a domesticated female reporter?" he asks, crossing the floor to taste her creamy oatmeal.

"Not particularly. You do have to keep yourself alive..." She dips a spoon into the oatmeal and holds it up to him. "Taste."

"It's hot..."

"Well, of course it's hot. Oatmeal should be hot. Blow on it."

He frowns, and blows, while she giggles. It's the giggle that does it. He doesn't just take the spoon, but her whole soft, warm hand with it and guides the oatmeal into his mouth. He meets her eyes as he slowly withdraws the spoon, savoring his mouthful, and it's surprisingly very good. Okay, now he's flirting with her, downright unashamedly; her expression reveals that she knows it.

He releases her hand, smiling into her uncertain eyes.

"Is there another bowl?" he asks.

She looks away, her cheeks pink. "Yes... of course."

While they eat it, he asks, "This morning in church, the whole service seemed complicated. Do you understand it?"

"I know the idea of it, yes. Understanding? Well..."

"And the Latin..."

"You might have noticed my missal..."

She had put her small prayer book on the hall table.

"...it contains the Latin as well as the English translation."

"But if the Mass is anything to go by, it must be difficult being a Catholic."

"Is this curiosity genuine, or are you looking for entertainment?"

"You looked peaceful, like you had left the worries of the world outside the doors of the church."

"Oh," she murmurs, "you are genuine."

"I can be – surprised?"

"I'm not going to answer that."

He laughs softly. "Since it's so difficult, why pursue it?"

"There is some prejudice, but it's not so hard. Like any religion, it can be as challenging as you want it to be."

Good answer. An intriguing mixture of reason and faith.

And it goes straight to his heart, like an arrow. Something inside him yearns for her to do it again. Touch him that way, deep inside his spirit.

"It makes you happy." He pushes his empty bowl aside.

"It keeps me on the straight and narrow," she says, utterly pragmatic now. "And I need that."

"And that doesn't make you happy?"

"It promises happiness," she says more thoughtfully this time.

"In this life?"

"I don't know. I guess. Definitely the next."

"Eternity."

"What an extraordinary word. I've always believed that from the moment a human being is conceived there is a promise."

"A promise?"

"It probably sounds silly to you that I believe eternity is not reserved for after the end of the world. I mean, if eternity has no end, then why should it have a beginning? And why wouldn't our own personal eternity begin with our earthly life?"

"No... not silly." It's not that he never wanted to think about it, he was never sure where to begin, how to start. "No time limitations back or front, I get that..."

"It's just that heaven is meant to be perfectly happy eternity, not the kind of half and half attempts at being happy we endure in our earthly life."

"It's often argued that everyone's just trying to be happy. I think I read somewhere that all men... amend to all *people*..." he says and receives an approving smile, "...are endowed by their creator with certain unalienable rights..."

"Life, liberty and the pursuit of happiness."

He smiles back.

"So... so how do *you* find happiness?" she asks.

"I don't... I haven't... found that kind as yet."

"But you have hope, don't you?"

"That's your secret," he says. "Hope."

"You hope to fulfill your destiny, don't you?"

"My destiny?" he grunts. "Is it all planned out for me, or do I have some say in it?"

"As far as I can determine, eternal reward is our destiny – the promise; but how we get there is up to us. We map out our lives by the decisions we make."

"Not strictly governed by the laws of providence?"

"You make it sound like Newton's law."

"From my experience, religion does not normally promote independence of belief, or even thought."

"As an institution, I suppose you're right. Yes, a church is a collective. But as individuals, faith and reason go hand in hand. We must choose; it should be personal."

"I think you are unusual. People prefer the collective. It's easier."

"If we say that our destiny is heaven because of the promise made to us, then we stay focused on that end."

"What if you don't believe in heaven, what happens then?"

Her eyes sparkle. "It's still there, whether you believe it or not."

"Ah," he says, and is spellbound by her gentle laughter.

"What have you heard about Catholics?" she asks.

"You have very strict rules," he says.

"That was polite, I'm sure."

"I am a guest after all."

She smiles. "Rest assured, beauty and mystery, artistic pursuits, humor and having fun are not forbidden or forgotten. And what rules are you referring to? – because we tend to be exceptionally adept at bending them; in fact, we make it our life's work."

"You are…" he says and stops himself in time.

Beauty, she is beauty…

With a look of sweet puzzlement, she holds his gaze for several moments. "I am…" she prompts.

Fair maiden are the two words wandering around his mouth and settling wistfully on the tip of his tongue. Lines of poetry entwine his thoughts.

And then Nan Morris walks in.

"Well, good morning, Sheriff. How pleasant to see you. At least, I hope it's pleasant. Nothing wrong I hope."

He gets to his feet. "Morning, Nan. Nothing wrong. Miss Roberts offered me a cup of coffee in return for walking her safely home."

"Oh, splendid. You being so good to her an' all. And you had your oatmeal, Emmaline. I suppose you added a dash of cream," Nan Morris chunters.

Emma catches his eye. "It was excellent, thank you."

He smiles, rather liking that look in her eye. "Well, I had better be going..." he says, pushing in his chair. "Let you get on with your cooking."

Emma retrieves his coat, handling it with a familiarity in those lively fingers that spins a thread of warmth inside him.

"I'll see you to the door," she says politely.

He takes his coat. "Thank you. Good day, Nan."

"Sheriff..."

They leave Nan Morris and head for the front door.

"I'd hide in my room when Nan is looking for her cream later, if I were you," he says.

"Plausible deniability."

He shakes his head. "The proof is in the pudding, or rather the oatmeal."

"We ate all of it. I gave you a very large bowl..."

"Hide," he says into her laughing eyes.

They stroll to the top of the porch steps.

He pushes his arms into the sleeves of his coat, ignoring the twinge in his healing wound. "Will you do me a favor?"

"If I can."

"If I'm going to call you Emma, which obviously meets with your approval, you could call me Cliff."

"Interesting name. Is it short for something?"

"No fuss, easy to remember..."

"You didn't answer my question."

"Just Cliff. Thank you for your hospitality, Emma. I won't leave until you go inside."

"Very well." Her eyes tell him goodbye.

And he likes that a lot.

His smile tells her the same. As she turns and moves away, he catches the curl of her mouth. She steps insides and the door closes quietly behind her.

He can't stop himself from grinning as he negotiates the slush on Nan Morris' front path.

Ben

The river running through Bright River valley iced over during the night. The morning sun flares off it, the impact intensified by the thickest coat of snow he has ever seen in his life. And at the front desk of the town's snug Fortune Hotel comes the news that: *the road is impassable, unless you are an expert rider and know where you're going. Ah, but the sky's wide and clear and blue at last, the sun's fully shining and the Chinook is sure to find its way here any day now.*

Impatient and nervous, he must wait.

Bright River is more like a village than a town; the end of it is visible from the second story window of his room in the hotel. The few streets, piled high with snow, are deserted. The huge general store is closed for business after the roaring trade it did early yesterday afternoon when he and the stage rolled into town just ahead of the snowstorm; the store was crammed with people buying supplies and discussing the approaching weather, while the street was frantic with activity. Now the place looks like a painting entitled *Still Life of a Town*; even the smithy has his livery doors firmly shut. A whole day stretches in front of him with nothing to do but sit around and read old newspapers from the lobby of the small hotel. And probably help the townsfolk shovel snow…

Suddenly, from out of the deafening silence, the church bell tolls. It resonates into every corner of the landscape. And watching from the lobby window, he espies figures emerging and moving towards the church.

"The reverend delays his services an hour or two after a snow-storm; gives folks more of a chance… takes a while to get out your door and shovel the snow… after a real bad'un it can take days." The hotel owner is standing at Ben's shoulder peering where he is peering. "You'd be welcome, of course. Some folks don't let weather keep them from Sunday services."

The hotel owner, Andy Rigg, can't do enough for Ben since he discovered who Ben is. *Young Tressa Keaton's brother* was one thing, but *Luke's cousin* brought great delight; and he informed everyone within yelling distance. It's been a struggle to keep a low profile ever since.

"They come a real long way but the Keatons don't let a pile of snow keep them from Sunday services; John went and made himself a real fine cutter… you know, a sleigh," Rigg continues. "Though with the baby an' all your sister ain't likely to make it, but John and Amy Keaton hardly ever miss. Might even come today. Well, think I'll be gettin' over there myself. Comin', young feller?"

He nods, hastily collects his thick coat, scarf and gloves from his room while Rigg waits for him. He figures a short walk through thick snow is better than no walk, considering the ache and pains he's experiencing from one of the worst stage journeys of his life, although the scenery was something spectacular. Much of it was snow-blanketed prairie, vast and open, but then came mountains, valleys, forests and streams; no one could do justice with words to the beauty of this place. But then something must compensate the traveler for the discomfort of the journey.

And to think Tressa did this while she was expecting a child. Why should he complain?

By the time they get to the church at the other end of town, the woman who owns the general store and several other folk have joined them. Rigg keeps saying, *this here is Luke's cousin from Omaha*, and the townsfolk shake his hand.

The yard behind the church is a jumble of horses and sleighs. There is a view across the graveyard to the expanse beyond that should be painted.

Inside he encounters a small, simple wooden building packed with people, who in spite of their reverent silence are busily nodding and smiling warm-hearted greetings to one another. It seems to be some kind of unspoken register of who survived the snowstorm, of who is present and who is not.

Rigg points out a couple sitting four rows from the front.

"John and Amy Keaton," he whispers with a wink.

Ben finds a seat at the very back, while Rigg and the others disperse to take up their regular places.

The service is short. The reverend is cordial. A hymn, a scripture passage, a brief sermon, prayers, a few announcements, another hymn. Sufficient, if they or their horses waiting in the yard don't want to freeze.

From time to time he casts a curious eye over the Keatons, but all he can see is the back of John Keaton's broad shoulders and silvery head.

When the service is over, the townsfolk hold an impromptu town meeting. The reverend conducts it. They inform one another of damage, of injury, of help needed, of those who are not present. All in all, it seems that no one is in peril and all can be accounted for. John Keaton and his wife sit quietly throughout. The reverend adjourns the meeting and the church begins to empty.

During this time, he notices Rigg disclose his presence to the Keatons. It is probably for the best; his nervousness has been growing throughout the morning. How was he to tell them? And how would they react? These people love Tressa and they could very likely see him as a threat to her happiness and tell him to clear off. His inclination at this moment is to shrink against the back wall of the church rather than face them; but Taylors are not cowards.

Before long, the man with the silvery hair and broad shoulders, and the finest of light blue eyes, stands before him.

"I understand from Andy Rigg that you are Tressa's brother?"

Ben holds himself tall. "Yes. I'm Ben Taylor."

"John Keaton. Tressa's father-in-law." He holds out his hand.

Ben takes hold.

"Good. A strong grip. This is my wife Amy."

"Mrs Keaton," he says.

"Well, I'm not one for surprises, but you are a welcome one," she says. She's a small, pretty woman with dark gray eyes and a fair complexion. There is a gaunt shadow about her, however, that he is not mistaking for anything but abiding grief.

He clears his throat. "I'm welcome?"

Amy Keaton frowns. "Of course. All this long time Tressa has spoken of your coming one day. She has never given up hope of it. I think such faith should be rewarded. No matter what you might think, we don't pass judgment, ain't that right, John?"

John Keaton is still scrutinizing him. His wife elbows him and he grunts. "You know, son, you bear a remarkable resemblance to your cousin..."

"Oh, John, don't start that, as if the boy don't feel terrified enough."

"Well, I'm just saying."

Ben says, "I keep getting told that, Mr Keaton. Not ever having seen my cousin, I'm not at liberty to agree or disagree."

John Keaton chuckles deeply. "Well, I reckon we got a photograph or two at home. You know, this is a momentous occasion. If only Luke were here, now then it would be downright perfect."

"John Keaton, I'm warning you..."

These people are nothing like his own parents; no wonder Tressa fled here when their father cast her out.

"I understood my cousin was supposed to be returning home."

"Hasn't made it yet, but that's Luke for you. He'll get here when he runs out of things to do along the way. And that's always more than he figured on." John Keaton slaps a hand on Ben's shoulder. "Come on, son, let's get on home. This is gonna be some day in the history of the Keatons and the Taylors. And we could use one right about now."

Cadie McClements

The dining car takes Cadie's money and considers it as good as anyone's. Her stomach full for the first time in two days, she makes her way back to the car. As she passes the Gents lavatory outside the first-class car, the hard-faced friend of Bodecker looms up in front of her. She gasps; his eyes go big and then narrow. He grabs her by the wrists and forces her into the Gents lavatory and locks the door.

"What are you doing here?" he says, his breath in her face.

"I decided to go on a holiday, not that it's any of your business."

"Whores don't go on holiday." He releases her wrists and puts one hand around her neck and one on her waist instead.

Breathless, she says, "I'm going to Bright River. It sounds nice."

"How do you know about Bright River?"

"I heard you and Mr Bodecker speaking of it last night."

"Is that so? I wonder what else you heard and might be taking with you to Bright River."

"What do you mean?"

"You know, most of anything Bodecker gets I usually get. But I'm humble, I don't mind his cast offs..." His grip around her neck tightens; his other hand begins to slide down over her hips. "You look like you're up for it, well-fed and watered, and of course if you make a sound, I can break your neck."

"You can't do that on a train, you won't get away with it."

"Smart girl, ain't you," he says, his hand easing up her skirt. "Thing is, I don't want you going to Bright River..." His big hand is so tight around her neck now she is just a fraction from being strangled. She moans but he laughs. "Hold up your skirts."

"No…"

"Do it."

In fear she obeys.

"Higher…"

"No…"

His smelly, sweaty hand slips from her throat to her mouth smacking her head hard against the wall; pain drills her skull. She can barely breathe.

"Do it."

She clasps her dress to her belly.

"That's right. Now your drawers."

With one hand she loosens them; they drop to her ankles.

He looks down at her. "Well, ain't you just like a little bird."

He presses himself hard against her.

His hand muffles her protest.

"I ain't gonna pay you, whore," he says, "this is for free, because I could kill you for going to Bright River, snap your scrawny little neck, so you better do what I want."

Ben

Bright River

"You don't have to put me up at your place," Ben says, "I can stay at the hotel in town."

Amy Keaton replies, "Won't hear of it. You're family. Family don't stay in hotels when there is a perfectly fine and comfortable room at home going to waste."

He doesn't want to think about whose room that is: Mart's room, or their daughter's.

"But you're still grieving; maybe it wouldn't be fitting."

"Well, some might see it that way," she counters, "but we don't. Both our children died a long way from home, we don't keep their rooms like shrines, and the best way to live is to keep moving on. I have their things, those things I wanted to keep, put away. Kelley's is a fine room overlooking the front yard. John built it with his own two hands..."

He senses her struggle with grief in the ensuing silence. Even so, as he studies her profile, he decides that this woman's strength, in spite of what she must be going through, is more confident than his mother's.

The moment passes.

"Besides, Andy Rigg seemed glad to be rid of you," she says; she glances sideways at her husband who winks.

He suspects he'll be the butt of much teasing during his stay.

He smiles to himself. "I reckon you're right."

Cadie McClements

He removes his hand from around her mouth. Licks the side of her face. "Like I said, I always get what Bodecker gets. Only he ain't got you now, I have. And I'm gonna have you again, anytime I want. Now fix yourself up. You look like you been screwed."

Shaking so hard she can barely move, the taste of blood in her mouth, her body burning with pain, she rights her dress, then picks up her drawers and balls them in her hand; with this done, he opens the door, carefully looks in the passageway and shoves her out. She loses her balance and crashes into the wall of the train, and winces as pain shoots up her side.

"I know where to find you when I want you again. Now get back to the cattle car where you belong."

He watches her all the way down the passage.

The train buffets her this way and that until she finds a Ladies saloon in the next carriage and locks herself inside. She throws up her breakfast in the lavatory, and sinks to the floor of the tiny room with her head in her hands.

Ben

The sleigh ride is very long, and cumbersome at times, but not uninteresting; in fact, John Keaton acts like a tour guide, attempting to give Ben a good grasp of the country. And he gets a distant look at his cousin's ranch along the way.

"There's a long association between Keatons and Taylors," John Keaton says. "Our son Mart and your cousin started it when they were young'uns. We came here from Philadelphia and Luke had just lost his pa. He and Mart struck up a friendship. I think Luke thought we were the most pathetic excuse for ranchers he'd ever seen..." and he chuckles deeply in the frosty air. "Of course Ethan and Luke and his mama, Sara, were the best help we could've asked for coming to a new life. And we stuck together through the good and the bad times. And the worst of times..." He shakes his head as if he's willing away those particular times.

"I don't know why my father deserted Luke's family all those years ago," Ben says. "Wasn't allowed to know exactly, but my father didn't respect my Uncle Morgan's decision to stay in Texas and fight on the side of the Confederacy in the war. He believes that the South ceding from the Union was a betrayal of our country."

"Mm..."

"He believes that the Democrats' stranglehold on the South is detrimental."

"I see."

"He can't tolerate other people's opinions very well."

"And the fact that your Uncle Morgan left Texas and came north straight after the war, that don't mean something to your father?"

"He believes that all men make decisions based on the need to make a living. He probably thinks that my uncle's decision was purely a financial one. The South was in pretty bad shape after the war, so they say."

Amy Keaton turns around a little in her seat at the front to look at him. "And what do you think, Ben?"

"I've never known what to think. That's why I'm here. Tressa knows the truth and I've come for it. Things she spoke about before she left home won't go away. About our great, great grandfather mostly."

"That would be Matthew Taylor," says John Keaton. "Tressa knows all about him, sure."

"But why does it make such a difference knowing?"

John Keaton shrugs. "I guess it's because once you know you kinda make sense to yourself."

Ben hopes that's true.

"Now, Matthew Taylor was a revolutionary, and fought hard for American independence from the British back then. Luke wears his ring; it's got an inscription on it: *We will not be slaves*. That kind of thing means a lot to Luke."

"He has Matthew Taylor's ring?" He doesn't like the feeling of envy, but it's creeping up on him now. "I would like to see this ring."

"Mm, just one problem with that. It's on Luke's finger. Gonna have to wait for him."

He stews. Stews with resentment towards his cousin.

"Soon be there. You hungry? Stupid question; 'course you are. Well, your sister turned out to be a real fine cook. I figure she's been baking something good. And hot. I don't know about you, but my butt is clear frozen solid."

"John Keaton! In front of a guest…"

Ben grins. They are amusing, these two.

Father would never talk about frozen butts, and even if he did, Mother would never reprimand him.

And another thing, John Keaton complimented Tressa; at home, fine and natural compliments like that are few and far between.

Cliff

Cliff raps on Nugent's door with weird and unnamable feelings driving him, almost as though someone he can't see is shoving him forward.

"Ah, Sheriff Ryan," Nugent greets him warmly.

"Afternoon, Father. Not disturbing you, I hope."

"No, no. Come in."

Nugent shows him into his modest but comfortable parlor.

On a small table beneath one of the windows, and bathed by the pale afternoon sun, stands a wooden crucifix. A fire crackles in the hearth. On the mantle above, a clock ticking contentedly... Nugent gestures for him to sit in one of two old but generous-sized cozy chairs. "No doubt about it, Cliff, your duties certainly take you into places you would never otherwise go. Take Mass this morning."

Cliff looks at his hands. "I'm Methodist, Father."

"Well, nobody's perfect," Nugent replies and when Cliff lets out a laugh, Nugent chuckles.

"But I want to know..."

"Yes?"

Cliff rubs his eye. "This is weird..."

"Well, I hear all kinds of things. Comes with the job. Bit like you, I'm guessing."

"Sure." He looks Nugent squarely in the eye and says, "How do I get to understand it?"

262

"It?"

Another nervous laugh he can't control.

"Oh, oh…" says Nugent. "Yes, yes, I understand. Well, you're right. This I was *not* expecting."

"I'm not usually so…"

"Yes, I know…"

"It's just that…"

"Something's driving you and you can't find the words for it."

He nods, since words are failing him.

"Strange when that happens," says Nugent. "You said you are a Methodist. Do you practice being a Methodist?"

He clears his throat. "No."

"Well, that could be due to any number of things; for instance, you no longer believe what a Methodist believes. Of course, if you don't believe in God the Almighty at all, that could definitely be holding you back."

"I haven't thought about it much, at least not for a very long time. Sunday School Methodist, think you'd say."

"She made you think about it, did Emmaline Elizabeth Eppy."

"Yes."

"She takes her obligation seriously. Although, don't ask me how her bishop let a confirmation name like that slip under his beak."

"Fourth century martyr."

"Uh, you're in the know. And God love you for it. Thank you. I can rest easy. She's got a world of spunk, that one."

"She didn't look to me like she's only keeping the rules because she's obliged to."

"So you noticed that."

"I notice everything about her," he admits out loud.

Nugent smiles. "God's peace was shining in her eyes, yes, I saw. You might not know, Cliff, but I was a chaplain in the war."

"No, I didn't know that."

"I was young, and it was hard. I saw a lot of men, young men, who wanted peace for their anguish and hope for their despair. I sat by them day after day watching as God poured out his peace. I saw it on their faces, in their eyes, and eyes are the window to the soul, that's what they say, you know."

"Those were extraordinary circumstances."

"Indeed, they were. But they don't have to be."

"That kind of peace and hope is not easy to come by."

"It's simple, my boy. You ask for it."

"No, Father. That's not so simple."

"I don't think you realize, Cliff, but you just have. You knocked on my door…"

Again, words fail him.

Nugent sighs. "Strikes me that you're a man who gives a lot but doesn't ask for much in return."

"I gain a great deal of satisfaction from my job."

"Haven't a doubt in the world about that. But I'm thinking your encounter with young Emmaline has made you think beyond that self-reliance to things that your work can't give you."

"She has this way of… saying things."

"Gives you stick, does she?'

"In varying degrees," he smiles. "Strange, but I kinda like it…"

Nugent has one of his merry chuckles.

"And she knows what she believes."

"She has had a great deal of practice. Cliff, if you're going to *be* something, you're better off practicing it."

He swallows. "Will you teach me to be a Catholic, Father?"

Nugent probes him with clear blue eyes.

"In essence you gave your life for that young woman, a brave and serious act, and a situation that produces powerful emotions, are you sure you're not mistaking *that* for something else?"

"That's one thing I am sure of."

"And if Emmaline Elizabeth Eppy doesn't reciprocate, will God be enough?"

"I'll need you to help me find the answer to that, Father."

After another searching gaze, Nugent says, "I can't ask you to be any more honest than that."

He half-smiles. "Thank you."

Nugent sits back. "Well, you're a busy man with a great load on your shoulders, when do think you'll have time for this?"

"I have some time right now."

Nugent's eyes twinkle. "Would you look at that, so do I!"

Ben

Keaton ranch

There is a figure on the porch as they stop outside the Keaton ranch house. The figure of his sister. She is calling out to them, "At last, I wondered what had happened..."

He steps out of the cutter into soft snow.

"Oh my God... *Ben*?"

Tressa always did possess a good sense of occasion: his name echoes around the yard and unsettles snow from the trees.

He grins, inside and out, as the thrill of seeing her, of finally reaching her, pours through him.

The figure of his dark-haired, pink-cheeked, slender-framed little sister strains towards him through the snow.

He goes to meet her.

"Ben..." She throws her arms around his neck. "Ben..."

Luke

Aboard the UP out of Omaha

As the afternoon wears on, so does their patience wear thin. Luke would give anything to be riding across open fields, and Caroline is fidgeting constantly.

Kearney was about three hours ago and North Platte is about half an hour ahead. They'll probably take on water and coal, which will give Caroline something to think about for a while.

"That young girl doesn't look at all well," Caroline whispers to him.

He looks up from his newspaper and a handful of nuts.

"Sorry..."

"The little blonde girl..." Caroline whispers impatiently. "She just went past, again. Pale and dreadful. And she looked so bright this morning. What could have happened?"

"I don't know."

"Dreadful things trains," Caroline murmurs. "One hears the most alarming tales."

Their little blonde friend returns a few minutes later and he gets a look at her. Caroline is right. The girl is pale and worried, a complete about-face from this morning. She keeps her eyes down and doesn't look at anyone, even though it has to be obvious to her that he is watching her. And she walks a little crooked.

He whispers to Caroline to keep her newspaper up. She replies that she's read every article four times. He tells her to learn them by heart and that he knows the second page word for word. She says she needs to visit the Ladies saloon. He reluctantly agrees.

Caroline clears her lap, gets up and promptly sits back down again. Her newspaper is hastily raised and he can see her hands shaking.

"What is it?"

"He's here, down there, more bad luck, coming this way."

"Who?"

"Him." Her voice wobbles and cracks. "The stranger." Then she clams up and tosses her head.

He follows the toss, which is impressive for tenderfoot, and sees what terrifies her. The hard-faced man from Loren Bodecker's hotel room. Donnelly.

"Easy, Caroline," he whispers. Her response is a small whimper.

Donnelly goes straight by them without a glance. He stops at the seat of their small blonde friend and gives her a nod; now he walks back again and this is their most vulnerable moment. They both hold their breath and stay behind their well-read papers. Donnelly doesn't see them.

"He's gone," Luke says. "Breathe, Caroline, or you will pass out and then everyone will know we're here."

He hears her gasp for air.

A few moments later their little blonde friend gets up and leaves the carriage again. Caroline exchanges a sharp look with him; his imagination gets to work on those *alarming tales*. He sits there feeling sick for about ten minutes.

"You remember what I told you, Caroline," he says.

Caroline frowns. "Yes, Luke, of course." Then she sighs. "What are you going to do? The girl? You can't. It's none of our business. You'll get into trouble…"

He flashes a smile. "You sounded like Ethan then."

"I wish Ethan were here right now."

"I trust you, Caroline." Then he gets up, preparing to follow the blonde.

Luke

Inside the first-class sleeper car he hears the girl's voice.

He tucks himself in the recess between the car door and the wall of a compartment.

"I'll pay you... here, you can have this... it's all I have... three hundred dollars..."

"You stupid bitch, what would I want with your pathetic money. Now get in there..."

Luke inches forward with the idea of wrapping his eyes around the wall to see them.

"No. I won't let you," the girl says defiantly. "Not again. I'm hurting... You hurt me."

Luke's eyes find their mark. They are standing in a long passageway. Donnelly has the girl pinned against the windows of the train by her neck with one huge gloved hand; she's tiny compared to him. He unglues her from the windows and slams her against the compartment wall behind him. Her head hits with a great thump and then lolls forward.

"Bitch," Donnelly rasps. Before Luke can take another breath, he hears a sickening, cracking snap; Donnelly releases the girl and her limp body falls to the floor. Luke's stomach lurches and he just manages to hold onto his apples and peanuts. Donnelly steps over her, snatches the money from her hand and stuffs it in his pocket; then, massaging his fingers, he strides away. Luke waits for him to leave the carriage and then rushes up to the girl. With one look he can tell she is dead. Still he examines her just as Jennifer would if she were here. He finds no carotid pulse; no breath comes from her mouth; there is no heartbeat when he puts his ear to her chest. Her eyes are closed. Around her girlish neck are the black and blue remnants of Donnelly's brutality. As he touches her bruises, a great pity rises up in his chest.

"Sweet Jesus..."

She's just a kid.

"Hey, what are you doing there?"

He looks up. A middle-aged couple is coming towards him. The woman screams when she sees the girl's limp, bruised body.

"Guard, guard," the man shouts. "She's dead. Murder!"

Almost at once, uncannily, a guard appears from the direction Donnelly left. He's a capable-looking man who pulls a pistol from his belt inside his coat and aims it at Luke.

"All right, you. Stay right where you are."

"You don't understand," Luke says, taking his hands off the girl, "I just found her..."

The guard approaches steadily.

"A passenger just reported screams coming from down here. We're a few minutes out of North Platte. You got something to say you can say it to the sheriff there. Now get up slowly."

"I'm telling you, I just found her. These people would have found her if I hadn't it. And I saw who did it."

"I said get up."

He stands up, the girl's body lying awkwardly at his feet. The guard asks the middle-aged man to fetch the other guard from the rear car.

"Now, if you got a weapon, put it on the floor."

"I tell you, I just found her," he says, unbuttoning his coat and extracting his colt from his belt.

The guard takes aim. "Steady, mister..."

Luke crouches slowly and lays his colt next to the girl's body. He stands up slowly, leaving his reunion with Jennifer on the floor and a very long way behind.

Caroline

Caroline clenches her hands together, resisting the temptation to go take a look for herself when Luke does not return. The girl never returns either; nor, thankfully, the stranger Luke calls Donnelly. Too apprehensive to visit the Ladies saloon, she stays in her seat, newspaper at the ready. Eventually, the train stops in a town called North Platte just as Luke said it would. On a fearful impulse, she drags Luke's saddlebags across the floor at her feet. She tucks them up against the wall beneath the window where she sits and stuffs his newspaper on top of them. She completes this in the nick of time, she realizes, for two men have boarded the train, both wear silver stars, both have hip holsters loaded with pistols and one has a rifle in his hands. They come straight towards her.

"M'am, who is the passenger that was sitting next to you?" asks one, easing his hat back.

"I have no idea," she says.

"You weren't traveling together?"

"Good heavens, no. He kept offering me peanuts and trying to converse. I had to hide behind my newspaper to put him off. Why do you ask?"

"I'm Ralph Walker, sheriff of Lincoln County. There's been an incident on the train. You sure you don't know who he is?"

These men we're dealing with… they're powerful and dangerous. We don't know who we can trust. What connections they might have…

"Yes, I'm sure," she says. "What kind of incident?"

"Did you see him talking to a young blonde girl at any time during the day?"

She has a think about this.

And shakes her head. "I've been reading most of the time. Train journeys are so tedious."

"Uh huh," the sheriff says and starts looking around. "Did he have any luggage?"

"Oh, I wouldn't know. I think the nuts came out of his pocket, but I couldn't be sure. What has he done, sheriff? He was pesky but he didn't seem dangerous."

The sheriff adjusts his hat; his deputy scans the passengers with suspicion. "We've arrested him on a charge of murder."

She gasps, a genuine one.

"No need to fear, M'am. We have him in custody. He won't be coming near you again."

Her heart quickening, she pants, "Thank you, sheriff."

"The train will be held up here in North Platte for an hour or so while we carry out our investigation. Appreciate it if you wouldn't mind staying on the train, and if there's anything you can recall, please give us a shout, M'am."

The sheriff tips his hat. The two men move on.

She stares out the window of the train just as daylight is fading. Her breath sticks in her chest and her heart refuses to stop its wild flutterings; she can only hope and pray no one suspected anything friendly between herself and Luke.

Tears well in her eyes.

I trust you, Caroline.

She takes a handkerchief out of her pocket and dabs at her eyes. It is a long time before she puts it away again. And when a deputy comes around to write down everyone's name and address, she tells him she is Winifred Hastings and she lives at Garden Street, Boston. Well, not so much a lie as a slight departure from the truth, for a Winnie Hastings truly lived there once, many years ago, with Caroline's Grandma Mab and Grandpa Henry.

Luke

Luke imagines what Cliff would do with him in this situation if he didn't know him. Probably exactly what this Ralph Walker is doing. But that don't mean he has to give Walker any joy. In fact, he waits until he knows the middle-aged couple has told Walker what they saw; and Walker admits in a whisper to his deputy that it is circumstantial, placing Luke at the scene of the crime but that's all. Walker looks like he might have to release him due to lack of evidence – Luke has stolen none of the girl's possessions, he didn't resist arrest or attempt to use his firearm, and he rationally proclaimed his innocence until they sat him down in Walker's office. And yet this Walker is reluctant.

Luke's stomach is knotted so tight it feels like it may never come undone. He could stay snug in the lockup for quite some time until Caroline gets some help. But concern about what has become of her fastens that knot so tight it gives him a bellyache.

"Well, Mr Taylor," says Walker, "what are we gonna do with you? Got any suggestions?"

"Wire Sheriff Cliff Ryan in Cheyenne, he will vouch for me; the murderer's name is Donnelly; I saw him do it, he'd thrown the girl against the wall and snapped her neck before I could stop him. After he left, I went to the girl to see if there was something that could be done, that's when those folks and the guard found me."

"How do you know this Donnelly?"

"He is the subject of an investigation in Cheyenne. He ain't a nice feller."

"Well, we'll just have to see what Cliff Ryan has to say, won't we? In the meantime, being a Sunday, you can bunk in my lockup."

The desire to break out, get back on the train before it pulls out and protect Caroline from Donnelly is as strong an urge as he's ever felt. Sweat pours out of him; Walker is noticing and he sits like a wound up spring and eyes Luke with understandable suspicion.

"What are you going to do about Donnelly? He's a predator. You shouldn't waste time picking him up."

Walker calls for his deputy. "Lock him up."

The deputy cuffs Luke with a pair of mighty uncomfortable manacles and escorts him down to the lockup. It's not the first time this has happened to him, and it calls to mind the day McCurdy delayed him in the Bright River hoosegow not so much for what Luke did (telling McCurdy what he thought of him) but because McCurdy liked to harass him. Ethan bailed him out that day, and since McCurdy was satisfied he'd made his point he didn't take it any further. As for this situation, Walker's not officially charged him yet, but sheriffs have been known to detain someone, anyone, rather than have the public think they ain't doing their job. And Walker strikes him as this brand of sheriff.

The Lincoln County jail has a row of half a dozen cells stretching the length of the interior; in the furthest one is a guest slumped in his cot. Luke's expecting the deputy to indicate where he wants him to go when there's a cracking thud and the deputy falls at his feet. He swings around with his heart in his mouth... someone grabs him by the collar of his coat and pulls him forward. He is staring into the face of Donnelly. Those dark eyes are like fury.

"Try somethin' and you'll never see that doctor of yours again," he rasps. With that said, Donnelly rams Luke's belly with his fist; Luke doubles over as pain drills through him, and his breath deserts him. Donnelly grabs him tightly by the scuff of his neck and pulls him along through a back entrance. When they get outside in the cold air, Luke tries to stop and breathe.

"No time for that, hero boy..." And again Donnelly finds Luke's belly with his iron-mean fist. He crumples like a sack, gasping for breath. Then he's yanked upright, and with the point of Donnelly's colt pressed into his side, he's dragged, breathless and in pain, along back alleys and dark streets until they reach a snowbound house on the edge of town. Donnelly raps on a door.

A man wearing spectacles opens it. "What do we have here?"

"A guest, 'til further notice." Donnelly shoves him inside. "First class treatment for this prize."

Breathing hard, Luke rights himself, thinking the blonde didn't stand a chance.

He looks around; sees he's in a kitchen.

The man with the spectacles closes the door. Rubs his hands together. "Cold night." He's bald, and wearing a full-length white apron that's smudged.

And there's a strange smell like pickling liquid wafting through the room.

"What's the story?" the strange man asks.

"Assaulted the deputy down at the lockup and escaped; he's wanted for murdering a girl on the express. Walker will be scouring the town."

Not a kitchen; more like a science laboratory, a bigger version of Jennifer's... much bigger...

"Not to worry," says the bald man with a weird grin. "The basement is always on hand."

"So is this your twisted version of the underground railway, Donnelly?" Luke grinds out.

"Shut your face, Taylor."

"What is this place?"

"Do you like it?" the weird man inquires hopefully.

"It stinks," Luke says, peering through the dim light at all the paraphernalia.

"Nobody asked you, hero boy," Donnelly retorts. Then to the weird man, "You gotta watch this one."

The hands rub together again.

He feels like a turkey the day before Thanksgiving. And if his stomach wasn't wracked with bruising pain at the moment, he knows it'd be telling him about the funny feeling in it.

The eyes shimmer keenly behind those spectacles. "Let's get started then; not a moment to lose..."

FOUR

How can I tell the signals and the signs
by which one heart another heart divines?
How can I tell the many thousand ways
by which it keeps the secret it betrays?

Henry Wadsworth Longfellow
Emma and Eginhard

Caroline

In the raw early hours the express steams into Cheyenne and chuffs to a halt. Caroline struggles down onto the platform with Luke's saddle-bags, trying not to look conspicuous about carrying them. In the numbing cold she waits for her luggage to appear, and as she collects it she asks the porter where she would find the sheriff's office.

"Always someone at 16th Street..." He gives her directions.

Overburdened, she drapes the saddlebags over one shoulder the way she'd seen Luke do, and takes her leather travel bag in one hand and her suitcase in the other.

She passes a large sign that welcomes her to Cheyenne, but she is too exhausted to care and too frightened to feel welcome. Her eyes dart about at everything and everyone, even though only three passengers alight when she does. There are plenty of shadows, however, and each one must be broached.

She shuffles out of the depot; looks this way and that at the dark and desolate street. And up at the heavens, where the sky is lightening to violet, and the stars are beginning to fade. Her heart is heavy with concern about many things, and about Luke, but she has made it just as she promised.

She struggles along, following the directions given by the porter; the town is deathly quiet and her footsteps sound eerily off the icy sidewalk.

Lamplight glows in the window of the sheriff's office. She puts her suitcase down and opens the door, picks up her suitcase and enters, closing the door behind her with her foot. The place is deserted. She finds a chair and places her bags safely beside it. How long she will have to wait for help she cannot guess. She must hold her nerve at this crucial moment. So close to achieving their goal...

A man wearing a heavy coat appears through a doorway at the back. He looks mildly surprised to see her.

"M'am."

"I need to see the sheriff, young man. It is an emergency."

He comes toward her. "What kind of emergency, M'am?"

"Are you the sheriff?"

"No, I'm Clary, night deputy."

"I'm sorry, Mr Clary, but I must see the sheriff, no one else will do..." She stops and draws a painful breath.

"Are you all right, M'am?" asks Mr Clary.

She wobbles on her feet and then drops onto the seat behind her.

"M'am?"

"The sheriff..." she croaks. "Please."

"Okay, M'am, I'll get him. I'll fetch you some hot coffee first. Just made fresh..."

She manages a weak smile. "Thank you, Mr Clary."

The young man is as good as his word; he fetches her coffee, steaming hot, placing it into her hands with care.

So she sits, and waits, numb with cold and terrible concern, but more determined than she's ever known herself. This will be done; no one rips her family apart and gets away with it.

After a while, a tall and rather handsome young man arrives; he's unshaven, wears a navy blue coat; he has longish black hair and blue-green eyes that sweep over her alarmingly as he sizes her up in an instant. Who is this woman who's woken him, disturbed his dreams, robbed him of precious sleep? It's all in his eyes, and yet his expression is not unkind. He draws up a chair in front of her and sits down.

"M'am, I'm Cliff Ryan."

She sighs with relief.

If Luke trusts him, that is good enough for her.

"My name is Caroline Taylor, Mr Ryan, and I have some very important things to tell you."

Mr Ryan frowns. "Taylor?"

"Yes. Luke is my nephew."

"This is about Luke?" he asks quickly and she nods. "Where is he?"

"The last time I saw him he was with me on the train near North Platte, Nebraska," she tells him.

"North Platte?"

"Mr Ryan, this is a long story, better if I just tell you everything."

He rubs his hand over his stubble the way men have of doing, and then he says to Mr Clary, "Go wake Mac for me, Clary. Very well, Mrs Taylor, I'm listening."

Ben

Ben wakes from a solid dreamless sleep, and yet thinking of his mother. It is still very early, pre-dawn, and gazing out his window he sees the sky lightening to violet and stars fading.

Recollections of the big sky back in Montana make him smile. Sometimes as a small boy he'd rise with his mother at this hour of the morning, they would watch the stars fade, and talk.

"This is the biggest sky you will ever see, Ben, and the most stars; in the whole universe everything has its place, even thousands of stars."

"I wish they weren't so far away."

"Their distance is their greatest charm... infinite beauty for us to gaze upon and inspire us... they don't say 'reach for the stars' for nothing..."

It didn't dawn on him, until they had left the ranch and were living in Omaha for some years, to ask his tender and refined Bostonian mother why she wanted to live on the frontier with a man like his father. He and Tressa were enthralled to hear her tell that when she was young she longed to escape the confines of Bostonian society; she wanted adventure.

And your father captivated me with his many adventurous and daring plans. In the beginning we were happy, but as it turns out, we realized that we should be more contented with adventures of a more citified nature...

As an adult, he understands that she had simplified a great many complex issues, not the least of which is that somewhere along the way she lost that initial spirit, and the disappointments were harsh.

He dresses in warm clothing and pads down the Keaton staircase into the parlor. The fire has long gone out, so he sets about making a new one with wood and kindling… more memories of Montana. The wood crackles, the fire comes to life. He stretches his hands towards the flames. After a spell, he hears murmuring coming from Tressa's room which is next to the parlor. The murmurs become clear; it is Adam awake in his crib. The murmurs become objections.

He steals into his sister's room; she is dead to the world beneath her quilt, whereas Adam is sitting up. He has stopped objecting and now his big eyes are fixed on Ben.

"What's up with you?" Ben whispers. The room feels chilly. He crosses to the hearth and pokes at the remains in the grate; upon a gentle protest of flame, he adds a small log or two. "Come on, baby boy, let's leave your mother in peace."

He lifts the dumbstruck infant out of his crib, grabs the crib blanket and carries him into the parlor to sit by the fire. The child stares up at Ben the whole time. His hair stands on end and his eyelashes twinkle with tiny tears as the firelight catches them.

"You're a handsome boy," Ben tells him; he strokes his upended hair and smiles reassuringly. "You look like your father apparently. You certainly don't look like your mother much, so there you have it. Why were you crying?"

Adam rubs one of his eyes and gives a grizzle. Ben wraps the blanket around him.

"Were you cold? Your blankets were at the end of the crib."

The boy blinks several times and seems happier with the blanket, so Ben settles back into the chair, hikes his feet up on the footrest, and makes both the baby and himself warm and comfortable.

"I use to live on a ranch once, a long time ago. I was a boy and I was happy there. Being here reminds me of it. You're a lucky boy, growing up here; you'll feel free and happy. That mirror I brought you won't mean much right now, well, maybe not ever, but it's an heirloom, not a Taylor one, it's from your Grandma Caroline's side of the family, the Hastings. They came from Boston. Your great grandfather was Henry Hastings, your great grandmother was Mab, and they lived on Garden Street…"

The baby's eyes blink shut and stay that way.

Cliff

Cliff jumps to his feet as Mac walks into his office.

"Gees, you're jittery." Mac hands him a telegram. "This is what you been waiting for. From Walker."

```
SHERIFF CLIFF RYAN, CHEYENNE, WYOMING, HAD LUKE TAYLOR
IN CUSTODY ON SUSPICION OF MURDER, HE BASHED A DEPUTY
AND ESCAPED LAST NIGHT, NO TRACE AS YET, TAYLOR NAMED
DONNELLY AS MURDERER, THIS IS DOUBTFUL, WHAT LIGHT CAN
YOU SHED ? WALKER,
```

"You planning on shaving anytime soon?" Mac asks while Cliff rereads the wire. "You might scare the customers."

"Mac, I don't believe Luke escaped, do you? All he had to do was sit tight until someone bailed him out and had the whole mess cleared up."

"Yep," Mac says. "Luke's sometimes impetuous though."

"He's smart and he doesn't go around bashing deputies."

"True. You reckon Donnelly spotted him and picked him up?"

Cliff rubs his eye. "More than likely. Shit…"

"Word just come through from Dickson. The telegraph is down between there and Bright River; they had a snowstorm night before last. John and Ethan'll be still working on the last wire you sent them about Swinton Carter. They might come to town. Not a good time to leave their families unprotected if Maverick's supposed to be following Ben Taylor to the Keatons."

"No."

"So…"

"So, we've got the Alliance under critical threat on one hand and Luke in Donnelly's clutches on the other. And here we are right in the middle."

Meanwhile, he's got a couple of murderers in the lockup and the probability that anytime now Dillon Kerr will be in here taking over for Marvin Tucker as per Loren Bodecker's instructions and making life hell for everyone.

"I know which one Luke would want us to deal with first."

Cliff nods. "I'm not scaring off Donnelly for all the gold in the Black Hills. Ralph Walker had better stay in the dark."

"Right, boss. You off to see Cam now?"

"He can break the news to the mayor and the governor about their favorite citizen."

Mac concurs. "Planning on going to Laramie yourself?"

He's used to Mac anticipating his next move, but this surprises him. "Can you handle things here for a while, Mac?"

"Hell, I know how to handle those reporters better than you. Besides, I don't think the boys in Laramie know what they're up against."

"We need to keep an eye on Caroline Taylor. Luke promised to take her to Bright River; she looks desperate."

"To get to her family… Can't say I blame her, but Bright River ain't the safest place for her now. If Bodecker ordered Maverick to stay out of Cheyenne like Luke says, then this is the safest place. We'll keep her hid; don't want Dillon Kerr knowing she's here; although when they realize she's left Omaha, they might think to look here."

"We can't anticipate *every* move they're going to make. We just have to play this out and do the best we can."

"Don't fret, Cliff. Caroline Taylor knows the risk; she did it for her children. So… You gonna shave before you go?"

"You asked me that already."

"A question don't go away when the answer ain't forthcoming."

"You're just full of old sage, ain't you?"

Mac rolls his eyes.

Emmaline

The Tribune

MURDER ON LAST NIGHT'S EXPRESS. LUKE TAYLOR WAS HELD IN NORTH PLATTE ON SUSPICION. THEN HE BASHED DEPUTY AND ESCAPED.

"This...this was wired to you this morning?"

Mr Quaid grins. "Pays to have friends."

"Indeed. But... well, you don't believe it, do you?"

Mr Quaid shrugs. "Not my place to believe it, just report it."

"Well, I don't believe it," she declares. "I only met him once, but you can tell that kind of thing about a person."

Mr Quaid laughs at her. "If you say so, Roberts. Now get down to Ryan's office and find out what they know?"

"How do you know that they'll know anything?"

"Because Ryan is an irritating little pr... so and so, who knows everything before it happens."

"Well, you will have to send Simons or one of the others because you may recall I'm going to Laramie."

Mr Quaid frowns. "Oh, yeah. Sure. Investigating Donnelly. Any links to Maverick. Sidestepping to Bright River. This Luke Taylor business is a big story, Roberts; sure you still want to go?"

She thinks this very odd. "Yes, I still think it is important to go. While it's not likely that Donnelly will have his biography pinned to his front door, I think a few questions around town won't go astray; but more than that I want to find out what properties he's been buying out and how they came into his possession. The widow Adams sold out to him for half value after Maverick killed her husband, don't forget. And I think a call on the Keatons and the Taylors to update their current situation and get their opinion on Luke Taylor's arrest would be extremely useful, don't you?"

"When you put it like that, Roberts..."

"Good. I'll see you when I get back; in the meantime, I'll be in touch."

In a dry tone not lost on her, Mr Quaid says, "Sure, Roberts. Have a safe trip."

Packed and ready, bound for Laramie, she heads down to the depot.

Faraday

Office of Acting Governor Elliot Morgan

"Are you insane, Faraday?" All is not well in Mayor Francis E. Warren's beloved Wyoming.

"If only that were the case... so to speak."

And anyone who thinks it easy to tell a man of Warren's stature what he needs to hear, along with an acting governor who is barely two weeks into the job, is sadly mistaken.

Faraday takes a deep breath. "The facts are these. Maverick is a Laramie man by the name of Donnelly; Donnelly is in partnership with Loren Bodecker; they conspired with Ed Parsons to steal the Taylor and Keaton ranches by whatever means at their disposal; Parsons covered up their involvement, for what reason yet to be determined – perhaps he was happy for Maverick to deliver the final blow by murdering Miss Keaton, final revenge so to speak.

"We believe, but have yet to prove, that the assassin is Swinton Carter, who is in the lockup after making an attempt to murder Miss Emmaline Roberts of the Tribune.

"Maverick has almost certainly shot or murdered other ranchers and that will have to be investigated further. But it will have to wait for now because Cliff Ryan is on his way to Laramie to inform Sheriff Dave Ransford of the situation and that the Alliance is in grave danger from Maverick.

"To make matters worse, Donnelly has disappeared from the train on which Bodecker's whore was murdered. Ralph Walker, the Lincoln County sheriff, arrested Luke Taylor in North Platte on

286

suspicion. As he was being escorted to the jail in North Platte, the deputy was bashed and Luke is missing. Cliff Ryan suspects, as do I, that Donnelly bashed the deputy and took Luke. The Alliance, gentlemen, is in grave danger."

Elliot blusters into his impressive moustache. "This situation is intolerable. Loren Bodecker was... is a long time friend of Bill Hale's administration. There will be a scandal."

"I am aware of your predicament," Faraday says. "Of your position. And of Bodecker's past friendship with Governor Hale, but innocent people will die, have already died."

"What proof have you that this Donnelly and Loren Bodecker are partners?" Elliot argues.

"Luke Taylor slipped unseen into their Omaha hotel room and remained hidden while they discussed their plans for the Alliance and the situation here to do with Maverick. Marvin Tucker is to be taken off Swinton Carter's defense and Dillon Kerr is to handle it. Maverick is to be sent to Bright River. If nothing else, Luke Taylor is a vital witness and he's missing."

Warren mutters savagely, "This is outrageous!"

"Is this secret witness to be trusted, Cam?" Elliot asks. "How do you know we can trust this person... the whole thing could be a fabrication."

"It is not a fabrication, Elliot. The witness risked their own life to come here with this information. We have been painstakingly gathering evidence and now it has suddenly got a lot easier."

Faraday would like to sympathize with Elliot because he understands the pain of a friendship gone sour. The administration has been lied to and deceived by a supposed friend, but politicians who maintain friendships at the big end of town for whatever reason need to be extra careful.

"I don't think you have anything to worry about, Elliot," Faraday says. "The public will just be grateful if we can stop these arrogant, marauding murderers."

Elliot nods. "I hear what you're saying, Cam, but I'm having trouble accepting it. And what disappoints me is that Bodecker has always been a strong advocate for statehood, for progress."

Warren snorts. "Well, obviously, Elliot, he intended it to be on his terms and for his benefit. Bill's death is probably just the kind of hiatus he needed. Very fortuitous. He's a baron in every sense of the word, and you fell for it! What would Bill say now? He's barely cold in his grave..."

"Francis, you are not being helpful," Elliot retorts. "Besides, we all fell for it! Bodecker has the wealth and the progressiveness to help make something of this territory. That's the point, isn't it?"

"But at what cost? This town and this territory are demanding fair representation. The Populists are on the march, Elliot, and this will help their cause, mark my words. We need to take clear and decisive steps to divorce ourselves from Loren Bodecker at once."

Bodecker, once seen as a healthy tree in the Republicans' political garden, threatens to be cut down like diseased wood.

"Renounce him before Cam has even mounted a case?" Elliot chokes out. "I don't recall Loren Bodecker ever being an enemy of yours, Francis."

"Anyone who would do this is indeed an enemy."

"Francis, you are getting ahead of yourself."

"Faraday is giving us fair warning of what is about to befall us and you plan to ignore it?" retorts Warren, understandably.

Faraday intervenes. "Gentlemen, let me remind you that Loren Bodecker has substantial financial interests in every major industry in this territory. Small time operators across those industries have been toiling to keep his greedy hands off their right to liberty and property for years. Some, bullied and overwhelmed, have already capitulated; and some refuse to.

"The Alliance, as you well know, is one who refuses. Already its resistance is a beacon to the others who are fearful and need support. Be assured, gentlemen, I *will* mount a case against Loren Bodecker; we *will* discover his plans and his schemes. If your political survival is as important to you as cattle and sheep and coal and produce is to your constituents, then number yourselves among them, because we want justice and integrity to be the traits of the fittest, not terror and greed. And it makes no difference if our enemy comes from within or without, we still need to fight." Faraday pauses momentarily. "So, now you are up to date with things, I have work to do. Good day, gentlemen."

Elliot checks his departure by raising his hand. "We are calm, Cam, be assured we are calm." He lowers his hand and slides it into his pocket.

Warren says, "I remember Mr Taylor from last September. He flatly refused to stand down when ordered by Marshal Hummer until Wilson Cutter was strip searched for a concealed weapon. There were at least three rifles trained on him and he didn't budge; he said he would kill Wilson Cutter if anyone tried to remove Cutter from Cheyenne. At first I thought him a contemptuous upstart, and if there hadn't been a concealed weapon on Wilson Cutter, Taylor would still be in prison right now. He refused to give up; you *all* did. And you won. Then Miss Keaton was murdered, which stole the victory from under you. That was Bodecker's doing? That is what you are telling us, Faraday?"

"Yes."

"Why?" Elliot asks with a searching gaze.

Faraday returns it. "As to understanding what drives the man I cannot say, but what he expects to achieve from all this I think that is fairly obvious. He intends to possess as much of Wyoming as possible."

"As if that was ever going to happen!" exclaims Warren, whose interests and influence across Wyoming are both extensive and undeniable. Perhaps he is missing the point, or wants to.

"And this foray into Taylor's uncle's company in Omaha – what is that about?"

"Cliff Ryan has wired the US Marshal's office for assistance in retrieving Mr Bodecker. When we have him back here in Cheyenne, Elliot, I'd like to ask him that question myself. For the present, however, it appears to be another form of manipulation and terror."

Elliot nods circumspectly. "Thank you, Cam. Be assured we will maintain strict confidentiality until this Maverick has been caught."

Faraday bids them a final good morning.

He returns to his office, requests that Josh not disturb him, and sits with his head in his hands. George is never going to forgive him if anything happens to Luke. He's not sure he could even forgive himself.

Cliff

Aboard the UP to Laramie

Cliff throws his duffle bag, and then himself, onto the train just as it begins to roll. The conductor, standing at the door of the car, looks somewhat alarmed, but Cliff straightens up and gives a reassuring nod. The conductor tips his hat and moves on to the next car, while Cliff retrieves his bag. Normally, he rides in second-class, he is a servant of the people after all, but as his priority was to get on the train before it left, that meant launching himself into the first-class car. He looks ahead at the plush and comfortable appointments. They don't call them palace cars for nothing.

He's about to turn around and follow the conductor when he notices a huddle of women in the middle of the car, talking a blue streak, with no regard for what's happening around them. He recognizes them as the wives of some of Cheyenne's prominent businessmen. How they manage to stand like statues while the train skids and bumps into its rhythm is anyone's guess. They are clearly agitated about something. So he goes to investigate.

"Everything all right here, ladies?" he says, pitching his voice between the noise of the train and their incessant chatter.

Two of them turn around; a revealing movement… in the center of their huddle stands a much frazzled-looking Emma.

"Oh, Sheriff Ryan… of course," says Mrs Baird.

Mrs Harrington utters a similar sentiment.

Mrs Kent prefers to elaborate. "We've just been telling this Miss Roberts that her work for the Tribune is not helpful. She's not from around these parts, don't you know."

Mrs Arnold adds details. "Our husbands are upstanding citizens as you know, Sheriff, and Miss Roberts' article insinuates that they are anything but, and this being a free country and all, thanks to Mr Lincoln..." a pointy eyebrow in Emma's direction, "... we are expressing our view."

Emma sighs and rolls her eyes. "Do you think you might have concluded? Because I would like to sit down before I fall down... in case you hadn't noticed, the train is moving."

The women look around.

Mrs Arnold says, "Oh, so it is."

"But you do agree with us, don't you, Mr Ryan?" asks Mrs Kent.

"I'm just the sheriff, ladies, I don't do editorial comment." He looks straight at Emma and says, "I have that information you were asking for, Miss Roberts, and I see an empty seat up ahead. After you. Good day, ladies, have a pleasant trip."

The women part and he focuses on Emma who has turned to look for the seat. Mrs Baird and Mrs Harrington finally move out of her way and she finds it.

He follows; reaches up, accustomed to the twinge in his arm by now, and stows his duffle bag on the rack above.

"The irritating side of the human face of ideology," she says. "Less irritating if I learn to speak like a Yankee."

Clutching the rack, he grins and says through his arms, "Don't. Learn to speak like a Yankee, that is."

Her smile warms his insides, until her eyes fall on his silver star, exposed by his reach, and her smile dies.

Okay, Miss Emmaline Elizabeth Eppy, I get it... He places his hat on top of his bag, then lowers his arms and adjusts his coat.

"Thank you for rescuing me – again," she says.

"It's always a pleasure."

"They ambushed me. Short of physically pushing them aside, I could not escape. Did you want to sit by the window? This is your seat after all."

He gives his head a shake. "I'm sure you would have got to it first if they'd let you." He sits beside her.

"I don't usually travel first-class, but there wasn't a second-class ticket left."

"I was on my way to second-class myself when I saw President Lincoln's fan club."

"I am amazed at how many people travel in this climate."

"You get used to it."

"I suppose. How is your arm today?"

"Fine. Did you have a pleasant day yesterday?" He settles his backside further into the upholstery.

"I did, thank you. I was warm all day. Nan Morris' roast was delicious. I read in my room and even managed a nap."

"Changed your mind about plausible deniability?"

"Something like that. I think the cat became the prime suspect."

"I had my suspicions about that cat from the start."

"Mm. And you? How did you spend your Sunday?"

"I visited a friend. We spent the afternoon talking."

"A friend?"

"Well, I do have one or two, as unlikely as that may seem."

"I don't mean to pry, it's just that I don't know many people in town and…"

"You're curious."

She looks mildly fed up and says, "Forget I asked."

"Are you going to Laramie?" he asks.

"You're not going to lecture me, are you?"

"Would you listen?"

"I don't see how I could avoid it since you are sitting next to me," she says and then looks out the window. "And *you* are going to Laramie?"

He tells her that he is.

"Is it colder there than in Cheyenne?"

"Probably."

She studies the view from her window. "I'm thinking you wouldn't be leaving Cheyenne unless there was something urgent happening elsewhere."

"There is."

"Did Luke Taylor commit murder on the train last night?"

"No. Luke's not a murderer."

"Then who did?"

"Donnelly is the suspect."

Her head swings around, her eyes wide and gloriously golden. "You're serious."

He shifts his feet; adjusts his legs in the space in front of him; picks a speck of fluff off his pants. "I suppose Quaid thinks he's got a jump on the rest of us."

She shakes her head. "I quote: *Ryan is an irritating little so and so, who knows everything before it happens,* unquote."

"*So and so?* How polite."

"He chose his words for my benefit."

"The day Quaid became a gentleman."

"Can you tell me what is going on?"

"You're heading in the wrong direction. Your newspaper's back that way."

"You know, when everything is finally disclosed, there will be a great deal of confusion. When all the facts come out, someone will need to draw the whole lot into one succinct body of work. I believe Mr Quaid expects it of me. Now, if Donnelly killed that person on the train, then it's likely that *he* bashed that deputy and kidnapped Luke."

He frowns. "Essentially, you're riding into hell, Emma."

She turns in her seat to face him and says in a hushed tone, "Donnelly is Maverick."

He doesn't reply; he doesn't need to; she's worked it out, the information is extremely sensitive, particularly on public transportation, and he's grateful that the upholstery and the clatter of the train absorb their conversation.

"He's planning an assault on the Keatons and the Taylors, I bet," she whispers like she's thinking out loud, "and that's why he's kidnapped Luke; he's the bargaining chip, the pawn in a sick game."

She wants his job now?

"How much do you know, Emma?"

"Sorry?" She looks up; her eyes are dancing.

"I said, how much do you know?"

"I'll know everything I need to know when you tell me."

And the time had come.

Very quietly, he tells her everything he knows, Caroline Taylor being the exception. Then he reveals what he intends to do. She takes notes. When he's finished he watches her read over them, scribbling a word here and a word there, mumbling things like *I knew it, I just knew it.*

Finally, she asks, "Why did you tell me?"

"You're my favorite reporter," he replies lightly.

"I know how you feel about reporters. Your severity on our first meeting stands as testimony to that."

"I seem to remember telling you that if you were genuinely interested in solving Miss Keaton's murder and getting to the truth I'd be cooperative."

"You were very rude. And I don't believe you meant it."

"I was wrong."

She laughs softly; her eyes sparkle. "I can't imagine the effort it just took for you to admit that."

"I'm glad I was wrong," he tells her. "Can we talk about something else?"

A change comes over her; hardly noticeable to some maybe…

"What else could we have to talk about? The news about Loren Bodecker will hit Cheyenne very hard, don't you think?"

"For sure. Mac told me that you have a twin sister."

Looking at her notes, she says primly, "Yes. Celina. She lives in Jacksonville. She was married six months ago."

"To a lawyer?"

"No," she smiles at her notebook. "Celina would never marry a lawyer. Harrison Kennedy is a banker."

"Are you identical twins?"

"Mac didn't tell you that?" she says dryly. "No, we're not."

"How old are you?" he asks and her glance flies off the page and collides with his.

"Do you think that's an appropriate question?"

"I guess a true gentleman wouldn't ask it, but we've already established my efforts in that department. So that leaves: yes, if it's something I want to know about you."

"Why do you want to know?"

"I myself was thirty in August."

Her eyes travel over his face, the observation reminding him of gentle waves trickling over a tidal pool and settling in the crevices.

"Celina and I will be twenty-three on Wednesday."

"*This* Wednesday? Black mink hat and muff day. Now *that's* appropriate."

"Yes," she smiles.

"Did you always want to be a journalist?"

"No, not always," she says. He waits patiently and she offers, "They wouldn't let me into law school."

"Wrong gender."

"Utterly."

"That's tough."

"As well as pathetic, unfair, discriminatory and chauvinistic."

"Is Celina as smart as you?"

"What kind of a question is that? Really, of all the..."

"You're the clever one," he grins.

"Now you are insinuating that Celina is married because she's not 'clever', and therefore because I am not married I am more interested in being 'clever', or because I want to be 'clever' then I am not likely ever to be married. That, Mr Ryan, is a very narrow-minded view. Celina is..."

"I know, and not one I hold to, but..."

"...an exceptionally well-informed and perceptive individual."

"She shares your pedigree, I realize..."

"You are beginning to sound like an intellectual snob."

"That was not my intention."

"Your intentions are peppered with sarcasm and artifice."

"You certainly know a lot of big words."

"Occupational hazard."

"You don't need to be so defensive."

"Then don't sound like my mother."

He laughs. "I wish I could say I was sorry."

"And do you consider yourself 'clever'?" she counters.

"I'm curious mostly," he tells her.

She gives him another searching look; it develops into something wonderfully intriguing.

"I'm curious about you," he murmurs.

"Why? Because I took the confirmation name I did on a dare?"

"Pretty much, yes. And, you're curious about me. Such as now."

"Why would I be curious about you?"

"You try not to be, like I try not to be about you, but we always end up the same."

"The same?"

"Mm. The same. Curious."

She opens her mouth to speak; nothing comes out and it shuts again. Her soft pink lips momentarily sidetrack him; still she says nothing.

"You were going to say something?"

A shake of the head.

"Because I don't think it's inappropriate to tell you where I was born, or about my family, or why I came to Cheyenne, what I've been doing since I got here, why I'm not married, and why you are my favorite reporter."

Her mouth tightens, like someone's sown her lips together. The color drains from her face and then she turns away and looks out the window.

Mm.

"I enjoyed talking with you yesterday," he says. "Some of those insights you shared spoke right to my heart."

"They did?" she asks, still staring out the window.

"I have never heard such ideas put like that before."

"I'm glad then."

Glad? *Look at me, Emma…*

He swallows and changes his tack.

"May I tell you the story of when I first met Luke?"

A hesitation. A nod.

"I arrived in Cheyenne five years ago. As I mentioned before, I decided to go into law enforcement, and coming from Chicago…"

"You're from Chicago?"

"I thought I told you that already. Well, I had a hankering to experience another kind of life and decided to come out here. The sheriff at the time was looking for a deputy; he said my law degree would come in handy since law was something sorely needed in Wyoming. He taught me to shoot, he taught me my job. Not long after this, Luke comes into town. He's got Mart Keaton in tow. They'd driven their cattle to Laramie and decided to get on the train and come to Cheyenne. Luke gets himself into trouble; nothing serious, just too much whiskey; someone complained he'd shot down a sign, which he hadn't, but it was my job to put him in the lockup for the night. The owners of the sign wanted reparation. Luke protested his innocence, so did Mart, but the sheriff wouldn't listen, that is, until the real culprit was caught red-handed..."

"By you," she interrupts. And finally looks at him, those golden eyes shiny with feeling.

His insides snap and roll, and deliver a very basic urge, one he's been trying to ignore for some time and is not getting any easier... move closer, take her hand, touch her cheek... kiss her.

"Er..."

"By you."

"Mm?"

"By you..."

"By me... yes. We've been friends ever since. They'd come to Cheyenne every few weeks for a beer and talk and cards. Even hammered a few nails in Luke's ranch house when he renovated the place a few years back."

"Beer and cards, quite likely. Talk, definitely. Hammer and nails, you?"

"I said a few."

"So you did," she says with a teasing laugh.

"The important ones."

More laughter. "Of course."

"But why he didn't confide in me about the extent of their problems with Ed Parsons he's never said, because we've always trusted one another, so I always assumed that Parsons was extorting their silence."

"You never asked?"

"Seemed a reasonable assumption with all that was going on, so I never asked, no. This much I know: Luke is a good man, and he'd never deliberately hurt anyone."

"You have a dilemma, don't you?" she asks.

"Do I?"

"To go after Luke, or help the Alliance. You are telling yourself that you have to do what Luke would do. But Luke is a key witness now, and protecting the Alliance is not your jurisdiction, surely? The Alliance families don't live in this county."

He looks away. "I know Luke would want me to protect the Alliance, but the thought of them losing Luke on top of everything else that's happened..."

"Just the Alliance losing him?" she asks.

"All right, all of us losing him," he concedes.

"You know, there are two schools of thought on this. One, that the cause is greater than the individual and therefore any individual can and should be sacrificed as long as the cause is won; and two, that the individual is intrinsic, the cornerstone in fact, of the cause, and to cherish and preserve the individual is to make the cause heroic, superior and invulnerable, and secured."

He looks at her, and wonders if her twin sister could have articulated that. "You read a lot, don't you?"

"I was just making an observation. I'm sorry if..."

"No," he says, "don't be sorry."

Silence falls between them for some time. Lost in thought about his 'dilemma', her two schools of thought holding class in his head, he doesn't hear her at first; then after a moment her words untangle themselves in his mind and find his ears. *I want to help you.*

"Emma?"

"I want to help you. If you trust me, that is. I think you do, otherwise you wouldn't have told me anything."

He told her because knowledge for Emma is her best chance of protection since he won't be around to do it.

He stays mute.

She sits back.

"My mistake," she murmurs.

Into the thick and difficult silence, he says, "I assume your help would be to carry the information to Dave Ransford, the sheriff in Laramie, on my behalf."

"Yes."

"I would have to deputize you."

"Why?"

"Because that's how it would need to be done, Emma."

She looks at her hands. "Yes, Sheriff Ransford in Laramie might not take me seriously otherwise; I mean, the story is so fantastic and I am after all a newspaper reporter…"

"You have an aversion to this Silver Star, Emma."

"Oh. You noticed."

"I notice everything about you."

She gives him a sideways glance. "It doesn't mean you can't trust me with it, and what it would represent."

"I trust you, but you …"

She raises her eyes to look straight into his.

Of all the words that could come out of his mouth, he says, "I've never deputized a woman before."

"It *is* legal?"

"Yes, in Wyoming women have the franchise, own land, and even hold public office if they want; it's considered a drawback to statehood… you can thank Mrs Esther Morris… talk to Nan Morris, she claims she's a relative…"

What is this – a civics lesson? What is she doing to him?

"Will you do it then? I promise to represent you faithfully. I will take the information to the sheriff and I will see that the Keatons, the Taylors and the Benchleys get their protection, although you will have to leave the operations to Sheriff Ransford for obvious reasons, but I can be his guide. I have firsthand knowledge of how Maverick operates, and if you trust Sheriff Ransford and his men to do the job then your dilemma is over."

"I know you would do a first rate job, Emma, I don't doubt it for a moment, but I can't send you into danger."

"I'm volunteering."

He can't decide if he is vulnerable to her persuasion or if she is truly persuasive.

"Wrong gender *again*," she groans with color in her cheeks.

In his mouth his tongue is restless with the words that would put truth to his emotions. He clamps his lips together.

She folds her arms impatiently.

"You're doing that… that clamming up thing again."

"I am? You're not so bad at it yourself, you know."

"How am I supposed to know what you're thinking? I have to guess, I suppose. Well, I'll never understand you, so just forget I even said a thing. I simply thought that since relating information is my line of work and chasing outlaws and looking out for people is yours that you'd be glad to distribute the work according to our strengths…"

"If anything happened to you, Emma, how do I tell your family that I let you volunteer for this? They will hold me responsible and they'd be right."

"Listen to me, Cliff Ryan, I was already going to Laramie to investigate Donnelly on assignment for the Tribune, I was already planning a visit to the Keatons, also on assignment for the Tribune. Mr Quaid didn't have a problem with it, so why should you?"

"Does Quaid care about your welfare at all?" he exclaims.

"Professional people put the job first."

"Journalists might, but not law enforcement. People come first. You come first, Emma."

"Thank you, I… I appreciate your concern for my welfare, truly, but this is extremely important to you and you can't be everywhere, do everything…"

Their rather passionate discussion is attracting attention; on top of this, the conductor enters the car announcing that Watts Landing is the next stop; that means he has about two minutes to make his decision. Emma's eyes search his with increasing urgency.

"Cliff," she whispers. "I *promise* you won't regret it."

"You can't make such a promise, Emma."

"I can," she breathes. She raises her right hand. "I do solemnly swear I will do whatever it takes to deliver this information, and to faithfully uphold the position of deputy sheriff in accordance with the laws and statutes of the territory of Wyoming, so help me God."

He can't believe his ears. She doesn't even know the laws and statutes of the territory of Wyoming.

"Give me your star, 'til we meet again…"

The train's velocity is decreasing in direct proportion to the escalating emotions coursing through his body.

He must decide…

Her hands grip the armrest between them. "You saved my life, you took a bullet for me; you take care of me, if I needed anything I would turn to you; for heaven's sake, I slept in your coat…"

"This one?" he squawks. "You *must* have been cold."

"I was frightened. Even though we are constantly bickering, I consider you my friend. If you consider me your friend, if you would risk your life for me, why can't you let me do this for you?"

Because he...

He swallows and echoes raggedly, "For me?"

"Yes, for you."

"Emma..."

"Never mind that now."

He thought he'd made this decision back in Cheyenne. Someone needed to stay in town – Mac. Someone needed to help the Alliance – himself. And they were leaving Luke to something that hadn't sat right in his gut from the moment they made the plan. School of thought number one.

And now this angel of mercy.

School of thought number two is now possible.

He reaches for his silver star and unpins it. He takes Emma's hand and secures it in her palm.

"I deputize you, Emmaline Elizabeth Eppy Roberts, to act on behalf of the Sheriff of Laramie County, so help you God."

The train pulls into Watts Landing, barely a settlement, more like a siding depot, close to the county line; mists of steam float upwards outside the window behind Emma's head, framing her flushed face with cloud.

"You can't fail, Emma."

"I know. I won't, I swear on my life, I won't. On your behalf I won't. Now go," she pleads, "and God bless you."

He leans towards her. Looks into her eyes. Caresses the small hand beneath his.

"Take care, my sweet friend Emma," he murmurs.

And kisses her cheek...

...reluctantly, he releases her hand.

He doesn't look at her after that; he reaches up for his bag and hat, strides down the car and steps off the train into the biting cold. The fragrant tenderness of her cheek remains on his lips and warms him to his very core.

Emmaline

She clutches the star in her hand exactly as he placed it.

Stares in awe at her notebook lying in her lap.

Breathe, Emmie!

I will…

She closes her eyes and attempts to breathe away the fervor clambering through her body.

But it's no use. The immensity of what has happened won't be quieted. It commands her whole being.

He's a sheriff, for heaven's sake! And he's not Catholic. Mama always warned you that journalism would lead you astray.

Be quiet, Celina, I know what I'm doing.

And the irony of YOU with a silver star! I couldn't believe my ears when you demanded he give it to you! I think he might like you, Em. A lot.

Celie, you don't understand. I wanted adventure, now I have plenty.

Who cares about adventure? I think you might have a man, darlin'. A very good-looking one.

In case you hadn't noticed, Celie, he has integrity.

I seem to remember you declared him ruthless.

I know, but…

That's a lot of trust he just squashed into the palm of your hand.

So?

So he has feelings for you.

He wants to save his friend.

True. Well, let's just enjoy the scenery, shall we?

She can do this job and she will see Cliff again to return his silver star. She regrets nothing she said to him, no matter what Celina might think.

Then she remembers she told him about sleeping in his coat.

Your secret's safe with me, Emmie.

He wasn't meant to know that.

Well, he knows now, sweetie. Oh, get a grip, Emmie, just think how he feels about that stupid old coat now.

Celie, you are not helping.

Well, what do you want me to say? That he won't figure out that what you really needed that night was him, and his coat was the next best thing? Don't be so hard on yourself; that was a very bad night, Em, and you were alone. He'll understand. Besides, you do want him to know you like him, don't you?

Look to your job, Roberts, and focus. That's all that matters now. To let him down is unthinkable.

Mac

Cheyenne

Mac don't usually run places, but now seems a better time than most – straight to Cam's office. Josh Bridger looks up as Mac skids to a halt in front of his desk.

"Need to see Cam, pronto," he pants.

"He's in court."

"Get him out, now!"

"Is it Mrs Faraday, Mac?" Bridger asks.

"No, it's not Mrs Faraday, don't go panicking him about that. It's about Cliff... it's URGENT!"

"Okay, okay. Just wait." Bridger scoots off, giving Mac a backward glance.

Mac wipes his brow on his sleeve. "Damn it, boss..."

He straightens out the telegram he'd crushed in his hand as he ran. The minutes feel like hours until Cam strides his way...

"What's the problem, Mac?"

Mac hands him the telegram. "This."

"SHERIFF'S OFFICE. CHEYENNE. REPORTER NAMED EMMALINE ROBERTS SAYS SHE WAS DEPUTIZED BY CLIFF RYAN TO BRING CRITICAL INFORMATION REGARDING SITUATION WITH ALLIANCE. SHE CARRIES HIS STAR. CAN YOU CONFIRM IMMEDIATELY. DAVE RANSFORD."

Cam looks up, frowning.

"I confirmed one thing, Cam. Miss Roberts was on the train to Laramie, Quaid told me. I just don't know what happened."

"Why would Cliff do this?"

Mac sighs. "To release himself so he can go after Luke."

"Precisely. He's deputized Miss Roberts, that's all."

"That's all?! But he must have told her everything."

Cam nods, a smile tickling the corners of his mouth. "Looks that way, Mac. Cliff doesn't give his trust lightly, so we can only assume, I think correctly, that he trusts Miss Roberts."

"I know he was in a dilemma before he left."

"I'm not surprised. We need to vouch for Miss Roberts, Mac, at once. She's probably frantic and Cliff is miles away by now trusting that the information has been delivered and that Ransford and his men will soon swing into action."

Mac gives a nod of approval. "You don't seem too worried about Miss Roberts, Cam."

"She's a smart, capable woman. Cliff knows that. And, I have to admit, I feel a great deal better now that he's gone to find Luke. Oh, I think you might like to know, Mac, that Swinton Carter pleaded guilty to attempted murder of Miss Roberts before the Judge this morning. Tucker represented him; he turned a pale shade of green and declared that wasn't how he had counseled his client."

"So Donnelly's stop over in North Platte with Luke means that Dillon Kerr ain't got his orders from Bodecker yet."

"It would seem so. We are ahead of the game in that respect. I think you had better start thinking of ways to keep Carter and Jacobs alive, Mac. Dillon doesn't exactly possess Tucker's ethics."

Mac feels like a circus juggler with more colored balls in the air than he knows what to do with; Cheyenne without Cliff is hard work. Keeping their witnesses alive and kicking, including Luke, is no mean feat for all of them. And that's aside from getting the evidence against Loren Bodecker and protecting the Alliance from Maverick. They need every kind of break they can get. Mac never figured that Emmaline would be one.

Luke

That potent chemical smell twists itself inside his nose like a snake uncoiling, slithering, deadly with venom. He must move before it sees him but he can't; he's trapped, held back. His heart pounds, sweat breaks out. Suddenly, he is picked up and thrown, his body hurling through the air which is filled with colored lights; if he could make a sound he would scream. He hits the ground: dumped into reality. A smelly, sweaty blackness. His eyes are open but he can't see; his tongue moves in his mouth but it can't escape, can't moisten his lips. Beneath his scalp a headache throbs in time with the pounding in his ears. His body has to be here, but even his most concentrated thoughts can't rouse it.

The smell. The smell. Welling nausea. Don't vomit.

Ethan said he'd seen men drown in their own vomit. *Come get me, Ethan...* But it wasn't Ethan who came; it was Mart. Found him in the old bear cave with his ankle sprained, his arm broke and his head banged up. Mart who calmed him and went for help. Then Ethan came and took him home. Simple days. Good days. Ethan took care of him; and in Mart he had a brother. But Ethan let him grow up a long time ago and Mart is dead.

Just as he considers the notion that his death is not far away, the darkness encasing him fades just a little. Light grows. And grows. Too quickly for his stinging eyes, but he hungers for sight and blinks away the tears.

A strange voice says, "Well, look at you. How did you enjoy that? Pleasant, I trust. You will experience such pleasant dreams."

306

He wants to struggle but can't move.

"Oh, there's no use doing that, my young hero, your body is almost separate from your brain. And if I keep you in this state long enough I can alter your personality. And then of course there's the addiction. Such a pity if that were to happen. I hope Mr Donnelly wires in a day or two with the good news that your family has agreed to give up without a fight. I mean what would be the point of resisting – when your brain has turned to mush and you are hopelessly addicted. But that's a few days off yet. For now you can relax and enjoy. In an hour you'll be able to sit up and eat; got to keep up your strength."

Somehow he manages to pee into a rusting old pot. He can barely swallow the odd soupy concoction his weird captor feeds him. He thinks about overpowering him; since he's smaller it should be easy, but suddenly Luke feels odd; his head swims and he has to lie down. His captor chuckles.

"It's in the soup. And I won't need to gag you this time. I've got you well-managed. Now you relax. This won't hurt."

A tourniquet pinches his arm.

"You have good strong veins. Very helpful."

He feels the sharp prickle of a syringe as it slides into him; the cold solution spews forth and he imagines clouds of colored dye floating through his blood. The tourniquet comes away.

Come get me, Ethan.

He begins to float.

He dreams about Jennifer. She comes to him, her hair like a chestnut cloud and her eyes like emeralds on fire. She gives herself to him, her body soft and warm and smooth. She is like a drug he can never give up. He won't give her up. He can never be whole without her.

Somewhere off in the distance he hears strange laughter. Jennifer is leaving. He calls for her; tears well up in his eyes; where is she? He must get her back.

A voice says, "Relax, my young hero. She'll come back. Next time. Be patient."

Emmaline

Office of Sheriff, Laramie

Emmaline cannot help it; she needs to pace. It clearly annoys Sheriff Ransford. In fact, he seems like one giant frown of suspicion.

"You're wasting time," she remarks.

"We'll see," he says. He's much older than Cliff, forty or more, with leathery skin; the epitome of an outdoorsman.

And somehow he seems to have more deputies, all of whom sit about waiting for the confirmation from Cheyenne, watching her as she paces, cleaning the barrels of their rifles with soft cloths. Every so often one or two make fun of her... they think it a huge joke that she carries a sheriff's badge.

"Come on, Mac," she breathes.

Suddenly, the youngest deputy flies into the room. He holds out a telegram. "Sheriff, it's from Cheyenne."

Her heart bounces every which way; butterflies take flight in her stomach. Her eyes are glued to Sheriff Ransford's face as he reads. His shrewd gaze is on her within seconds.

"Mac's confirmed," he says. Relief.

Murmurs of excitement ripple across the room.

"Well, Miss Roberts, it looks like you are Cliff Ryan's deputy. Come into my office and we'll plan our next move."

She nods and follows Sheriff Ransford into his office. Three other men, senior deputies, do likewise.

"This is Crogan, Mason and Deloight."

"How do you do, gentlemen," she says. "Roberts will do fine. I don't use the *miss* myself."

"Right, Roberts," says Sheriff Ransford. "Let's go over this again. Where's that notebook of yours? I want to know every detail and I hope you know what to expect from Maverick because we sure as heck don't."

"Actually, you do," she says as she produces her notebook. "He's been targeting Albany County folks for some time. Mr Adams in Dickson for one."

"The sniper?"

She nods. "The only reason I'm alive right now is because of Mac and Ryan."

The deputy Deloight, thirtyish, blond hair, blue eyes, says, "We have a special file on all those shootings."

"Get it out, Deloight, as much as I hate being reminded that we ain't yet been able to get to the bottom of them."

"It seems," Emmaline says, "that if Donnelly has Luke Taylor hostage he intends to bargain on Bodecker's behalf. Something like: hand over your land or Luke dies. Or to Luke, instruct your family to hand it over or they die."

"Plain old threats don't seem likely with these stakes."

"It's about capitulation."

"Mm, the Alliance ain't well known for that. Taylor would let himself be killed first."

"Well, even if he does for that very reason, Maverick sharp-shooters will be used."

"Shoot one of the family, that way it terrorizes any survivors into keeping quiet and giving up. Why wouldn't you? You wouldn't hang around to die. But like I said, the Alliance ain't known for capitulating, but with Luke Taylor's life in the balance they might just do it. And vice versa for Luke. The fact that they're miles apart is really gonna test the family bonds."

"I understand that they are exceptionally strong."

Sheriff Ransford gives a nod. "It's called survival."

The deputy Crogan, late thirties, brown hair, brown eyes, says, "So Donnelly doesn't know we know about his plans. Come to think of it, how do we know?"

"Ryan wouldn't disclose his source," she tells him.

"He's protecting someone," Sheriff Ransford concludes. "I hope

Mac and Faraday have got that someone well hid." He looks over at the deputy Mason, who's bald, on the stout side with a pair of piercing eyes. "I'm gonna need someone here, Doug."

"Sure, Dave."

"The press might get wind of it. Roberts, what's the situation in Cheyenne regarding the newspapers?"

"Well, the Tribune knows about Luke Taylor and the bashed deputy. Mr Quaid has connections. So that story will break. But whether he knows to bring Donnelly into the picture? – I don't think so; I don't believe his source is that close to the Lincoln County sheriff. According to Ryan, Mr Faraday has informed the governor and the mayor of the situation, so in their case I'd say they will have to plan to separate themselves from Bodecker to save their own necks, but I'm certain Mr Faraday will have asked for their co-operation. He is thoroughly determined to indict Bodecker and wouldn't want anything to go wrong at this stage."

"The story breaking in the press will have Maverick running in the opposite direction, Dave," Mason remarks. "We'd never catch him."

"I want the press kept in the dark, Doug. And send word to Cheyenne – the same. We can't do much about the Tribune's knowing about Luke and the incident on the train, but at least we can stop it going any further."

The journalist in Emmaline is appalled. She bits her bottom lip. Sheriff Ransford notices.

"I know how you feel, Roberts, but just think of the story you'll have at the end of this."

"Although that is a great consolation," she says, "I know for a fact that's what Ryan would want. I'm sure Mac is suppressing every detail on Ryan's orders at this very moment, so you won't need to risk another telegram."

Deloight returns with the special file, and something else.

"Found a map of the Bright River district. Sure hope some of that recent snow's melted down by the time we get there."

Emmaline shivers...

With the information delivered as promised, her thoughts drift to a determined young man in a blue coat, now so very far away.

FIVE

What is begun
at daybreak must at dark be done,
tomorrow will be another day;
tomorrow the hot furnace flame
will search the heart and try the frame,
and stamp with honour or with shame
these vessels made of clay.

Henry Wadsworth Longfellow
Keramos

North Platte Extrication

Day One
February 2, 1885

Cliff rides steadfastly for hours through the eternal snow and a pale wash of sunshine on a sturdy mount he commandeered from the livery in Watts Landing. He follows the rail line, giving Cheyenne a wide berth, until he reaches the settlement of Hillsdale ahead of an east-bound Union Pacific that will take him to North Platte. Here he stables the horse and heads to the ticket office where the clerk recognizes him and gives him passage in the first-class sleeper car. When Cliff tells him second-class will do fine, the clerk insists.

"There ain't a ticket left in second-class. Lotta folks on the move at present, Sheriff, don't ask me why."

After riding most of the day, Cliff's not about to complain.

Once aboard and underway, he checks with the conductor when they might expect to reach North Platte.

"Lotta snow and ice about. Can't see us going full steam, and we have a few stops to make, but we should be there before breakfast tomorrow morning. Can't guarantee nothing though…"

The westering sun casts long shadows of the train across the snowbound upland prairies. It's a lonesome view.

Vast.

Monotonous.

Pure.

Prairie by prairie, town by town, they make progress.

Eventually, the Wyoming plains recede into the dusk.

Nebraska. And he no longer has jurisdiction. For most of the journey he has focused relentlessly on his objective. Only now does he feel like a man pulled in two directions. In his heart he knows he has done the right thing, and because of this he doesn't need to rationalize his actions, particularly as he's moving closer towards his destination. But that doesn't mean for one moment he's stopped thinking about Emma. Her voice is in his head; her beauty in his eyes; her spirit in his blood. And that's a lot for a ruthless sheriff with a difficult task ahead of him to be getting on with. He doesn't doubt for a second that she has done the job he entrusted her to do; she's the type of person who does everything the only way she knows how: with distinction. Her safety *is* his concern, but she's smart and she's learnt a lot over the past several days.

Keep on telling yourself, Ryan, just keep on telling yourself…

He eats a solitary supper to the leisurely rhythm of the train, and after a long cold day the hot food is welcome. The windows darken and transform into mirrors as night settles in; he sees the reflections of the other diners. A car attendant moves about drawing down the shades.

You miss her, Ryan.

Exhausted, he tosses his duffle onto his bunk, crawls in after it and fixes the drapes, enclosing himself in his own little world for the night.

And it's only going to get worse.

He strips down and turns onto his stomach with his face in the pillow.

Face it, Ryan, something you never expected has happened.

The train clatters and clicks over the line, rattles and rolls into the deepening night.

She wore your coat to bed. What does that tell you?

The question carousels in his head until he finally falls asleep.

Third time lucky, Luke hopes, as he squeezes his eyes shut and then firmly blinks them open. He swipes his hand in front of him again. Back and forth. He can feel the disturbance in the air, but sees nothing. He presses his fingers into his flesh; pinches.

Awake. Not hallucinating. In fact, he feels more lucid than any-time since...

The mad doctor hasn't been back for some time. The power of the drug begins to wane.

He moves his head; blackness to the side, and the other. But then which way is up? The basement lies in deep darkness; or he's blind.

There are no bindings on his wrists, or across his mouth. But around his vision, around his sense of perspective, the restraints are taut and very real.

There is no light. None. Not a skerrick.

He needs to pee real bad. But there's no way he can locate the old bucket.

How long has he been here? Hours, days, weeks...

What happened to everyone? Where'd everyone get to? Has the world ended? Mart said the world would end one day. He used to say the only way to get to the end of anything tricky is one step at a time. But Luke's lying down. Or so he thinks. He feels the cot beneath his back. So the ground is still there. The walls? The ceiling? If he can feel with his fingers, maybe they can be his eyes. He reaches out around him into nothingness. Right and left there's nothing. Above, nothing. But there is floor and he can crawl on that. He heaves several deep breaths into his lungs and counts to three. Nothing happens. His body doesn't move.

Again. This time he puts some grunt into it.

His body hurls through the black abyss. The floor catches him and sends shock waves of very real pain through his body. As he heaves more breath, the smell of earth hits his nostrils. The floor is dirt, reeking dirt... If he could get to his hands and knees, he could find a way out. Sweat drenches his brow; his brain is so dizzy in its black cocoon he's on the verge of throwing up. But he begins to crawl, dragging himself, arms, knees, everything he has, into the blackness.

He spits dirt from his mouth; the sound plays like a favorite tune in his ears. Sound. The sound of himself. He creeps, he crawls. A snake in a black pit. He moves his tongue around his mouth.

Words. *Make words.*

"Jennifer. Just... wait..."

Day Two

Cliff pays for a cheap room over an inconspicuous-looking saloon in the low end of town and stows his gear. The morning is rigid with frost and intense cold. North Platte looks like it would shatter like glass if someone threw a stone. Under a blanket of immaculate snow, the town is crystallized into the banks of its icy rivers and frozen streams. The train, although slow, suffered no unscheduled delays as it steamed through the night and across the plains, and from sheer exhaustion Cliff slept through most of it. Beneath a sky the color of lusterless pearl, it chuffed into North Platte with the sun barely able to raise a glimmer. In essence, it all amounts to one thing. He has no idea where Luke is or what's happened to him, and this kind of weather is deadly.

Luke lies faces down in the dirt just inches from his own vomit. He hasn't moved for so long now he's frozen to the floor. His whole body aches and his skin crawls. He's shivering mercilessly with cold, even though there are flames beneath his skin. He can't move. Can't see. Can't anything.

He has no idea how to fix this.

Sound, speech, sight – all gone.

How long? *How long!*

Something is touching him, pulling at him. Weird sounds reach his ears. He feels a sharp prickle somewhere on his skin and then everything, including this hell, goes away.

Cliff begins his search of North Platte by having breakfast in the busiest eatery in town. *Nell's Nebraska Bite.* Catchy. Cliff doesn't eat as much as he listens. A few conversations center on the escaped murderer, the one who 'killed the whore on the train'. A few mutter that she got what was coming to her.

His waitress tells him he's come to North Platte at a bad time; there's a murderer on the loose and no one's safe.

"On the loose?"

"He knocked out the deputy who was trying to lock him up and got away."

"No sightings since then?"

"It's like he disappeared. Rumor has it he's got an accomplice who's hiding him somewhere."

"Here in town?"

"Yesterday's newspaper reported that the sheriff could find no evidence that the murderer had left town." Her eyes narrow and she whispers, "They think he's still here."

"Any of your customers seen suspicious types hanging about?"

"North Platte ain't like that usually. We're kinda friendly. We got our share of odd-folk but we know who they are."

Before he can discover the identity of those odd-folk his waitress is called away. He pays for his meal and heads off to his next stop, the general store in the next block. It's a large, well-stocked store with a 'let me pass the time of day with you' type of shopkeeper tending the till. A few townsfolk, mostly women, attend to their selections quietly, so Cliff approaches the till.

"Hear tell there's a murderer holed up in town somewhere."

"Yep."

"Folks are getting jittery."

"Some."

"Now who would do such an unneighborly thing like stash a murderer?"

"'Til the heat's off, I reckon."

"Yeah? Could be. You know, I reckon there's a way you can tell who's doing the stashing."

"Oh?"

"Mm. Notice anyone buying more than their usual supplies? You know, extras. Food, clothes, shaving gear and such..."

"Ah. Some folks have relatives and friends coming to visit..."

"But you'd know who they were..."

The shopkeeper gives a nod. "True. Yep, that's true."

Cliff lifts an eyebrow. "So who is purchasing more than usual and hasn't got relatives staying?"

"Hey, you're a cluey feller, ain't you?"

Cliff shrugs.

The shopkeeper's eyes narrow. "You got a personal interest in this, mister?" His eyes fly wide. "You're a reporter! Decked out like you are, you sure had me fooled."

"Well, I'm under cover and I don't want it blown. But you could be my source. I won't name you in my story, but when I mention my source, you'll know it was you who helped break the story, catch the murderer. So, how about it?"

The shopkeeper serves a customer. Thanks her by name.

"Good day, Mr Lumsden," she says and leaves.

Cliff gives the man a lazy smile. "So how about it, Lumsden?"

Cliff dumps his box, packed to overflowing with supplies, on his bed. No reason why he wouldn't need any of this stuff at some point in his life. He extracts the list from the inside pocket of his coat. There are ten names on his piece of paper, and all have been buying extra supplies. And Lumsden tossed in a couple of town odd-folk for good measure. *You can't miss the odd-folk. We never know what they're up to, and they don't like folks knowing, but they're there all the same, and their money is as good as anybody's.*

What Lumsden doesn't realize is that some odd-folk have a way of knowing more about townsfolk than the townsfolk. They need to know who they can trust and who to avoid.

He lifts a candy bar from the top of his box and breaks into it. Every town has them. The eccentrics. The marginalized. Isn't Mrs Landers one of Cheyenne's? They keep secrets. March to the beat of a different drum. Look different. Express different opinions. Are persecuted. Harassed. Ridiculed. Laughed at. Blamed when things go awry. Among the first to be accused. Create holes in what would be a perfect patchwork of town life. He's fought for these people from the moment he took his oath. They have their rights, same as everyone else. Ever since he began chopping wood for Mrs Landers people treat her differently. Now she's sweet old Mrs Landers, not the weird old lady who appears and disappears like a ghost.

People's uniqueness is the stuff of life, not their sameness.

But not if their uniqueness harbors menace.

There is one particular point Lumsden seemed determined to make. It appears that North Platte has its very own scientist. *He's a doctor, you know, and a chemist, but no drug store in this town deals with him; he's real odd and we all steer clear of him; strange smells come from his place; but the sheriff says he ain't doing nothing illegal; has a permit for inventing chemicals to kill insects; you know, the ones that attack crops; he's got these funny eyes, see, like he's seeing one thing and thinking another; lives on the edge of town; hear tell he has a buyer in Omaha for whatever it is he concocts in that laboratory of his; in my opinion, I think he should be asked to leave town.*

Before Lumsden mentioned Omaha, Cliff thought the scientist was merely another Mrs Landers. As much as he hates to admit it, Omaha puts this man under suspicion. Criminals spread their evil deeds far and wide, a known fact. And they like to wear a mask of innocence. He munches on the remainder of his candy. What is it Mac likes to say? *I'd rather have a hunch crawling with coincidences than no hunch at all.*

He runs his eye down the list one more time. The following people bought extra supplies from Lumsden in the last few days.

Dieter Svensen, farmer

Jules Wishard, rancher

Mariah West, widow

Cooper McLaren, bank teller

Miss Emerald, saloon girl at the Bijou Saloon

Miss Sapphire, her twin

Louis Porterfield, scientist

Wilma Young, loner

Eliza Bensen, loner

Steven Knox, he paints.

No prizes for guessing who the odd-folks are.

If Luke is being held in town, there is a chance that someone is being forced to take care of him. Lumsden said the Bijou twins were nice girls, but prostitution is a notorious cover, and local working girls tend to talk, so quizzing them is likely to blow his own cover. Still, later on he's likely to need a drink to warm his cold insides. They bought extra soap.

Farmers and ranchers live too far out of town; it's too obvious and Ralph Walker would have already searched all the outlying ranches and farms.

Widows are vulnerable for sure. But many are also tough as old boots and have to be. Still, he'll be able to tell about Mariah West as soon as she opens her door to him. She bought a whole bolt of cheesecloth and dried fruit.

Bank tellers. Targets for extortion.

Cooper McLaren purchased items from nearly every department in the store. Needed a wagon to take it all away. Setting up house? *Could be.* A tad obvious.

So what now about the scientist, the painter and the loners?

Dr Louis Porterfield.

What kind of extra supplies did the scientist purchase? Extra vegetables, carrots and potatoes. That's all. More soup? Stew? An experiment? Does he do this occasionally? *Nope; can't say that he does; but he came yesterday afternoon.*

Knox the painter bought more canned food than usual.

Nearly filled a crate.

Cliff knew an artist once, back in Chicago, whose view of the world was completely different to anyone he'd ever met; but the artist type tends to be intent on expression, in a world of their own. Why a businessman like Donnelly would chose an artist's home as a lair defies logic, unless the artist is so compliant and in need of patronage he'd take a lodger on Donnelly's behalf.

Wilma Young and Eliza Bensen are probably North Platte's version of Mrs Landers: Eliza bought a blanket and Wilma two pairs of men's socks.

On the edge of town beside a frozen stream, there's a dark gray house set back in a fenced yard spiked with at least half a dozen bare trees. Dr Porterfield's. The nearest house is about three hundred yards up the street. It's a march to the front door; no one has shoveled the snow in recent times, and ahead of Cliff deep footprints pattern the way. The window shutters are all closed up tight. Clutching carrots and potatoes in their brown bag, he knocks firmly on the door.

And again.

At last the door is pulled back by a smallish bald man with bright round eyes. "What do you want?"

Cliff smiles. "Mr Lumsden said you left these groceries in the store yesterday. Carrots and potatoes? Said you might be needing them. I happen to mention I was coming out this way and he asked if I wouldn't mind dropping them off to you."

He holds out the bag. Dr Porterfield blinks; his eyes flit from Cliff to the bag and back.

"No, Lumsden is wrong. I didn't forget my vegetables. They must be someone else's. Now excuse me, I'm a very busy man."

Cliff looks confused. "That's strange. He seemed so sure." He sniffs the air. "That sure don't smell like soup on the stove..."

"That's because it's not..."

"I'm new in town, but that ain't like nothing I've ever smelled before."

Dr Porterfield starts to close the door. "You should get around more. Take a course perhaps. Good day." And the door snaps shut.

Cliff taps again.

The door snaps back. The eyes are bulging with impatience.

"What?"

"You wouldn't happen to know where Wilma Young lives, would you? I know she lives here in town, but we lost contact and..."

"So," says the woman called Wilma.

She's tall and big bosomed but wrinkled and weathered, with leathery eyelids drooping over intense blue eyes. "So, you reckon that your cousin knew me from school. And before she died she wanted you to come to tell me she was sorry for all the mean things she said when we was kids?"

Cliff smiles. "Here. I bought you some soup vegetables."

Wilma's blue eyes narrow on him. "Son, I don't remember your cousin. And if I went to school one day in my life I think I'd remember that too."

He looks perplexed. "Mm. Must be another Wilma Young."

"And you can take your vegetables. I ain't needing charity. I got me a house and a fireplace."

He thinks for a moment. "Got an axe?"

"And I ain't gonna let you murder me with m'own axe neither!"

He grins. "To chop wood."

Wilma's eyes light up. "You chop wood?"

"For a hot cup of coffee."

"Chop those logs out back, I'll accept your cousin's apology."

Half an hour later Wilma inspects his work. "Mm. You done this before. Apology accepted. Come inside and get a hot drink. You deserve it."

While he's sipping coffee, Wilma says, "Sorry there ain't no pie to offer you, Cliff."

"This is fine," he says. "I figure you live here alone, Wilma."

"Sure I do. I like my independence."

"So what's with the men's socks on the bureau over there?"

Wilma tosses her head. "Keep my feet warmer, and I got big feet. I'd show ya, but that wouldn't be polite, now would it?"

"Guess not." He shares a laugh with her. "There's someone else I'm looking for."

"Yeah?"

"Eliza Bensen."

"Your cousin terrorize her at school too?"

"I haven't decided yet."

Wilma belly laughs. And an infectious laugh it is, too.

"Well, if you're going over to Eliza's you'd better take some of that wood you just chopped. Make sure she takes your vegetables too. Finish your coffee and I'll fetch a crate."

Eliza's small decrepit bungalow shivers on the bank of a frozen waterhole. The remnants of someone's past life lie scattered about the ice-encrusted yard. A broken down wagon with its wheels half buried in the snow. Farming equipment. Ploughing tack. The back-yard can be seen through walls of the barn. It looks like no one lives here. Except that someone has shoveled a path to the rickety front stoop. The shovel rests by the door, rusted, with a broken handle.

He knocks. Snow falls from the eaves and the house seems to shudder.

The door squeaks open. A tiny old woman wrapped in a blanket appears. She looks up into his face as he towers over her.

He swallows hard and removes his hat. "Mornin', M'am. I was

chopping some wood for Wilma Young and she said you might be needing some."

"Oh, my… that Wilma is so thoughtful, so thoughtful. But I don't know you, young man."

"Why I'm a cousin of the woman who used to terrorize Wilma back in school."

"Oh my…"

"This sure is a pretty piece of land, Mrs Bensen."

"It's condemned you know, this house. No one knows I'm here except Wilma. Expect they'll chase me out soon enough."

"They?"

"Yes. You know the ones who do that sort of thing. You can put that wood in here by the hearth," she instructs him, opening her door and allowing him access. Inside consists of one large room.

"There are some fresh vegetables as well. Don't let them go to waste."

"Wilma got more than she needs, has she?" Eliza asks cannily.

"She's all set, M'am."

"Ah."

"M'am, you wouldn't know anything about Dr Louis Porterfield, would you?"

Her eyes slide down into her wrinkles. "The scientist feller…"

"Mm." He sets about making a larger fire in Eliza's hearth.

"Nasty that one. One tracked people often are."

"How so?"

"Got in his way once. He pushed me aside, said he was in a hurry. I fell in the snow and a nice young woman helped me up and told him he should be ashamed of himself. But not that one. Don't think he'd know what shame was. Ah, just look at that fire. Does me good just to look at it. You won't tell no one I'm here, will you?"

The smell lingering at the door of Steven Knox's alleyway entrance is unusual, but recognizable and kind of comfortable compared to the scientist's odor. Linseed oil, artist's paint, candle grease…

Cliff knocks loudly. The door is reefed open. A tall, thin man about his age, with blond hair and a moustache, says, "What do you want? He sent you, didn't he? Look, I'm just trying to do my job. Why can't he see that? I'm not interested in his wife, okay? She sat for me. She's an interesting subject. I bet he never took the time to see her the way I did. That's the problem, ain't it?"

"Is she here?" Cliff asks.

The man's nostrils flare.

"Because I can come back if you're busy."

Suspicious glare.

"You *are* Knox, the artist? Portraits are your specialty?"

"He didn't send you?"

"Who?"

A long sigh. "Never mind. Yes, I'm Steven Knox."

"So are you busy?"

"I have a few irons in the fire, so to speak."

"May I come in and take a look at your work?"

Knox steps back. "Sure."

Once Cliff's inside, Knox sticks his head out and quickly looks right and left before closing the door.

On an easel near a window stands a large portrait of a very beautiful woman. It's not particularly provocative, but there is a seductive air about her, which appeals to Cliff…

"Her husband hates it. He refuses to pay me. *She* on the other hand loves it, but he won't allow her to pay me either."

"Beautiful woman," Cliff murmurs.

Knox pushes his fingers through his hair. "It's her mouth. She has a great mouth." He sighs and starts wiping a brush on an oil soaked rag.

Cliff leaves Knox to stew a bit and wanders around his studio. There's a staircase leading up to an attic level, and a kitchen, with a rumpled brass bed in the far corner of the studio.

Cliff catches Knox's eye.

"I didn't sleep with her," Knox mumbles in an open-ended tone: not that it didn't occur to him, or even that he didn't try. "There was more to her. I just helped bring it out. That's what an artist does."

Cliff studies the portrait nonchalantly. No, he slept with her, more than once, because her want is in her eyes and the shape of her mouth; artists take a different slant on things.

His art is good. There are a variety of compositions and land-scapes, as well as numerous portraits, all differing in size. There is also a small table set up with an eclectic mix of items, featuring an arrangement of canned food.

Knox says, "A still life commission." And he shrugs.

"You shouldn't have a problem selling these."

"They're nearly all sold. I have three other commissions."

"You make a pretty good living as an artist out here."

"There are art lovers back east who pay well for frontier art. But, even the locals it seems like to look at their own back yard. I'm doing okay, but I don't need jerks that won't pay me for a major work."

"Have you a sponsor or an agent out here?"

"I work alone. I have an agent back east…"

"You're not trying to support a family?"

"No. So do you want me to paint for you?"

"I'm thinking about it. I might be back later."

"Take your time. I'll be here."

"You know, Knox, to my way of thinking, that woman's husband wouldn't need a three foot reminder of his wife's infidelity staring down at him from over his fireplace."

Knox gazes at the portrait; his fair cheeks begin to glow pink and his eyes caress his subject.

Especially when the affair is still in progress…

Mariah West is a young widow who owns and runs a popular fancy restaurant, the sort of establishment that Emma would find agreeable. He drops in for lunch and as he waits to be seated he notices that her tables are spread with neatly trimmed cheesecloth squares and matching napkins. Her food is delicious and hearty with a lot of trouble gone into making the food look nice on the plate. There is a pudding on the dessert menu that boasts tender dried fruit soaked in brandy as one of its ingredients. And it's damn good. With the right food filling his once empty recesses, he decides to return to Porterfield's place before the afternoon cold comes down any harder than it already has.

He skirts the perimeter of Porterfield's property and heads

round the back of the large gray house. The snow is dense with ice and his breath freezes as soon as it leaves his mouth. He's not even sure what he's looking for particularly; basically anything that increases his already healthy suspicion of Porterfield. He's working off hunches again. And the premise, if you're innocent you have nothing to hide, just like the others.

The backyard consists of more deep snow and wintering trees. He imagines this place in summer with every tree a billowing cloud of green leaves and swaying branches, a veil for this man's odd science. At the back of the house, clearly visible and darkly contrasted against the thick layer of snow all about them, are the basement doors – everything else is groaning under the weight of past snowfalls, but these are padlocked and exposed. The back windows of the house are shuttered like the front. A small porch protects the back entrance, accessible by a short stoop.

Using the trees as cover, he moves from one to the next to reach the back of the house. The snow is very deep here. He makes it to the entrance of the basement, his throat stinging and his chest aching. Other than the key itself, the heavy lock would need a couple of direct hits from his colt or a pair of bolt cutters.

Keeping low, he treads softly to a window; after slowly reaching up he tries to pull back one of the shutters. It won't budge; it seems to be rusted in place.

Clearly, there's not a quiet way of breaking into this house.

Unless… a different tack altogether.

He treads stealthily around to the front again and creeps to the front door; very slowly, he tries the door handle. It turns and the door pops open. He draws a steadying breath and knocks hard.

"Hello, anyone here?" he swings the door wide and takes a step inside. The smell of chemicals assaults his nostrils.

There's a scuttling sound and Porterfield appears. "How dare you? What do you want?"

Cliff grins.

"Remember me? I went back to the store with the vegetables. Told Lumsden that they weren't yours. He was confused, but what can I say? The man probably gets customers confused every day; it's a busy store…"

Porterfield makes a shooing action with his arms… "You'll have to leave."

"But I just found out that you experiment to make chemicals for eradicating insects from crops. I guess you're working with arsenic, sulphur, et cetera. Such a coincidence. I have a cousin who is a chemist. In Chicago. He's written a paper on some work he's been doing. Industrial stuff. The way of things is mass production, he says, and industry needs science. He's due for a letter from me and he'd be thrilled if I could tell him about your work. Have you published, Dr Porterfield?"

The man's eyes bulge. "You have to leave."

"But you don't understand. What you're doing here is unique. I mean, look where you are. North Platte, Nebraska. I sure would love to see your work and write my cousin. Hear tell in town that they're kinda chuffed to have a scientist."

"That's a lie. They hate me," Porterfield retorts.

"If you're anything like my cousin, you like to work in secret so nobody steals your achievements. It happens. Lotta jealousy out there. And as for the folks in town, people who keep secrets are kinda scary."

"You're ridiculous. I don't care about you or your cousin. Get out."

Cliff sweeps a glance across the entrance hall. "I can almost hear your experiments bubbling, although I guess you gotta love your work to stand the smell, eh?"

"What part of get out don't you understand?"

"You know, people will like you more if you're more sociable, Dr Porterfield. You got no competition in town, so you should let your hair down…"

Porterfield immediately puts his hand on his bald head.

"Er, sorry… just an expression. Say, you wouldn't happen to have some coffee on the stove, would you? I could use a hot drink."

Cliff sidesteps Porterfield, strides down the hall to the back of the house. He reaches the kitchen with the scientist close on his heels.

"You have to leave."

A coffee pot steams gently on a large cast iron range.

Beside it, also steaming, is a boiler.

Cliff saunters right up to it.

"Mm, is that soup? Ah, potatoes, carrots… no meat?"

Porterfield jams a lid on the pot.

"That's a lotta soup there, Doc. You already got a visitor." Cliff smacks the side of his head. "That's why you want me to leave. You're entertaining someone already. A colleague?"

Porterfield says nothing.

"You know, over a bowl of that soup, I could tell you and your colleague all about my cousin's work." Cliff starts opening cabinet doors looking for bowls. "You know, my cousin says that industry is turning Chicago into one of this nation's most important cities. Factories of every conceivable kind. Industry needs science… new stuff, all the time."

He finds the bowls in an otherwise ordinary-looking kitchen, the exception being several used bowls soaking in murky water in the sink. Then, somewhere in the house, a clock starts chiming the hour.

Porterfield's eyes dart about. "You have to go. One of my experiments is ready and I need to attend to it."

Cliff grins. "Can I watch?"

Porterfield squeals, "No." And mops his brow.

"I won't touch anything. My cousin…"

"Stop this about your cousin. You have to leave. Now."

"But it's cold out. I'm just a traveler passing through, looking for a little hospitality."

With speed Cliff didn't think possible, Louis Porterfield opens a drawer and extracts a small revolver.

Cliff stares at it, and at Porterfield's tremulous hand.

"Is that loaded?"

"Yes, it's loaded," Porterfield squawks. "And if you don't leave, I'm going to shoot you."

Cliff nods. "You're right, you're absolutely right. No one, and I mean no one, can be too careful about strangers these days. Hear tell that there's an escaped murderer probably holed up somewhere in town. Folks are scared. I'm not surprised you got that gun there. Sensible. Because you just don't know who's gonna turn up on your doorstep."

He sweeps back his coat and draws his colt with well-practiced speed. Porterfield's eyes pop.

"I got one too, because you just never know."

Porterfield, stunned and inert, allows Cliff to take his revolver from him. Cliff pockets it. "Okay, Louis... you don't mind if I call you Louis... let's go attend to that experiment."

They go back up the hall. Cliff locks the front door. They head into a different part of the house, where the smells become intense, and enter a large room decked out like a laboratory. Concoctions hiss and bubble. The room is dark but for low burning lamps illuminating various sections of equipment. There are two doors apart from the one they just came through. He guesses that one leads to the basement and the other outside, a side entrance for the laboratory itself, bolted top and bottom.

"What do you create here, Louis?"

"You won't get away with this," he says.

"No, I think I will. So, show me the experiment, Lou."

"Louis. There's nothing to see, just what you see here."

"That door there leads to the basement?"

Porterfield just stares.

"Silence is always such a definitive answer."

"It's... there's nothing."

"And what kind of fool would I be if I believed you?" He pushes Porterfield towards the basement door. "Let's take a look, shall we? Open it."

"This is my only work, up here..."

"Very ho hum, Louis. Now open the basement door or I'll shoot you."

Porterfield opens the door.

Cliff reels, almost pushed back by the rank odor.

"Are you keeping dead bodies down there, Louis?"

Porterfield shakes his head. "No. No. I don't kill anyone."

"I'll be the judge of that. We'll need some light."

"Yes."

Cliff reaches for the nearest lamp. "You see, Louis, now you're cooperating..."

Holding the lamp high, he shoves Porterfield through the doorway with the point of his gun. Slowly, with Porterfield both nervous and purposely dithering, they descend a set of wooden stairs.

"Gees, Louis, this wouldn't happen to be where you dump all those failed experiments, would it?"

They get to the bottom of the stairs. The basement is an expanse of dank and bitterly cold darkness.

"Is there another lamp in here, Louis?"

"Ceiling, but…

"Light it."

"But…"

"*Now*, Louis."

"I can't see."

"Light a match, you… I assume you carry matches in your pocket. Now find the damn lamp. And don't go getting any stupid ideas because I can and will shoot you."

The jittery scientist finally shuffles off to do as he's told, babbling something under his breath. Cliff turns away, using his lamp to inspect the space around the stairs; he hears Porterfield scrape a match; there is nothing in the blackness of this putrid space, so he places the lamp on the bottom step to light the way out and returns to Porterfield.

"Who… who are you?"

But Cliff doesn't answer. The ceiling lamp has revealed something – and everything. Mariah West's lunch surges precariously in his stomach. He holds onto it. Just.

"What have you done?" he rasps.

"Who are you?" the Porterfield whispers.

Cliff's chest explodes with rage. "This man's friend."

He thrusts his fist into Porterfield's face; the man crumples to the floor and the only sound thereafter is Cliff's heavy and pained breathing.

Luke went flying with Jennifer again. They soared above clouds the color of sunset. Made love high above the world. Descended to earth. Lay side by side on the grass, shivering with happiness.

Then she faded away…

…and he stood up on the Diamond-T.

Home.

It's Jennifer I love, Sara.

You loved Kelley. I know you, Luke. This other woman is just a distraction. You loved Kelley, you will always love her.

Not the way I love Jennifer.

I don't believe you, Luke. You love Kelley.

He screams. "No!"

Darkness.

The power of the drug begins to wane. Again.

Smells return.

The smell of dirt.

The intense scent of a warm human being. The freak. Get away.

And sounds. The rustle of clothing. Boots on earth.

"No…get away…from me…"

"Easy, Luke, just take it easy."

"Get away…"

"Luke…"

"No."

"Take it easy. You're safe."

"Not safe."

"I can see that things have been a bit grim, but now you're safe."

His heart is in his mouth. Not the freak?

"I promise."

He begins to think he recognizes that voice.

"Not real…"

"It's Cliff."

"Not real…"

"In the flesh."

"Dreaming…"

"No. I'm here."

"Blind. Can't see you."

A pause. "Shit."

"Not real."

"Can you get up?"

"Can't move. Drugs. Dreams."

"It's over now. You're safe, I promise."

"Where's...?"

"I've dealt with him. Time to get you out of here."

A new strength takes over; it seems to belong to the voice.

"You know, pal, you don't smell the best."

"No control." He is hoisted to his feet. "Dizzy..."

"Take a minute."

"Fainting."

Not soup. No. No.

"It's just water, Luke. Come on, swallow."

Cold. Cold.

He swallows. Not soup. "Cold."

"I've stripped your soiled clothing off you. Porterfield's got a bath back here."

"So...cold."

Blanket.

"Can't see."

"Nothing? Light, shapes?"

"No."

"Did he do anything to your eyes?"

"Drugs. Darkness."

"Well, it will probably wear off soon. Just hang on. All you got to do is soak in this tub. Warm you up. Get clean."

He can hear well enough. The sound of Cliff's voice. And what that means.

"Home."

"It's being taken care of."

"Gotta get...home."

"I told you. It's being taken care of. Even as we speak. This is deep enough. Time to get in."

Cold. Cold biting his body.

Water. Warm. Clean. Fresh.

Swooning...

Fresh clean warm water...

His hand being grasped and something smacked into it...

"Soap, Luke. Wash."

He can barely move. "Let me...lie here...a minute."

"Sure, Luke."

"The freak…"

"Tied up in the basement. Listen, Luke, since you're lying about like this, might be a good time for me to go back to town, get you some clothes and a doctor. Can you manage?"

"Can't move, Cliff…can't see. Ain't sure…you're real…"

Warm hands, warm water, washing his face.

"I'm real. And you're sick. But I'm going to make sure you get better."

He swallows. "The drugs…when they wear off…"

"I won't be long."

Cliff finds relief at the sight of Wilma's astonished but friendly face. "Well, look who we got here…"

"Afternoon, Wilma."

"Have you come a-calling on old Wilma, young feller?"

"I need a doctor. Who would you recommend?"

She gives him a droll look. "Let's see. A doctor for the cousin of the woman who terrorized me back in the old school days that I never had. You hurt? Sick?"

He shakes his head. "A friend."

"Doc Kincaid on Dewey Street. Know where that is? Want me to show ya?"

"No. Stay out of the cold. I'll find it."

"He's a fine gentleman. He comes and sees Eliza and me regular. Never charges a penny. Never tells nobody where Eliza's squatting. He's your man."

"Thanks, Wilma."

"Don't mention it. Hope your friend gets better."

Cliff dons his poker face as heads into Lumsden's general store.

"So, what can I do for *you*?" Lumsden greets him.

"I need more clothes than I bought with me."

"Well, there's all the gentlemen's gear over in that corner. Go get what you need."

Cliff gathers armfuls of garments, including woolen long johns, socks, woolen shirts, jacket and coat, and boots.

Lumsden is bug-eyed. "This lot won't come cheap."

"I forgot the nightshirt."

He tosses a hat on the pile as well. Lumsden makes his total and Cliff hands over the money.

Lumsden is grinning from ear to ear. He wraps the lot in brown paper and string, saying, "You know, I never figured I'd make any money out of you."

Cliff shows Kincaid through the front door of Porterfield's house of terror.

"Remember, Doc, you can't tell anyone about this."

"Don't worry," says Kincaid, looking around. "You know, I've often wondered what went on in this house."

"Well, you're about to find out." Cliff locks the door. "There's a bath…"

"You left a sick man in a bath on his own?"

"Desperate times, Doc."

"In all my years…"

Cliff reckons there's been about sixty of them.

"Come on."

The fire burns low, but the bathroom is warm. Beneath a slick of soap scrum the bathwater lurks, discolored and smelling oddly like the basement. Luke is asleep with the soap floating on top of his chest.

"The patient?" Kincaid deduces.

"Found him in the basement; he was half frozen, lying in his own filth and doped up on this stuff." He hands Kincaid a vial of liquid he found in Porterfield's pocket. "What is it, Doc?"

Kincaid looks at the vial, then removes the lid and cautiously sniffs. "Symptoms?"

"He mentioned dreams, and he's disoriented. Can't distinguish what's real. Falling in and out of consciousness. He's barely able to move. Blindness."

"Blindness?" Kincaid echoes sharply and hands back the vial. "How long has he been on this stuff?"

"I estimate three days."

Kincaid plunges his hand into the putrid water and extracts Luke's wrist. After taking Luke's pulse, he says, "He's going to be a very sick young man, I'm afraid. I'll do what I can. Now, it's time we got him into bed."

Cliff grabs several towels from a shelf behind him. "What is that stuff, Doc?"

"Morphine, although that alone…" Kincaid's expression turns grim. "To cause blindness… essentially, he's been poisoned. A controlled over-dosage, if you like. And I should warn you, he'll be in a great deal of discomfort and I dare not give him any more drugs than he's had already unless it's absolutely necessary. This won't be an easy time, tonight and the next few days."

Cliff's heart sinks. "But you'll stay tonight."

Kincaid nods brusquely. "And I'll be here as often as I can after that. He's lucky to be alive and even luckier you found him when you did. We can only hope there's no permanent damage."

They take Luke, unconscious and wrapped in blankets, to one of the upstairs bedrooms, and deposit him in an armchair. Meanwhile, Cliff finds clean linen and pillows in a closet and makes up the bed. They dress Luke in the new nightshirt and put him to bed. Kincaid draws the bedcovers over Luke's chest. Takes his pulse once more. Checks under his eyelids.

And chunters, "Never in all my years a doctor…"

Cliff returns to the basement to check on Porterfield. He's awake and struggling, protesting, despite the gag on his mouth, about Cliff manacling his hands not only behind his back but to the stairs as well. Cliff lowers the gag and holds a cup of the soup to his mouth.

"Here, drink this."

Porterfield's eyes bulge.

"Don't worry yourself, Louis. Unless you've tampered with it, I didn't touch it."

Porterfield refuses it. "What are you going to do with me?"

"Leave you here. Once Luke is well enough to travel, we'll be on our way and the place is all yours. Of course, you'll still be down here enjoying the many unique comforts it has to offer."

"Why don't you fetch the sheriff?"

Astute question from the doctor.

"It's not in the plan, Louis."

Cliff makes a fresh pot of coffee.

Upstairs, Luke's sleep is becoming fitful, and Kincaid is busy arranging a wet cloth over his forehead.

"He's coming out of the stupor now," Kincaid murmurs with a worried look on his face.

Cliff hands Kincaid a cup. "Sit and drink this. I'll tend to him."

"Thanks. You know, you haven't told me your name, or his."

Cliff pretends he didn't hear.

"He's the young man from the train, isn't he? The one they think murdered the prostitute and bashed the deputy to escape. Why would he end up here?"

"Listen, Doc…"

"He didn't do what they say he did, did he? Someone has taken away his right to defend himself and has no qualms about abusing and torturing him."

Cliff, struggling to maintain his sheriff's poker face, his hands trembling, stares helplessly at Kincaid.

"And you came to rescue him." Kincaid gives a wry grin. "You know, things are going to get pretty dynamic real soon…"

"Luke. His name is Luke." Cliff swallows.

"And you? So cautious. A lawman breaking the law perhaps. He must be a good friend, someone very important."

Suddenly, Luke croaks, "Cliff?"

They both flinch.

Cliff sits by Luke on the bed. "You're safe, Luke. You're safe."

"Can't see. Hurts, all over."

Kincaid comes forward. "The blindness will pass, I believe, as the drug passes from your body."

"Who are you?" Luke asks.

"I'm Arthur Kincaid, your doctor."

"Cliff?"

It's a desperate sound for a desperate-looking character.

"The drug…what is it?"

"Morphine."

"Jennifer said no morphine…"

"Who is Jennifer?" Kincaid asks.

"Doctor. No morphine…"

"Your body has an intolerance?"

"Bad. What will happen to me?"

"You have a healthy body and a strong heart…"

"Yes. Strong…"

"Then you can fight this. Every discomfort is bringing you one step closer to being free of the drug. Remember that, if you can."

And so it begins.

He vomits.

He sweats.

He's in constant pain. As useless as his eyes are, their dark blue pupils almost disappear into bloodshot as they weep.

As his ability to move increases, so does an unforgiving restless agitation. And he makes demands upon Kincaid who calmly offers words of encouragement and that's all – *remember, one step closer*. He goes on like this for an hour, like a cranky old man one moment and a child on the verge of a tantrum the next; then he lies curled up on top of the bedcovers, exhausted, and shivering in a strange doze.

Kincaid wrings out the cloth and sponges Luke's face and arms and legs. It seems to Cliff that the touching hurts but the soothing coolness overrides the pain. Then, he retches; Kincaid thrusts forward an enamel basin. Luke regurgitates the mouthful of water he took ten minutes ago.

Kincaid says, "He's vomiting bile; wasting and painful."

"Am I addicted to this stuff, Doc?" Luke whispers.

"I'd say more like poisoned. You received it in the past from this doctor of yours?"

Luke nods weakly. "Never did this."

"Carefully administered, no doubt."

"Careful, yes…"

"It's likely that in future you will not be able to tolerate it again. Now, if you're all right for a while, I want to go down to that lab and check out a few things."

Cliff nods. Luke grunts.

Apart from the sound of Luke's pained breathing, the room is quiet and still for a spell.

Cliff sits pensively before Luke's poisoned body: rigid with pain one moment and quivering in relief the next, his clouded face with its dark bloodshot eyes staring into space, complexion drenched with sweat and swinging rapidly from deathly pale to deep flush.

Cliff wishes Jennifer were here.

They both sorely need her reassurance.

"What did you say?" Luke breathes.

"Nothing."

"You...you said you wished...Jennifer were here."

Cliff frowns. "I didn't know I said it out loud."

"I haven't stopped...dreaming about her since...Real dreams, like she's right here." His eyelids close and his voice drops to barely a whisper. "The first few times were bad...but then they were all about her...but I can't see her in this state...it's like she gone... Sara says you're never far...from the ones you love. But...Jennifer's far, very far..." Suddenly, he's asleep; or dormant at least.

Cliff would never have matched Luke and Jennifer; only when he saw them together that first time, after the arsonist Jake Murray tried to torch Jennifer's surgery, did it occur to him, and by then there was already an understanding and a bond of trust between them. He mentioned it to Cam just the once; Cam's response had been typical: *your soul mate can be difficult to ignore.*

Cliff gets to his feet and moves restlessly to the window. Draped, shuttered, only because he knows night has fallen can he say with confidence that it has. This is a dark world with no distinctions.

Kincaid returns, holding a cup of steaming liquid, whispering, "Porterfield has a box of peculiar dried mushrooms in that lab of his. Wonder how *he'd* like them crushed up in his soup. And I found his supply of morphine. There should be no lasting effects from the mushrooms. You found him in time."

"They made him dream about the woman he's in love with," Cliff murmurs.

Kincaid nods. "Literally the woman of his dreams."

"What's that you have there, Doc?"

"Of all things, I found some peppermint tea in Porterfield's kitchen. It's dried, and an infusion of fresh peppermint would be better, but this will do. My mother swore by it all her life for nausea, that and ginger, but Porterfield doesn't have ginger; but this might work and if the lad can keep it down, should rehydrate him and generally make him feel a little better without giving him any more drugs. I'll let it steep a little longer and cool."

Cliff regards the curled figure on the bed in miserable silence.

"You know," Kincaid continues, "when I started medical school my mother was very proud, but what did I do? I told her that her simplistic farmhouse remedies would be swept away by science. This is a woman who raised four sons to healthy and successful manhood in an era when there were barely half the drugs and medical procedures we have now. She made us wash our face and hands and kept an immaculately clean home in a time when scientists didn't know where many basic diseases came from, and still don't in many cases. But she knew. *Dirt is bad, son, remember that when you're a doctor. Peppermint tea will make any sick person feel better, remember that when you're a doctor.* God rest her soul, she lived till she turned eighty-three, went down with pneumonia winter before last. But here am I, giving this sick lad peppermint tea."

Cliff rubs his eyebrow. "What are Eliza Bensen's chances of surviving this winter?"

"That is anybody's guess. But, you know, a lot about being a doctor is hope, as well as science. For example, I would never give up on this lad, just as he hasn't given up on himself. He's in a lot of discomfort and, yes, it's making him agitated and depressed, but he's been fighting the battle with courage and determination. He has hope, he remembers *one step closer* and he's using it. When you see a lot of suffering it is easy to lose hope, but it is the courage of people that makes you think twice about giving in to despair. You are not to give up, Cliff, because the lad hasn't, no matter what he might say while the morphine works its way out of his body."

Cliff stares at Luke till his eyes sting.

"You were right about him. He is important, more than I can tell you. I can't fail in this, Doc."

"You won't. You're as determined as the lad. By the way, you are favoring your left arm."

"Old bullet wound."

"Not so old, I think," Kincaid says, but lets it go at that.

When Luke next stirs, a violent spasm seems to shake him out of his odd doze. Clearly, he's in pain; very soon he's drenched in sweat. Kincaid tries to soothe him in a calm voice and coaxes him into sipping the tea. But Luke starts shuddering and rocking; his moans become sobs; he's crying.

Cliff grips his hand but it does nothing to help.

If Jennifer, who is compassion itself, were here, what would she do? If Ethan were here, or Mart, what would they do? A father... a brother...

Cliff sits on the bed and clasps Luke in his arms, good and tight... "It's all right, Luke, you're not alone, I swear." And absorbs the racking pain until Luke's body has slumped and the sobs die to whimpers. "Everything is going to be all right."

He sets him back against his pillows.

Kincaid, holding the tea up to Luke's mouth, catches Cliff's eye. He gives a solemn nod. "Indeed it is."

Luke whispers something Cliff can't make out.

But he hears Emma's voice clearly in his head... *you can't always be a sheriff, sometimes you just got to be a human being.*

It becomes apparent after a while that Luke is able to stomach the tea. Moments after this he tells them he can make out light.

"You're getting better," Cliff tells him, sponging his face.

"Progress," declares Kincaid. "We can try salicin, lad, it may help a little, now that your stomach is improving."

"Save it, doc...my stomach...ain't the best...I ain't gonna die?"

"No, lad, not now."

"Then this is how it has to be."

Kincaid looks up. "We'll keep up the tea. His temperature is still high and the salicin would bring it down, ease those pains, but he has to be able to stomach it, so we'll keep sponging for now."

Cliff nods.

"I'll be back," Kincaid says, and he scoots off.

Luke rasps, "What...have you done...with Porterfield?"

"Tied up in his basement."

"Donnelly wants to use me to get…the Alliance to…give in. We have to get word to them that…that I'm all right."

"No one, well two, probably three people, know I'm here, but that's all. We have to get you back to Cheyenne and safety as soon as you can move. Ralph Walker will have thrown a dragnet over as much of Lincoln County as he can to find you so it won't be easy. I'm not telling anyone anything until I get you out of here."

"The others…"

"Dave Ransford and his boys were moving in yesterday to protect them. Luke, you've got to trust me."

"Like I trusted…you and Cam…with my file." He sits slumped against his pillows, his blinded eyes staring out, unseeing but nonetheless accusing.

"For God's sake, will you grow up?"

"If I…if I could stand up…I'd rearrange your face with my fist."

"Maybe you're feeling better then."

"No, I've had…a hankering to do it…since you pulled me out… of that hole in the ground."

They pause while Luke deals with a spasm.

Cliff says, "Maybe on some level I deserve it, but this whole business *will* be played out, not necessarily with happy endings and good constantly triumphing over evil."

He thinks about the bullet he took for Emma and swallows hard. Thinks about the one that narrowly missed her outside Cam and Meg's home.

"We suffer losses and failures and disappointments, but I swear I will not fail getting you back to Cheyenne and that can only bring us one step closer to shutting Donnelly and Bodecker down. Isn't that what the Doc says, *one step closer*? So put a lid on it and concentrate on getting better. This house gives me the creeps."

Moisture pours down Luke's face, from his nose and eyes. He gasps and says, "Which three?"

"What?"

"Which…three…know…?"

"Mac, and therefore Cam… and Emma."

Luke swallows hard.

"You're pitiful," Cliff says.

"I…know."

Cliff puts the cup of cooled tea in Luke's hand and helps him track it to his mouth to drink. He takes several good sips. Cliff takes back the teacup and replaces it with the wet cloth, freshly rinsed; he's no longer in the mood to be the fever nurse. "Here…"

Luke grunts and moves the cloth over his face with a trembling hand. His relief is obvious, and he relaxes.

"You said Emma."

"Emmaline Roberts. You met her…"

"Cam's trespasser. The reporter."

"That's right."

"I remember her. What I…don't remember is…you trusting…a reporter. If ever…there was a woman…with trouble…written all over her it's…that one…"

"Well, you'd know since you're the expert on trouble."

"Guess they're…all trouble," Luke babbles on breathily. "Never do…anything the way you…expect. Why is that?"

"I don't know."

"They say too much…they cry…they make you…miss 'em when they're not around…"

"I guess," Cliff says. They get inside your head so that all you hear is their voice. "What happened with you and Jennifer in San Francisco?"

"Long story. Long…they make everything…long."

Cliff hasn't known Emma long enough to experience the *long* Luke's talking about, but the potential is definitely there.

"And then that turns into long*ing*," he concludes and closes his eyes. He whispers hoarsely, "There's an ache…inside of me that's got nothing…to do with morphine…or trying to save…the Alliance from Donnelly's…clutches. It's all Jennifer. I hope she's…proud."

Cliff observes Luke for sometime as he sleeps. It shapes up to be a good sleep. His breathing has improved; the shivering slows; the spasms don't jolt him quite so hard.

He finds Kincaid in the kitchen putting a meal together.

"Got to keep up our strength," he mutters as he spoons sizzling chunks of bacon and fried potatoes onto two plates. "Here, eat this. If the lad is sleeping, we can take a moment for supper."

"Thanks, Doc." Kincaid's food hits the spot immediately. "I think he's improved in the last half hour."

"Good. What are you going to do about Porterfield? He's been down there a long time."

"I've been thinking about it. I'll let you know what I decide."

"Mm. I was thinking of the humane thing to do actually."

"Let's just eat our supper, Doc. It's not bad."

Kincaid grins. "Thank you. My wife taught me."

"What does your wife think about you being out all night?"

Kincaid swallows his bacon. "She's a doctor's wife, Cliff. She's used to it. I'll be back in the morning, she knows."

Cliff winces. "You didn't tell her where you were going?'

He shakes his head. "She's used to that, too. There are a lot of folks who don't want to be found, such as Eliza. My Belle knows if I tell her then she's supposed to know; otherwise she doesn't ask. She's a mighty good woman. Stuck by me all these years. The life of a doctor's wife is not that easy. I don't know what you and the lad think are important qualities in the women you love, but you can't beat loyalty."

They finish their meal in silence.

Cliff suspects Kincaid is thinking about his Belle, and he can't escape thinking about Emma. Only she's not *his* Emma and it's likely that she never will be. And that amounts to 'longing'.

Luke opens his eyes. There in front of him the world has returned. The room looks nothing like he'd imagined; Cliff and Kincaid made it appear to his unseeing eyes like a comforting stronghold of care and concern, but it's actually dull, colorless and lacking in warmth but for the fire crackling in the grate.

Porterfield's world.

Objects within it bend and blur as his vision struggles to get it right. It makes him queasy, more than he is already.

Weird, but now that he can see he doesn't know where anything is. Troubling as this sensation is, he's not closing his eyes again until he feels the need to sleep.

And sight brings something else.

He turns over and sits up; the world expands and sends him reeling. And there is more pain, more sweat, more work to be done. Exhausted and fed up, he looks down at his hands. If he can't control their violent shaking, how is he ever to stand up?

He inches to the edge of the bed; he forces each leg over and each foot to the floor. Flashes of darkness, of grasping in the dirt, of crawling and failing strike him. His hands shake worse than ever. And he's not sure if his muscles have the strength to do the most basic of movements and get him to his feet. He feels thin and wasted. Everything on the inside seems to be jumping, darting about like insects in meadow grass, not responding to his command. He will do this; Cliff says he won't fail to do his part. With all that he has left in him, neither will he.

Cliff drags Porterfield up from the basement and tosses him onto a wooden chair in the corner of the laboratory. The scientist shields his eyes from the lamplight.

Cliff removes the restraints and the gag, and thrusts a plate of fried potatoes, courtesy of Kincaid, in the scientist's trembling hands; he trains his colt on him while he eats.

"Don't put me back down there," Porterfield mutters.

"Shut up."

"I'll help you, just don't make me go back down there."

"Shut up."

"I need to use the lavatory."

The scientist is pathetic, but Cliff feels no compassion and there are no mitigating circumstances that would tempt him to be lenient.

Porterfield eats slowly and quietly, his strange, bright eyes behind his spectacles watching Cliff ceaselessly.

"You damn near killed him," Cliff mutters.

"No, no, I wasn't to kill him. My orders were to keep him alive. And the morphine was pure, not rubbish."

"You take away a man's mind and his body, you kill him."

Porterfield spoons the last of the potatoes into his mouth.

Cliff stares hard at him. "How long will it take for him to withdraw from the amount of morphine you gave him?

"The acute withdrawal two or three days, but he will experience withdrawal symptoms for up to a week or more."

"You poisoned him."

"In a manner of speaking."

"You would do this to a perfectly healthy man who hadn't threatened you or done you harm?"

"What are you going to do with me?"

"I haven't decided."

"Don't you want to know why I did this, who asked it of me?"

"I already know."

Cliff allows Porterfield to use the lavatory and then throws him back into the basement, manacled and gagged as before.

When Cliff returns to Luke's room, he's confronted with a totally unexpected sight. With Kincaid's support, Luke is upright; he is the picture of ill-health on two legs, but he's standing.

"I can see," he says simply, while his whole body quivers.

Kincaid is beaming.

"How long 'til you can throw a punch?" Cliff says.

Kincaid's smile vanishes. "Eh?"

Luke spends the rest of the night wandering restlessly around the room draped in a blanket, in pain and constantly shivering; when inevitably he breaks out into profuse sweating, he curls up on the bed and is barely coherent as though in a delirium, heard to be murmuring *one step closer,* until he falls asleep for a spell. Then it all starts again. When he wakes, he is irritable and anguished. But his sight improves with each passing hour. And he drinks a lot of peppermint tea. When Kincaid insists on nourishment in the form of soup, Luke retches ominously and pants, "Never again offer me soup."

Kincaid checks his heart, lungs and pulse and grunts a lot.

Snatching some sleep for themselves whenever they can, they pass the night.

Day Three

At first light, Doc Kincaid bundles himself into coat, scarf and rubbers and heads off home, promising to return around midday.

Cliff rummages through Porterfield's kitchen for food. Stumped as to what Luke might eat, he goes up and asks.

"No food," Luke says, shaking his head; actually he's in the middle of a sweat, so Cliff can hardly blame him. "But you go ahead. One of us…needs the strength to…get me…out of here."

Cliff prepares his breakfast. More of the bacon, and a couple of eggs cracked beside.

He's plating it up when a loud thump on the front door startles him. He steals up the hall and places his eye on the peephole in the door. A warmly clad man in his twenties stands there. Someone from the town? No, Porterfield is odd-folk. Even Kincaid had never been here before.

Cliff races through the laboratory, unlocks the basement door and fetches Porterfield. The scientist is sleepy and cold; he smells food and complains through his gag about his hunger. Cliff shoves his colt into Porterfield's stomach and tells him to shut up and listen.

"There's someone at the door. You're going to answer it, get rid of them if it's a stranger or if it's someone you're expecting let him in. Do you understand?"

Porterfield regards Cliff as if he's gone mad.

"Move. And I'll know if you try and signal my presence." He removes the gag. "The front door. Now."

Cliff opens the door, making a narrow wedge for Porterfield to speak to his visitor. Cliff conceals himself behind the door with his colt pressed into Porterfield's side.

"Porterfield, you remember me? Larry Fulbright. Donnelly said you'd be expecting me."

"Oh, yes," Porterfield mumbles. "Er… what news?"

"Donnelly said it's time to start bargaining with Taylor. He capitulates or Maverick will start shooting his family and friends one at a time. His boys are in the area right now. Can I come in? It's like ten below out here."

Cliff grabs hold of Porterfield's manacles and pulls him back. Fulbright pushes the door and enters. Cliff places the barrel end of his colt to the back of Fulbright's head.

"Don't move."

"Hey, what is this?" Fulbright objects.

"You move again and I will pull this trigger."

Fulbright lifts his hands in surrender. "Okay, okay…"

"Hands behind your back." Cliff reaches into his trouser pocket for his second set of manacles. He fastens them around Fulbright's wrists and then pads his hands over Fulbright's body. "Where have you concealed your weapon?"

"I'm just a messenger. I don't have a weapon."

"You better not be lying." Cliff shoves Porterfield forward in the direction of the laboratory. "Let's follow Louis, shall we?"

They start walking, more like shuffling.

"Move it along, Porterfield."

"I'm just a messenger, don't hurt me," Fulbright whines.

"Shut up."

When they reach the laboratory Cliff warns Fulbright not to touch anything.

"I keep telling you, I'm just a messenger."

"What message are you suppose to give Donnelly in return?" Cliff pushes Porterfield into the basement with a swift kick and says, "MAVERICK LARAMIE TELEGRAPH NIGHTHAWK LULLABY perhaps?"

Fulbright shoots Cliff a look over his shoulder. "Who are you?"

"Keep your eyes front. Is that the message?"

"The message begins with MAVERICK. It depends on whether Taylor agrees to capitulate or not."

"Go on. What if he agrees?"

"MAVERICK ROUND UP AND DRIVE. Means that…"

"I get the meaning." He presses his colt tighter into Fulbright's head; the man catches his breath. "Then what?"

"Then we're supposed to transport him to Bright River."

"Doped up?"

"'Course."

Donnelly had seized upon happenstance; from the moment the opportunity presented itself he intended to enslave Luke with addiction, to break his courage and determination with dreams he could never make real, and then throw him down on the Alliance's doorstep to die.

Fulbright continues, "If Taylor won't cooperate the telegram is to read: MAVERICK BEGIN."

"How is this arranged?"

"Donnelly gets my telegraph in Dickson. One of Maverick's boys is waiting at the telegraph office in Bright River for Maverick's signal."

"Which is?"

"Either NIGHTHAWK LULLABY ROUND UP AND DRIVE or NIGHTHAWK LULLABY BEGIN."

"And if Donnelly doesn't get any message, then what?"

Fulbright replies churlishly, "If I don't send him the telegram by midday, he'll know something's wrong. He knows how reliable I am."

"Yeah, I've heard it all before. So, Mr Reliable, what will Donnelly do if you don't report back by midday?"

Fulbright holds his tongue with almost girlish defiance.

"Why go to all this trouble? Has Donnelly got a code fetish or something? Why not just murder them all and have done?"

Fortunately, Fulbright can't resist blabbing what he knows.

"Heard tell that Donnelly made some mistakes in Cheyenne and the boss ain't happy. Heard that Donnelly is trying to make up for them by nabbing Taylor."

"Who is the boss?"

"Someone in Omaha. Donnelly's partner I think."

"Will he tell the others that he has Taylor?"

Fulbright suddenly cracks. "I don't know. How do I know his every move? Stop with the questions now."

"How does he think he's going to get away with it?"

Fulbright groans. "As far as I know, no one knows what he's up to. But Donnelly has friends in high places. Don't know who. They leave him be," he gulps, "is what I'm told."

The hairs on Cliff's head prickle so sharp it hurts.

"You've been a wealth of information."

He shoves Fulbright into the basement and locks the door. Then he drags several pieces of furniture across the doorway; meanwhile Fulbright starts kicking the door.

"I'm going to be right outside this door, Fulbright. You try to escape and you'll regret it."

"If I don't report back to Mr Donnelly, Maverick's gonna start killing the lot of 'em, I tell you. Kill the lot."

"Well, I'm just going to have to see to it that he doesn't."

Clearly, NIGHTHAWK LULLABY is a macabre game for Donnelly.

Nothing gives him more pleasure than killing… like folks plan their day, he plans his next kill. Cold-blooded and calculating. And someone to keep Bodecker's hands clean so he can spruik about how his big ideas and his business are just what the Territory needs.

"You can't keep me here with Porterfield. He's weird. It's pitch black. And it smells. Let me out…"

And so it goes.

Cliff rushes up to Luke's room. He's awake but irritable.

"What's up with you?"

"We got company."

"Donnelly?"

"Not quite; his little messenger friend. He's in the basement with Porterfield."

"Now what?"

"Have to get into town and send a telegram."

"And how do you propose…to do that without being noticed? Western Union is in the same block…as the jail. Have you…and Ralph Walker ever met…?"

"Yes. Once. And it wasn't love at first sight."

"What about his men?"

Cliff shrugs. "Wouldn't have a clue."

Luke's eyes bore into Cliff's. "They're gonna die, ain't they?…if you don't…send the telegram?"

"From the arrangements he put in place, Donnelly will assume that his plan has been compromised. I have to be honest, Luke, and say that it's more than likely a diversion or a distraction. A great

deal has happened since you left Cheyenne and I need to fill you in
– later."

Luke's expression turns kind of wild. He gets unsteadily to his
feet. "We need a plan of our own…"

Cliff has already formulated one; planning comes as naturally as
breathing. But Luke is also a planner, and a proud man who has
had to let others save him, so it seems efficacious to Luke's recovery
for Cliff to hold back and let him contribute.

"I'm listening."

"Do what you can…at the telegraph office and…then get us seats
on the next train. I'll get dressed, be ready to leave…If you give me
a colt…I'll keep watch over the basement…'til you come back for
me."

Cliff nods. "It's a plan. You'll have to come up with some kind of
disguise. Your wanted poster is all over town. But without those
whiskers. Keep them."

Luke runs his hand over his chin. He narrows his eyes. "If you
keep yours we could travel like a couple of hobos with the livestock."

"Out of work itinerants looking for a break."

Cliff receives a look almost like the Luke of old; irony is never
lost upon Luke. But a huge racket from the other end of the house
disturbs the much-needed encouragement provided by their connection with the old days.

"It's amazing how quickly plans can change. If that's Fulbright
making enough noise to raise the dead, we may have more than we
bargained for."

Luke nods. "You go see. I'll get dressed."

Cliff almost flies through the house to the door of the laboratory;
he holds himself back, bending his eyes around the doorframe.
Fulbright is climbing over the furniture Cliff stacked previously.

Most of it lies broken or trashed as Fulbright systematically
demolished it. Porterfield is in his wake, mumbling into his gag.

"Good idea of yours, Porterfield, grabbing that acid stuff to melt
the lock. And in the dark too. Backwards to boot. Who would have
thought a scientist could actually be useful?"

Before they get too far, Cliff pulls his colt and rounds the door. "Hold it, Fulbright."

Fulbright looks up. His mouth drops. "You still here?"

"I told you I would be."

Fulbright grimaces. "Thought that was just a load of bulldust, you know..." And shrugs. "Can I move now? Think I got a splinter up my butt."

Luke struggles into the clothes Cliff bought him; it won't make that much difference – on the train he won't smell any different to the livestock. Still, to be out of that sweat-ridden nightshirt and into real clothes almost makes him feel human.

He fumbles his way through the house and down the stairs, his body drenched in sweat by the time he reaches the bottom. He's breathless, dizzy and his bones ache. He tries to move quickly, but he's not sure if his efforts match his intention.

Following the direction of voices, he comes to the laboratory. The sight of it, the smell of it, sends him reeling. He pours all his concentration into not retching and moves into the room.

Cliff smacks a colt into his hand. "This is Fulbright. Mind him."

He thinks it pretty hilarious; he can barely hold the gun, let alone keep a steady aim. Still, he stares down the skinny kid who he assumes is Donnelly's messenger, while Cliff grabs Porterfield and re-manacles him to a shelf bracket beneath a row of containers.

"What's in these, Porterfield?" Cliff taunts him. "Not something you'd like to unleash by pulling down I hope."

Porterfield says nothing. Luke finds his attention wandering to the weird man with the bald head who caused the raised red sores on the inside of his elbows. Porterfield stares back at him. Fulbright makes a move; Luke's attention swings back, but Cliff catches him.

"Whoa there, Fulbright. There's another shelf over there for you. Yours has got pretty colored stuff all neatly stacked."

Luke wipes his face, and tries to focus. His empty gut contracts, followed by a spasm in his back. He grits his teeth.

Meanwhile, both Porterfield and Fulbright, gagged and disgraced, seem to be hanging from the shelves. A sight he won't ever forget, so bizarre it could be one of his dreams.

Outside the intense cold breaks upon his sweat-drenched body. His lungs seize and he can't breathe. He feels like a brittle twig ready to snap. Cliff adjusts his wool scarf around his face for him and murmurs encouragement. He grips him firmly and hustles him through thick snow, across Porterfield's yard, onto the street and towards town. The only time Luke felt worse than this was... no, there is no worse time. This is it. He will never feel any more weak, sick, useless, degraded or demoralized than this. All he can do is hold on. Ethan would say if holding on is all that's required then that is what you do.

"Ethan..." he whispers.

"Hold on, Luke."

"Yes, Ethan," he breathes.

Then all is black again.

He comes to in a strange place. It's warm but dark. He sits up, blinded, struggling for breath.

"Easy, lad, easy does it. You're safe here with old Wilma. No harm can come to you here. Got some nice warm milk, how does that sound?"

A decrepit room moves into focus, followed by a smiling old woman, with a small crackling fire behind her that flickers orange light onto her thin gray hair.

"Where's..."

"Your friend went on an errand. Be back soon."

"You're Wilma?"

She gives him a gappy grin. "That's right. Got plenty to share. Nell brings me her leftovers ev'ry mornin' before she opens the Nebraskee Bite. Got a decent pale of milk today. Keeps fresh in this weather. Want some? I warmed it. Do you good."

He nods weakly. Sara used to give him warmed milk.

"Good lad."

Wilma puts a chipped cup into his trembling hands and helps him drink. It's fragrant and tastes sweet.

Sara...

"Not too much to start. Your friend said you ain't had nothin' to eat in days."

"Thank you," he breathes as she lowers the cup again.

"Did you know that your friend had a cousin who terrorized me at school?"

He shakes his head.

"Mm. How do you think that could happen when I never even went to school?"

He stares at her. And likes her. "He's fibbing."

"I think that young man would tell a hundred fibs if it meant gettin' you out of trouble."

He wants to smile. Like he used to. But smiles just don't seem to want to sit on his face anymore.

Now that Kincaid knows not to return to the house, Cliff returns to his cheap hotel room, retrieves his duffle bag, stuffs into it what supplies he can from the crate of goods he'd bought from Lumsden, pays the desk clerk what's owing and clears out. He makes his way into North Platte's courthouse precinct. Kincaid warned him that Western Union would be closely watched. Apparently, the town's second office at the depot was shut down when Luke 'escaped' and will stay that way until he's caught.

Cliff surveys the customers coming and going at the telegraph office from across the street. A deputy stands by the window, occasionally taking a short walk to the edge of the sidewalk and back. Not a comfortable job in this weather.

Cliff doesn't recognize him and proceeds to cross the street.

He senses the deputy studying him as he draws level with the office window.

"Morning, stranger," the telegrapher greets him. "Write what you want."

Cliff takes up the pencil, keeping track of the deputy out of the corner of his eye. In the **SEND TO** box on the telegrapher's paper he scribbles: *Dickson telegraph.*

And then writes: *Maverick round up and drive.*

The telegrapher gives him an odd look. "Conundrum, eh? Where to?"

"I wrote it on the paper."

The telegrapher glances. "So you did. Dickson telegraph."

The deputy sticks his head in Cliff's space. "Didn't have time to shave, Mister?"

Cliff pretends to be interested in what the telegrapher is doing. "Heading off to the barber when I finish my business in town."

The deputy peers. And grunts. And withdraws his gaze. "Just grabbing a hot drink and a spell by the fire, Fletch. Pete, my replacement, is coming right along now. Be seeing you."

"See you, Mike. Sure you don't want to say who it's from?"

"Sorry, Fletch?"

"Not you, Mike. My customer. You get along now."

Cliff waits for Mike to move away. "What's a conundrum if you give away too much?"

"Well, I guess. As long as the person on the other end is waiting for it, otherwise no one's gonna get nothing from you. That'll be seventy five cents, Mister."

Cliff fishes the coins from his pocket, and Fletch starts tapping on his machine. "Just getting Dickson's attention."

Cliff takes a casual look around for Mike's replacement.

Fletch waits; Cliff's pulse starts to throb in his neck.

A long series of clicks has Fletch looking thoughtful.

"What?" Cliff asks.

"Dickson district got hit by a snowstorm a couple of days ago. Reckon the wire's down all points to the northwest. First I heard of it. You reckon someone would tell me these things. Guess not many folks here wire points northwest of Dickson, Wyoming. Anyhow, yours'll still get through. Lucky for you."

Fletch finally stops talking and starts tapping.

Cliff feels a nearby presence.

"How do ya, Fletch? Anything to report?"

"All done, Mister," says Fletch. He spears Cliff's hand-written message onto a metal spike. "They got it."

Cliff thanks him and moves away.

"Not a thing, Pete," says Fletch to Mike's replacement. "If that Taylor feller is trying to send word to his murdering gang of outlaws to come get him, he ain't doing it through this office."

L uke is shaken from his sleep.

"Luke, time to go."

Wilma's house wanders in and out of focus.

At least he remembers where he is this time. Last time Wilma woke him to give him milk he screamed and dispatched the poor woman to the furthest corner of her house.

"Luke, come on..."

"Don't bully the lad."

"It's all right, Wilma," he croaks and sits up.

Cliff is stacking firewood in Wilma's wood box.

"Enough," Wilma says. "I forgave your cousin, remember?"

"Can't thank you enough, Wilma," Cliff is saying to her. He wipes his hands on the back of his coat.

Wilma shrugs. "What's an old woman good for... You know, I'm gonna miss you. You're interesting, cousin of my enemy."

They're grinning at each other. Luke looks from one to the other.

"Can I have some help please?"

Outside, tramping along in the snow, he feels the nourishing benefits of the milk. They head in the direction of the depot, with him trying to manage on his own.

"What happened...at Western Union?"

"I got it sent. There's a deputy posting guard duty round the clock, checking in with the operator, probably after every wire gets sent. The operator likes to chat and the deputy got a good look at me, so the sooner we leave the better I'll feel. One thing, the operator informed me that the wire's come down in a snowstorm northwest of Dickson. I already knew this, but it looks like no one's got around to fixing it yet. It may buy us some time."

"You know, I'm confused...about a lot of things," he pants.

"I'll bring you up-to-date on the train," Cliff assures him.

He promptly stumbles in the snow. Unable to break his fall, he lands face down. Strong hands pull him upright and brush him off. He can't be sure if he blacked out or not; his head still objects to taking reality seriously. Who knows what happens between one moment and the next... With a trembling hand he gloves away the snow stuck to his sweaty face. They start off again.

"Want me to hold your hand?"

"Piss…off."

However, Cliff is all but carrying him by the time they reach the depot. They huddle behind a wooden building and observe. To their surprise and relief, there are two Union Pacifics, heading in opposite directions. Deputies with Winchesters patrol each side of the tracks. A station guard blows his whistle beside one of the trains and calls, "All aboard! All stops for Omaha!"

The whistle shriek jangles Luke's nerves, but at least now he can pick east from west. The hustle and bustle of the disembarking and boarding passengers and the sheer bulk of two trains steaming away happily seem like an answer to prayer, but not one that he uttered. Maybe someone is watching over him. Maybe K put in a good word for him with the angels. He finds a pocket of strength as Cliff maneuvers them towards the livestock car of the westbound UP.

A couple of men are goading a cold, recalcitrant Arabian up a conveyor into the car. The effort almost produces as much white cloud as the steam from the train.

"They're doing it all wrong," he mutters.

"I only hope it likes us," Cliff replies.

"Here comes another…"

They wait behind a stack of hay bales. Three horses are stabled in the car before the men clear off for some reason and present him and Cliff with an opportunity. They seize it at once and charge up the ramp; and, avoiding the rear end of disgruntled horseflesh, they find a dark corner.

He gasps, "This is good…this is good." The smell of horse and hay washes over him like a healing balm. This is who he is. Horse and hay.

Cliff chuckles as he lowers him into a pile of hay; its surface is cold. It's come out of winter barns, but it was cut from the fields when the sun was high and warm.

"This is great," he murmurs.

He lies back and remembers the Diamond-T in high summer. The green and gold pastures. The river running bright blue, sun-sprinkled diamonds on the surface. Moving the herd through the pass where the air is so thin it makes you light-headed and the light so sharp you can see forever. And the ranch corrals, where the dust floats in the heat and stains the inside of your nose and gathers beneath your eyelids...

"Hey, are you still in there?"

"What?"

"We're about to move."

He sits up and blinks.

He is so used to darkness he hadn't noticed the car door was shut. The only light comes from three high window vents near the roof. Beside him, Cliff sits on the hay. Not *in* the hay, the way he is. Although Cliff is no slouch when it comes to horses, he's a city boy at heart and he'd rather sit on a chair.

"I can't smile...anymore," Luke says.

"It'll come back, like your eyesight."

With trembling fingers, he picks up a long strand of hay and brings it to his mouth. His aim is off and he stabs his cheek several times before his tongue can savor it.

"What's to smile about anyhow?" Cliff asks.

"What would make...you smile...right about now?"

"Breakfast in the dining car."

"You should try...the hay."

The train jolts and begins to move; the horses object, but their neighing and stomping brings more sunshine into his shadowy existence. It doesn't last long. Another round of deep chills and sweats arrives. They feel like death is knocking on his door and the pictures of diamonds and sunshine scatter.

He hunkers down into the hay; every shiver causes pain; sweat pours out of him, runs into his eyes and soaks his clothes; dark thoughts penetrate his imagination. After each bout he prays that it will be the last, but it never is. He feels Cliff's gloved hand grip one of his gloved hands and tighten.

Hold on.

He squeezes his eyes shut and holds on tight.

Cliff holds the flask of tea firmly in Luke's hands and guides it to his mouth. Luke takes a long and much needed draft.

"What else…have you got…in your pockets?" Luke asks.

"Besides the flask of peppermint tea you have there, Kincaid gave us a canteen of water, biscuits made by his Belle left over from last night's supper which he says he ate for breakfast, and barley sugar. There are some supplies I bought in town yesterday in my duffle as well. Needless to say, Kincaid wasn't happy about you traveling. I gave him a generous commission, but he waved it in my face and said he still wasn't happy and I was to wire him with your *therapeutic outcome.*"

"You can tell him…the hay was…very beneficial."

They hit a crick in the track; the horses whinny and steady themselves. A railcar full of horses and hay is not the therapy Kincaid could have imagined for his patient.

"Did you meet Belle?" Luke asks, screwing the lid back on the flask with all the dexterity of a town drunk.

"Yes."

"What's she like?"

"Nice. Are we going to talk about women again, because I'm pretty sure I don't want to."

"If my chuckle was working…"

"Yeah, well, it's not."

"I spent most of the time…I knew Jennifer…pretending I didn't feel about her…the way I did…and she did the same."

"You're talking in the past tense," he observes out loud.

Luke's silence is telling and just a little surprising; the clacking rhythm of the train fills the void.

"You know…" Luke says after a while, "one of Jennifer's…best qualities is her…compassion… it's also the scariest. She is totally… passionate about helping people. She helped me…all the time. But back then…I could help her. And I did. But I don't…need a doctor who's passionate about…curing me; that's her first instinct…the scary part."

He falls silent again. Cliff digests what he's said.

"You won't be like this forever, Luke. In a week or so you'll be feeling a whole lot better."

"In a week…my whole world…might be gone."

Kincaid said this would happen. *He'll get melancholy. The toxic effects of the drug are relentless. He'll feel trapped within the cycle. Be patient. Be positive.*

"Not if I've got anything to do with it."

"But you're here...with me."

Cliff shifts his position in the hay. "Listen up, Luke."

"Listening."

"I was on my way to Laramie. Emma was on the train. She was also going to Laramie, to investigate Donnelly. I told her everything, except about Caroline, and then she pleaded with me to let her help. She knew I had a dilemma, and how much I wanted to come find you. I gave her my badge and I deputized her. I left her on the train at Watts Landing. She was to take all that critical information to Dave Ransford, which would set in motion the protection of your family and the Keatons from Maverick. Dave is a good man and he would see it done. But I trusted Emma with the very thing that I wouldn't trust anyone else to do. It was weird; I knew it was right, that I could trust her."

Even in the gloom of the car he feels Luke's eyes boring into him. "Go on."

"Luke, you should know that I've arrested the man who I believe shot Kelley."

"Go on," he urges with breathless impatience.

"The night you met Emma, that was the first time Maverick tried to kill her; the second was on the street the next day. From a rooftop. I was walking her back from court. She stopped on the sidewalk. She was exposed so I stepped back to her and the bullet meant for her struck me in the arm. I turned, looked up and spotted him; he was trying to work out who he'd hit and dallied too long. I fired my colt and wounded him. Mac and the boys squared him away. His name is Swinton Carter and he's in the lockup, interestingly with Loren Bodecker's attorney as his counsel. I sent John and Ethan a wire, telling them. They should have received another telling them not to come to Cheyenne, to stay put and defend themselves against what Donnelly is about to unleash, but the telegraph's down... Still, every delay that slows Dave Ransford's progress similarly hinders Donnelly's."

He continues until he's told Luke every detail, and because he doesn't have to protect Caroline's identity he talks about her too. His voice is hoarse by the end as the cold penetrates the protective layer of hay and equine body heat.

Luke says barely anything; asks no questions.

They suck on barley sugars and fall into utter silence, which is quickly absorbed into the rhythm of the train. After miles of it, Luke mutters, "I'm still...gonna rearrange...your face...with my fist."

Although the train stops at a number of towns on its westward journey, no one comes near their car or the horses.

"Makes you wonder...where they're bound," Luke remarks.

Cliff paces up and down the carriage, tramping a path in the hay. Luke can't really see him; he's a shadow that shuffles.

"Will you quit that?"

"I'm thinking."

"About what?"

"What we are going to do when we get to Cheyenne."

"I already know...what I'll be doing."

The pacing stops. "Oh?"

He snatches a couple of quick breaths. "Staying right here on this train and...going on to Laramie."

"What are you talking about?"

"You know...what I'm talking about."

"Luke, you are a key witness..."

"I know that's why...you came for me..."

"...and a wanted man. And that's not the only reason."

He deals with a sharp spasm in his back. He's too weak to argue, especially with someone like Cliff. "I appreciate everything you did, but...I'm going home, Cliff...do you hear me, *home*...to Ethan... don't try and stop me."

He falls silent before he sounds so weak and pathetic that Cliff thinks he can toss him over one shoulder and carry him off the train.

Cliff, however, crawls back to his position in the hay; Luke can feel the heat from his body. Quietly, he says, "You may be the only witness we will ever have to stop Bodecker."

"I ain't arguing with you, Cliff...I gotta save my strength to get home. I will crawl if I have to…and I don't care if it ain't in your plan…or Cam's plan or anyone else's…this is what I have to do."

Cliff is quiet, although Luke can hear his breathing, a little fast and uneven. The noisy rhythm of the train breaks in.

"Luke, I can't show up in Cheyenne without the man I risked my job for."

Luke swallows hard. "I don't mean to be ungrateful."

Cliff gives a harsh laugh. "Cam and I did discuss the risks in going after Bodecker, but you being a ruthless, ungrateful bastard never entered my head."

"And you…and Cam…deceiving me…about Bodecker…never entered mine," he retorts, struggling for breath.

He falls back into the hay and can't speak another word. More words are unnecessary; the right ones have been spoken.

The night progresses, mostly with silence between them.

They doze, he fitfully as the dissipating effects of drugs continue to undermine his body.

Surprisingly, Cliff never leaves his side.

Whatever the words spoken between them, none seem to discourage Cliff from attending him in his discomfort or need – the significance, and the benefit, of being a key witness.

Day Four

Cliff is shaken out of his sleep by the train coming to an abrupt halt. A glance at the small windows reveals that it is still dark.

"This doesn't feel right," he murmurs.

"Where are we?" Luke asks groggily.

Cliff listens hard; loud voices surround the train.

"Probably at the border," he whispers. "I'm turning you into a haystack."

In the pitch darkness, he heaps as much hay as he estimates would look natural over Luke's body. He crawls on all fours into the corner of the car adjacent to the sliding door, dousing himself in hay and pressing himself against the wall.

The voices get closer and closer until someone is standing outside their car. Lantern light reaches the car's small high windows, yellow and glowing.

"Horses in here?" a deep male voice asks.

Another voice joins him. "Yep. Loaded in North Platte and not opened since. This door's the only way in and it's locked, see?"

"Someone could've snuck on while they were being loaded."

"Aw, it's gonna stink and my toes are half froze. There ain't damn *fools* in there. Hell, it's too cold for rats."

"Get the key."

Cliff's heart begins to race. He hears the jangling of keys.

"I tell you there ain't no one..."

"What's taking you so long?"

"My hands are near froze... "

"Give it here... tarnation!"

"You had to go drop the keys, didn't you? I'm telling you, we're wasting our time. Ain't no one is desperate enough to ride in there in this weather."

"Murderers are desperate."

"Murderers don't like freezing their butts off just like the rest of us. Let's go."

A moment's silence.

Someone decides to rattle the lock; it resounds through the deep chill. The horses snort and whinny.

"All clear down here," a hoarse voice yells.

The lantern light moves away, taking its gold glow with it and leaving them in total blackness once more.

The train remains stationary for a very long time; exactly how long he loses track of. Voices can be heard in the distance, then close by, and then far off again; clearly the whole train has been disturbed while a search is carried out.

Luke murmurs, "There's an angel... watching over us."

When at last the train jerks into motion again, Luke says, "They might have left someone on the train."

"It's likely."

"Will they have jurisdiction in Cheyenne?"

"If Union Pacific called in a US marshal with a federal warrant for your arrest, which at this stage is unlikely. They'll put their own detectives on the case first. So the longer we stay on the train…"

"Nice try."

"Worth a shot."

"What if that acting governor…"

Cliff sighs.

"…feels obligated to…"

"The governor knows what's going on, I thought I mentioned that."

"Gotta get home," he says, fading.

"Just go back to sleep."

The train finally arrives in Cheyenne late-morning; from their hideout in the stable car at the back end of the train, Cliff can just make out the depot's hustle and bustle in the distance.

After its tardy arrival, the UP will take on water and coal, gold and currency consignments and their guards; load and unload live-stock, freight and bags of mail; and busily exchange disgruntled and relieved passengers. And it's very likely that Mac or one of the others will be standing watch on the platform.

It was Monday morning when Cliff stepped onto the train to find Emma on it; now it's Thursday, the day after her birthday. Where she is and what she's up to bothers him squarely into frustrated silence. Almost as much as fixing his butt to the darkest corner of this frozen corral on wheels, hiding like a wanted criminal. He glances across at Luke's sleeping form huddled beneath a deep pile of hay. He's not sure why he expected anything less of Luke than he was getting…

Suddenly, the car door is hauled open and blinding light pours in. The horses stomp and whinny their objection.

A voice yells, "Horses are fine… didn't they come with a groom? No? Well, they seem fine. Not a mangy peep outa them… Got heaps of hay. Ah… where are they getting off? Buford, you say. That's still a ways. I'll get someone to check them. As if there ain't enough crazy going on this morning…"

The car door rumbles loudly and crashes shut.

Gloom returns.

The horses protest the noise and take a minute to settle; but no one comes to take care of them and the train leaves Cheyenne, with the car door unlocked. At this point, Cliff believes in Luke's angel.

"Are you all right?" he asks.

"Yes," comes a breathy reply from beneath the hay.

"I'll need to send Mac a wire in Laramie."

"I'll organize our horses."

Cliff shakes his head and bites back, "You do that."

However, when they stealthily emerge from the car in Laramie late in the afternoon, after even more delays along the line, it's abundantly clear that they will never reach Bright River by nightfall. Luke can barely stand and they both need a bath, a proper meal and a decent night's sleep.

Panting, Luke says, "We can at least get to Dickson tonight...set off for home...first thing tomorrow."

The briskness of Laramie's business day is coming to a close. Soon the streets will be quiet. As it is, people are staring at them, a couple of hobos hanging about the depot.

"We're heading to the Sheriff's," Cliff announces. "I want to hear what Dave has been up to, see if there's any word."

Luke pulls himself upright, wincing, but determined.

"Let's go then."

It's obvious he uses all his remaining energy in the process. He falls into a slump on a chair inside Dave's office.

Doug Mason appears.

"Ryan? Is that you behind those whiskers?"

"Mason." They shake hands. "What news?"

"The wire's still down between Dickson and Bright River, so there's none to speak of. Three days and no word. Dang weather. Everyone's stuck right where they're at. I was just about to send off a couple of the men." He glances at Luke's draped form. "Luke Taylor?"

Cliff nods.

Mason grins widely. "Well, good for you."

"We're heading off for Dickson ourselves…"

Mason looks skeptical. "You ain't going nowhere that I can see, at least 'til tomorrow morning."

"No," Luke pipes up. "We're going today. We need horses…and provisions."

Mason looks to Cliff.

Cliff removes his hat. "Miss Roberts… where's she?"

"She did all right, Ryan. Brought the information and stood her ground until we got Mac to confirm her position. Once that came through, she was no end of help to us."

"Where is she?" he asks again.

"Ah, she went with Dave and the boys."

He blinks. "What?"

"Dave assigned her the Diamond-T with Deloight. She wouldn't take no for an answer. Dave figured she could try and get there on her own, so she might as well be with Deloight. She wants her story something bad, that one."

He can't speak.

"Ryan?"

"He needs a moment," Luke says from his chair.

"Organize those horses and provisions right away, if you would, Mason."

Mason stares wide-eyed for a moment. "Sure, Ryan. I'm on it." And he disappears.

"You got it real bad…Sheriff," Luke taunts.

"Shut up," Cliff mutters.

Dickson

Luke's hands tremble and shake too violently to shave (better that no one recognizes him anyway), but he can sit in a bath and with a soft brush slowly work soap into his filthy skin.

The hot water surrounding his sore, exhausted body soothes and comforts him.

The fragrant soap reminds him of Jennifer, and he lies there thinking about her and only her for some very long minutes.

Then, melancholy, he rounds up his thoughts back to the present, only to have Cliff interrupt them. Washed and shaved, he barges in unceremoniously.

Luke figures after what he's put Cliff through, Cliff don't need to be polite.

"There's a crew going out tomorrow to fix that broken cable."

Luke studies Cliff's closed, remote expression with suspicion.

"What about Donnelly?" he asks.

"The telegraph office confirmed that he got our telegram. Picked up provisions and headed out hours ago, according to the feller at the general store."

The soap pops out of his hand. "And we're lolling about taking baths and shaving and…"

"Making sure we get there in one piece. Because as desperate as I know you feel, and as worried as I am, we won't make it if we don't…"

"All right," he snaps.

"Donnelly's already a long way ahead of us. We knew he would be. Actually thought he'd be further. We won't catch up to him at night, in these conditions and with you unwell."

"Okay."

"Dave Ransford is there. Deloight and Crogan are good men."

"Fine."

"Can you eat?"

His stomach lurches. He and food ain't the best of pals lately.

"No."

"Something?"

"Just help me out of this hog-wallow, will you?"

The Laramie Defense

Emmaline's Day One
February 2, 1885

On Sheriff Ransford's desk, Deloight's map of the Bright River district lies stretched out beneath a paper weight made of glass with an unfortunate butterfly preserved inside it, a brass letter opener with a mother of pearl handle, two colt .45's and a Bowie knife. There is a tendency for men to breathe heavily when wordlessly grouped around something. All that close proximity…

"So," she says, "is there another way apart from the stage and telegraph route?"

"That's what we're looking for, Roberts," Sheriff Ransford says. "The map don't show the snow cover. So we have to rely on our local knowledge of the conditions."

She swallows his sarcasm. "I understand."

Deloight taps his forefinger on a spot. "Here."

Sheriff Ransford gives his head a shake. "Steep gorge… here." And taps.

It seems to Emmaline that the stage/telegraph route is the only way. On the map it extends for miles across the prairies and then winds like a black snake up into the mountains. It crosses a river several times, helping to segment the land into several ranches and homesteads which are all clearly labeled.

She spots the Diamond-T nestled below a mountain plateau and stretching down into a wide valley with a river running through it.

On the other side of a high pass to its north lies Ed Parsons' property.

"What happened to Parsons' ranch after he went to prison?" she asks.

Sheriff Ransford scratches his chin. "It was bought."

"Did anyone think to ask by whom?"

"We asked. Loren Bodecker."

She meets his eye. "Anyone living there?"

"Can't say. But if you're thinking what I'm thinking, then yes, it would be a perfect staging ground for an assault on the Diamond-T and the Keaton Ranch. As you can see, it borders both properties."

Crogan speaks up. "Remember, boss, when John Keaton got his cattle rustled by Parsons' agents, he reckoned the rustlers came down through the north-east pass and left the same way. See here? – there's concealed access to that from Parsons' ranch, obviously why it was used in the first place. And at this time of year no one will be up there."

"At this time of year, no one's anywhere. Those boys keep their stock in close and hand feed them like pets. Diamond Pass – here – will be deserted too. They can creep in and out from Parsons' ranch house if they want."

"I don't know," Emmaline muses. "Seems too obvious. Donnelly laying claim to Loren Bodecker's new place, stocking it with rifles and ammunition and staging his grand assault on the Alliance from there. And it's not how Maverick usually works. His sharpshooters are unknown to him and each other. They get clear instructions from Maverick via the telegraph and work alone until they get the job done. Where they hole up until the job is done is up to them."

Deloight says, "If that's the case here, they could end up shooting each other."

Sheriff Ransford's glance shifts between herself and Deloight.

She says, "They've always known who their victim is. In a town with many women walking the streets at any given time, Swinton Carter knew exactly who I was." She swallows at the memory and looks Sheriff Ransford in the eye. "They know their victims. They have a description. They stalk and they watch. They probably have one victim each."

Sheriff Ransford's eyes narrow. "Two women and a baby, John Keaton and this Ben Taylor: four at the Keatons. Then Sara Taylor, Ethan and Tip Benchley. Seven hired guns in one operation." Sheriff Ransford rubs his chin once more. "That kind of operation requires military-style coordination. No, I'm inclined to think Maverick's arranged a gun for each house and probably someone to cover the middle ground.

"So. Crogan, Deloight, we're going to Bright River, defend the Keatons and the Taylors, and stop Maverick. Stealth is the key to this. Maverick doesn't know that we know and we're going to hang on to that advantage, and if we can, we take prisoners."

They nod their heads.

"Good. Now I want one of you to be at each of the ranch houses with the families. Crogan, at the Keatons. Deloight, the Diamond-T. Go in by the Stewarts' stock trail and cross the stream; the forest will give you cover for a while. And keep your eyes open and your-selves out of sight. Stay out of town. Donnelly knows all of us and if he is out there, he'll figure out the rest."

"And you'll be at the Parsons' place, Dave?" asks Crogan.

Sheriff Ransford nods. "Taking a careful look around. Then I'll swing out and keep a look out for that third gun."

Emmaline frowns. "And what will I do?"

Silence.

Sheriff Ransford clears his throat. "Well, Roberts…"

"I hope you're not intending to leave me here."

"Roberts, it seems like the thing to do – after all…"

"You wouldn't leave Sheriff Ryan here, would you?"

Deloight exchanges glances with Crogan and says, "If you're going into a fight, M'am, you wouldn't leave Cliff Ryan behind."

Sheriff Ransford sighs hard. "Roberts, Maverick's already had two goes at you. You think you're up for a third?"

"Sheriff Ransford, you promised me a story," she declares unable to keep the wobble out of her voice.

"Even you can't be in three places at once."

"Then choose one for me," she demands.

Deloight and Crogan stiffen; their eyes widen.

Sheriff Ransford says simply, "Deloight, you take Roberts."

She smiles at him. Deloight blinks. Crogan breathes a sigh.

"I would take you with me, Roberts, but I could find myself wandering around in this weather. 'Least at the Diamond-T you can stay put. I know this ain't what Ryan had in mind for you, Roberts, I know him well enough to know that much."

So does she. "Don't worry, Sheriff, I'll make sure he knows you protested vehemently."

Crogan snickers. Deloight is still in shock.

The young deputy barges in. "Excuse me, Sheriff…"

"What is it, Kid?"

"Just got word. This afternoon's stage and tomorrow morning's to Dickson and Bright River are cancelled. The last two are already held up in Dickson and the town's crowded. Nowhere left to stay 'til the road's open."

"Thanks, Kid. Right. We start first thing in the morning."

"In the morning?" Emmaline chokes out. "You can't be serious."

"Listen, Roberts…"

"Would Ryan just stand here and not protest about this?"

"It's the same for everyone," Sheriff Ransford declares, and then looks contrite for raising his voice. "Maverick doesn't know that we know what he's up to; his sharpshooters don't want to be freezing their bu… look, Roberts, they're probably in Dickson with everyone else waiting for the weather to clear up so they can move in. We wait 'til morning. Do you ride?"

Deeply frustrated, she gives a curt nod.

"Experienced?"

Again, she nods.

"Good. Get yourself geared up for a very long and very cold excursion. There's a comfortable hotel two blocks down; I'll send the Kid to get you a room. Albany County will foot the bill. Just rest up and get a couple of good square meals into you. You're going to need them. I'll organize your horse and provisions. We meet out front eight o'clock tomorrow morning."

"Right, boss," Crogan and Deloight respond.

They clear out in haste.

Sheriff Ransford reaches for the map and starts rolling it. "This'll be some story, Roberts, if you live to write it."

Emmaline's Day Two

Her horse, she was told, is called Timmy, and there was never an animal more sturdy, good-natured and reliable. She can't recall when she first fell in love with horses, just as she has no recollection of when she started loving her mother; it was natural and taken for granted. Celina also liked horses; she and Emmaline rode together all the time, but Emmaline jumped fences and creeks, terrorized the town, and raced boys, while Celie sat back, enjoying Emmaline's antics, encouraging her because it made her laugh. Made them both laugh. And it wasn't the constant teasing for her unladylike antics that reined her passion for them. Her mother did it with an innocent observation, in a single sentence, when Emmaline was fifteen.

You and horses, Emmaline, you're just like your father.

Her mother realized the impact of her comment when Emmaline stopped riding and began talking about applying for college and having a career in something that would change the world. Horses subsequently became little more than an essential mode of transportation. For a time she followed Celie into her world of fashion and friends. Celie understood that for Emmaline it was a means to an end. They both ended up in college. One turned out young ladies destined for the homes of high profile, wealthy or important men, such as Harrison Kennedy. The other turned out young citizens who relished the idea of making the world sit up and take notice of them because they were going to do something great.

Celie and Emmie's mama had lovely, conventional dreams for her twin daughters. Well-educated, refined and prepared for life, they would marry Roman Catholic boys and raise Roman Catholic families. One out two wasn't bad.

Hours out of Laramie they finally stop and dismount.

"How far from Dickson are we?" she asks Sheriff Ransford.

"About half way," he murmurs. "Eat something, Roberts."

She rummages through her provisions.

Amongst the beef jerky and other assorted pieces of men's food, she finds several candy bars. She extracts one, peels the paper wrapping and starts snapping and munching. The others, pulling on their jerky, stare at her.

Deloight cracks a smile and looks away.

Their progress depends on the varying conditions. Heavy snow or light snow; and there's prairie after prairie of it, vast lands of purest white. Every so often there will appear animal tracks in the snow leading off into the distance, but no human prints. The telegraph poles are deeply buried but guide them effectively through the landscape, linking the familiar world to the unknown.

The country changes from prairieland to hills, mountains, valleys and meadows, and extraordinary vistas.

They reach Dickson as it is getting dark... cold, exhausted and hungry. In the tiny settlement, still overcrowded with visitors with no place to go, Sheriff Ransford gets very jumpy. They split up and must find their own billets for the night, and then leave separately in the morning for their destinations. Emmaline and Deloight give themselves the cover of brother and sister visiting relatives in Bright River. After Sheriff Ransford dismisses them with a firm 'good luck', he and Crogan disappear into the town and that is the last she sees of them. She looks up at Deloight as he surveys the town for a place to stay.

"Don't worry, Roberts," he murmurs as he looks around. "Hot food is on the way."

There's a cottage on the edge of town. Deloight dismounts and she follows.

"Who lives here?"

"A friend."

The cottage is occupied by a wizened old man; there are only two rooms, but the fire in the hearth warms the place nicely and it's good to be inside.

"Beecham, this is my sister," Deloight says.

"You got a name?" Mr Beecham asks.

"Emmaline."

"Pretty. Sit." Mr Beecham indicates a chair by the fire and she does as she's told. "Got yourself a good looking sister, Deloight."

"I take after our mother," she says. "Is that food ready by any chance, Mr Beecham?"

Over supper, Deloight asks if they are any strangers in town.

"Town's full of them."

Ask a stupid question.

Emmaline's Day Three

Despite Mr Beecham's odd little cottage, she sleeps soundly on a cot by the fire. In the morning, Mr Beecham feeds her a bowl of oatmeal, bacon, fried eggs and several cups of coffee.

"Thank you, Mr Beecham, for your kind hospitality," she says as she mounts up.

He waves them off.

They skirt the town and head out.

"Who is Mr Beecham really?" she asks Deloight.

"I told you. A friend." Deloight glances sideways at her. "Are you ready, Roberts, because this won't be an easy day. We'll be following the telegraph line as much as necessary."

She nods. "I'm ready."

Deloight is right; the going is tough and slow. The sky is clear and bright but a raw wind is blowing, and the snow is deep. She takes Deloight's lead in everything. He doesn't talk to her at all. He watches the landscape continually, reminding her a little of Ryan as he strode through Cheyenne.

Mr Beecham's excellent breakfast begins to wear off by mid morning. Even for Deloight. He indicates a large outcrop of rocks; they dismount and take cover there. Time to rest the horses and break out some food.

"How are you, Roberts?" Deloight asks.

"I'm used to a little more conversation."

"Sorry," he sighs.

"Sorry you got stuck with me."

"I didn't mean that, M'am."

M'am? He's M'am-*ing* her?

"Don't answer to M'am. If you get tired of Roberts, my name is Emmaline."

His eyes catch hers before she stuffs her candy wrappings in her saddlebag. "What do you think about hour upon hour?"

"I'm just doing my job," he says.

"Mm. So am I, I suppose. I mean, I'm writing my story, in my head, almost constantly..."

"Almost?"

She is not about to tell Deloight that Cliff Ryan is in her head with her.

"Where are you from, Roberts?" Deloight asks.

"Florida mostly."

"Mostly?"

"How long to Bright River?"

"Snow's getting deeper. Hard to say."

He can't guess?

"Am I slowing you down?"

He glances sidelong. "No. The snow is. Have you ever rode through snow this deep?"

"Never."

"Mm. Can't say I've rode this deep kind of snow much myself. Almost makes more sense to leave the horses and don snow shoes. Mostly people got the good sense to stay indoors and let it melt. On a summer day Dickson to Bright River is a pretty outing, if you like that kind of thing."

"I don't want to get lost."

"Easy to do."

"I haven't seen where the telegraph is down yet."

"Me neither."

At last, they ride over a rise and espy the telegraph wire adrift in the snow.

"There."

"I see it," she says. "It looks so forgotten and forlorn."

"Yep."

Much later, Deloight says, "So, Roberts, how you holding up?"

He reins his horse beside her and they both stop.

She looks up into Deloight's face. "Fine."

"Born in a saddle, were you?"

"Something like that."

There's an amused twinkle in his eye. "Wouldn't have picked it. Although Ryan obviously did."

"Where are we?" she asks.

For a while back there, but for the virgin snow, she could have sworn they were going in circles. They lost sight of the telegraph for a long while, until Deloight got them back on track; she appreciated his calm and dogged disposition. Now, the air is still and brittle with frost. The landscape closes in with ghostly light and low on the horizon a silver moon is rising in a cold lavender sky.

"Bright River's not far."

"Are we going in?"

"Afraid we have to. My horse is favoring a leg."

"How long should we stay?"

"Just long enough to get some hot food. Change my horse. Head off for the Diamond-T soon as possible." He pulls a tight smile. "These things happen, Roberts."

Indeed.

The hot food at the Fortune Hotel is very welcome. Deloight eats fast and then goes in search of a horse. At this late hour he warns her it could take some time. She falls asleep on her arms at the table.

She is shaken out of a muddled dream.

"What time is it?" she asks groggily.

"Very late."

"You look worried," she whispers.

"It's nothing."

"Horse?"

He nods. "Let's go."

They collect their animals from the livery in the next block.

Timmy looks well fed and ready to go. Deloight's horse is a little smaller and stockier than his other.

"Cow pony," he whispers and shrugs.

Sometime later Deloight pulls up and Emmaline follows.

"Stewarts' stock trail is in that direction. It's the quickest way. We should be at the Diamond-T in an hour or so, depending on the conditions."

"I'm glad we've got this big moon to light our way," she says.

"To light our way, but not give us away; this is now officially maverick-occupied territory. Keep out of the moonlight."

She nods. "Of course. I understand, Deloight."

"There's some brandy in that pack of yours. Suggest you have some. Keeps yours insides from freezing."

Deloight retrieves it for her and removes the lid. "Here."

She takes several small but effective sips and hands it back.

Deloight repacks it.

"Haven't seen anything suspicious, have you?" he asks.

"Don't know what constitutes suspicious for you, Deloight, but I haven't seen anyone on the road or in the countryside all day long. *That* is suspicious, don't you think?"

He actually gives chuckle. "It just seems that way. High country ranching is specialized."

In Deloight's mind that must answer her question. She'd still like to know where everybody went.

She asks, "The Stewarts – they won't mind us using their trail?"

"Not many people know this, and Dave won't mind me telling you, but the Stewarts sold their herd last October and moved out. Heard they took fright when Miss Keaton was murdered. Figured it was the last straw. They haven't sold out, mind. Just quietly sold their stock at market and left. Mentioned something about holding out for better days."

"No doubt they believed with Ed Parsons incarcerated life would get better."

"Everyone around here did. The Stewarts smelled a rat."

"How come this wasn't mentioned back in Laramie?"

"If the Stewarts wanted everyone to know, they would've made an announcement."

"What happened to their breeding stock?"

"Ethan Benchley and John Keaton bought it."

She catches her breath.

"Ethan and John each have a key to the place, I'm told. To keep an eye on it."

"I can't believe Donnelly never noticed."

"Well, we don't know that for sure, do we?"

"So the Stewarts' place should be deserted?"

"Unless Maverick's found a use for it."

"Let's hope not. Coming this way was a risk then?" Frosty whiteness billows out of her mouth as her breathing becomes rapid at the thought.

Deloight shrugs. "Would you have changed your mind?"

She feels a familiar, peculiar pain in her chest, like a tug of sadness. It comes and goes, particularly since the train pulled away from Watts Landing.

She sniffs back the cold and says, "Let's go."

They enter thick forest with no clear trail to follow and Deloight increasingly looking about.

The brandy continues its warm ascent inside her, slightly easing that pang in her chest. She looks upwards through the tops of the trees. The moon rides high in the star-studded, inky sky.

"*Look at the stars! Look, look up at the skies!*"

"What's that, Roberts?"

"A line from a poem called *The Starlight Night* by Gerard Manley Hopkins."

"Very nice. You look up if you dare, Roberts. I'll keep my eyes on the ground."

"You do that, Deloight."

Even with the beauteous starry sky, this long day is not how she ever imagined she would spend her twenty-third birthday.

❖

With a bad feeling taking hold inside of him, Dave eyes the dark hump in the middle of the trail and approaches with caution.

As he dismounts, a horse trots out of the snow-covered brush and scares the bejeezus out of him. He steadies the horse, then bends down and turns that long dark figure.

The eyes are frozen open; the face is ice-white and opaque in the fall of moonlight... except for the bullet hole in the side of the head that's left a dark stain.

Dave crouches quietly for several moments and removes his hat. Jim Crogan. One of his best deputies; a good friend; a good man.

With his hat once again firmly on his head, he fetches Jim's bedroll from his horse. He wraps up Jim's cold, lifeless body, drapes it across the saddle of Jim's horse and secures it.

"Sorry, Jim. So damn sorry..."

He mounts and changes his plans.

Emmaline's Day Four

The Diamond-T ranch buildings figure darkly in the gloom, with the barest blink of easterly aspect in the snow.

"I thought you said an hour or so. I can see a trace of light over in the east."

"Did *you* memorize the map perfectly?" Deloight counters.

"No," she admits. "Sorry."

"We're here now, that's all that matters," he says.

"Of course."

Their previous apprehension about encountering a maverick as they were crossing the Stewarts' property had thankfully amounted to nothing. There was the other challenge though...

"Landmarks get disguised in the dark and under all this snow," Deloight continues, peering out from their cover, a small clump of pine trees.

He was right; the forest was more like a huge maze. Good thing they both possessed the resolve to see it through.

"Perfectly understandable," she says.

"We got to get to the house without being detected."

"The moon's set."

"That should help."

All is silent.
It is deeply, abominably cold.
Her bones begin to shiver.

❖

Jed Tyner, silent, careful, peers through the murk and shadow of Taylor's hayloft as two figures lead their horses inside the barn. They whisper to one another; they stable their mounts and stalk out of the building. Jed skulks from his hiding place to the barn door and watches the pair cross the yard to the door of the first house. They'll find the house empty, just like he did… He waits patient for them to reappear.

Who are these two?

Sure enough they emerge and move on to the next house. They'll find one of his possible targets asleep. And that's all, unless they go to the bunk-house. There are half a dozen cowpokes snoring in there. Things weren't exact in how he was told they were going to be. And now this.

He watches as lantern light springs out into the gloom from a window and then goes out.

❖

In the pearly gloom of a promising morning, smoke curls from the Keatons' chimney, and there's a smell of bacon on the wind.

Dave rides in from the cover of the forest behind the Keaton ranch house and cautiously leads both horses into the barn.

He casts his eye around the building; there don't appear to be anything unusual except that at this hour of a deep winter morning, activity in the ranch house notwithstanding, all of John Keaton's horses are fully awake and alert like he ain't the first person they've seen today.

Bright River Siege

Day One with the Alliance
February 2, 1885

Ben wakes for the second time that morning; the parlor is full of light and there are tantalizing breakfast smells coming from the kitchen; bacon, pancakes, coffee – steak? He hasn't had steak for breakfast since Montana… He glances down at the bundle still sleeping in his arms; the small pink mouth is moving. Does the smell of bacon whet this little guy's appetite as well? He sits forward carefully and then stands up. Adam stirs a little; one eye opens then shuts; then two together. He blinks himself awake and gives Ben a smile that reveals two perfect bottom teeth.

"Well, they're just fine."

Adam makes a throaty noise that sounds like a cross between a chuckle and an attempt to speak. They stroll into the kitchen.

Amy Keaton, placing a platter of bacon rashes and thin steaks on the table, looks up. "Did he kick off his covers again?"

"I guess."

"Mm." She straightens, folds her arms. "How did you sleep?"

"Like a log. I woke early is all, concerned about my mother."

John Keaton barges in through the front door as though morning is his favorite time of day even in the depths of winter. "Smells good," he's muttering; when he sees Ben and Adam, he says, "Now there's a sight you don't see every day."

"Give the baby to me," Amy says, taking the kid from him.

"You two start eating. I'll wake sleeping beauty."

John sits down. "He's a special kid that one. Don't know what we'd have done without him after all our loss. He's a Keaton, see... Sit down, son." John Keaton starts forking steak and bacon onto a plate. He passes the plate to Ben, saying, "Tressa gave him Taylor as his middle name."

"Thanks. She told me and he's a great kid. Have you thought any more about what I told you last night?"

"About my daughter's killer being in jail in Cheyenne? Thought about it all night. I got a wire from Cliff Ryan, came just before you did. Ethan'll be here any time now; we're gonna discuss whether one of us should go to Cheyenne."

"Do you and Ethan do everything together, like partners?"

John Keaton piles bacon and steak onto his own plate and starts cutting. "Guess it could look like that to an outsider. Eat up, son. Amy's breakfasts always hit the spot."

He's right. The steak and bacon is the best he's ever eaten.

Half way through, a man bursts open the door. He's about his father's age, with a face leathered by years of working outside in extremes of weather, and the canniest eyes Ben has ever seen.

"Dang, it's cold," he declares. He strips his hat from his head and pegs it by the door all in one motion. His eyes meet Ben's abruptly. "Sorry, John, you got a visitor."

John Keaton chuckles deeply.

"Sure we have, Ethan. You might be interested in meeting him. Ethan Benchley, Ben Taylor... Ben, this here is Ethan, he and your Uncle Morgan were partners, long time ago now, but..."

Ben doesn't really hear what John Keaton's saying. He's too busy keeping track of Ethan Benchley's shrewd eyes sizing him up.

Finally, the man says coolly, loaded with barbs, "Now ain't this a day to remember. You'll pardon my accent. It's Texan."

Ben nods. "I noticed. I don't have a problem with it."

"Sit down, Ethan," says John Keaton. "Steak's getting cold."

Ethan Benchley takes a seat opposite. So Benchley doesn't like the look of him, so what? Ben didn't come for this man's approval, although approval from such a man would be something.

"Ben here brought us confirmation of that wire from Cliff Ryan.

On his way through Cheyenne he heard that Kelley's murderer is in jail. Ryan shot him. The feller who told Ben reckoned we'd be celebrating. What d'you think, Ethan?"

Ethan Benchley chews his steak thoughtfully. "That why you came? To bring this information?"

"Not exactly. I have my reasons, Benchley, and they're none of your business. And I thought the information might be of interest to the Keatons."

John Keaton says, "Ben came to see Tressa, Ethan. Decided it was time; ain't that a fine thing?"

"Where are the women?" is all the man says in reply.

"They'll be along; give us time to work out what to do."

"One of us should go to Cheyenne and talk to Cliff Ryan."

"Figured you say that, Ethan."

"We need to gauge if there's someone else behind this besides Parsons, another threat…"

"Yep, just what I thought. I'll leave right after breakfast."

Ethan Benchley shakes his head. "You got a guest, two women and a baby to look after. I'll go. Nothin' much happenin' at home. Tip and the boys can handle it."

"You sound kinda melancholy, Ethan."

"I wish the boy would come home," Ethan Benchley mutters and then helps himself to coffee. He slurps it steaming from his cup, while John Keaton observes him sympathetically.

"You go to Cheyenne, Ethan," John Keaton says.

Ethan Benchley mumbles his agreement.

Day Two with the Alliance

Ethan surveys Tip's approach from his front porch. If he weren't so worried about other troubling matters, he'd be able to take more pleasure in how strong his good-natured son is becoming, manly and full of purpose.

He manages a grin as he watches his long-striding offspring negotiate his way towards the porch.

"Well, son?" Ethan asks as Tip reaches him.

The young feller is exhaling plenty of white clouds into the air between them. "Unless you intend to walk out of Bright River on snow shoes, you're better off waiting, Pa. Maybe a day or two."

Ethan suspected as much. He nods his thanks. "Go on in and get some hot grub."

Tip's dark eyes go soft with sympathy. "I'm sorry, Pa."

"Aw, that son-of-a-bitch ain't going nowhere, behind bars, under lock and key. I just don't want some fancy lawyer talking up the case without one of us there."

"Have faith, Pa. It's gonna be all right. You'll see."

Has his mother's quiet heart, this son does. A good legacy that. Of all the things she gave him, the many wonderful, worthwhile things. He appreciates it all the more because it's something he could never have given the boy. When he was young he was like Luke. And then Red Sky came along with her quiet heart and gave him peace and this prince for a son.

He smiles and places his hand on the boy's shoulder.

"You're of an age, Tip…"

"I know, Pa."

"Tip, you're the grandson of a chief."

"When it's time, I'll know. And so will you."

Ethan gives him a shake and a lop-sided grin. "Go get your grub. I'll ride over to John's tomorrow morning and let them know what we've decided."

Tip folds his arms; he's a muscular kid, strong and lean like his people. "Take another look at Ben Taylor while you're there. Don't rush back. Then bring him over; I'll show him around."

He frowns. "I ain't bringing him here. What would Sara say… what would Luke say?"

"Luke and Sara ain't here. Ben Taylor ain't responsible for what his father did, just like you weren't responsible for the slaughter of my mother's band. We both know that overcoming prejudice ain't easy. If Ben Taylor has found it within himself to do it, then that is something even Luke can't ignore."

Day Three with the Alliance

Ethan spies John's barn doors pulled back, so he steers his pinto towards them and ambles in. It's a darn sight warmer inside.

John has one of his quarter horses on a halter, walking the animal studious-like.

Ethan dismounts.

"Snowshoe weather," John says.

Ethan removes his hat and wipes his sleeve across his forehead.

"Cheyenne'll have to wait."

John leads his horse into its stall.

"That animal looks ginger," Ethan remarks.

"Thought so, too." He closes the stall gate. "Fresh feed and water – help yourself…"

The pinto needs no encouragement after the cold ride.

"So," John says, giving the pinto's neck a soothing stroke, "you came all this way to tell me you ain't going to Cheyenne just yet? Kinda figured that out myself. What's on your mind, Ethan?"

Ethan folds his arms. "How's the boy?"

"Ben? He and Tressa haven't stopped talking since he arrived. I think he's hearing what he came all this way to hear. Not a bad storyteller Tressa. Seems to remember a lot of details. Guess it runs in the family seeing how Luke never was short of a story."

Ethan sighs hard. Talking about Luke and the way things used to be only makes it worse; he ain't sure if he can do as Tip suggested…

John brings his hand down hard on Ethan's shoulder. "I know you're worried because you figure he should be home by now, but you know what he's like. Besides, worry does nothing but give you sleepless nights and a stomach ulcer."

Ethan appreciates the talking to; John wouldn't say it if he didn't mean it.

"Come inside and see the boy?"

Ethan shrugs.

John grins. "Amy will be pleased to see you. You know how she loves feeding people in this weather."

Ben begins to understand. But if so much of his identity is bound up in the story of Matthew Taylor, why did he not feel his heart questioning or hear the whispers in his mind long ago?

How could he let himself be so firmly controlled by his father?

Why was he so complacent until the day Tressa left?

And how fantastic the circumstances that brought her here, to lead him here also.

She has the baby on her knee, a careful eye on him as he plays with a toy horse – 'a cherished gift from Luke'. When she stops talking for any length of time, her eye falls on the horse and sticks; a far off place takes her attention away from him and Adam, who almost gets the horse into his mouth.

Ben distracts him.

Tressa comes back again and smiles, stroking her son's blond head.

"I'm sorry," she murmurs. "Where was I?"

"I don't know but I'm glad you go there sometimes."

She shakes her head gently. "No, no. I mustn't."

He takes the horse and makes it gallop over Tressa's lap and Adam's knees. The little boy laughs, reaching with his arms.

"How long can you stay?" Tressa asks.

"With the Keatons, can't outstay my welcome. But here in Bright River, as long as you want."

"I think you look fine away from Omaha," she blurts out and then looks stricken. "Sorry…"

"Don't be sorry for saying what you think, not ever," he says. "Omaha is no longer the place it was, Tressa."

"But you didn't bring it with you, Ben, and I'm proud of you."

There are loud voices in the kitchen; they both turn their heads in that direction, leaving Adam to make a grab for the horse. By the time Ben has worked out that Ethan Benchley has returned, Adam has the horse's rump in his mouth and is drooling happily.

"Ethan… maybe he has news," Tressa murmurs.

Adam baby-talks his delight in the horse, waving it in front of Tressa's face.

"Yes, my darling," she says distractedly and lowers the toy.

"It's surprising he came back, with me here."

"No. They're not like that," she says. "They're proud, yes, but not...."

He meets her eyes. "You want me to try again."

She nods.

He sighs. Gets to his feet and saunters into the kitchen.

Amy Keaton is settling a cup of coffee into Benchley's hand.

"Here, Ethan, warm up."

"You're not going to fuss, Amy, are you?" Benchley counters.

"Yes," she retorts. "You need it."

Benchley spots him standing in the doorway.

They eye one another. Ben keeps a poker face.

"Coffee, Ben?" Amy Keaton asks.

It means he'll need to sit at the table with Benchley.

"Thanks," he says. And sits opposite him.

"Pie?"

Benchley accepts pie; Ben is still full from lunch.

"So," Benchley says, chewing, "you wanna give me the lowdown on what's going on in Omaha?"

Ben frowns. "What do you mean?"

Benchley swallows. "No one decides to up and leave a comfy life like yours 'cause they woke up one day and felt like it. Gotta be a reason."

"I wanted to see Tressa."

"So I heard. There's more. You're a Taylor. There's always more. Now spill it."

Ben realizes that the only way to earn this man's trust is to do as he says. "My father decided to expand his business from sand, gravel and limestone into Wyoming coal. A businessman named Loren Bodecker is the man who is going to help him to do it..."

"Bodecker?" Benchley echoes. "You sure?"

"Speaks volumes for my father, does it?"

"Never met Bodecker, but I heard plenty. I know the type."

"Yeah, well, he doesn't appeal to me either. He's slick, arrogant and he smiles too much. The kind of attributes my father admires in a business associate."

"And you don't, I take it?"

"I don't care for the kind of life men like Bodecker lead. Despite his shortcomings, my father has managed to remain in the realms of decency at least."

"Far as you know," Benchley says.

Ben may be tough, but that dart finds its mark.

"Yes, Mr Benchley, as far as I know."

John and Amy Keaton have also taken a chair at the table – the same one, until they bump behinds and Amy finds her own; meanwhile, John's bright blue eyes stare intently at him.

"Go on, Ben, we're listening," John encourages him.

"Bodecker's partner goes by the name of Donnelly, a Laramie businessman. On the train from Omaha he corners me in the dining car at breakfast. I'd been reading the Cheyenne papers and I asked the waiter who owned the Bugle. I'm told Bodecker owns it. It's full of Republican sweet talk, Association propaganda for the cattle barons and Bodecker blowing his own trumpet.

"This Donnelly character wants to know why I want to know. Then he decides he recognizes me from the meeting Bodecker had with my father and me the day before. He asks if I'm related to Luke Taylor of Bright River – it's obvious he already knows that I am – says he's a nuisance and a troublemaker. He said he'd heard I was none too fond of my cousin, still he believed I was going to Bright River to see him. He informs me that Luke has been in San Francisco the past few months. He reckoned I'd know all about it since my cousin's best friend was married to my sister.

"When I suggested that he seemed to know a lot about it himself, he said you people were all famous. He wanted me to think that your private business was common knowledge.

"I wired my mother to inform my father that Donnelly needed investigating for the sake of the company, but I can't say if they went and followed through. Foolhardy not to. And my father may respect this Bodecker but I never could.

"Look, I came to see my sister. My only regret is leaving my mother to deal with the aftermath, and my only consolation is that she wanted me to go and gave me her blessing."

Benchley and John Keaton exchange looks.

Amy Keaton straightens and pulls back her mouth to a tight line.

"Well," Benchley says, "he's got it, John."

"Yep," says John.

Ben frowns. "Got what?"

"You know, a lotta people assumed Luke got it from Sara, but that's only 'cause they didn't know Morgan."

"What?"

"Tressa's the same," Amy sighs. Then she grins. "I like it."

"Mm," Benchley nods. "It can fill a spot."

"What?"

"The talk," John tells him.

"Reckon they might get on all right," Benchley says.

"Who?"

John grunts. "I don't know, Ethan. You gotta be prepared to let the other one speak his opinion on occasion."

Benchley grins. "I got Luke trained, you know that."

Then all three start chuckling.

"You're not the least bit interested in anything I just told you?" Ben asks.

"What about what *we* just told you, boy?" Benchley says. "Ain't you interested in that?"

"You're talking like I'm not in the same room and my name's Ben, not boy. If you can't be interested in that, then we have nothing to talk about." Ben scrapes back his chair.

"Whoa, whoa, now," Benchley declares like Ben's a horse.

Tressa appears at Ben's side, Adam in her arms. "I'm ashamed of you, Ethan Benchley, behaving this way toward my brother."

Ben stares up at her, dumbfounded.

"He's come here for a noble purpose and all you can do is... is..."

Ben reaches up and wraps his fingers around her wrist. "It's all right, Tress. Hush now, don't fret."

Adam, seeing Ben, reaches out his arms and squirms.

But Tressa and Benchley are eyeing one another, one with resentment and the other taken aback.

"Ben is an important guest in this house and... and..."

Ben gets to his feet. "Right, come on, Tress. We got some things to sort out." He takes Adam from Tressa's arms. "Let's go."

Ethan grumbles, "Just when we were gettin' somewhere."

"Yep," John says, stretching.

"And where would that be, Ethan?" Amy inquires in a tone to be wary of.

"Amy, that is one tough kid," he says. "Cup of coffee and a chinwag about the niceties of train travel ain't gonna cut it."

"The baby adores him," says Amy.

"Go figure," Ethan returns. "Amy, a kid like that... how can I explain it..."

"It's about respect," John says. "He wants it from Ethan and he's prepared to work to get it."

Ethan glances at John. "Why do you think that is?"

John shrugs. "For Tressa most likely."

"Well, anyway, for all our sakes, but particularly Luke's, I gotta try and find some middle ground here."

"Heal the rift of how many years and how many disappointments?" Amy asks.

"Too many, on both counts. They weren't the boy's fault. Richard Taylor don't cut the mustard, but somehow his offspring do. Don't ask me how."

Amy gets to her feet, starts gathering coffee cups.

Ethan scratches his chin. "He's got a lot to say but I reckon he means every word."

"Yep," John says. "He got it all off his chest for sure. Now, who this Donnelly is and why Bodecker is interested in Luke's uncle's business are questions I'd like to find the answers to."

"Amen to that."

Amy puts her cups in her sink. "You will call him Ben this time, won't you, Ethan?"

"What was all that about?"

Ben knows his sister too well to think he can just shrug this off.

"I'm doing what you want, Tressa."

She sits Adam in his crib. He grizzles until his chubby hand comes in contact with an object with a tinkling bell hidden inside.

"You have to understand something. I bet when you arrived on Luke's doorstep he took one look at you and thought how could this sweet, pretty girl be any threat to me or my family, how could any of the bad things her father did be her fault? And he was right, what he did was right. But look at me, Tress. I am my father's son. It's different for me. I have to prove in any number of ways that what our father did isn't my fault either. So if you want me to reconcile with Luke's family, then you're going to have to let me do it my way."

Tressa folds her arms. "Even if it means fighting with Ethan?"

He gives a laugh. "That wasn't fighting, you goose."

"I thought you'd left Omaha behind," she accuses.

Smiles reassuringly. "These people are far more honest than I've ever had to deal with, I know, but in a way it gives me a freedom I've never known before. To be myself, to say what I think and believe, and not fear their disapproval or rejection – because I don't. They don't have to like me; they just have to acknowledge that I am not responsible for our father's actions. I cannot carry that burden anymore, Tress; it's not mine to carry. Nor is it my duty to be like him. Mother made me see that."

Tressa, wide-eyed and soulful, says, "I miss her."

"And she misses you."

Ethan remembers a time when he sat at this table and not only was Luke there with them, but Mart and Kelley, as well as Tressa. It was like fate closed her eyes for a moment and let them have a spell; and then she opened her eyes again and all hell broke loose. He slides his fork around his plate like skaters over an iced pond. Just something of Luke, some small insignificant thing, would ease his concern right now. The boy sitting in Luke's place resembles him. Fine-looking, strong and smart. Gifted with words. And no doubt many other gifts besides. But the difference between a boy raised with love and one raised with authority is interesting to see. Ethan don't want to compare them, and judge Ben, but he has to and deep down he knows why. *Morgan, you left me with a mighty charge.* He wouldn't have swapped a minute of raising Luke, but now this?

"Something not to your liking, Ethan?"

He lifts his head in the direction of Amy's voice, but instead catches the boy's glance. His navy eyes, similar color to Luke's, are cold. Luke always has a pack of sparkling mischief in his. But in Ben's cold eyes is something Luke's never have: neediness.

Ben looks away but it's too late for that.

Ethan puts down his fork.

"What do you know about your uncle Morgan?" he asks the boy.

Ben looks up again. "Stories Tressa has told me."

"Mm. What do they tell you about him?"

"That he was courageous, smart, prepared to take risks."

"He would've made a canny city businessman, like your father. What else?"

"He had a preference and skills for raising cattle; he had an eye for real estate; he knew good grazing land when he saw it."

"What drives a man like that to be successful?"

Ben lowers his fork. "A man like my father, power and money. Not that he didn't try to hold onto his heritage; it didn't suit him. Cattle, acres of land, and a ranch house with a wife and young family in the middle of nowhere. It hurt to leave, you know…"

"You?"

The boy's eyes flash. "Yes."

Ethan glances at Tressa. She's biting her lip, head down.

"I never had the privilege to know my uncle, but do you think if my father had allowed me that privilege I would have ended up the company secretary for my father's business, doing deals for coal with a man like Loren Bodecker? So my father is the rotten fruit in the whole barrel full of apples bent on living the righteous Matthew Taylor heritage, but that has never been and never will be my fault."

He picks up his fork and starts shoveling food into his mouth.

Ethan just rolls his eyes and goes back to skating his fork around Amy's hearty stew.

After supper, Ben helps John Keaton bring more firewood inside the back porch, which is large with a substantial stove to warm it; John explains that it often doubles as a warming room for newborn calves, and then they head off to the barn to check on John's horses. The man's crazy about them. He likes to tell about his daughter's love of them and he shows Ben her gentle mare, Dancer.

"You would've liked my Kelley. She felt things deep inside and wasn't afraid to speak her mind, kinda like yourself."

No one has ever described Ben this way; it seems to him that he's been scared to say what he thought all his life, now John's comparing him to his legendary daughter.

"And this pinto here is Ethan's," John says.

Ben strokes the animal's strong, warm neck.

John continues to bed down his collection like children in a dormitory and then heads for the door.

"You coming, Ben? It's getting late."

"I'll be along soon."

John winks at him. "Sometimes I prefer the company of horses myself."

When he's alone, Ben rests against the pinto's stall, which is full of fresh hay, turned and smelling sweet…

As a boy he would have dived over and over into a stack of hay like that, until he had hay storks sticking out his ears. He would have thrown himself onto the pinto and ridden bareback across the fields chasing the horizon of the Montana sky.

But the ways of boyhood are not the ways of a man…

Ethan finds the boy gnawing on a hay stork, staring at the pinto, contemplating.

He looks up, sharp.

"Relax," Ethan says, "I ain't dogging you."

"No?" The boy tosses down the hay; he straightens up, folds his arms.

"John and me were talking about this Donnelly character."

"And?"

"Day after tomorrow I'm heading off to Cheyenne. 'Til then, I reckon it might be a good idea if you come to the Diamond–T, meet Tip, my son…"

The idea registers in the boy's eyes; again their candid blueness reminds him of Luke.

"I came here to be with Tressa," he says.

"Well, where do you think Tressa found out what she knows and put it altogether?"

"I've put it altogether."

Ethan frowns. "I got an old photograph of your uncle Morgan somewhere. Your Aunt Sara's got one or two in her place. She's in New York right now, spending time with John's sister. Her house is empty, so there's plenty of room for you to stay."

The boy's eyes go narrow; far too suspicious, this one. Always thinking there's something else going on.

"I couldn't stay in someone's house without them knowing."

"Then stay with Tip and me. Got heaps of room. Tip's keen to meet you; told me so himself."

The boy unfolds his arms and jams his hands in the pockets of his britches instead. "I don't get you, Benchley."

"Nothing to get. I realize I can't be holding you to account for your father's actions. That would be just plain wrong, unless of course you agree with them, agree with him."

"My father created this prejudice and we have all lived with it and suffered because of it."

"Plain to see that you've made up your own mind about your Uncle Morgan."

"It matters little to me which side my uncle fought on during the war. I don't care if he lived in Texas or on the moon. I'm not staying here indefinitely, Benchley, this visit will come to an end and I will be gone. I don't need reminding every day for the rest of my life of my father's shortcomings as a brother and an uncle. There's plenty more where they came from, believe me. I know my heritage now and I'm proud to know it, but I think I can work out how to live it for myself."

The boy strides past Ethan and heads out. Ethan douses the lamp and hurries out, latching the barn door behind him. "Wait up..."

"What for?"

"You're a tough kid," Ethan breathes.

The boy stops; they face one another darkly, with just a trace of light from the porch lantern, in air so cold you could slice it with a blunt knife.

"So?"

"You don't have to be. Not with me, anyway."

"I don't know what you expect of me, but I'm never going to be like Luke. Face it, Benchley, he's as much your son as your real son."

Ethan's breath gets stuck in his chest. He tries to pull himself together. This ain't the time to discuss how he feels about Luke...

"This ain't about me or Luke. You're off track. Don't you ever want to be happy, Ben? 'Cause you don't look it."

The boy's pause is painstaking.

Ethan waits.

"Staying at the Diamond-T will make me happy?" the boy asks, annoyed and disbelieving. "I'll only have to do this all over again when my cousin returns."

Ethan clears his throat. "If you leave here never having been to the ranch, you won't have finished what you came here to do. Prove to yourself that the prejudice is all in your pa's mind. The demons won't go away by themselves, Ben, you gotta chase them away."

Another pause. "I'll think about it." He strides off again. And then stops and turns back around. "How do you know I'm not manipulating you?"

"I just know."

"You just know," the boy mimics.

"Mm. Always annoys the heck outa Luke too, so don't worry about it."

"I won't," the boy says with sarcasm.

Ethan watches him head towards the glow of the porch lantern.

Day Four with the Alliance

Ethan wakes early and heads out to the kitchen to make coffee. John, though, has beaten him to it.

By lamplight they greet one another croakily.

John sits down with his coffee, frowning and mumbling.

"What is it, John?" Ethan asks.

"You hear something during the night, notice anything?"

"Nope. Slept like a baby on Amy's cooking. Why d'you ask?"

"Horses seem kinda jumpy this morning. Took a look around but didn't see anything."

Ethan shrugs. "Stray critter."

"Maybe."

"Take a look myself after chow if you want. Better light."

John nods. "You leaving today?"

"Okay with you if I spend more time convincing Luke's ornery cousin to come back to the Diamond-T with me?"

"Stay as long as you like, Ethan, just make sure you tell Amy when you plan to leave. I don't wanna be eating the leftovers of two grown men. I wanna be able to get myself on m'horse come spring round up."

Amy emerges looking sleepy.

"Guess I'll start breakfast; there's no more sleep to be had once you two start chin wagging."

She begins fixing them a feast for breakfast. A feller could get downright portly living at the Keatons in winter.

"*Deputy Chase Deloight.*"

"*Tip Benchley. Who is this?*"

"*This is Acting Sheriff of Cheyenne, Emmaline Roberts.*"

"*She's a girl. What do you want?*"

"*Extinguish that lamp at once...*"

"*What?*" *The young feller does it anyhow. Gloom returns.*

"*The Alliance is in serious trouble.*"

"*Luke... is Luke all right?*"

"*We don't know. Where's your father?*"

"*At the Keatons'. What do you mean the Alliance is in trouble?*"

"*We'll explain soon. Who else is here? The other house is empty.*"

"*Sara is in New York with John Keaton's sister.*"

Chase nods in relief at this piece of news.

"*What do we do now?*" *Roberts asks.*

Her cold, weary face peers up at him from out of the gloom.

Chase smiles, then says to Tip, "What's on the breakfast menu?"

Keeping his eyes peeled, Dave stalks up to the Keatons' door. He wouldn't be so worried except for the fact that Jim Crogan was murdered by moonlight and therefore anything's possible now. He knocks. John Keaton pulls back the door.

"Morning, John. Sheriff Dave Ransford. Sorry to bother you so early."

John stands transfixed momentarily. Then he steps back.

"Sheriff, come in."

Dave steps into the warmest, most fragrant kitchen he's ever known.

Amy Keaton and Ethan Benchley are there.

"M'am," Dave says politely and removes his hat.

"Sheriff."

"Ethan."

"Sheriff, what brings you by?" His eyes go wide. "Luke..."

Dave puts up a steadying hand. "I can explain. Who else is in the house?"

"Tressa, our daughter-in-law, her brother Ben Taylor, and our baby grandson."

"Wake them. I think it's best to explain this once to everyone. What about the bunkhouse?"

"Just three; the others went south for a couple of months."

"I'll talk to them while you wake your family."

Chase squints as morning sun bounces off long, deep drifts of snow.

"Come on, you bastard," he mutters.

The move to the Taylor house has afforded him a better view.

"Chase?"

"What?"

"You said anything that moved, correct?"

"Yep," he calls back. "You see a rabbit, Emmaline?"

Chase assigned her the kitchen, with her eye on the backyard.

"I saw the sun glint off something, you know, a reflection. Maybe off metal or..."

"Get back," he barks. "I'm coming to take a look. Tip?"

Tip responds from his post at a front window on the second story.

"Did you see anything?"

"No. I'll take a look out back."

"No, stay put. And out of sight. You're a target, remember?" With his black hair the maverick won't mistake him.

Chase joins Emmaline in the kitchen. "Where?"

She steps aside to give him access to the window and points to a stand of cottonwoods about fifty yards away.

"A glint," she whispers.

Chase watches patiently. "You got eagle eyes, Emmaline?"

"There," Emmaline says. "Again..."

Chase's heart quickens. "I see it."

He stands up and draws her back into the hall.

"Can I count on you to stay here and keep an eye on Tip?"

"Of course."

Chase lets himself out the front door into the stinging cold and follows the side of the house around to the back. Under cover he waits but the reflection does not occur again. Would Maverick even know or care that things around the place ain't what they should be? Tip should be in the other house, or the bunkhouse or the corrals or barn. Sara Taylor should be busy in this house. And where would Ethan Benchley have got to?

Chase heads back into the house.

"What did you see?" Emmaline greets him.

"Nothing. All doors still locked and secured?"

"Yes. And curtains, drapes and shades are drawn."

"Tip? – come down here."

"What are you going to do next?"

"Always with the questions," he mutters as he waits for Tip.

I'm sure it's the same conclusion Chase Deloight has come to over at your place, Ethan," Dave says in the most soothing voice he can muster. "We wait for Maverick to make the first move. And believe me, that won't be shooting any one of us."

Ethan's red-rimmed eyes stare blankly at him, but he's still thinking – thinking what Dave is hoping with every bone in his body, that Chase made it.

"The fact that none of you are going about your daily routine, which he probably knows, is gonna frustrate and confuse him eventually. He'll come to us."

Amy Keaton catches her breath and puts her arm around her daughter-in-law holding the baby.

"We're well armed, M'am, and you and your family will be safe, I promise."

Ethan gets shakily to his feet. "What about *my* family, Sheriff?"

"Chase Deloight is a capable man, Ethan. And I reckon you probably know what kind of a man Cliff Ryan is. So try and stay calm. We all need to be alert until this is over. We discussed what you all need to do, so let's get on with it."

Ethan strides out of the kitchen into the parlor. Ben Taylor's eyes follow Ethan's movements.

"Any more of that fine coffee, M'am?" Dave holds out his cup.

Amy Keaton murmurs, "Yes, Mr Ransford, of course."

At the Dickson telegraph office Donnelly finally picks up what's been waiting for him; confounded weather...

NIGHTHAWK LULLABY. ROUND UP AND DRIVE.

Triumph winds through his blood.

Taylor capitulated. Good for him.

He's finished — now it's time to finish off the rest.

He crushes the telegram paper in his hand and stuffs it in the pocket of his britches.

"Send this," he orders the telegrapher.

He tosses his reply and payment on the counter.

The telegrapher stares at the reply like he's confused or something.

"It says NIGHTHAWK LULLABY. FINISH THE PROJECT. *Can't you read?"*

"A word or two," snaps the telegrapher, and gets down to business.

When it's done, Donnelly moves away.

He looks up and surveys Dickson's main street. The town's full of people who can't move on. Pity for them, but no such pity for the Alliance.

He mounts up and heads out of town for Bright River.

Ben finds Sheriff Ransford leaning against a stack of crates on the back porch. He must be staring at the snow melting because apart from the wind blowing, moving the trees, nothing is happening. The weather has cleared completely; the sky is blue and the sun shines as bright as it can at this time of year.

"Sheriff..."

Ransford shifts his feet. "Ben."

"It's been hours and hours and nothing."

"What time is it?"

"Two o'clock. Look, I've been thinking. With you and John here, don't you think it'd be all right if Ethan and I slipped away for the Diamond-T? He's out of his mind with worry about his son."

Ransford looks around and scrutinizes Ben long and hard. "I get that, Ben... he's as patient a soul as I've ever come across..."

"Well?"

Ransford sighs and returns to his lookout. "It'll depend on how this plays out. I'll think about it."

Ben nods and goes to find Ethan. It's not hard. He's been sitting in the same chair for the past three hours, just staring, seeing things in his mind, going crazy with worry.

"I spoke to Sheriff Ransford about slipping out later for the Diamond-T."

Ethan turns his reddened eyes on him.

"I'm going with you," Ben says.

"You're staying here with your sister."

"I seem to recall you invited me..."

"Like I said, you're staying here with the Keatons."

"I don't like this waiting around any more than you, Ethan. But, I reckon we'll get through it."

Ethan looks away.

Ben decides to check on Tressa and Adam.

"Why is it taking so long?" Roberts moans, pacing back and forth in front of the fireplace.

Chase stretches himself out on the sofa to try and get some shuteye.

Roberts is just one of those women. Too inquisitive. Too good-looking.

Just one step ahead of trouble.

"The maverick is watching our movements," he says.

"Essentially we're under siege. We have no movements."

"He doesn't know what you and I are doing here, he's been told certain things about how the ranch operates, who should be here and where, but it's all wrong, so he's confused and wondering what to do next. So he thinks and thinks and decides to wait until someone sticks their foot out the door. But we're not sticking out a single toe. So like I mentioned before, we don't know where he is and I have no intention of making anyone the bait, so he's gonna have to come to us. And that, Emmaline, is why it's taking so long."

"Oh," she says.

He lifts the lid of one eye a fraction; she's plonked herself down into an armchair. "Patience, Emmaline. Don't worry. We'll be ready for him. Now go watch the front. Wake me in ten."

She does as he asks.

Donnelly rides hard through the difficult conditions and reaches his destination as evening begins to fall. He rides in cautiously, dismounts, and strides though heaped snow to Keaton's front door. He looks around, scrutinizing everything. But everything is still, except for the wind blowing the trees… Time for complete and utter capitulation. He thumps on the door. No one comes directly. He scans the yard. They can't all be dead. It was only meant to be one of them, maybe two, 'til he arrived…

The door opens slowly. Keaton's face appears from around back of it. "What can I do for you, stranger?"

"Respite from the cold?" Donnelly mutters.

"I think I can offer you that," Keaton says.

Donnelly enters, wondering why Keaton looks so calm.

The kitchen is warm and smells good.

"You all alone in this big house?" he asks.

"No, he's not," a voice says.

He swings around. "Ben Taylor…"

"Ah, you remember me. 'Cause I sure remember you, and I saw you coming."

"So you made it. Three cheers." Ever so slowly, Donnelly inches his hand towards his holster, saying, "Does your father know you're here?"

"Oh, yes. My father knows. And you know he does. What you and Bodecker have done with him is anyone's guess. But you made a mistake, Donnelly. You think I care. And I think he has it coming."

Donnelly grasps his six-shooter and whips it out.

A shot rings out; he feels sharp, burning pain and his pistol flies from his grasp. He brings up his hand; blood is oozing from it. He glances around. Someone else is in the room, by the back porch door.

"Benchley," he breathes.

"Make another move like that and I'll make a more permanent arrangement for one of my bullets."

Somewhere between the searing pain and the dripping blood he pulls himself together.

"If you've harmed one hair on my son's head..."

He stands erect. "So..." he begins, but he hears the distinct sound of boots on floorboards coming from the parlor and swings his eyes in that direction.

Dave Ransford appears. He's clutching a Winchester between his hands. "Mr Donnelly. Take a seat. We have some matters to discuss and then you're gonna call out your maverick and make these people safe again. Is that clear?"

Very.

Donnelly dives for the front door.

The Winchester explodes; he feels the bullet zoom over his head. It hits a plate on the wall and it smashes to the floor.

A baby cries in another room within the house.

"Sit down, Mr Donnelly," Ransford says.

Before he even knows what's happening, John Keaton has the Winchester and Ransford is securing manacles around his wrists.

"My hand," he winces.

"Yeah, I got blood on me," Ransford remarks. "Now sit down."

He's shoved to the kitchen table and pushed into a chair. He looks around at them all. There are three guns trained on him.

"Where's my boy?" Benchley grinds out.

He feels strengthened by Benchley's anxiety; the man looks a wreck. "Which one? Oh, you mean the one who murdered the dirty whore on the train, brained the deputy and escaped."

"No," Benchley breathes, sweat across his brow, "you did that, Donnelly."

"Is that what Ransford told you?"

"Where is he?"

He glances at Ransford. "Don't we have more pressing matters to attend to, Sheriff?"

"Answer Ethan now or I'll make some other part of you uncomfortable."

He swallows and moves his head side to side, trying to loosen his collars and scarf. "He's... not dead. He's in North Platte. Alive. But he's capitulated."

"Meaning?" Ransford prompts.

"He'll give up the Diamond-T to me so none of you get hurt."

Benchley lets out a barking laugh. "You're crazy."

"No, but Taylor will be – soon, if you don't clear off."

Ransford scratches his chin. "You know, Donnelly, you're the lamest excuse for a human being I've ever known. That being said, you might be interested to know that Cliff Ryan went after Luke and, if I know Ryan, he's found him."

But the telegram...

Donnelly takes a deep breath. "It'll be too late for Taylor."

"So you say."

"Ain't nothing you can do for him now."

"We'll see. You never intended to bargain, Donnelly, we know that," Ransford continues. "That's why I'm here and my deputy is at the Diamond-T. Before Luke fell victim to your plans for him, he got word out about you and Bodecker. Ryan acted on that word and on the fact that he and a lot of people know Luke too well to believe him capable of those crimes. So, how many shooters are out there, Maverick?"

"I thought you said you knew everything," he says, throwing in a smirk for good measure.

Ben Taylor lets out an exasperated sigh.

Donnelly fixes his gaze on him. Only a tough kid don't care about his father.

"We figured three," Ransford says.

Donnelly chuckles.

Ransford shrugs. "No matter. We got plenty of time."

"It's almost dark out," he says.

"But there's a big moon rising," Ransford replies.

efore the moon gets too high, and while the evening gloom over the ranch is still thick, Jed makes the distance between the barn and the house. He reaches the back porch and crouches into a ball by the back door. Every drape, every shade is drawn; he can tell that the lamps are positioned so they don't throw shadows and only bright enough so the occupants don't fall over the furniture. Even so, now he stretches up as best he can and tries to find a tiny crack in the drapery to peer through.

Not knowing who those two strangers are who arrived in the early hours confounds and bothers him. Since they came there's been no movement from either house. They hunkered themselves inside and he hasn't seen anyone since. Maybe if he'd already shot one of them they'd act this way...defensive and such. But he can't risk not getting paid, or being killed off.

There's only one thing to be done.

He reaches up and very careful tries the door handle. It moves and clicks open.

What kind of strange goings on can he expect to find in this place?

Inch by inch he pushes the door back; it hardly makes a creak. Like everything he's seen around the ranch it's in good repair. He squeezes himself inside the house; there's a lamp on the table burning so low there's just a pale orange haze coming off the glass.

Just then a strong gust of night wind howls into the room and blows out the light. Something crashes in another part of the house. He sucks in his breath. His heart is beating wild. Maverick never said this house was haunted.

His eyes take time to adjust to the gloom. By then he detects faint light within. Someone must be here; he never saw them leave.

Clutching his rifle, he stands up slow and edges himself towards the next room. He steps into a hallway where a lamp is burning low on a small table. He looks left and right; nothing.

On the other side is a doorway to a room where pale light also glows; he can just make out the shape of parlor furniture.

He takes several careful steps forward; suddenly a figure appears by the lamp, tall and commanding, rifle in hands.

Jed raises his gun.

A voice behind him growls, "Don't move."

Dave shoves Donnelly towards the door. "Get moving."

Donnelly balks; no wonder, since he's holding a lamp.

Ethan prods him hard with his rifle barrel and says, "Get out there or I'll shoot you myself."

Dave opens the back porch door and together he and Ethan push Donnelly outside.

"Anyone'd think you're scared, Donnelly," Ethan taunts.

"We're all gonna get shot… this plan is stupid…"

"Call off your shooter," Dave orders him.

Ethan pushes him down the porch steps.

Donnelly clings onto the hand rail. "He don't know me. There was supposed to be a sign…"

"You got a lamp, what more do you want," Ethan says.

Donnelly is shaking and stuttering. "Don't shoot, maverick," he shouts at last. "It's all over. Nighthawk lullaby is over. Don't…"

A shot rings out. Dave and Ethan duck, but Donnelly falls, the lamp crashes and gloom returns. Donnelly starts groaning.

"The barn?" Dave rasps.

"Reckon. Just hope the boys in the bunk house remember to lay low like you and John told them. A good fight is hard to resist."

"They will. And they know the sign if we need their help. Let's get this fool back inside."

"He ain't worth it."

"He might be, in the long run. Cover fire, if you don't mind, Ethan. I'll grab Donnelly."

Jed feels the end of a rifle barrel between his shoulder blades. The figure in front of him takes aim. "Hand it over – now!"

Jed swallows hard.

"Do it."

He hands over his rifle.

"And the six-shooter."

The barrel in his back gives him a shove.

"Nice and slow."

Jed complies.

"Right. We're moving into the parlor. If you try anything, you will be shot. Is that clear?"

"Yes."

As they go in the parlor, a girl stands by another low lamp with a rifle in her hands.

"Put your hands behind your back."

Again he complies.

"Him I recognize," he says, nodding his head towards the half-breed whose rifle barrel had been in his back. "Who are you?"

"Deputy Chase Deloight, at your service."

Cold, hard manacles bite into his wrists.

"What's your name?" the deputy asks.

"I don't have to tell you anything."

"Tough guy, eh? Well, Mr No Name, you are under arrest."

His tall figure comes into Jed's line of vision. There's a silver star on his lapel with the word deputy engraved in it. Jed gapes at it.

The deputy smirks. "Roberts here has one even more impressive."

Jed looks across at the girl, confused.

She produces a chunky silver star from her coat pocket and holds it up for him to see. It reads Sheriff.

"So," she says. "Are you the only one?"

The moon is in the wrong position to be of any use to them, but Donnelly's maverick doesn't seem to have any trouble with it.

Dave is pinned behind a large tree in the yard, moonlight illuminating the snow around him. He fires a shot in the direction of the barn; a double report echoes back through the stinging cold.

On the porch John Keaton is trying to get his attention with a signal that Dave can't quite make out. Then John takes off around the side of the house. When Ethan Benchley follows after him about a minute later, he figures they've worked out a plan between them.

The maverick in the barn is out-manned and out-gunned. His position, coupled with his uncanny aim, is his only advantage. And there no denying it's a good one. No one said this was going to be easy. The main concern: young Ben Taylor is left to guard Donnelly by himself in the house with the two women and the infant.

As Dave bends himself and his rifle around the tree, a bullet zooms by him. He returns fire. The maverick does likewise. He and the maverick blast away at one another for several minutes, the cold air cracking and hissing with gunfire, each time Dave just evading the shooter's astonishing aim. If he were to try to move to another position, he can't even be sure he'd get there.

He slides his spine down the trunk of the tree, looking for something to distract the maverick. He spots a good-sized branch but he'd have to reach for it. He leans out and snatches it up with no shot from the barn. He takes a deep breath and hurls the branch across the yard opposite to the direction he wants to run. A volley of shots overwhelms the silence. He scampers, fast. He dives onto the porch and rolls, coming to rest and lying flat on the icy boards. He wriggles backwards into the house, his rifle at the ready.

Huddled in the frigid cellar, Tressa keeps Adam's ears covered, one with her hand and the other pressed against her shoulder. The little horse keeps him occupied, while she rocks him.

Suddenly, silence.

She and Amy look upwards through the light of a dimmed lamp.

"What do you think it means?" she asks.

"I don't know," Amy replies; her voice trembles, even though her grip on the rifle she holds is steady enough.

"Are we going to die?"

"I don't know."

"John and Ethan... and Ben."

"I don't know, Tressa," Amy says. "We have to hope..."

Silence falls between them. It all could have been so different...

Once inside, Dave takes stock. Donnelly sits on the bottom of the stairs, gagged, and bound body and feet to the banister with rope. Ben Taylor has a six-shooter trained on him. The young feller don't even blink as Dave makes his entrance.

"How goes it, Sheriff?" Ben Taylor says; his voice is hoarse, like he's the one who's been out in the cold.

"Ethan and John?" Dave pants.

"They're using your cover to trap the maverick."

"The women?"

"Safe."

Donnelly makes an effort to protest. Ben kicks him in the shins and takes aim. Donnelly's eyes go wide in his hard face. He looks pale, although the bandage on his leg has a woman's touch.

"Don't kill him," Dave mutters.

"Don't you worry about a thing, Sheriff," Ben replies.

"Amy Keaton did the bandaging."

"She did."

"Right. Keep up the good work."

Reassured, Dave eases himself back out onto the porch just as shooting breaks out across the yard in the vicinity of the barn and the corrals. The reports are crisscrossing now at different angles from before, distortion ballooning in the ever-thickening chill.

The gunfire from the barn won't let up. Now Ethan and John's cover fire works to Dave's advantage. He creeps across the porch and through the heaped snow to the corral fences where he weaves his way from one post to another until he reaches the barn doors. He slips inside and crouches behind a water barrel to listen to the maverick's reports and determine their precise source.

But silence comes, followed by scuttling sounds somewhere in the barn; he gauges from the hayloft. He decides not to wait too long while everyone reloads... just long enough...

Carefully, he reaches up for the lid on the water barrel and tosses it out, sideways. The shooter takes the bait and fires; Dave, fast to the lookout, glimpses movement in the hayloft above the third stall along.

Gotcha.

He targets the hayloft and blasts away, three times; in those seconds, hay and splinters fly in all directions, including onto the frightened horses below; someone cries out, then, as his rifle fire fades away, comes groaning and hard-breathing.

"I got your position. Throw down your weapons and get down here," Dave shouts. "If I have to come up and get you, I can't guarantee you'll stay alive."

"Don't shoot no more. I'm hurt," comes a young voice.

"Get down here. Now."

"Who are you?"

"Sheriff Dave Ransford. The game's over, young feller. Got your boss all tied up and you can't escape. You can't achieve your aim, and there's no point to it. It's all over now. Throw down your weapons and present yourself."

The guns fell silent some minutes ago. Every nerve in Tressa's body stings in expectation that they will soon fire up again, just as before. Her glance strays to the rifle; their last defense.

Movement noises from above. Her heart jumps into her mouth.

Amy looks sharply at the cellar door.

More noises.

What should they do next?

Adam wriggles; Tressa turns him onto her other knee and fixes the woolen wrap around him.

"None of this would be happening if…"

"Hush, now," Amy whispers.

She shakes her head. "…if I'd just told Luke about Mart in the first place."

"Hush…"

"Some of the responsibility is mine."

"Does it bring you comfort thinking that?" Amy gives a grim sort of smile. "There are a lot of players in this game, Tressa."

"I guess. Yes. Then, why mayn't we win this time, for a change?"

"I know how you feel."

Tressa strokes Adam's cheek; it's warm in the middle but his jaw feels chilly. The tip of his nose is turning pink.

"He's cold and I think I've grown tired of waiting."

"You and me both. I'll look."

Suddenly, the cellar door opens.

They flinch and gasp, but Ben's face appears.

"All clear. The sheriff's arrested the maverick. He's all tied up. I think Ransford wants to use the cellar to hold him. You must be frozen. I've got a good fire going in the parlor. Here, pass Adam up to me..."

Day Five

February 6, 1885

Ethan gives Ransford a shake. "It's time, Ransford."

The sheriff lifts one eyelid and grunts.

"Sunup in a couple of hours."

Ransford shifts, and sits up. "I've been thinking carefully about this, Benchley."

"What are you talking about?"

"I need to ride Donnelly and Raz Cole into town and secure them in the lockup. Deputize someone to watch them. And I need to deliver Crogan's body to the undertakers. I want you to stay here until I get back."

"Are you crazy? What about my son!"

"Ethan, listen..."

"No, you listen, Sheriff. You head into Bright River. Ben and I'll head off home. John has been taking care of his family in these parts for fifteen long years. Indians, Ed Parsons, rustlers, you name it. I think you can trust him for a day while we clean up this mess."

"I do trust him... all of you. You're amazing folks, but you recall what I told you, there's a maverick for Ben. Now Cole may be it or maybe there's another out there. We can't say for sure. Donnelly's mind ain't in this county any longer, if you get my drift, and even he don't know what's going on with his mavericks. If you wait a few more hours 'til I get back, then I'll leave John in charge and ride with you and Ben to the Diamond-T. It's a better plan. Besides, Deloight is there and he's one of the best, believe me."

410

"Damnation, Sheriff!" Ethan explodes.

"Listen, Ethan. I know how hard this is for you, I know, but I need you to sit tight. If there is another maverick out there, you and Ben will draw him out for sure, a good thing, but I ain't about to let that happen without me being there. Clear?"

Ethan wrestles with his disappointment. "I ain't about to give up the Diamond-T without a fight."

"And I wouldn't expect you to. If Tip Benchley is anything like his father, I don't think he will either."

The day turns out bright; there's glare off the deep snow, which makes watching for mavericks tricky and wearisome. Ransford had got back from town later than Ethan would have liked. Said it took longer than he thought it would to secure his prisoners. Ethan was afraid of that from the start, and Ransford looked tired. But now they are on their way. Ethan and Ben catch each other staring from time to time; sizing up a man can be a lengthy business when trust is an issue. It takes observation and consideration; sometimes a good long look at the man as he goes about his business is the only way. Ethan's been alive too long and past vanity to worry about what the boy sees when he's studying him, but the boy on the other hand has plenty to be concerned about. His quiet intelligence and sullen streak could be mistaken for offishness, but Ethan ain't fooled by it. A boy who gets hurt does things; acts out, puts up walls and the like. Yep, there's plenty to be getting on with.

Mavericks. Reputations. And just plain getting home.

The boy rides alongside him, silent, his eyes peeled for the maverick. Ethan wished Ben was seeing this country in June. Ain't a prettier place anywhere. Luke's favorite time of year...

"We're nearly half way," he announces.

Ransford gives a nod in reply.

Then, out of the blue, Ben says, "You said your son would be happy to see me?"

Ethan glances sidelong. "He suggested it."

"He feels no grudge."

"He's half Comanche, Ben. His grudges, as you call them, lie elsewhere. And he's a right to them, except..."

"Except what?"

"I would never have met his mama without what created them."

Ben appears to digest this, and then follows up with, "If you don't mind me saying so, Ethan, you live in a strange world."

"I guess." He gives a chuckle. "It's just the snow; ain't been this deep and uncomfortable for a few seasons."

"Did you lose any cattle?"

"Tip reckons not."

"Your mind hasn't been on your work."

Ethan sighs white clouds. "No."

"Does my cousin know how lucky he is?"

"You think having an old coot like me worrying after you is something to be grateful for?"

A gunshot crackles through the air.

"Down!" shouts Ransford and dismounts instantly.

"Ride, we should ride," Ethan screams.

"Snow's too deep. We can't outride. Down!" Ransford screeches, while he struggles to hold the reins of his mount.

Another gunshot. Ransford has to let go of his horse. "Ethan!"

Yet another... the sound of the bullet pings across Ethan's ear.

Ethan grabs Ben by the sleeve and hauls him down into the snow with him. They come up panting and trembling.

All the horses are spooked and take off as fast as they can.

"Where did that come from?" Ransford rasps.

"That shot across my ear?" Ethan thumbs his reckoning at a clutch of snow-covered lodgepoles to the northeast. "We need to take cover in the trees behind us."

Ransford nods. "Ben, with me."

Ben's eyes are round and dark in his pale face.

"I'll be right behind you," Ethan tells him.

They flatten themselves at once as another resounding crack hits the air. Ethan doesn't feel the path of the bullet this time, but he senses something nonetheless. "Different direction, Sheriff."

"Shit!"

"There are *two* of them?" Ben squawks.

"I'll keep northeast maverick busy while you get to the trees," Ethan says.

"Right."

Ransford tugs on Ben's sleeve and they half crawl, half slither on their bellies. Shots splinter the brittle air; Ethan's reports burst in reply. The northeast maverick falls silent. The other maverick starts up. Ethan picks up the direction. Northwest.

He wriggles around quickly. Northwest maverick must be on the edge of the forest where they are busy trying to take cover.

"Northwest," Ethan shouts at Ransford.

Both mavericks start firing.

Ethan is pinned down with bullets flying over his head. He spots Ransford advancing through the trees, firing his rifle in the direction of the northwest maverick.

Ben starts shooting at the northeast maverick. "Ethan, get out of there!"

"Don't shoot me by mistake, boy!"

Ethan begins his retreat. The trees are further than they look; he rolls and crawls and dodges for several long minutes; the trees seem further and further away, not closer; bullets fly over his head and he must press himself into the snow; his mouth fills up with the stuff and the iciness cuts into his skin; his face feels raw by the time he finally rolls to a position beside Ben and behind a thick tree trunk dressed with snow-laden boughs. His chest feels like someone is sitting on it; he's sure his lungs have frozen solid.

The shooting stops. Ethan coughs instead.

Ben's hand comes down on his chest. "Take it easy for a moment, Ethan."

And because the boy takes up aim again, he relaxes.

"Where's Ransford?"

Ben looks around. "Can't see him. Tree cover is too thick. Lucky for us."

"No. We should've dug our spurs and took off out of here."

"We couldn't leave Ransford."

Ethan nods. "He'd made up his mind. Made his point, too."

"We'll get the horses back, Ethan."

"Maybe," Ethan wriggles into a better position. "Well, if we want to get out of this now, we're gonna have to make our stand here and kill those bastards."

Together they hear movement on their right and turn their weapons.

"Don't shoot," Ransford calls out.

"Any sign of the horses?" Ethan asks as Ransford appears.

"No. No sign of the mavericks either."

Ethan turns northeast again.

"They're gonna freeze us out, Sheriff."

"I'm going to look for those horses," Ben announces, getting up on his haunches.

Ransford grabs his coat sleeve. "No, stay with Ethan. I'll scout around."

"Keep your head down," Ethan says as Ransford slinks away.

Sure enough the gunfire starts up again.

Sounding closer.

"A maverick has spotted Ransford."

"Which one."

"Northwest maverick, I reckon. He's moved into the trees; he's looking for us."

"Shit."

"Yep. Do you want to watch the trees?"

"No, I'll watch the northeast maverick, if that's where he's still positioned."

"I'll watch the trees."

They hear Ransford's reports; the exchange is frantic and quite close.

"That don't sound too good. I'm going after him."

"Ethan?"

"Hold tight, Ben. I'll be back."

Ethan steals a path from tree to tree, following Ransford's tracks in the snow. The gunfire becomes louder, fresher and he's very close… he stalks about until he spots Ransford's cover and then follows his aim through the trees. It ain't easy to see gunsmoke with all this snow, but if he gets it just right he might just spot…

Ransford fires; the maverick returns fire. Ethan sees it; a bright flash from the trees fifteen yards away; his eyes focus in on the rifle barrel and then hone in on the maverick. Got him.

Gunshots ring out freely now.

He steadies his nerves; moves silently through the snow and trees until he finds a position behind the maverick; moves forward until the maverick's back is in his sights. Then he hears the northeast maverick start up again, and Ben's reports.

It's closer, much closer... he snatches a brittle cold breath...

The maverick turns around and takes aim, but Ethan fires. The crack of his rifle blasts snow from the trees. The maverick falls like a mule deer into a pile of snow.

He lowers his rifle and fixes his gaze.

Ransford's rifle is silent.

He pushes through the snow; reaches the maverick and turns him over; he's a boy. He gulps and examines the kid. It's a mortal wound. He's dead.

"Ransford! Over here!"

But Ransford doesn't arrive.

Ethan clambers through the snow and trees to where he approximates Ransford's position. After a several minutes he finds him; slumped in the snow, clutching his belly.

"Ransford..." Ethan drops to his knees.

Ransford works hard to breath. "Ethan... This... this..."

Ethan inspects the wound. He shakes his head.

"Thought so," Ransford pants. "He got me just as I moved to get closer."

"Well, I got him. He's dead."

Ransford nods and gives a crooked smile. "The boy..."

Ethan crouches down, slides his free arm beneath Ransford's shoulders and prepares to move him. It's time to regroup and stick together. "Told you to stay at the Keatons, but you wouldn't listen."

The northeast maverick starts up again.

Ben's spasmodic reports sound lonely and scared.

"Leave me, Ethan, take my ammunition... and get back to the boy..."

❖

"What's happened?" Ben asks while Ethan catches his breath.

"The maverick's dead."

Ben gets his head around this and says, "You?"

Ethan nods.

"Where's Ransford?"

Ethan busily organizes ammunition...

"Ethan?"

"Ransford's dead."

Ben gulps; Ethan stops what he's doing and clamps a firm hand on Ben's shoulder. "I'm sorry..."

Ben hangs his head. Grieves for a long time before he says, "Ransford didn't deserve that."

"Nope." Ethan returns to their ammunition.

"It's unforgiving," Ben mumbles, half to himself.

"This land? Reckon it is, at the moment anyway."

"What'll we do now?"

"This is all the ammunition we got left. Some of it belonged to the maverick. Some to Ransford."

"I got three left in my six-shooter. Rifle is finished."

"Here... load these. Reckon Ransford had a box in his saddle-bags. But this is all he had on him. One round."

Ben quickly loads his Winchester. "This won't last long."

"All the maverick has to do is wait and I grant you he's a dang sight more comfortable than we are. Dang pest of thing..."

"What's that, Ethan?"

"What's what?"

"That tear in your left sleeve, just below your shoulder."

"What the hell are you talking about?"

Ben takes hold of the sleeve and inspects the hole. Then, when he presses the fabric against Ethan's arm, dark red fluid oozes forward and Ethan grimaces.

"Ethan... you're shot."

Blood seeps into the fabric of his coat.

"Maverick must've grazed my arm. Didn't even feel it, it's that dang cold. Don't feel so good, maybe that's it."

The stain is spreading.

"That's no graze, Ethan."

A bullet flies past their tree and hits the one on their right, dislodging snow from its branches. Ben shivers and meets Ethan's eyes. Then he bends his arm around their tree and fires his colt.

❖

A lotta time has passed, but exactly how long Ethan can't say. Long enough to freeze them into stupor and relieve them of nearly all their ammunition.

"I got two left in my six-shooter," Ben says. "That's all."

"One in Ransford's Winchester. I got four."

"Been a while since the maverick fired on us," Ben remarks, an observation not lost upon Ethan.

"He knows what's happening to us. He's moved."

"Moving in for the kill?"

"If you want to put it like that."

"Shouldn't we move then?"

"Shame when we just got the place all warmed up…"

Ben looks about them. "Where to?"

Ethan sighs and looks around. A bullet whizzes past them. They dive into the snow and raise their eyes a fraction.

"Which way?" Ben whispers.

Ethan fires his Winchester into the trees; a maverick report follows at once but the shooter remains unseen. Ethan fires again; again the reply but neither he nor Ben can spot the maverick.

The maverick fires on them again; they scramble around their tree and take cover. Bark flies off the trunk and peppers their faces.

"Shit… No, save the colt."

In the break, Ethan fires the Winchester only to be blasted back behind their tree.

"Can't see a damned thing. Where the hell is he?"

"Cover me," Ben says, "and I'll…"

Then a strange thing happens.

More rifle fire… Over their heads… Coming from behind.

"What the…"

Ethan and Ben turn in desperation to find their new enemy. Two men on horseback, rifles drawn and firing into the trees. They split up and take off in different directions.

"What is it, Ethan?"

"Don't know," he breathes. "Keep your head down and don't move."

A firefight ensues; then silence, and then spasmodic shots, then silence.

Voices resound eerily through the stillness.

They hear the approach of horses…

"Don't shoot…" Ethan whispers.

"I'll wait for your signal," Ben replies.

Ethan nods.

They wait.

The riders come into view, moving through the trees.

A voice calls out, "Ethan!"

Ethan freezes.

"We spotted your pinto about half a mile from here…"

He swallows hard. "They're dismounting…"

Ben says, "Who is it?"

Ethan struggles to his feet, his heart in his throat.

"…what are you doing, Ethan?"

He rises and moves away from the tree. He can't believe his own eyes. Two tall figures stand there, trailing their mounts, rifles in hand.

One of those men gives him a whiskered grin, swaying on his feet, saying, "I'm home, Ethan…"

Ethan rushes forward, catching a glimpse of those dark blue eyes before they close.

"Ethan…" His body crumbles.

Ethan reaches him in time and gathers him in. His injured arm gives way and they both sink into the snow.

"I got you, son… I got you."

❖

Emmaline stares hard through the approaching dusk at a group of figures on horseback moving slowly towards the yard.

"Chase, who are these coming?"

Tip and Chase rush to the front window, squashing her between them in their haste to take a look.

"Thank God," Tip mutters thickly.

"What?" asks Chase.

"That's my father's pinto. And that's my father…"

"You sure?"

Tip makes a move.

Chase stops him. "Wait 'til they get closer."

So they wait.

Emmaline studies the group carefully. There's the man on the pinto, three other men on horseback, two of them with a draped load each, and over the fifth horse…

She catches her breath.

"Steady, Roberts," Chase murmurs.

The group moves into the yard.

"Right. I'm going out to meet them. You two stay here."

Emmaline and Tip follow orders, until Tip, convinced the man on the pinto is his father, declares, "That's my father, and that, Emmaline, is Luke!" and rushes from the room.

She watches as he tears past Deloight and meets his father.

Even though the man dismounts rather gingerly, he and Tip embrace heartily.

Meanwhile, as these two help an unsteady figure who appears to be Luke Taylor, and more manful embraces follow, another young man dismounts and stands back looking on. Then there is the fourth figure…

She's never experienced a feeling quite like this one. It steals through her, working its way around her body until she's almost overwhelmed by it.

"Ryan," she whispers. And drinks in the sight of him.

He dismounts. He and Deloight shake hands and then talk.

She threads her arms into her coat and prepares herself to join them. From the top of the porch she notices Deloight inspecting the draped figure on the fifth horse. He hangs his head.

Her feeling at seeing Ryan takes a back seat as a new emotion – namely dread – takes hold. She rushes out. And even though she stops at Deloight's side, she looks up at Ryan. As she gazes at him, and he at her, warmth circles her body and floods her face; as much as she wants to, she can't stop it. She's longed for this moment for days and now it's here... But it's not right.

"Roberts, it's Dave..." Deloight says croakily.

"Deloight?" she asks, confused.

"Dave," he repeats. "He's dead."

"Sheriff Ransford, no," she whispers. "But he... he..."

She never expected this. Violent trembles unsteady her; Chase's hand grips her elbow, a gesture that steadies her body but triggers her emotions. Her eyes fill with tears.

Chase swears and pushes his other hand through his hair over and over.

She hears Tip's father say, "Who's that, son?"

"That's Emmaline. She's acting sheriff of Cheyenne."

She looks straight up into Ryan's eyes. Shimmering blue-green eyes full of feeling. She wipes shakily at her cheeks.

"What happened to Sheriff Ransford?" Tip asks then.

"Died bravely in the line of duty," Tip's father says. "You're the young woman who brought the information about Maverick to Laramie?"

She looks across the noses of several horses to Tip's father. He favors one arm, cradling it against his chest.

"I ain't sure I can ever repay you for what you did."

It wasn't her... she looks at the draped figure of Sheriff Dave Ransford. Never has she felt so far from home as at this moment. She is trapped within a nightmare with a bunch of strangers.

Overwhelmed by so many emotions, she can no longer think.

What should she do now? Where does she turn?

The men are on the move.

"Emma," Ryan says in a crusty voice.

Her throat is choked with emotion; she can only stare at him.

"Come on, Emma. I need to talk with you."

Go with him, Emmie.

Cliff guides Emma out of the snow and onto the porch, as far from the front door as he can. Over her head he glimpses the men making their way into the house. Ranch hands have appeared, laughing nervously in relief and taking care of the horses.

"Are you all right, Emma?"

She looks up at him, tears dropping softly onto her cheeks. "Yes. I... I think so. What happened?"

"There was a shoot out at the Keatons'. Dave, Ethan and John Keaton captured Donnelly and the maverick there. Dave took them to Bright River and locked them up."

"Donnelly..." she echoes, like a shiver up her spine.

"Ethan was determined to get home, but Dave wouldn't let him and Ben Taylor go by themselves..."

"That other young man..."

"Luke's cousin from Omaha. They encountered two mavericks about half way; there was another shoot out. Dave was mortally wounded, Ethan killed that maverick but was injured, then he and Ben Taylor got pinned down. They were out there for ages, frozen, and almost out of bullets. Eventually, Luke and I arrived and took care of the other maverick."

"In the nick of time."

"Luke wouldn't have it any other way. Deloight just informed me you have another maverick tied up here."

"Yes... Tyner... the Keatons, are they..."

"They are all fine. But there's one more thing you're going to have to bear, Emma, and I'm very sorry..."

Those sad eyes gazing up at him suddenly glint with familiar defiance. "Well, tell me..."

"Jim Crogan. He's dead. He didn't make it to the Keatons'. A maverick got him along the way. Dave found him."

She gasps and sobs all in one breath.

"Don't take it so hard," he tries to console her.

"You don't understand. When we set out from Laramie, Sheriff Ransford had to choose who I would go with; he chose Deloight but it could have been Crogan."

"Oh. I see."

"Poor things," she murmurs, shaking her head.

"Yes..."

"And Luke, how is he?"

"He's had a rough time, but I think he'll make it." He tries a smile. "You did a fine job, Emma. Thank you for what you did. I'm grateful and I'm proud of you."

She sniffs; rummages for a handkerchief.

"I only did what I told you I would do."

"You did more. And they all know just how much. And..."

She blows her nose. "And what?"

"And I'm glad you're all right."

She dabs her eyes. "So am I... you, I mean."

He smiles. "And I'm glad to see you."

She smiles back; then frowns and looks away. "It's cold out here. We should go inside."

"Before you go in, Emma," he says, "there's something else."

"What else could there possibly be?"

"Tomorrow your maverick will need to be locked up with the others in town. The deceased two from the forest need to go to the undertakers, and Dave's body as well. Laramie will have to be informed and we'll need a US marshal out here to clean up. But right now Luke and Ethan need a doctor, and the Keatons need checking on and to be told what's happened. I promised Ethan and Ben I would. Deloight will stay here with all of you until I get back."

"You?" she gasps. "Chase is rested and..."

"Chase just lost his two best friends."

She swallows hard. "Look at you. You're exhausted. It will be dark soon. You can't go back out there... it might not be safe."

"Emma..."

"Oh, don't Emma me," she declares and rummages again in her coat pocket. She reaches for his hand and slaps an object into his palm. "You'll need this."

Cliff drags his eyes from her tear-stained face and looks at his palm... his Silver Star lies there, almost throbbing with her emotion. He looks up again; she's trembling, staring hard at him.

"It could have been you," she says.

He opens his mouth to speak but shuts it again; where does he start?

"Oh, don't bother," she says. "There is nothing you can say that I haven't heard before."

He frowns. "What does that mean?"

"Never mind," she says. "Goodbye, Ryan…"

Confused, he watches her rush into the house. Ryan? – she's been hanging out with lawmen too long.

He closes his eyes for a moment to try and clear his head. With a deep sigh he reattaches his star, straightens his hat and heads off to the barn for a fresh mount.

SIX

Stay, stay at home, my heart, and rest;
home-keeping hearts are happiest...
weary and home-sick and distressed,
they wander east, and they wander west
...to stay at home is best.

Henry Wadsworth Longfellow
Song: Stay at Home

Faraday

Cheyenne Courthouse
Faraday's office

Mac careers to a halt in front of him before they collide.

"Check this out, Cam."

A telegram is thrust into Faraday's midriff. He reads...

WITNESS RETRIEVED AND SAFE. MAVERICK APPREHENDED AND SECURE. LARAMIE INFORMED. ALLIANCE FAMILIES SAFE AND SOUND. SEND U. S. MARSHAL AT ONCE TO BRIGHT RIVER. HOW GOES THE INVESTIGATION ? RYAN.

He reaches for his chair and sinks into it.

"I almost don't believe it... Reply?"

"I'm that dang excited, Cam, I can't hardly think of one!"

Faraday smiles. "Okay, Mac. Let's start with Hummer..."

"He got in this morning. Thinks he's going to Nebraska to look for Bodecker."

"Dispatch him to Bright River at once instead. We can't risk these prisoners. And send this..."

Mac pulls out a notebook and pencil, not with quite the same panache as Cliff, but no less determined.

"...Marshal Hummer en route to Bright River. Investigation has taken several twists. Elaborate upon your return. Glad all are safe. Need more information on condition of witness. Congratulations on your outstanding result. Mac and Cam."

427

Office of Acting Governor Elliot Morgan

Elliot glances up as Faraday enters. "Cam?"

"I thought you might like to know, Elliot, that Cliff Ryan has retrieved Luke Taylor and taken him home to Bright River where is he safe at the ranch. We have our witness safe and secure for now. Also, and equally impressive, Donnelly has been captured, which should mean no more killings at the hand of Maverick."

"What! This is excellent work, Cam. Damn good work."

Faraday happily nods his agreement. "I don't have any details at this stage."

"Casualties?"

"Cliff's wire was brief."

"Deliberately so, perhaps."

"Certainly, it could not have been easy to achieve all this."

"Mm. I am overwhelmed by this achievement, Cam."

"Yes, Elliot. Frankly, so am I."

"Although I'm somewhat perplexed that Cliff Ryan didn't bring Mr Taylor here to Cheyenne."

"I'm sure there is a very sound reason, and considering the outcome it appears to have been the best course of action."

"So it seems. I should send off my congratulations to Laramie at once. Well, Cam, everything in our power must be done to ensure Donnelly's successful extradition."

"Dan Hummer has been dispatched to Bright River for that purpose. He and Cliff Ryan will see it done, I'm sure of it."

Faraday's residence

He storms home to Meg and Caroline (aka Winnie Hastings) to tell the good news, only to have Caroline greet him with a solemn expression.

"Where's Meg?" he asks and holds his breath.

"She's resting."

He breathes and then hands her Cliff's wire. "Good news! Read this, Winnie Hastings, and then tell me how you feel."

"If you insist. But Meg received some news earlier which cannot have been good because she's been lying down ever since."

He finds his Meg reclining on their bed with a telegram paper scrunched up in her hand.

"Meg…"

Her eyes fly to his face. "Cam… at last. Oh Cam, wait till you read this…"

"Bad news? Because I have some of the very best news."

"Oh?" she murmurs, her frown lifting.

He sits beside her and takes her hand. "Cliff found Luke and took him home. He's safe. Doesn't that cheer you up?"

Her eyes fill with tears. "Oh, Cam, read this…"

He takes the paper she offers him.

DEAREST MEG. DERMOT REQUESTED MY RETURN TO PROVINCETOWN. HAVE SPENT MANY HOURS WONDERING WHAT TO DO. DECISION NEEDED VERY SOON. HAVE YOU HEARD ANYTHING OF LUKE ? WRITE SOON. PLEASE. LOVE JEN.

"I want to tell her, Cam. She deserves to know."

He strokes her forehead, her curls soft beneath his fingers.

"We have to do this for them, Cam, because they are so far apart, so unknowing. Bad things are always conspiring against them. They need a friend, Cam, you must see that."

He sees very clearly that not helping George is detrimental to his wife's health. "First let me discover more information about Luke's situation from Cliff."

Her gaze upon him is intense, demanding his integrity in the matter. Suddenly, her eyes widen. "*Took* him home, you said. You think he's hurt?"

"It's possible, I think."

"Oh, Cam. This has been the worst week of my life. Without Winnie Hastings I'm not sure what I would have done – gone utterly mad, I think."

"You don't look like you're on the verge of utter madness to me. You look beautiful, and I love you."

429

Her eyes sparkle, her smile less doleful. "I won't rest until they are together, Cam." She lies back against her pillows again.

"Oh yes, you will, Mrs Faraday. You have our baby to think about."

"I must write to her, Cam..." She closes her eyes. "And I can hardly wait to see our baby."

Cliff

"Well, Ryan, we meet again."

"Good to see you, Hummer," Cliff says and extends his hand.

They shake firmly.

"Always happy to be of service."

Hummer deftly twizzles his cigar from one side of his mouth to the other. "So – what mongrel have you got for me this time? – a mangy critter with the handle Donnelly, I hear, and some of his pals. This here's the lockup, ain't it?" Hummer draws breath and looks around at the street. "Amazin' how these puny cattle towns look kinda picturesque in winter."

"I assume Mac filled you in about everything."

"Oh, sure. Mac ain't as persnickety as you, mind, even so he gets the job done. But I like to read between the lines of a telegram like yours. You lost some people, didn't you? This ain't your jurisdiction and you look kinda uncomfortable about it. I think we lost someone important, mebbe..."

"Dave Ransford, and his deputy Jim Crogan."

"Dave..." Hummer grunts. "That explains it." He shakes his head. Removes his cigar momentarily. Puts it back between his teeth and says, "Dave Ransford. That's a loss, Ryan, a terrible loss. Gotta say, Ryan, I seen you look healthier. When was the last time you got a decent night's sleep?"

Cliff opens the door of McCurdy's old jailhouse and mumbles, "I can't remember..."

"Buck up, Ryan, got some good news for you... I'm instructed to grant you emergency temporary jurisdiction here in Bright River to carry on your duties. McCurdy's old job, don't yer know, such as it was. I had a hunch and I always act on my hunches. Ah, here we are... On you go, Sheriff, introduce me to the prisoners."

Half an hour later, Hummer has interrogated his prisoners and told them how things were to proceed. They sit pathetically in their cage, Donnelly on one side, while the two mavericks, Raz Cole and Jed Tyner, stay as clear of him as possible on the other.

Hummer emerges from the lockup and closes the door. "That Donnelly, mean character, don't recall ever seeing him before."

Cliff pours two cups of coffee. "Me neither."

Hummer is strangely silent. Cliff hands him a coffee and flicks a glance at his face. Hummer is staring at him, piercingly, and grunts.

"Sit. Tell me the situation at the Keatons and the Diamond-T."

"John Keaton has everything under control at his place. His wife, daughter-in-law and grandson are fine. Ranch hands are back about their business. Everyone's a little jumpy."

"Can't say I blame 'em."

"At the Diamond-T, Deputy Chase Deloight has been doing a fine job, but the situation there's not as good as the Keatons'. Ethan Benchley took a bullet in the arm in the shoot out with one of the now deceased mavericks. He'll be all right. Luke, on the other hand, is very sick from his little adventure with Donnelly and this..." Cliff gulps, "...this mad, crazy scientist. Long story."

"The doc's been out there, has he?"

Cliff nods.

"Feel like telling me what happened in North Platte, Ryan."

Cliff relates the main points.

"Anyone bother to tell Ralph Walker to call off the search for Luke?"

"I'm leaving that up to..."

"Me? Good idea. Send off a wire soon as we finish here. I'd be happy to tell old 'iron pants Ralph' he's been barking up the wrong tree. Now what's this about Bodecker? Mac tells me you wanted me to take myself off to Omaha and pick him up for questioning."

Cliff nods. "But I don't know the current situation regarding Bodecker. Where he is, or who knows where he is."

"Mac told me Bodecker's not to be found; mebbe the manhunt for Luke gave Bodecker the perfect cover to slip away."

"Damn," Cliff mutters.

Hummer barks a laugh. "You can't do everything at once, Ryan. Retrieving your witness and stopping Maverick were your priorities and that's what you did. Not bad, Sheriff, sneaky and underhanded, could have cost you your job, might still, but not bad at all."

"I need to get back to Cheyenne…"

"I'm taking Chase Deloight with me. You are staying here for a few days, hospitality of the Alliance."

"What the devil are you talking about, Hummer?"

"You been sleeping right here and keeping guard over those prisoners. That'll be enough of that. Go back to the Diamond-T and take Deloight's place. I don't want to see you in Cheyenne 'til – what's the day today… 'til Wednesday at least. Make it the end of the week. Got it?"

"No."

"Benchley's injured, Taylor's ill. They could use some help. Keep an eye on the Keatons while you're at it."

"Are you pulling rank on me, Hummer?"

Hummer laughs uproariously. "Hell, yeah! Sure as you're sitting there, Ryan. I know you took a bullet for that girl. You look like hell. When you're rested up you should go over to Parsons' old place and check it out. See if it ain't a maverick lair, eh?"

Cliff opens his mouth to object, but Hummer leans towards him, removes his cigar and says in a low voice, "Let it go, Ryan. I promise to do the job as good as you, honest. I want you fit for the likes of Bodecker, understand?"

Hummer sits back, staring Cliff straight in the eye. He replaces his cigar. "So that's three prisoners. How many bodies, then?"

"Four."

"Ah… two too many…" Hummer leans forward again. "But it could've been much worse, ain't that right, sheriff?"

❖

With a week's worth of fine weather and persistent clearing wind since the snowstorm, excited and relieved Bright River towns-folk come out on Monday morning to watch as Donnelly, Cole and Tyner, dumbly submissive and looking miserable, are manacled and chained together on horseback by Dan Hummer. Donnelly was stupid enough to give Hummer some lip earlier; he's gagged.

Emma stands nearby on the sidewalk, scribbling madly in her notebook; she'd already interviewed Hummer, much to his delight, and eventually his annoyance, particularly when she pestered him to be allowed to interview Donnelly. Hummer flatly refused her, a lot, which made her very grumpy. She talked to a few townsfolk instead, but they were more interested in the proceedings than a pesky reporter; she retreated to the sidewalk to observe and write.

Tip, who had brought Emma into town, hovers vigilantly nearby, his keen eyes on Hummer's business. Needless to say, a detailed account would be required on his return to the Diamond-T.

The Reverend Percival Cosgrove of Bright River Congregational Church, meanwhile, stands beside the undertaker's wagon saying a farewell blessing over the coffins. Chase Deloight is supervising this part of the operation. His distress over his colleagues has given his somber mood a defiant edge... he can't believe it, don't want to believe it, but can't escape it. Cliff shakes his hand firmly and leaves him to his work. However, Chase's final gesture is to walk over to Emma and say goodbye; they shake hands. Cliff knows Emma is keeping her feelings over the deaths of Dave and Jim close to her chest, but with Chase there is no pretence; they are comrades-in-arms and feel each other's pain.

Hummer leans towards Cliff and says, "That reverend said a heap of prayers yesterday, you think God've heard by now."

"Speaking of God, Hummer, when you get back to Cheyenne, if you see Father Nugent, tell him I said sorry and I'll be by later."

Hummer removes his cigar. "Nugent. Sorry. Be by later."

Jams it back in.

"Good luck, Hummer."

"Do what I told you, Ryan," Hummer says boisterously as he mounts up. "See you in Cheyenne!"

Cliff watches them until they disappear around the street corner. He turns to find Amy and John Keaton.

"We thought you could use a good home-cooked meal, Sheriff," John says.

Cliff nods. "Thank you."

"We are the ones who are grateful," Amy Keaton says.

"Got some things to purchase here in town. I'm staying for a few days over at the Diamond-T. Marshal's orders."

Amy Keaton smiles. "I'm glad."

"Take your time. We're just visiting for a spell..." John looks in the direction of the cemetery, the hill beside the church.

"John and I have been thinking. Sheriff Ransford saved us. Is there any way we can repay his sacrifice? His wife? Family?"

"Dave wasn't married."

She sighs. "Perhaps it was just as well then. And Mr Crogan?"

"Jim lost his wife a few years back."

"Such courageous men."

"They will be remembered."

"They surely will," John says. "See you back at the house."

"When your business is concluded, Mr Ryan. Don't rush."

"Please," he says, "call me Cliff."

They smile and nod, then saunter off in the direction of the cemetery, discussing their plans to attend Dave's, and Jim's, funeral and that they should pay for a suitable headstone...

Cliff observes Tip and Emma preparing to head out of town on horseback. No wonder she got Deloight's respect; the girl can ride, a natural. She has on riding clothes. He approaches them as she is stowing her notebook in her saddlebag. A pencil is still perched over her ear beneath the brim of her hat. Her skin is pearly white with cold, the tip of her nose slightly pink, the ridgelines of her cheeks a flaring shade of rose. She is so pretty it takes his breath away. He removes the pencil and hands it to her.

"Oh... thank you," she says.

"You're welcome," he murmurs.

Wispy breath clouds form and dissipate between them.

"Tip, would you mind letting Ethan know that I'll be bunking at the Diamond-T till the end of the week?"

"Sure, Cliff, I..."

"Why?" Emma asks before Tip can finish his sentence.

"Hummer's orders."

Tip grunts. "Wish you'd been doing McCurdy's job a couple of years back. Mart would be alive; Kelley would be alive. Luke would be himself and Pa not shot up. None of this would have happened."

Without making any comment, Cliff watches Tip mount.

Then he catches Emma's eye. What he sees there finds a home with his thoughts. They would never have met.

"I'll tell Pa, Cliff, and I think we'll be more than glad to have you around. Mount up, Emmaline, we're heading out."

Tip turns his horse, waiting for her.

"What will you be doing while you are here?" she asks.

Before Cliff can respond, Tip complains, "Emmaline, it's too cold to interview out here any more. You can talk to Cliff later. He's staying with us, remember?"

Emma sighs and mounts. "For crying out loud, Tip, I swear you sound more like my little brother every day."

As she settles herself tall in the saddle, Tip is grinning.

"I like to make all my guests feel at home," he says.

"I'll be seeing you," Cliff says.

She nods and turns her horse.

Tip, already on the move, goads her, "Come on, Emmaline, don't dawdle."

"Boys," she declares softly and rides off.

Cliff locks up the jailhouse and heads toward the barber and bathhouse, making a mental list for the general store.

Later that day...

"Anyone home?"

He tosses his duffle bag to one side and closes the door of the Taylors' ranch house behind him. The house is nice; roomy but welcoming and cozy at the same time. When there's no one to greet you on arrival, an enormous moose head (with sprawling antlers) on the wall opposite the door and a black bear skin rug (head and teeth attached) do the job in style.

Quick, light footsteps and then Emma appears. The sight of her, back in female attire and pinked up by the warmth of the house, ties his stomach in knots. How does she do that?

"Oh, it's you," she says.

He doesn't respond. He just wants to look at her and blissfully suffer his knots in silence.

"Cat got your tongue?" She has her notebook and pencil in her hands; her fingers are also stained with ink.

"How's the story coming along?" he finally asks, and removes his hat. Emma's eyes react at once, all golden and doe-like, but she says nothing. Amy Keaton remarked a dozen times how nice he looked...

"Luke recounted for me what happened in North Platte, his side anyway."

"Did he? He's well enough to speak to reporters – there's a good sign."

"What he endured... I can't find the words."

"Well, if *you* can't find the words, Emma."

A fleeting smile. "You saved him, Cliff."

He shrugs. "Not without your part."

"Well..."

"Well..."

"What have you been doing?" she blurts out. "I mean apart from having your... your..."

Her attention wanders momentarily.

"...your hair cut."

He pegs his hat, grinning. "Amy Keaton decided to feed me. When you eventually get over there to interview the Keatons, she'll probably feed you too. It is an experience not to be missed."

"Do I look like I need feeding?" she asks.

"A little," he says, still grinning.

"You think I'm skinny?"

"No, I think your perfect," he says without thinking. "Well... well, what I mean to say is that a lot of hearty food keeps the cold at bay."

"They keep on saying that," she says, with an intense gleam in her eyes, "around here."

He stares dumbly back.

"Your hair cut looks very nice."

"Thank you."

Then he remembers the narrow but oblong package in his coat pocket. He retrieves it and holds it out to her.

"For you. Happy Birthday for Wednesday. I was shopping in the general store in North Platte and I saw this and thought of you…"

"But…" She tucks her notebook under her arm. "I…" Slots her pencil over her ear and takes the package; she removes the string and starts unwrapping the brown paper. "I wasn't expecting…"

With the paper discarded, she opens the box.

The blood-red quill with its well-crafted nib presents itself handsomely between layers of fine-leaved paper.

Lumsden told him a craftswoman in town made them, often coloring the goose feathers… *I'm told they write real good…* As soon as he saw it, he imagined her writing with it in…

"Oh… and this…." He reaches into his other pocket and pulls out a small, leather-bound journal.

She's still staring at the quill. "I love quill pens. And this is very fine… and the color…" She looks up at him. "Thank you."

"Don't forget this…" He hands her the journal.

"This is very thoughtful."

"A lot of people think you deserve a lot more."

"One of my uncles likes to say you get a whole lot more out of life if you put a lot more into it…" She shrugs.

"Your uncle would be proud of you."

Her cheeks turn a delicate shade of rose.

"Emma," he sighs. They have to make a start… somewhere…

"I have work to do," she announces abruptly and turns away. "Thank you for the birthday gift. It's very lovely."

Not so fast. "I know it's the job, Emma."

She stops. Her shoulders stiffen.

"I don't know what you mean," she says, and half turns so that she's looking at him along the line of her shoulder.

"You do," he insists.

He watches in astonishment as her eyes fill with tears.

"Emma," he murmurs.

"Don't stand there and Emma me like that…"

"Like what?"

"Like your job is a walk in the park or a day at the beach or a ride in the hills. I know what your job is, and I know what it does to people who…"

"Who *what*, Emma?" he persists, taking a couple of steps towards her.

"My mother wouldn't do it and neither will I."

"What are you talking about?" he asks, shaken.

But she rushes away. "Ethan… Sheriff Ryan is here…"

Ethan gives him a run down of current sleeping arrangements; Ethan sleeps on the couch in Luke's study, which is next to his bedroom, to be close by; Ben Taylor has taken up residence with Tip at the Benchleys' house.

"I put Emmaline in Sara's room. It's big and comfortable and has everything she needs. But there's a good room facing south that gets the sun, and you look like you could use some. Let's get your gear squared away."

"Sorry about this, Ethan; I promise not to get in your way."

"You won't. You eat proper today?"

"Two words: Amy Keaton."

"Say no more."

"How's your arm?"

"Just a scratch."

"What did the doc say about Luke?"

"He's weak, needs feeding up and bed rest, but he's going to be okay. He ain't complaining about having to stay in bed, so that's telling you something."

They begin climbing the stairs.

"Can I see him, Ethan?"

"He'd never admit it, but I think he's been waiting for you to drop by."

But when Cliff drops by, Ben is standing by the window and the room feels kinda... chilly. Luke has a humorless look on his face, standard these days, but it clears a little when he sees Cliff.

"Well, look what the cat dragged in..."

Cliff stands at the end of his bed and studies him. "Doc says you're okay."

"I feel like shit. You?"

He shrugs.

"That *long* subject we spoke about..."

"Getting longer," Cliff concedes.

"Fascinating though."

"If you say so."

"Mind like a bear trap."

"Yep." Cliff turns to Ben Taylor. "How goes it, Ben?"

"Never better," is the terse response.

"I have some news for you."

"My father?"

"Mac wired me an update on your father. He's gone missing, according to the authorities in Omaha."

"Missing?"

"The police department is trying to track him down."

"Like I told Donnelly, he probably had it coming, dealing with men like Bodecker. So desperate he allowed himself to be used. Put us all in danger."

"Apparently so," Cliff muses. "But, I have better news..."

He tells Ben about his mother; what happened between her and Luke in Omaha, what they encountered on the train, and how she brought the information to him in Cheyenne.

Ben regards his cousin with a critical eye.

"She's a hero," Luke murmurs. "A very nice one."

"Mm. You promised her a visit with her children and grandson," Cliff says.

"The least I could do," Luke quips.

"Well, she's coming, now Maverick's been shut down."

"Caroline? Coming here?" he asks, almost childlike. "I'd like to see her again. When?"

"Soon as Mac and Cam can arrange it."

Ben says, "Does my sister know about this?"

"I had dinner with the Keatons today. I told her I'd tell you."

"If you'll excuse me, I have some things to do."

"Sure. See you later. I'll be around for a few days."

Ben departs without a backward glance at his cousin.

"So, how's it coming along with you two?"

"I'm not in the best mood for making peace with my cousin, and I'm wondering if he's *ever* in a good mood. We're trying... Caroline coming here will help. "

"He seems like a good man. Ethan thinks highly of him."

"He earned that, you know."

"And you can't ignore it."

"No." Luke closes his eyes and takes a shaky breath. "So, a few days, eh? How's Dan Hummer?"

"Sends his regards. About Jennifer..."

The frown returns to Luke's face.

"Cam and Meg have been asking after you. I think they want to tell her what's happened."

"I don't want her to see me like this and I don't want her around here while all this crap with Donnelly and Bodecker is going on. It ain't safe."

"Her father has asked her to go see him in Provincetown."

"Oh. Where's that again... Cape Cod?"

"Mm. Massachusetts."

Luke looks disgusted, saying, "Her father... what good can come of that..."

"You know something, Luke, I don't think she should come here. You're about as jolly as that hole I found you in."

Luke's eyes fill with moisture. He sticks a thumb and finger into them and stays like that for several moments. There is a look of agony on his face that is hard to mistake.

"I'm sorry," Cliff grunts.

"No. It's settled. No Jennifer."

"For now."

Luke removes his hand from his eyes. "I don't know if I can do this, Cliff."

Cliff can hear the panic in his voice. And to be honest, he's not exactly sure what it is that Luke thinks he can't do – get better? Be without Jennifer? Or get his mind out of a very dark place? – he's scared and that's not something he's used to being.

"Sure you do... you've been doing it, one step at a time, like Kincaid taught you."

"Easy for you to say."

"I'll be around for the next few days to remind you..."

Hummer was right. For now, this is where he needs to be.

Emmaline

The following morning

Mystified, Emmaline wanders from the kitchen to the sitting room, searching for her errant notebook...

The Taylors' house is lovely and definitely loved, welcoming and comfortable, brimming with character and charm, making her very curious about the absent Sara Taylor, whose bedroom she currently occupies...

And there in the sitting room, perched upon the arm of the Chesterfield is Cliff, his legs stretched out, his head down, lost in his thoughts, and holding her notebook.

"What are you doing with that?"

He looks up and his blue-green glance is like a snare in the underbrush she failed to see. "I found it lying around, and I thought if I held onto it for long enough, eventually you and I would meet."

"I thought I left it..."

"Sorry?"

"Never mind. Were you reading it?"

His smile is fleeting. "No."

"May I have it back?"

"Mm... no."

So, that's how it's going to be...

"It's of no consequence as long as you don't lose it." She turns and starts to walk away. "I have another upstairs."

"There is, however," he says, "the matter of the content on page twenty-seven. Good of you to number the pages, by the way."

She stops; page twenty-seven? What is on page twenty-seven?

You cannot let him win. But what is on page twenty-seven...think.

"Would you like me to refresh your memory?" he asks from behind her on the arm of the Chesterfield.

"Since I only write content of the highest quality, I doubt I have anything to be concerned about," she says and takes a step to leave.

"In the margins on page twenty-seven is the darndest thing."

She stops again. "You said you didn't read it. A lie, Sheriff?"

"Well, I fanned through and this caught my eye."

"Convenient," she says and turns.

He raises one eyebrow, deftly opens her notebook at the page in question, and reads...

"See the mountains kiss high heaven... and the sunlight clasps the earth, and the moonbeams kiss the sea... what are all these kissings worth, if thou kiss not me?"

"So?" she says, pretending his reading of Shelley has no effect on her.

"So."

"Shelley's kiss poem." Absolute poker face.

"*Love's Philosophy*, I believe is its true title."

"I know."

"Considered to be one of the most romantic poems in English literature."

"Really? Who knew? How clever of Shelley. He does have a way with words."

"He's a poet... they invariably do."

"And you read it *very* well," she patronizes him.

He laughs. "Thank you."

"And how amazing, truly, that the sheriff of Cheyenne even knows which poems are considered as the most romantic in English literature."

He looks wryly amused but says nothing.

"Do you want to make a point?" she asks. "Or may I have my notebook back now?"

He holds it out to her. She makes her move, steps towards him and goes to take it. He whips it away, out of reach.

She sighs. "A little childish, don't you think?"

"Explain for me *my mother wouldn't do it and neither will I.*"

Poker face, Roberts. "That is none of your business."

Holding the book behind him, he retorts, "Well, I think it is, and since you mentioned it in the context of our topic of conversation…"

"We were not having a conversation."

"Two people talking constitutes a conversation, and you and I have had a great many in the relatively short time we have been acquainted."

"Give it back."

"No."

Poker face slipping… "Oh, for heaven's sake, why not?"

"Because I want your attention, your conversation and your… your…"

Her…? Her.

Her cheeks suddenly feel warm. "Oh, dear."

"Oh, *dear*?"

"Not you. The predicament."

"Oh, I see."

"Well, if I thought that was likely."

"Mind sharing?"

"Yes, I mind."

His eyes sweep over her face and become very sparkly. He's thinking. She knows him well enough to know that when he keeps anything to himself it's a very calculated move. And a less secure personality could be forgiven for feeling a little self-conscious. She, on the other hand, is highly suspicious, and annoyingly curious.

But the color of his eyes is so beautiful… sparkly, yes, but so reminiscent of a tropical lagoon lazing in the sultry summer heat… They are magic… And it would be so easy to… so easy…

What are all these kissings worth, if thou kiss not me?

A bucket of cold water, someone?

"There is another poem on page fifty-two," she says in a rush, "when you've finished reading that, put the notebook back where you found it. I have to go…"

Suddenly, her notebook drops onto the sofa behind him with a faint thud. She's not sure what he's going to do next; she only knows she has to leave and leave now.

Too late... He's too fast. He springs from the Chesterfield and grabs her arms.

The trap was set and sprung.

She was supposed to win.

Think of it as winning, Em. I'm sure it will help.

He draws them together.

A realization is before her...

He slides one arm around her.

...she has no resistance to the bait.

And with his other hand he caresses and cradles her face.

"Emma."

There must be something...

She looks up at him. Nothing springs to mind.

Oh, why won't something spring to mind?

And on his handsome face, the most irresistible expression of all.

Shelley put words to it... the words she and Celina have adored and recited and giggled about and delighted in, and re-titled, since they discovered *Love's Philosophy* at age fourteen.

Emmie, try not to be as analytical about kissing as you are about everything else. When you find the right pair of lips, just kiss them. The trouble was that the right pair was not that easy to find...

"You saw mountains coming here," he murmurs.

"Yes."

"And moonbeams..."

"A sea of snow..."

"Emma." His lips touch her cheek, kissing her... "Emma."

Heaven...

Mountains kiss... moonbeams kiss...

"Kiss not me?" he says, his lips almost touching hers.

"No..."

But there was never any doubt... his is the right pair of lips.

Entwined... suffused by warmth... at last their lips part and their eyes meet. Even *she* can't think.

Sheriff Ruthless just executed a master seduction... and yet... his eyes, now turned to melting viridescence, reveal there is something he hadn't expected... she knows because she feels it too... the desire to follow it almost sweeps her away... with the words on her tongue and floating in the breath of distance between them...

Kiss not me...

But at that moment two voices converge in her head:

You will come to no good as a reporter, says one.

You might just win some respect for your gender in this business, if you can hold to that promise, says the other.

Although how they got in she has no idea. The connection between her and Cliff seemed so... so romantic, so impervious to common sense.

Shelley's poem of kissing and clasping begins to lose sway.

Kiss not me?

Common sense.

Kiss not me?

Common sense.

"Cliff..."

"Emma," he whispers, his lips a breath away from hers.

"Cliff..."

"Don't talk. I think we should go back to what we were doing..."

"No, I... we have to..."

"What is it, Emma?" he asks softly. "There is nothing but good between us."

"I know it seems so, but... think about it for a minute... you have your job, I got mine. They, we, aren't compatible."

"Recent events would suggest otherwise."

"Yes, well, I really cannot go into that now, but... I promised Mr Quaid... something..."

"Emma, stop..."

"And I can't get involved with a man who's... who's..."

"Who's what?"

"A sheriff.... A sheriff, all right? You picked it before."

"A sheriff is a man like any other."

"Well, hardly."

"How can you say that, Emma?"

They could argue this all day and get nowhere.

"You kissed me and we both liked it, the end."

"You felt a lot more than liking it..."

"You think so, do you?"

He gives a warm, gentle laugh. "You really need more practice at fibbing."

"I do not fib."

A lover-like grin.

She can't believe that description popped into her head.

"It doesn't change the fact."

"You know, you could give us a chance."

"At what?"

He looks flummoxed. "What do you mean *at what*?"

"I suppose this was bound to happen eventually, and now it has, but that doesn't mean anything more should."

"*That* was no ordinary kiss, I know you felt it; how can you be sure?"

"It was nice, but I'm sure."

"*Nice*? Emma," he says, "you don't think I'm sincere."

"Why would I? It is a separate issue after all."

"I see. So you would prefer I kissed your hand. I don't think that's what Shelley had in mind."

"It's just a poem."

"Mm, you could have fooled me."

"May I have my book back?"

"Not yet. I'd like your permission to write in it."

"What are you talking about? And you asking permission is novel."

"Well, you bring out the best in me."

"About my notebook?"

"I'll write my account of what happened on one side of the page and leave the other side blank. Later you can ask me questions and use the other side to write what you want."

Now it's her turn to be flummoxed, and stares at him.

"Emma?"

"You. Write your account…"

"Who, what, when, where, why, grammar, the works."

"Grammar as well," she teases.

"My grammar's pretty good."

"And dotting your 'i's and crossing your 't's."

"That's Mac talking."

She gives a laugh. "Very well."

His eyes twinkle. "You'll find it interesting, I promise you."

As she gazes at those twinkling eyes, two things dawn on her; they are still holding one another exactly the same, and, how very agreeable it is to have one of their conversations in each other's arms.

Very, very agreeable.

She smiles at the thought. When he smiles back, it occurs to her that this could go on for a very long time. They could lose themselves for days… in 'conversations'.

Yet it was not long ago that he hauled her out the snow, scared and shaken, and put her in irons. He threatened to arrest her for trespassing, but instead cocooned her in his blue coat, gave her comfort and took care of her.

And cared about her ever since. And she him.

Yet another dire revelation is upon her. Their conversations are a metaphor, and have been from the start…

"What are you thinking, Emma?"

What are all these kissings worth, if thou kiss not me? All this time? Every time?

"Emma?"

"I…" Common sense, *common sense*…

That whatever he thinks he wants to give them a chance at… the surprising passion uncovered in the kiss, the transient love affair, the brief encounter, the casual liaison… he is not her future, and certainly not the one she has in mind for herself. Long ago she decided on ambition, not a sheriff-come-lately…

Better.

"…nothing…"

She disentangles her arms and hands from around his neck.

Distance is what they need…

…and less conversation.

His arms, however, don't budge, and she gets stuck against his chest.

"Your nothing equates to a full analysis of any given situation, I've noticed."

"We are not doing this, Cliff."

"You want to be miserable while we're both working and living in Cheyenne… I like running into you every place I go."

"You take rather a lot for granted."

"Then, you want me to be miserable?"

"Of course I don't want you to be unhappy, but you work hard, work means everything to you, and you won't be unhappy."

"You say that like you've known me for years."

"I… know someone like you, Cliff."

"Your father," he says with such directness that she catches her breath.

"This *conversation* is over," she says and pushes at him so that he must release her.

"Emma, wait… please…"

Taking a steadying breath, she looks up at him. His expression is utterly contrite. How can he be so ruthless one moment and so vulnerable to her the next?

"I was going to ask you before…" he says.

"Before…"

"Yes, before…" and clears his throat.

"Ask me…?" she prompts him.

"I was planning to take a trip out to the Parsons' place first thing tomorrow. I need to look around and I could use some help. Your help. Will you come?"

"Mightn't it be dangerous?" she asks.

Emmie, you can ask that? You know he's dangerous. I think we just established that fact. Anyway, who cares? You get to investigate and snoop to your heart's content, as well as be with him all day even though you shouldn't. Sounds utterly perfect.

Not now, Celie. I'm busy.

"It might," he says. "But I'll protect you – Sheriff of Bright River, remember?"

"You're sheriff too much if you ask me."

But not one part of her is interested in mustering the required effort to refuse him and he knows it. His eyes are sparkling like magic again; well, he has his way again, something he is very used to getting.

She does her best to focus on the investigation. "I can't deny this would be excellent for my story. What time?"

"The sacrifices we make, eh? Dress as warm as you can, and I'll meet you in the barn after you eat a hearty breakfast."

"Very well."

They part company.

She wanders off a ways; he turns back to the sofa where her notebook fell. From the corner of her eye she watches him pick it up; he catches her snooping.

"Anything else?" he asks.

"No," she replies.

"Well then…"

"… goodbye."

Of all things, she feels that stab of pain inside her, like the ones during her journey with Deloight that came and went from the time Cliff left the train at Watts Landing… the one the brandy soothed and the stars comforted.

Less conversation… more distance… really?

She swallows hard. If there is anything she detests more than being confused about something she has yet to discover it.

He gives her a strained smile.

Emmie, don't you know what's happening?

No.

And she continues on her way.

Cliff

The morning is cold and crisp with an intensely blue sky; so blue in fact he can't understand why Emma hasn't commented on it, extolled its virtues, or renamed it cerulean or azure... Or remarked on anything else for that matter. She hasn't uttered a word since they left the Diamond-T, and only offers a gentle grunt in response to an occasional comment he makes.

He clears his throat.

After a moment's delay, she responds, "I'm sorry, did you say something?"

"Possibly."

Something's different. Even her hair is different. Did he hear somewhere that the way a woman wears her hair reflects her mood or something? Emma's honey-blonde tresses are woven into one loose braid down her back, with her hat jammed on her head.

"How much further?" she asks.

"Did you sleep all right?"

"I... I was working on parts of my story last night and I lost track of time."

That's her excuse then. *Academic.* He thought about her for hours before sleep finally rescued him.

"You *are* watching, aren't you, Cliff? These fields are wide and exposed..."

"I'm watching," he says.

"I mean, how far does a shot from a rifle reach? I think Sheriff Ransford might have told me once, but I can't remember. Poor Sheriff Ransford. He didn't deserve to be killed. I'm relieved he wasn't married, that he had no children – bad enough for us mere colleagues, friends and acquaintances. I dreamed about him last night. I dreamed that someone was trying to shoot me and Sheriff Ransford took the bullet for me and died. But it wasn't really Sheriff Ransford who did it, Cliff, it was you, and in my dream Sheriff Ransford became you…"

"I didn't die," he jumps in, irritated. "Now, turn around. I'm taking you back."

Her cold face peers defiantly at him from under her hat. "I'm dreaming about you dying, Cliff, and that's all you have to say to me?"

"I didn't die in Cheyenne, it was Dave in your dream and I don't plan on dying today or any other day until I'm an old, old man, too old and cranky for you to want to know, get it? Now pull yourself together, Roberts, or I'm taking you back."

She looks away; she's intensely silent for several minutes.

He continues his watch.

Then she says, "I'm sorry."

"Got it off your chest now?"

"I believe so."

"Fine."

"We won't talk then, until we get there?"

"We won't talk."

He orders her to stay with the horses behind a stand of aspens on the edge of the Parsons' ranch settlement. He searches the perimeter outposts, the ones Luke warned him about, and finding them deserted heads towards the barn. Except for a couple of cold rats, it too is devoid of life. The vacant bunkhouse feels icy cold; drab and deserted. Old cots line the walls. One of the windowpanes is broken and the wind whistles in. The odd bit of tack lies about, pieces of old newspaper and tin cans. There is a covering of rimed dust on everything, no tracks or prints, and like the barn it seems clear that no one has been in here for a very long time.

He makes his way back to Emma; she has her hands tucked into her armpits and looks so relieved to see him that his heart skips a beat.

"All clear, except for the house. We'll do that together."

"I was keeping watch on the house while you were gone," she says, following him, "and I saw no signs of life."

"Good."

The house is deceptively big. And the solid front door is locked. There's a sign over it warning trespasses what will happen to them.

Emma reads it and gulps. "If Bodecker owns this now, it seems incredible to think he wouldn't have someone watching the place," she says. "But there are no prints about, neither human nor horse – perhaps around the back?"

"Cole and Tyner and the other mavericks moved on the Keatons and the Diamond-T after the snowstorm, so if they holed up here together and planned the attack there should be prints."

Emma starts to move; he stops her with a gentle hand.

"Anything we find here, inside or out, could be evidence."

"I understand. I'll be careful. But I doubt anything we find here will be admissible if you don't have a warrant."

"Thank you, Judge Roberts."

They make their way around to the back of the ranch house trailing their horses. There are no tracks and the house appears sealed up and vacant.

When they reach the back entrance, Emma remarks breathily, "When Marshal Hummer suggested you take a look out here, he probably didn't mean for you to break into the place."

The back door is locked.

"You should have a warrant."

"I heard you the first time."

All the windows are shut tight; he moves along the back porch testing them until he discovers there's some wobble in one near the corner of the house and starts working on it.

"Bodecker could have us charged with trespassing," she says.

"That will go nicely with the charge of concealing a prisoner and enabling his escape."

"For retrieving Luke?"

"Why do you think Hummer's pulled rank on me and ordered me to stay put?"

"Because obviously you're exhausted and need a spell?"

He looks around as he's trying to force the window to quietly laugh at her. She looks nettled by it.

"Maybe," he grins. "And thank you for your concern for my well being. But Luke is charged with murdering the prostitute on the train, assaulting a deputy and escaping custody until Ralph Walker, the sheriff of Lincoln County, can be convinced that Donnelly did it, and until that happens..."

Finally, the window gives way. He raises the sash as high as it will go, then turns and raises his eyebrow at her.

"...you, Miss Roberts, aided and abetted me."

"I know," she says matter-of-factly. "When the Lincoln County sheriff finds out what really happened he will need to mount a search for Porterfield and Fulbright. It must have nearly killed you to leave them behind..."

"I try not to think about it. So, shall you go first or shall I?"

"I'm still aiding and abetting," she says.

He chuckles and hoists a leg through the open window.

He enters into a small dank room with a large metal tub in the far corner, and, down the centre, a long scrubbed wooden table with several small basins scattered on top. A laundry room.

Emma, who has followed closely behind, remarks, "Even evil conniving men like a clean, starched shirt."

He draws the window down behind her, leaving a few inches spare at the bottom. "Why am I not surprised that you are adept at climbing through windows."

He leads her beyond the laundry room into a small pantry and beyond that to a large kitchen geared up with table and chairs, a huge stove, an old pump and sink, and a large dresser still decked out with plates and cups with their pattern faded beneath a coating of dust.

"This hasn't been touched for months. No one holed up here in the last couple of weeks," Emma whispers. "When you think about it, it would be too obvious, wouldn't it? And prove a connection between Donnelly and Bodecker that would make a prosecutor do handstands."

"Well, maybe there is something around here that will still do that."

In the eerie stillness they pick their way about the derelict house, from room to room, until they come to the old man's study. Emma catches her breath; Cliff whistles softly.

"It's like a shrine," she whispers and rather quaintly removes her hat.

There are great maps hanging on every wall.

Shelves are crammed with crusty papers and books.

A dead parlor palm droops in its brass pot.

And a massive mahogany desk is centered beneath an equally impressive portrait of Ed Parsons.

"The man himself?" Emma asks.

"Looking a darn sight more healthy than when I last saw him."

"The maps..."

"Mm."

"I've seen this one. In Sheriff Ransford's office. Chase brought it out."

"I'm guessing it wasn't framed."

She shakes her head. "See – all the ranches and homesteads are carefully marked. Chase and I used this map to get to the Diamond-T. Of course, we carried it in our heads. And not all that successfully either. It all looked different in the snow."

"This map here," he says, moving along, "the rail network. Look at the detail."

"Every station, every siding and water tank..."

"Even Watts Landing."

"Look at the key. These colored dots indicate the approximate populations of each town, these stars how many passengers, and these markers what type of freight and consignments..."

"Every coal mine, gold mine, silver mine..."

"Why would Parsons need this kind of detailed information?"

As Emma asks, he moves to the next map.

"These show far more detail than a UP tourist map. This one, most of the south-east quadrant of Wyoming. Laramie, Albany, and Carbon counties."

Emma steps into the space between him and the map and stares up at it.

"What's that scribble in the corner?"

456

They both hone in on it.

"Can you make it out?" she asks.

He studies it over her head. The letters congeal in his brain...

"Cliff?"

He clears his throat. "It says: The Empire of P D B."

"P D B..."

"Parsons Donnelly and..."

"Bodecker. Are you sure? Their empire?"

He nods and steps away from the maps to think.

But Emma has other ideas... "We know that Parsons was on the rampage, terrorizing homesteaders and small ranchers and taking their properties. The Alliance stood in his way; he needed help to remove it. Bodecker and Donnelly. They collaborated. What one achieved they all achieved; great, if all their plans succeeded."

"This supports the theory that their plan is to take over the south-east."

"It's fantastic!"

"Mm."

"How could they imagine it would ever be possible?"

"Well, Bodecker works at the top level: the governor; all his Republican pals; Association members and affiliates. Meanwhile, Donnelly covertly takes care of those that get in the way. And Parsons takes the fall..."

"They are truly mad I think."

"They think they can manipulate Cam and me, and they would be right to a degree, but they never figured on Luke. He is determined to push the boundaries of the law; what's lawful is not his first thought. He follows his instincts for justice..."

"Such a scheme would take years to bring to fruition. And then there's the changing political, social and economic climate. How did they think this could be done? What about all the cattle barons that congregate at the Cheyenne Club for a start – did they honestly believe that those men would allow it?"

"Do you remember me asking Mac to round up Bodecker's association members for questioning..."

Emma's eyes widen considerably. "Are there enough of them to achieve this?"

"At some point Bodecker obviously thinks there will be. This is not the kind of empire in which you garrison armies to defend your borders and make war on your neighbors. This is an economic empire, it eventually controls politics, business and society, and the only way to stop it is to bring down Bodecker. You may have noticed that for some time Charlie Quaid has been alluding to the damage Bodecker's ideology wreaks. It might surprise even him to have proof of Bodecker's intent."

"Mr Faraday, I recall, wrote something in one of his letters to Miss Keaton... they were discussing liberty and property... about Thomas Jefferson's 'empire for liberty'... about you all living in the heart of it..."

"Mm, that sounds like Cam."

"What I'm trying to say is: doesn't 'empire for liberty' title the noble cause for the spread of democracy?"

"I guess you and I and all other idealistic saps would like to think that it started out with noble intentions. But I can't see it. We just replaced one empire with another. They tend to come and go anyway."

"That is highly cynical."

"Where do you think this nation will be in a hundred years from now with men the likes of Bodecker, Parsons and Donnelly allowed to flourish?"

"Shall I check my crystal ball?" she replies jauntily. "I brought it with me, in my saddlebags..."

"Very funny."

She sighs at him. "Democracy, and our Republic that we hold so dear, allows that there will always be unscrupulous people such as Donnelly and Bodecker to inflict what they please on society, but, more importantly, there will always be people like you and Mr Faraday and Mac and Luke and Mart Keaton as well."

He stares at her; holds himself very still.

People like her.

She is extraordinary.

A beautiful, rare creature who walked into his life and (no matter what that crystal ball may or may not reveal) will never truly walk out of it. And she touches his heart so unexpectedly, with a kind of swooping artlessness that leaves him altered somehow… or rather, with a revelation of himself, leaving it to him to be the judge of it.

She is his Emma. For always.

Her eyes register the moment.

She slights him, albeit gently, with a look. And she moves away, saying, "Such a shame we don't have a warrant. We could tear these down from the wall. I think Mr Faraday would be very pleased to see them."

He looks up at the maps. "Who could have known…"

"The problem with men like Donnelly is that they are too arrogant to think they will ever be caught and then they leave evidence like this around."

"Donnelly is a cold-blooded killer; he doesn't think like you and me."

"There's a chilling insight. Never thought of it quite like that."

"Mm… first rule of law-enforcement: if you want to catch a criminal, think like one."

"Now *that* I have heard before, but it's not exactly the same as contemplating on the twisted workings of a cold-blooded killer's mind by comparing them to those of a normal person."

She has no idea that her attempt at dealing with 'the moment' by speaking about criminal activity makes her more endearing and desirable, not less.

"Oh, there's a safe over there," she continues. "I don't suppose you can crack the combination."

"I've cracked one or two safes in my time. You?"

She looks as though she thinks the better of answering.

He can't stop himself from grinning.

She looks away.

He investigates the three-foot high metal box behind Parsons' desk. "No need to worry." The door is open slightly and he peers inside. "There's nothing in here."

"You know, I've been thinking about something…"

"Be surprised if you weren't."

"No, seriously…"

He abandons the safe; she is studying the first map again.

"This map reminds me of something Chase told me. He said it

wasn't public knowledge, deliberately so in fact, but I think I could tell you."

"Tell me what?" he asks, moving to her side.

"The Stewarts' place, see…" a small, gloved finger points out the Stewart ranch, "…here. After Miss Keaton was killed, they decided they'd had enough and moved out. Not permanently though. They sold their cattle at market last October, then secretly left their ranch. John Keaton and Ethan Benchley bought the breeding stock, Chase said, and are supposed to keep an eye on things. I believe he said they each have a key.

"Anyway, we came into the area along the Stewarts' stock trail… here. That's when Chase told me. Even though it was supposed to be the fastest way in, and believe me it wasn't, it was also the riskiest because he thought it possible that Donnelly might have noticed the Stewarts were gone and then taken over the ranch. But there wasn't any trouble along the way, so we figured that Donnelly didn't know. But that's not real proof, is it? Clearly the mavericks were already in position. You know, Cliff, Sheriff Ransford planned to come out here to Parsons' place; Jim Crogan was supposed to go to the Keatons… so…"

"The mavericks used the Stewarts'."

"It's highly probable."

"John Keaton has a key?"

She nods, a sparkle in her golden eyes.

"You're good."

"So I'm told."

He smiles and says, "Suddenly I'm very hungry… You?"

"I could eat," she grins.

Emmaline

"I'm going with him," John Keaton declares.

"You certainly will not," Amy Keaton argues.

"Aw, Amy…"

"Cliff is the sheriff, it is *his* job."

"Amy, Sheriff Ransford died saving our necks, the least we can do is give Cliff help by watching his back."

In the parlor, before the warmest, coziest fire she has enjoyed for quite some time, Emmaline cradles Adam on her lap while he sucks on the rump of his toy horse. Holding a baby releases a curious kind of pleasure inside her. And who would have thought something so special was to be found in all this strife?

She catches Tressa's eye. But Tressa's thoughts are elsewhere and she raises an eyebrow and shrugs.

"Can you blame her?" she says softly.

The discussion in the kitchen continues until Cliff returns.

"Ah, Cliff, did you saddle m'horse?" John says.

"No, John," Cliff replies, sounding perplexed, "just mine and Roberts'."

"Emmaline's!" Amy cries. "You're taking that slip of a girl with you?"

Tressa bites her bottom lip.

Emmaline removes the horse rump from Adam's mouth.

"You could use an extra rifle, right?" John asks.

"You cannot take that girl into a den of mavericks."

Den of mavericks – Emmaline wishes she'd thought of that.

"Now just hold everything, Amy," Cliff says, "John, both of you.

461

Roberts is with me. What you think about that, Amy, I have no control over, so I'm sorry but that's that – although I'm sure Roberts will appreciate your concern for her welfare. As for you, John, as sheriff of Bright River I'm ordering you to stay home. All I need you to do is give me the key to the Stewarts' and your permission to search the property and inside the house."

Silence.

Then: "The key's in my bureau. I'll get it. And you have my permission to search whatever you like."

John Keaton's gracious-in-defeat footsteps can be heard on the stairs.

Emmaline strains her ears to the gentler exchange that follows.

"Thank you for that, Cliff."

"Concede Roberts without fuss," Cliff says. "She's got enough to be going on with."

"She's a lovely young woman, and very well brought up. Why would she want to go back out there, traipsing around with you!"

"Because it's her job, Amy. She's a journalist, you know that. If I don't keep her with me, she'll go by herself – and considering the risks I would be derelict in my duty. I know this is difficult for you and I understand why…"

"But she and Tressa get along just fine, it would be no trouble if you leave her here and collect her later. Cliff, will you…"

Suddenly, he's standing in the doorway between the parlor and the kitchen, barking, "Roberts!"

Emmaline jumps; her gaze flies to his face, which is dark with a rather fierce expression. He stares back for a few moments, during which the fierceness wanes and *her* Ryan (the one who whispers *kiss not me* like a sultry summer afternoon by a tropical lagoon) makes an appearance, causing her heart to skip a beat.

Then it's gone again.

"We're leaving," he growls.

Ten minutes later they're in the saddle, heading out with the key in Cliff's pocket, very full stomachs and…

"Amy stuffed my saddlebags with food and packets of herbs. Herbs to toss into a long hot dreamy bath."

"That spell by the fire has made you soft, Roberts."

"The Keatons are the nicest family I think I've ever met."

More grunting.

"Don't be cranky."

He lets out a loud sigh. "A hard ride in freezing conditions will knock it out of you."

"Do *you* want to get something off *your* chest now?"

"No. Shape up, Roberts... "

"She got to you, didn't she? Amy Keaton. Dragging off a slip of a girl into a den of mavericks. "

"...or I'll send you back to the cozy house, the hot food and the sweet cuddly baby."

"Mean old sheriff."

She hears him laugh, a highly amused chuckle, that causes her to smile. She urges her patient horse forward and catches up.

Nearly two hours later it seems to her that Cliff has got his wish; she's slowing turning into an icicle and the Keatons' parlor seems a very long way away.

As the afternoon deepens so does the cold, reminding her of her journey with Chase. They follow a similar procedure to the one they used at Parsons' place, only this time there are prints, both human and horse, everywhere... all around the yard, the barn, the corrals, up to the front door and circling around to the back. And all must be investigated.

Cliff returns to her with the news that, as at Parsons' place, all the ranch buildings and structures are vacant.

"This place is much nicer, don't you think?" Emmaline whispers as they tie up their horses.

"I agree." He reaches beneath his coat and pulls out his pistol. He catches her eye. "Stay alert."

The Stewarts' front door opens up for them without the key. Evidence of recent human habitation is everywhere, although not all the rooms have been used. They go from room to room, with Cliff jotting notes in a small notebook he keeps in his breast pocket. He searches every shelf, every closet, every cabinet, desk and dresser and under the beds.

Then they separate and execute individual searches.

"There were four," he says as they meet up in the hall.

"Four beds slept in, yes. Enough refuse for four young men, and from the looks of the kitchen and the state of the leftover food, you could safely say that no one has been here for at least several days. To put it simply, they have converted a thoroughly pleasant home into a pigsty."

"Looks that way. Their belongings are all over the place, so they believed they would be returning."

"Have you found any evidence of Donnelly or Bodecker?"

"Just this." He hands her a creased telegram paper.

NIGHTHAWK LULLABY. WAIT FOR THE SIGN. MAVERICK.

"Where did you find this?"

Cliff brings forth a rumpled flannel shirt from under his arm. "The breast pocket. Peculiar for the mavericks to work together."

"Indeed." She hands back the telegram. "But this campaign was meant to be the final blow, wasn't it? Donnelly made the rules; he could change them at his own discretion. Although, this change in his strategy turned out to be his downfall and the Alliance's salvation. That and the fact that the rest of us knew what he was up to and had a strategy of our own."

"Got your story already written, Roberts?"

"Irony always makes for interesting reading."

"I guess we can now lock the place up properly and head on home."

"Home?" she murmurs with a shiver. "Home..."

A small, warm haven far, far, far away.

Her mother.

Letters from Celie every second day.

Their house on the sunny side of the street, with the orchard out back; the tall sweet grass and the fragrant manicured lawn; the standard rose bushes, the lilacs, the honeysuckle and the fruit trees in blossom.

Birds everywhere, singing their hearts out.

And neighbors. The aromas of their supper cooking adrift along rosy streets as you walk *home* at sunset.

"Roberts."

Her brothers. Their families.

All the children eager to play.

A sunny, easy life…

"Emma."

She wonders out loud, "Where is home for you, Cliff?"

The next thing she knows he is taking her hand and pulling her along into the parlor.

Cliff

He stands her in front of the hearth. "Wait there while I get a fire started. And don't pass out on me." He busies himself, saying, "I could have sworn with all that food of Amy Keaton's inside you you'd be warm for hours."

"It *is* hours," she says as she shivers beside him.

Quickly, the flames spring to life.

Thoughtful of those mavericks not to use all the firewood.

She thrusts her hands before the fire. He adds plenty of fuel.

"Oh, my, that feels good."

He glances again at the outstretched hands at eye level beside him. "I promise I won't mention the word home again."

"It just came over me."

"I think you're homesick."

"It's never happened before."

"For a start, you're not used to the cold... on top of everything you've been through..." He stands up and dusts off his hands. "Have you written home since you've been in Wyoming?"

"I wired to say I had arrived safely, just as I promised, but as for a letter I haven't had the time. I had intended to write a letter on the train to Laramie and post it when I got there."

"Will they be concerned?"

"Celina will be thinking the longer I take to write the more fun I must be having. My brothers probably don't even notice I'm not there. My mother saw me to the train with the words *I won't sleep a wink until you write me a proper letter.*"

"Your mother might be cranky from lack of sleep by now."

"She is already cranky because she didn't want me to come here. I will wire her again when I return to Cheyenne. You didn't answer me before, where's home for you?"

"For now, Cheyenne, I guess."

"You guess? Don't you know?"

"Not everything in life is black and white. When my grand-mother died, Chicago lost its shine..."

"So wherever you hang your hat then?"

"Not exactly."

"You don't like Chicago?"

"At the moment I'd rather be in Cheyenne."

"Is Chicago cold?"

"Freezing in winter. Arctic blasts sweep in from Canada."

She shivers.

The incessant questions, the dainty shivering, the small hands warming, the air of Southern quaintness that charms her intensity... she bewitches him completely. He puts his hands on her shoulders and closes the distance between them. Reluctantly, which amuses him, she looks up at him. He recalls how pretty she looked with the Keaton baby on her knee, the deep desirable warmth of her, how it took his breath away, and how he felt... They're not things he can ignore. But as compelling as the situation is between them, it is also ticklish...

"You..." She clears her throat. "You stood up for me with Amy Keaton."

"Well, you were going soft in there. I don't know how John gets out alive."

She laughs. "It's a home, Cliff. I think John Keaton likes it very well and he's not soft."

"Then you would have stayed, if you were given the choice?"

"I have been known to speak up for myself occasionally," she prattles jauntily.

"Just answer the question."

"The baby *is* very nice," she says, examining her fingertips. "Oh, look, they're pink again. I must admit, I like Tressa very much, and with these dreadful weather conditions I'm sure she doesn't get to talk to other young woman very often. She told me a great deal about Mart. At first I thought it might upset her, but I formed the impression that she needed someone other than his parents to talk to about him; I think she worries about upsetting them... the secret she and Mart kept, that she knew what he was doing and didn't know how to deal with it."

"It couldn't have been easy for her."

"No. All the same, I wonder at his love for her and her loyalty to him. Anyway, I don't believe many men would have chosen Mart's way to deal with Wilson Cutter. You certainly wouldn't have."

Her tone of voice suggests that she is pleased about that.

"No," he murmurs.

She considers him momentarily, then looks down and starts fiddling with one of his coat buttons.

"Talking about Miss Keaton, though, is a different kettle of fish. None of them would say much and I didn't have the heart to press them."

"With Mart they knew something was wrong; what happened to Miss Keaton was purely a shock."

"She died in vain."

"A quaint turn of phrase, but it all depends on how you look at it."

"Yes, I see. Her murder was a significant catalyst. If Maverick had kept his gun in its holster, she would still be alive, and perhaps Bodecker's empire plans would still go undetected. Stupid really."

"It goes back to Parsons, I guess. What they agreed upon."

"Bodecker is so arrogant."

"Mm."

Their eyes lock. And while he smiles, she looks intense, and he wonders what's coming.

"I... I discovered that I didn't like talking about Miss Keaton either; that is why I didn't press them, because there are ways of asking, but I... what kind of reporter am I?"

"A rare one; you have a conscience.

"The way Amy was concerned for me..."

"Made it worse."

"You were right, I would have followed you. I would never have stayed behind, let you come here without me. It would be like saying it's fine for Miss Keaton to step out onto the sidewalk as a bullet is about to kill her, just as long as Emmaline is safe and warm."

"Emma, you've forgotten."

"No, I have an excellent memory."

"Gordy Jacobs and Swinton Carter."

"Oh. Yes. But I had you. And Mac. Miss Keaton had no one."

"No one knew Miss Keaton's life was in danger. Certainly, you are in a unique position. You are able to empathize as a victim and as a victim's friend. That will make you a better writer, Emma."

The intensity abandons her face, leaving a gentler glow in her eyes… she turns away, looking into the flames.

"I just deal with the facts," she murmurs. "That's my job."

But he understands her, much more than she realizes.

He turns towards the fire as well, putting his arm around her, keeping her close to his side. "It's been a busy two weeks for you and me, Emma, since we met."

She sighs and puts her head against his shoulder. "I've never had anyone make me a fire before. Thank you."

"Glad you like it."

"I'm sorry I give you so much trouble. I'm not usually this bothersome. Ask anyone."

"What trouble?"

She chuckles and says, "How will I ever know when you are telling the truth?"

"Because I swear I will never lie to you."

"Your professional integrity will be enough, I'm sure."

"When did I achieve professional integrity in your eyes?"

"You're right. What was I thinking?"

"Well, it's been a long day."

"All this gadding about, I'm tired. Think I'll have a writing day tomorrow."

"Me too," he says, thinking of her notebook and the recount he promised her.

More chuckles. "You do that, Sheriff."

Emmaline

After breakfast, Emmaline shuts herself away in Sara Taylor's room, writing by the fire, determined to be thoroughly warm for one whole day. At about one o'clock, hunger drives her downstairs; she makes herself a sandwich and warms some milk, slices a wedge of Amy Keaton's spicy fruitcake onto a napkin, arranges it all on a tray and heads back up the stairs for an afternoon very like the morning had been. With her second notebook already crammed with stories from her visit to the Keatons, as well as all her notes from yesterday's excursion, there is much to be done.

She places the tray on the end of the bed and picks up the warmed milk. As she takes a long anticipated sip, she notices her original notebook, returned and in tact, on her pillow. She glances at the door, and back at the notebook. She takes another sip. She picks up the book. Then she tosses it aside.

Picks it up.

Tosses it aside.

And picks it up.

And tosses it aside.

Emmie, darling, just read the darn old thing...

Picks it up.

Tosses it aside.

And picks it up.

She downs her milk, licks her lips and places the cup on the tray.

The spicy fruitcake catches her eye. It's very good cake.

Spicy fruitcake or notebook.

Spicy fruitcake.

Notebook.

Emmie Roberts, if you don't attend to that notebook right this minute…

Notebook. She fans through the pages until she finds the place where her handwriting ends and a new and different script begins. Page after page is filled with Cliff's writing, the verso pages blank, just as he said. She sits by the fire to read. But there are words written in the margins, starting at the top and running all the way around the edge of the first page…

'The fountains mingle with the river, and the river with the ocean, the winds of heaven mix forever, with a sweet emotion. Nothing in the world is single. All things by law divine, in one another's being mingle. Why not I with thine…'

The first half of Shelley's kiss poem, Love's Philosophy.

She goes hot then cold in quick succession. If his intention was for her to remember their kiss, then he has succeeded. If it was to seduce her into thinking beyond it to something more, he is very sadly mistaken. He must learn to consider them not more than friends… This distraction notwithstanding, curiosity and the need to know what happened to him in North Platte impel her to continue.

Emma, I will begin with my stepping onto the train in Cheyenne on Monday morning. I was torn between what I wanted to do and what I had to do. My stomach was churning, I felt troubled, weary and burdened. And then you were there, in the midst of those gaggling women, and I rescued you. I like rescuing you, Emma. What man wouldn't enjoy saving a beautiful, passionate woman from the clutches of whatever happens to be threatening her at the time. We took a seat together. We talked. Like normal people do. Like we did after church over the oatmeal. And I found my burden sat a little lighter because of you. You were wonderful and delightful and lovely. And also incredibly smart; and the way you fascinate me was a welcome distraction.

Against all expectations, you then offered to help me. A defining moment, wouldn't you say? Not for an instant did I doubt your ability to carry out your promise. I just couldn't bear the thought of anything happening to you and me not being there to rescue you. So I did what you thought I couldn't do, Emma, I let God take care of you in my place.

I got off the train at Watts Landing and watched the train until I could no longer see you. There is a particular feeling inside me that I only know when we part company. Even though my heart felt heavy with leaving you and the job ahead, in my mind I could hear your voice, a voice I heard every minute of the day and night I was away from you. That oh so sweet sound. Encouraging me. Comforting me. Telling me what I'd done was right. I commandeered a horse and bought supplies and rode for hours without stopping until I came to a town called Hillsdale which was expecting a train heading east. I went to sleep on the train that night still with the taste of your cheek on my lips.

And I wondered what it meant when you said that you slept in my coat. We had only known one another a day then. Did you need me, Emma? And where was I? Working? I did watch over you, and I worried after you.

Anyway, the train reached North Platte in the morning. North Platte reminded me of a town in a snow globe. I'm not sure you would like North Platte in winter, Emma, and yet it's full of fascinating people going about their lives. You would like that part. I will tell you about some of them. I should warn you that from this point on I told more lies and carried out more deceits than you will ever be comfortable with."

Cliff

Emma is so uncharacteristically quiet at supper that Ethan keeps staring at her.

"What is it, Ethan?" she asks eventually.

"You okay, Emmaline?"

"Of course."

"You're a filly off her feed, I reckon."

She sips her water and says, "Still full from the Keatons."

Ethan chuckles. "Been known to happen."

"The baby's sweet. Resembles his father, I'm told."

"Can't decide if that's a good thing or something to worry about. You know how it is, a constant reminder of tragedy..."

"There's something about the dear little chap. When you spend time with him... In spite of everything, he's such a bonny, happy boy. I think he's a blessing, Ethan."

"Think maybe I oughta bring him over to visit Luke?"

"Well, I'm no doctor, but I can't imagine it would do anything but genuine good. Tressa and Luke are close, from what I'm told. She was at pains to tell me how much Luke loves the little boy, and how much she wants to visit."

Cliff, who's been enjoying the sound of Emma's voice (while curiosity for her reaction to what he'd written in her notebook slowly consumes him), notices Ethan's eyes on him. Clumsily, he picks up the thread of the conversation. "I'll... see to it, shall I?"

"Much appreciated, Cliff. After everything that's happened, I don't think John would let them out of the house without a proper escort."

"Understandable," he murmurs.

"So, Ethan, how is your arm feeling this evening?" Emma asks.

"Kinda sore… you know," he says with a lopsided smile.

"Well, perhaps you will be pleased to know you will have one less houseguest from tomorrow. I have finished all my interviews and gathering what I need for my story, so if I may have a ride to town in the morning…"

"Sure, you'll have your ride. The stage will take you right into Laramie. Darn sight easier than how you got here."

She smiles and thanks him for his hospitality.

"You'll be missed, Emmaline. If it weren't for you two…" He clears his throat. "Think I'll check that Luke's eaten something. Drop by later, Cliff?"

"Sure, Ethan. I'll tuck him in and tell him a bedtime story."

Ethan walks off, chuckling. "Tell him you said that."

And so Cliff finds himself alone at last with Emma.

She immediately starts clearing the table of plates and cutlery.

"I'll clean up," he says. "You had better get packed."

She unloads her hands by the sink. "Thank you, but I can do my share."

"No, I insist. Go pack. From what I've seen, your bits and pieces are all over the house."

"Oh," she murmurs, "I tend to be…" and, wiping her hands on a towel, she turns around.

"I'm… curious," he says.

"Oh?"

"You don't have any questions regarding my recount of North Platte?"

She starts wringing the towel. "No. But I really believe that you and Luke should buy Wilma a nice house, and then Eliza could live with her and they wouldn't freeze every winter."

He examines her face as she tries not to look at him. "That's it?"

"That's it."

"Are you sure?"

"I'm sure."

Dejection is squarely on the cards when suddenly the towel is discarded, those small hands become fists and her eyes like fierce sparks. "For God's sake, Cliff Ryan, you wrote me a love letter, and in the middle of my notebook."

"Did I?"

"You know you did."

"I'm relieved; for a minute there I thought you..."

"I'd have to be Adam's age not to notice! Why did you do it?"

"*Why?*" he chokes out.

"Of all the nerve. In my *work* book. Anyone could read it."

"*Why?*"

"I should have chosen the fruitcake."

"I can't speak for the cake, but what was I supposed to write, a hate letter?"

"You could have just kept to the facts."

"I did. I thought it quite good. You didn't like it?"

"For a ruthless, shameless and deceitful sheriff it is beautifully written. Don't ever do it again! What if I were some unscrupulous journalist who decided to use your... your feelings to spice up my story and sell twice the newspapers?"

"I know you're not. But so what? I'm not ashamed of my feelings for you. Write what you want. *I* won't feel guilty..." That sort of slipped out before he could catch it.

She gasps and glares at him, dumbstruck.

"Sorry," he says.

She continues staring, her gaze fixed and unnerving.

Now he feels guilty, right down to his bootlaces... that's if his boots had laces.

"Emma, what do you think is going on between us – has been going on since the moment we laid eyes on one another?"

"Attraction," she blurts out. "Something that can be overcome by discipline and will power because, Cliff, it won't come to anything. Against all reason, we like one another..."

"*Against all reason?*"

"But it is *not* going to go anywhere. Nowhere. No further."

"Speak plainer will you."

"Even you are not that dim-witted and..."

"Temper, Miss Roberts."

"...impercipient!"

"Interesting word, but you're getting nasty."

"Sometimes the truth hurts."

"Ouch," he feints and clutches his chest.

"You are impossible."

"You like that about me."

"I do not."

"Emma, be reasonable."

"Fine. I will be as reasonable and *professional*..."

"Double ouch."

"...as I can be. I promise I won't write anything to undermine the position you hold as sheriff and as the solid, uncompromised man the people you serve have come to expect."

"How decent of you."

"Nor will I refer to any part of your extrication account that would jeopardize my position at the Tribune, so don't be offended if some of your heroic exploits never see print."

"I don't recall writing 'off the record' anywhere on..."

"I gave my word to Mr Quaid, I shook his hand, that I would not become romantically attached to anyone during my employment with the paper."

"Oh, now you're pulling my leg."

"I certainly am not. Mr Quaid wants my full attention on my work and considering the scope of the story I'm working on, I don't disagree with him."

"Well, I do."

"I will not break my word. My reputation as a female in my profession is on the line and nothing is going to damage it."

"Is that what you truly think, Emma?"

"Furthermore, I don't want either of us to get hurt, so it's only fair to take control of our feelings right now, this very minute, and be entirely sensible about the matter. And now I have said all I'm going to say."

"Fine. You had your say, now listen. Charlie Quaid is a sore loser. He was very attached to that Daniels woman who went to the Bugle. She was extremely efficient and when she left it made him look bad. He doesn't want that to happen again, so he's cooked up this… this agreement between you. In my opinion, Emma, the fact that he made it is damaging to your reputation as a female in a man's profession. Do you think he would have said that to a man applying for the job? You should have told him to stick it…"

"Oh, charming. He's my boss. When was the last time you told your boss to… to…"

"You compromised, Emma."

"I wanted the job."

"I know. And you're damn good at it. But don't stand there and give me Quaid as an excuse because, frankly, I prefer the sheriff thing. That I can appreciate, that I understand in you, authentic and genuine. But not Quaid. Not you."

"Have you finished?" she asks, trembling, her chin raised.

"Oh, it's never finished between you and me, Emma."

"We shall see," she says and storms out.

"Yes we shall," he mimics to the air.

Meg

My dearest Jen,

I hope this letter finds you well. We all miss you terribly.

Please do not be anxious. I have never lost faith in my belief that everything will turn out in the end.

I know that Luke loves you. I am entirely certain of it. I know that whatever he chooses to do in his life he is always thinking of you.

You must believe this, Jen, and hold onto it, no matter what.

I cannot tell you anything else, but Cam assures me that you and Luke will find your own path together.

I think it comes down to this: you must do what you feel you must and Luke the same.

If you are torn between the need to go to Provincetown or wait for Luke, you must put that anxiety to rest in whatever way you see fit.

I can hardly believe that Dermot has asked to see you after all this time. Indeed, you must be curious.

It might be important, significant, or even affect the rest of your life.

Be strong, Jen, like I know you can be.

All my love, Meg.

Luke

February 15, 1885
At week's end

"So, you're leaving in the morning?"

"Time to get back."

"All good things."

"You know, there's something about this house…"

"Every window has a view, remember?"

Cliff smiles half-heartedly over his shoulder.

He's been studying the view out of Luke's bedroom window so hard you'd think something interesting was happening.

"That must be some sunset," Luke remarks.

"The snow's pink and apricot."

"Think I'm the wrong person to be watching it with." He sits forward, whacking at his pillows behind him, and it fast makes him breathless.

"And I *know* I'm the wrong person to be telling you bedtime stories."

"Guess you're thinking about what's waiting for you."

Cliff turns his back on the sunset; he picks up a chair, turns it back to front and places it bedside next to Luke. Then he straddles it, folds his arms along the top of the backrest, and fixes his chin on his arms. "Mac will have Bodecker's association members ready for questioning, Dan Hummer will be ruling my lockup, Cam indicting people left, right and center while cracking the whip over the search for Bodecker; there'll be lawyers all over the place, Dillon Kerr on my back, the mayor, the governor, the newspapers…"

Luke feels nauseous thinking about it, but the fact remains that as soon as the Maverick trials commence he will be in the thick of it himself.

"You don't like slowing down, do you, Cliff?"

He shrugs.

"Do you ever think about doing something else?"

"Do you?"

Luke folds his arms across his chest. "I could never stay away from here forever, but…"

"Bet a month's wages you haven't told Ethan that."

"What does the sheriff of Laramie County make a month?"

"Never enough." He gets up and wanders over to the window again.

This is a restlessness that Luke understands only too well. "So, you're going back to…"

"To Mac and Cam and Hummer and Dillon and Donnelly, the mayor, the governor and the newspapers." And he slides his hands into his pockets.

"She's gonna make you choose."

"I know."

After a long silence between them, Luke says, "You know something, I can hardly wait to get on my horse and ride the length and breadth of this ranch again."

Cliff looks up and tries a grin. "I like my chair back at the office, it's hard and it squeaks and I usually can't see it behind a stack of files, but it's my chair."

"Amen to that."

"Amen to that."

"You know, Cliff, I'm having a hard time trying to figure out what's happened to Ben's father."

"Mm, me too. Want to run a few ideas by me?"

"Porterfield?"

"Nah, he and Fulbright would have run for the hills after they figured out how to get loose."

"Can't imagine Bodecker would want anything to do with him."

"Mm, I think Porterfield is Donnelly's man."

"Richard Taylor might have gone home to any empty house…"

"He could be looking for Caroline..."

"The search may have led him into trouble."

"From what Ben was saying, his father is obsessed with that company of his, so I doubt he would have deserted it."

"Unless he was in danger himself."

"Mm." Cliff's eyelids flicker; his attention wanders.

Luke leaves him to it for a while. Besides, his arm prickles; he pulls up his sleeve and inspects the red blotches on his skin in the crook of his elbow. He reaches for the glass jar on his nightstand. Amy's ointment, he and Ethan call it. It smells fierce, but it has already worked wonders on his sores. More than this, he rubs Amy's love and care into his being. He's taken to cherishing these things. Last visit Amy not only brought enough cooked food for three days, bread, soup, cake, biscuits, stew, jam, cookies... but she brought Tress and Adam as well. He let Tress hug him for as long as she wanted because secretly he needed it; and then she placed Adam into his hands. He wasn't sure at first if he should hold the kid after what happened in Porterfield's cellar...

"Love don't care what people look like, or what troubles life dishes up," Tressa said, "and Adam loves you, and you love him."

It sounded like something Mart would have said.

Healthy and strong, wide sunny smile, fly away yellow hair and sparkling dark gray eyes, Adam brought Mart to life before his eyes. And memories of Mart chased away the dark visions that won't quit haunting him. Hundreds of revered memories that all rolled into one beloved remembrance...

He made progress that day.

The ointment dissolves into his skin, leaving an oily sheen on the surface. He could never be who he is without the Keatons. He wouldn't want to even try. His life is bound up with the boyhood friendship he and Mart thrived on. The hand Mart reached out to him from a dark and lonely place and spoke the words, *we can be friends...*

Luke wipes moisture from his eyes with the back of his hand.

"Luke?"

"Amy's ointment... makes my eyes water..."

Unbeknownst to him, a comradery existed to fill the gap.

Cliff was a revelation.

Where would you find a greater indication of what's inside the heart of a human being than in a willingness to sacrifice themselves?

By this, too, Luke is bound.

And so, he realizes, is Emmaline.

Cliff probably ain't even aware it, but he'd bet a month of Cliff's wages that Emmaline hasn't forgotten.

"How much trouble are we in?" he asks.

"Ralph Walker won't back down. Up to our necks."

"We can talk our way out of it."

"We might."

"I won't ever forget what you did, Cliff."

"Sounds like you have changed your mind about rearranging my face."

"Don't push it."

"Are you sure you're going to be all right?"

Nothing was for certain anymore. He came close to Ethan talking over him laid out in a pine box. Never has he known anything like these feelings of helplessness and self-loathing born in the hell that was Porterfield's basement. Whether he will ever feel clean again he can't say. But he knows that somewhere inside of him there's some fight left to get stronger and do what has to be done. He just needs some time.

"Give me a couple of weeks."

...Emmaline

BRAVE BRIGHT RIVER ALLIANCE RETURNS

CHEYENNE, March 5 - On the eve of the Maverick Trials, the forces are continuing to gather.

The arrival of the noted Bright River Alliance in Cheyenne has been highly anticipated for some weeks.

Today was the day.

The long expected Union Pacific from Laramie City huffed and hissed to a stop and doused the sizeable crowd that had gathered at the depot in copious clouds of steam, which expanded in volume as it hit the frosty air. The clouds parted and car doors were thrown open.

Undaunted Bright River rancher Ethan Benchley, part owner of the Diamond-T ranch, emerged from the first-class car. Mr Benchley extended his hand and Caroline Taylor took it, joining him on the platform.

Mrs Taylor is the wife of Omaha businessman, and owner of Aurora Mining Co., Mr Richard Taylor.

Following in like manner was Amy Keaton. Careful hands placed her grandson, Adam Keaton, aged eight months, into her arms.

John Keaton, owner of the Keaton ranch in Bright River, appeared next, raising his handsome head to peruse the depot, his steadfast hand at the ready for his daughter-in-law, Tressa Taylor-Keaton.

The women fixed their hats and fussed over the baby.

Luggage began to appear at their feet as Union Pacific porters went about their business in their usual efficient manner.

Ethan Benchley kept a protective arm hovering about the women. John Keaton continued his vigilance as more figures appeared, one by one, until three tall young men stood side by side on the platform.

Luke Taylor, the first of the three, swept his keen and vivid blue gaze across the depot and the assembled townsfolk.

His enemies had tried to keep him down and they have failed. His return to Cheyenne is the story of one of the great journeys, from the very pit of darkness to the resurrection of determination and endurance.

All who cared to look closely at Tip Benchley on his left saw the young and proud glance of the once great and fierce Comanche nation. Two-feathers-one-white is the son of Red Sky, and the grandson of Chief Black Wolf of the Nakoni people.

Lastly, Ben Taylor, also of Omaha, surveyed the scene with blue-eyed steeliness. He and his cousin Luke exchanged a fixed look of serious intent, until the trace of a knowing smile appeared on both their faces.

On this day one year ago, March 5,

1884, Mart Keaton was murdered by notorious outlaw Wilson Cutter, who was hanged for his heinous crime last September in Cheyenne. Luke Taylor explained the moving significance of returning to Cheyenne on this anniversary in a statement exclusive to The Tribune:

"With this gesture the Bright River Alliance remembers and honors with pride a beloved son, husband, father, brother and friend, Mart Keaton, for his valiant, resolute and heroic efforts in protecting the Alliance, and the sacrifices he made. These efforts were his contribution to the ongoing and just cause of freedom and liberty. Once again, we take up the banner and continue what he began. Let this be a sign to those who seek to destroy us."

A dazzling flash and a photograph was taken. The crowd gasped. The photographer departed in a timely manner befitting the occasion; the group was ready to move.

The man they had all come to see stepped out, flanked by his cousin and his Comanche brother.

They strode down the platform with uniform swagger, parting the excitable crowd as they went; their long, flapping coats filling with air and throbbing like the wings of great birds of prey, their boots sounding with ever more purpose.

The Alliance is back in town.

Bigger, brighter, better.

And stronger than ever.

THE END OF VOLUME TWO

THE LIBERTY & PROPERTY LEGENDS
A saga of The West and Gilded Age America

by

TERRI SEDMAK

America 1880's. Lives taken, justice sought. Love won and love lost.
Friendships forged and families fractured.
As terror grows, heroes rise.

HEARTLAND
On the Side of Angels

VOLUME ONE

WYOMING, 1883... Three families, one Alliance. A cold-blooded murder.
The conflict. The secrets. The passion. And the fight for justice.

ADVENTURE AND ROMANCE WILL NOT BE DENIED ANYONE WHO HAS THE COURAGE TO BE FREE.

———◄◆►———